Fuel-Injected Dreams

James Robert Baker

BANTAM PRESS

NEW YORK · LONDON · TORONTO · SYDNEY · AUCKLAND

TRANSWORLD PUBLISHERS LTD
61–63 Uxbridge Road, London W5 5SA

TRANSWORLD PUBLISHERS (AUSTRALIA) PTY LTD
15–23 Helles Avenue, Moorebank NSW 2170

TRANSWORLD PUBLISHERS (NZ) LTD
Cnr Moselle and Waipareira Aves,
Henderson, Auckland

Published 1986 by Bantam Press,
a division of Transworld Publishers Ltd
Copyright © James Robert Baker 1986

British Library Cataloguing in Publication Data

Baker, James Robert
    Fuel-injected dreams.
    I. Title
    813′.54[F]   PS3552.A42/

    ISBN 0-593-01190-2

Printed in Great Britain by
Richard Clay (The Chaucer Press) Ltd,
Bungay, Suffolk

For South Bay Ronnie

ACKNOWLEDGMENTS

"Wild Horses" by M. Jagger/K. Richard
© 1970 by ABKCO Music, Inc.
All rights reserved. Reprinted by permission.

"Hurt" by Jimmie Crane and Al Jacobs
© 1953, 1954, Renewed 1981, 1982 Miller Music Corporation.
Rights assigned to CBS Catalogue Partnership. All rights controlled and
administered by CBS Miller Catalog Inc. All rights reserved. International
Copyright secured. Used by permission.

"Remember (Walking in the Sand)" by George Morton
Copyright © 1964 by EMI Music Publishing Ltd. and Tender Tunes Inc.
All rights for the U.S. and Canada controlled by Screen Gems-EMI Music Inc.,
6920 Sunset Blvd., Hollywood, California 90028.
Used by permission. All rights reserved.

"Pale Blue Eyes" written by Lou Reed.
Copyright © 1969 Oakfield Avenue Music, Ltd. Used by permission.
All rights reserved.

I thought of you as my mountaintop,
I thought of you as my peak.
I thought of you as everything
I've had but couldn't keep.

—Lou Reed, "Pale Blue Eyes"

1

Well, I see by the cracked face of my Princess Grace wristwatch that it's four A.M., and the City of Angels is a glowing necropolis for as far as my wind-tunnel eyes can see. You know, boys and girls, I've got quite a view from my bulletproof glass tomb up here on the eighteenth floor of the Sunset/Vine Tower. On a good day looking east I can see Pico Rivera, and on nights like this, when it's hot and clear, I can see a ten-car pileup on the 405 in the suburbs of San Diego. It's hot in here tonight too, and that's no accident either. I'm suffocating in a fishbowl, gasping for breath in a plate-glass vault, drowning in pools of my own masculine sweat. I'm stripped down to my frayed Soldier of Fortune jockstrap, my rock-hard Mel Gibson torso gleaming in the soft amber light, my golden skin slick as a piston after a valve job, all because I refused to let myself be turned into a male sex object. That's why the air conditioning is out tonight. It didn't break down, that's a load of crap. They set it to shut off at midnight, knowing I'd be trapped here for the next six hours with nothing but a bottle of moldy Gatorade and a warm six-pack of Coors. All because I wouldn't let them wrap my bulging biceps in cellophane. Because I wouldn't let them sell my washboard stomach to Mattel. Because I wouldn't appear nude, with a glistening erection, in certain so-called women's magazines. Because I wouldn't go to bed with a powerful sixty-year-old broad in Palm Springs. And because I wouldn't make novelty records like "Disco Duck." They showed me the *lyrics to one they wanted me to do. It was called "Post New Wave Nouveau Rock Frog." They said it would make me a millionaire overnight. I'd be barnstorming shopping malls over Southern California, and that was just for starters. Today Orange County, tomorrow Nebraska. I'd be MC-ing dance parties at the Santa Barbara ranch, I'd have my own Playboy jet, I'd do Johnny and Merv, be on the cover of Peo-*ple *and* Rolling Stone, *put out a rock-and-roll diet book, start a chain of exercise parlors, endorse condoms and douche bags for big bucks, have to hire a goon squad to keep away the screaming teenage girls. I'd be on top of the world, miserable and lonely, but too blitzed on the world's finest drugs to care. And all I'd have to do was agree to take the drive-time slot, six to ten* A.M., *five days a week. Now, there's nothing intrinsically wrong with that time of day, unless you're a vampire, which, despite this dried blood on my mustache, I'm not. No, when I clock out at dawn, I'm just like anyone else after work; I like to get down. So while most people are scratching their pubes at Jane Pauley, I'm having a sex party with a couple of sultry Siamese twins still joined at the hip. When all the TRW engineers are stuck in their Subaru bumper-to-bumper, you'll find me stagger-dancing nude with a Ubangi princess, brain-dead, in a stupor of love. And after nearly a decade as the Igor of rock radio, my patterns are set. You can't teach a rutting dog new tricks. Though that's what they'd do, boys and girls. They'd rip me from the graveyard and tear off my Baloramas, pump me full of Ritalin, and make me stare at the rising sun. Then they'd chop off my jellyroll and my biker goatee, and call in the plastic surgeons to redo my face and teeth till I looked just like Art Linkletter circa* House Party. *Then they'd stick me in a tight federal-blue Jimmy Swaggart double-knit suit with a George Wallace tie, they'd throw scalding coffee down my throat and push my raw face to the microphone and make me say, in a Wink Martindale voice, "Now, here's a great one from Olivia Newton-John." And that would be it. They'd have my brains in a* microwave, my nuts in a Cuisinart, and my heart squirming like a baby in a cardboard box in the fast lane of the Ventura Freeway. I'd have a playlist of five songs, four of them by Barry Manilow. All our reeling, eclectic sleigh rides would be gone forever, a thing of the past. These nights when I've reached through the radio and held your hand as we strolled together from Little Richard to Bryan Ferry, from the Marvelettes to Shriekback, from Annette to the Sex Donkeys, from Bartok to Tina Turner, from Patsy Cline to Public Image—they would all be gone like an unhinged Southern belle with the wind, like the blond head of a sex goddess in a sheared-off Lincoln, like my ex-wife's dream of a Fourth Reich.

But I was saved at the last minute. They weren't going to take no for an answer. It was either accept or be banished from the L.A. airwaves forever to a Polynesian mood-music station in Arkansas. But you came to the rescue after my appeal last week, and the response was overwhelming. Dump trucks backed up to the KRUF offices, burying our born-again war-criminal manager in tons of letters and pornographic postcards. Some of what you said was really quite moving. You opened up your hearts, and the results are smeared here before me right now. Like this letter, written on the back of a Smith & Wesson warranty form. "Dear Scott," she writes. "I am a psychopathic teenage girl with a mood disorder and a weight problem who used to dream of killing her parents. One night I was standing over my sleeping redneck father with a container of sulfuric acid when your voice leapt out from his clock radio and licked my diamond-hard nipples one by one. I was so moved I threw the acid at the radio, thus sparing my dad. I have since undergone a lobotomy and am currently incarcerated at the Tehachipi Reformatory for Evil Girls, and I just want to thank you for turning my life around. The night is a grim time, Scott, and I know you must have interfered with the sick intentions of more people than you know. If they put you in the morning slot, just check with the

coroner after a week, and see if the mutilation and disfigure-
ment rate hasn't shot through the roof." Signed "Peggy."
Well, Peggy, I think you just about said it all. When I passed
your letter around yesterday there wasn't a dry glass eye in
the entire labyrinthine KRUF facility. And I've got literally
stacks of mail here from people like you, Peggy. The shut-ins.
I never knew there were so many shut-ins. One from a couple
of twins in El Monte confined to matching iron lungs since
1955. "Scott, we live to hear you play Tony Martin's version
of 'Lady of Spain.' Nobody else plays it anymore." Signed
'Elmo and Elmer.' Fellas, she's cued up right now. Cards
from victims here. I never knew there were so many victims.
People with diseases I've never even heard of, who only want
to hear "Kashmir" one last time. We've got letters from all
kinds of people. Republicans, Democrats. Syrians. Here's a
thick letter from the IRA that hasn't even been opened yet.
Rich people, poor people, girls who've sent their pictures to
Hustler, girls who haven't. I never knew before who was really
out there. I always figured it was a janitor somewhere Win-
dexing the lipstick smears off the boss's chair, or a couple of
Cambodians in the back room at Winchell's, or a whore with
a stolen boom box on Yucca. But I never really knew it was
so diverse. Like this—in a tasteful hand on White House
stationery. "Keep it up." Signed "Nancy." And the very next
card is a group photo of a bunch of the gals out at Frontera.
"Just don't play anything off the White Album," it says.
Then: "P.S. Just kidding. It's cool now." Signed "Sadie," but
that's crossed cut and "Susan" is written in a lovely, peaceful
hand. Now, who wouldn't be touched by that?

  So it looks like I've been saved, I've been redeemed—thanks
to you, the listener, in all your myriad permutations. You
know, it warms my heart, and heats my crotch, to know I'm
not alone in the night. Yeah, I feel pretty good right now.
You know, I feel all right. But I'm a little restless. I'm hot
and sweaty and all sexed-up with nowhere to go. I feel like
getting down and punching someone out—maybe even my-

*self. I wanna piss in the face of the status quo, I wanna make
my mother weep and my old man crap, I wanna make decent
people everywhere avert their eyes in sickened horror, I wanna
see those flashing red lights closing in,* I wanna hear the
sirens wail! *I wanna get on a* death trip, *boys and girls! I
wanna rip my brains out and set 'em on fire; I wanna stay up
for ten days straight, speedballing my way from the reeling
pleasure domes of Beverly Hills to the decadent sin pads of
Zuma Beach. I wanna go out in an orgy of wanton self-
destruction, I wanna paint my star on the sidewalk in blood.
I wanna go for a moonlight drive with no brakes. I wanna
slam my Z-28 into a cinder-block wall at 140 miles an hour,
I wanna shoot my GTO through the burning ozone in that
final chickie run with God, I'm on a death trip and I will be
till dawn. And to get things rolling, rolling like a Mack truck
toward an autistic children's playground, here's an epic trash
masterpiece, a twisted girl-group classic from 1963. A real
death trip from the demented mind of Dennis Contrelle.
Some of you may smile soft-headedly and remember this
gem. Others may simply cringe and wish to forget. This is
Scott Cochran, macho superstud, male feminist, and untreatable schizophrenic. You're listening to Radio Noir and
the crazed death sounds of the Beehives with "Angel on the
Highway." Hit it, girls, sideways or anyways. Rev it up and
blow it out.*

I spun the scratchy Beehives platter, three Brooklynoid
girl voices, larynxes like subway brakes. The tale began with
girltalk banter, a crude version of the style ultimately per-
fected by the Shangri Las. "Hey, Sharon, is that Scumbag's
ring you're wearing?" "Um-hum." "Well, did he fingerbang
you in his car last night?" "Well, I gave him some tit but not
any twat." Okay, I'm exaggerating slightly. "By the way, are
you eloping with him tonight?" "Yeah, we're leaving in his
car. His treads are bad but we'll go far." Of course it's raining
that night when they slip away. The radio doesn't work, a

bad sign. They cuddle close, the wipers slapping back and forth. Her eyes are wet. So is the asphalt. Their lips meet then POW! A blowout! They skid to a halt. They're all right, oh thank God. They scramble to safety as the cars go rushing by. But she forgot—*the ring!* Goes running back.

A semi—LOOK OUT! Horn blaring.NO! NO! NO! NO! CRASH CRUNCH SHATTER hubcap ringing gives way to celestial scuzz chorus:

> Now I'm his angel on the highway
> I see his lonely car below
> Now I'm his angel on the highway
> He loves me still oh this I know

I was mopping sweat off my chrome pectorals with a maxi-pad when the phone lit up with several calls. The first was from a short-order chef at Denny's who just wanted to tell me what a great guy I was and request the Gun Club's "Sex Beat" as a dedication to Yolanda, a stuck-up waitress who wouldn't put out.

The second call was from a flight atttendant in Marina Del Rey who'd just got in from Rio and wanted to drift off to Dusty Springfield's "The Look of Love." "Sorry, baby," I explained. "Too upbeat. I'm on a death trip tonight." She thought for a moment and then asked for "Sister Ray." "Now you're in the groove," I told her and wished her sweet dreams.

The Beehives were into the clattering instrumental break as I took the third call. "KRUF," I said, "Francis the talking Mule speaking."

"You vomitous fuck," he said.

"Wasn't that a Pet Clark B-side? Let me check the library."

"Who the fuck do you think you are, you simpering puke? How dare you belittle 'Angel on the Highway'? That song is a sublime expression of emotional truth." His voice was embalmed, like Clint Eastwood six days without sleep.

The Beehives' chorus was repeating.

"You've got to be kidding, pal," I said jauntily. "Either that or you'd better cut back on the Mai Tai suppositories. That song was a piece of cynical derivative pap when it came out—"

"*That song is my soul,*" he said with considerable fervor. Then: "Look here, my friend. I know where you live. I know your exact address."

"Hey," I said with facetious anger. "Don't you threaten me, you ignorant geek. Don't you call me up at four in the morning and threaten me. I carry some weight in this town, you understand what I'm saying? I'm on Chief Gates's bowling team, and I've got an orange shirt to prove it—"

"How'd you like to have your tongue cut off and shoved up your ass?"

I disconnected him and took another dedication. It was no big deal. In a megalopolis of psychopaths a few were bound to crawl out of the fiberboard occasionally, especially between the hours of three and six A.M. In a nation as diverse as America, even the gentlest satirist inevitably stepped on toes. There was just no accounting for some of the inane dreck some people held dear.

I went on playing death songs till dawn. Obvious stuff like "Tell Laura I Love Her," "Teen Angel," "Dead Man's Curve," and "Death Cab for Cutie," as well as songs that were Ironic in Retrospect or that Foreshadowed Doom: "Love Me Two Times," "I Don't Live Today," "Happiness is a Warm Gun." I included some songs that seemed to have nothing to do with death at all, but had always reeked death to me. "Sunshine and Lollipops" (I always saw charred babies in the Mekong Delta), "Someday We'll Be Together" (Yeah, like when we're both dead), and the Blue Cheer version of "Summertime Blues" (you could smell the brain cells burning).

It was great to be able to play anything I wanted. I was the only one at KRUF who could. The day jocks were all

straitjacketed—MTV without the pictures: a format that had
worked for a while, but was sinking now. Which was why, in
total desperation, they had turned to me. I did have the
largest graveyard audience in L.A. But putting me in drive-
time and shackling me with a playlist would have made
about as much sense as having Keith Richards take David
Hartman's job on *Good Morning America*.

The phone threat didn't cross my mind again until I left
the station after six. Walking to my car in the lot behind the
building, I had a premonition. Somebody might be crouching behind that Barracuda with a knife. Or I'd be unlocking
my door when a voice said, "You *fuck*—" as I felt a sting in
my lower back. But nothing happened.

A lot of it was the weather, the dry, windless, pressure-
cooker heat that fed feelings of imminent violence. It frayed
nerves, people drank too much, shitty remarks led quickly
to stab wounds. It was Watts-riots weather, Tate/LaBianca
weather, days when the neighbors called the cops to report
a stench in a boarded-up tract house. You expected to see
blood on the asphalt sparkling in the Minicam lights, a
crowd of spectators with beers in their hands, shirtless guys,
girls in shorts.

Delivery trucks groaned down the dead movie lab streets
as I unlocked my car, a 1963 Lincoln Continental convertible restored to mint condition, a gleaming assassination
black. I shoved the key in the ignition before the alarm went
off, fired the engine, lowered the top, and jammed in an
early Stones cassette. "It's All Over Now" rumbled from the
speakers as I roared into the harsh dawn light.

Streaming up Sunset I thought about the call. *I know
where you live. I know your exact address.* That didn't bother
me. If he followed the phone book he'd find a vine-covered
cottage in Beachwood Canyon and three young reception-
ists having topless pillow fights where my ex-wife and I had
once stared each other down. *That song is my soul.* What a

bizarre, histrionic thing to say. Demented really. Like referring to an old Fritos wrapper as the Virgin Mary.

Suddenly it hit me. Waiting for the light to change at La
Brea, I realized with inexplicable certainty who I'd been talking to. The voice matched, that had to be a big part of it. I
had a memory of that voice, from an interview in the mid-
sixties, perhaps a chat with Dick Clark on *American Band-
stand*. I remembered being surprised, a little disappointed.
It was a desperate hustler's voice, a little moronic or stupid.
If I hadn't known who he was I'd probably have dismissed
him as a jerk or a loser—you somehow expected a *genius* to
be more cultivated or eloquent, like Orson Welles or John
Gielgud. But Dennis Contrelle's manic voice created the
sense that he might be a kind of *idiot savant*, a helpless
retardate in every area of his life except one: his music.
There, no one else even came close. Dennis Contrelle was
the Richard Wagner of rock.

Or at least he had been, until it all blew up in the fall of
'69. He had withdrawn into notorious seclusion after that,
holed up in a posh and tasteless citadel high on a distant
Malibu bluff. The years that followed had been shrouded in
contradictory rumor and myth. There were tales of insanity
and drug-addled violence, of bizarre cures and restorative
surgery, of vendettas against anyone who attempted to violate the sanctity of his twisted mind.

It all fit. *That song is my soul.* Who else but the actual
creator of such monumental drivel could have possibly believed in it that much?

I had a bad feeling as I pulled into my slot at the Tropicana Motel and cut the engine. A sane man would let my
clearly affectionate joshing slide. But then, a sane man
would not believe he had invested his soul in a cracked vinyl
go-go boot like "Angel on the Highway." Of course his mind
was probably so far gone by now that he had already forgotten my offense and moved on to new and more horrific

imagined wrongs. What if I dropped him a short apology note, stating the truth: that I considered him a true and great genius, that I was deeply and emotionally attached to much of his music, that I'd certainly meant no harm? No, why stir it up? Better to let sleepless dogs lie.

I cut past Duke's Coffee Shop, where people were waiting to get in for breakfast, and paused for a moment to say hello to Norrine, a winsome nineteen-year-old Jewish cowgirl who lived downstairs from me at the Tropicana and sang with a post-punk country-swing group called Decapitated Flicka. She invited me to join her for breakfast even though she was hanging on a skinny young guy with whom she'd obviously spent the night. That was fine with me (we'd ridden each other till we dropped a few times, but she certainly didn't bear my brand), but I passed. I was exhausted and just wanted a beer, or several beers, and sleep.

I climbed the green outdoor-carpet-covered steps that led to my room on the second floor overlooking the pool. It was a historic room in its own way. The Ramones, it was said, had a sex party here one night. That cracked commode in the yellow-walled john? Jim Morrison used to clutch that and puke his lizard guts out, man. The lumpy double bed? That's where Patti Smith wrote a song about Jim Morrison, or so it was said. A girl who wasn't anybody lived here for a while too, but Tom Waits used to come around and bum cigarettes off her and lean in the doorway and talk.

I opened the windows to air the place out, got a Coors from the small, dying refrigerator, and looked through my record collection. It filled six milk crates. Containing most of the best (and some of the worst) moments in the history of rock, it was worth a small fortune to anyone who cared.

Lynn hadn't—that was what killed our marriage. No, just kidding. The way it ended with Lynn is a baroque psychological horror story unto itself, which I may sell to television someday for a mini-series about a stunning Vassar blond studio vice-president and a virile, boyishly handsome all-night deejay who only wants to listen to old Joe Tex records and make slow, beautiful love. It's so fine at first: the courtship's a whirlwind of good talk, good sex, and genuine rapport. Only after the honeymoon does this poor chump discover that he's married to a functioning schizophrenic, a classic case of multiple identity: the Four Faces of Lynn. There's "Lynn" of course, the witty, intelligent, sensual workaholic he thought he knew. But she can give way without warning to "Gwen," the belligerent feminist zealot: "For your information, *buster,* 'being on the rag' is a women's issue!" Yet no sooner has she professed to admire men like Alan Alda, who are "in touch with their feminine side," than she flips over to "Jan," the hungry slut who has no stomach for "pseudo-sensitive crap," who just wants to get fucked dog-style in a glass elevator by Harvey Keitel. Which is okay, except that right in the middle of that she turns into "Cynthia," the crushed romantic with a heart full of old Rock Hudson movies, who feels "used," "brutalized," and "cheap."

He does what he can to help this conference-call Sybil reintegrate her shattered psyche, but he's no Joanne Woodward. He's forced to admit her case is hopeless the night "Gwen" chases him from the house with a pair of heavy-gauge bolt cutters, "Cynthia's" tears on his chest and "Jan's" scratch marks on his buns, while "Lynn" calmly smokes a cigarette, watching, *All That Heaven Allows*—Rock Hudson, Jane Wyman, 1955—idly wondering who owns the rights.

Not long after that I became, I admit, totally obsessed with my record collection. Though it crossed my mind that she might try to claim half of it, or some such shit, I knew she considered it a smelly, dust-collecting half-ton of worthless cultural debris. (She liked movie music exclusively: *Psycho* for aerobics, *Jaws* for making love.) What I really feared was that she might destroy it some night in a fit of vindictive Valium-addled rage, one brittle disc at a time. Or worse still,

just give it all away to Goodwill, where a sweet old Navajo
lady in leg braces would sell off my priceless Elvis Sun 45's
at twenty cents a crack.

I'd heisted it back one night, entering the house when I
thought she was out. I was making my last trip when I heard
sounds coming from the bedroom that could only have been
made by "Jan."

Now, in my lonely Tropicana Motel room, I fingered
through the albums, many of the edges frayed and illegible,
till I came to Dennis Contrelle's landmark 1964 production,
the Stingrays' *Fuel-Injected Dreams.* On the yellowed cover
the five Stingrays slouched around a gleaming blue '63 Corvette split-window coupé, the four guys in skinny slacks,
slinky shirts, and shades, scowling under greasy blond jelly-
rolls like metal-shop morons, Youth Authority punks bound
for the Ford plant in Pico Rivera or a Fourth of July OD.
That was how baby-faced Bobby had gone out. Frank and
Billy were up in heaven now too. Jimmy was a Jesus zombie
these days. Back then there were rumors that he liked to
sniff gas.

But the guys were, finally, just background. They were
four blond actors designed to look like Dennis, props to
complement the main atraction. There was really only one
Stingray. In a stiff brown beehive and slippery snakeskin
sheath, her butt pressed against the rear spine of the coupé,
Sharlene faced the camera with a blue-eyed glare that could
burn through fiberglass.

Now, here was a girl you could be proud to be ashamed
of, a tough little dolled-up working-class slut, libidinous jail-
bait with an evil streak, a juvenile offender with a cherry-red
mouth, with Cadillac chrome-bumper breasts you would
mow down a crippled nun to get to. Here was a girl who got
down, put out, got knocked up and had to leave school, a
girl who got drunk but didn't puke out your car window,
who didn't have to be in by eleven, who didn't wear little
white gloves, who wasn't in love with her horse, who didn't

drive a T-bird but took the bus, who popped pills and wouldn't think you were sick if you went down on her, who wouldn't make a face if you suggested she go down on you. She was a cheap brunette angel, the stuff of dirty jack-off dreams, not one of the refined blond girls you were supposed to marry. But she never understood this. She was a girl with real, intense emotions who always fell in love after just one night and then, spurned, spent the next three years plotting revenge, inflaming her subsequent lowlife boyfriends against you. "Oh, baby, I'm so sorry," she would dream of crying when at last you bled to death in the parking lot.

I pulled the translucent blue vinyl disc from the sleeve, knowing without looking what the first song would be, what it had to be. Though there'd been perhaps a half-dozen hits, there was still only one song for the Stingrays, just as there wa; only one song that kicked in the padlocked door of my heart.

"Love Me Tonight" began high on a blue wave of pure shimmering euphoria, the Contrelle Sound come into its own. I felt a chill, as I always did, though I'd heard it surely thousands of times in the last twenty years. Though I wouldn't have admitted it under all circumstances, for fear of being thought sentimental, it was my all-time favorite song. In fact, I considered it the greatest rock-and-roll song ever made.

Objectively, it was an incredible song, the clarity of production astonishing for 1964. Where Dennis had been derivative before, with "Love Me Tonight" he surpassed himself and everyone else. It was the perfect synthesis of a layered, glistering studio surf sound with a swelling cathartic girl-group romanticism. Though velvet black girls slid through the background, there was really only one voice on the record: Sharlene's—relentless, inexorable, near-insane.

The lyrics were pap; most Contrelle lyrics were. They all said the same thing in slightly different ways: love me now, right now, tonight, now, this is it, not tomorrow, not next week, not after we graduate. *Now!* The thing was, you believed her. *She meant it!* It was not a pose, she wasn't acting. She was giving herself away to someone totally, irrevocably, forever, and if you knew anything about them at all you knew it was to Dennis, though of course she spoke for everyone who had ever been in love, or totally obsessed, or both, just once, unequivocally.

I lay back on the bed, lit a stub of Hawaiian dope, and let the music surge through me. It was like listening to a soundtrack album, the score of my favorite and most personal film. It was as if I had appealed to Dennis Contrelle late in postproduction, six months after the completion of principal photography, asking him to compose a score that would somehow exteriorize all the naive romantic emotion left unexpressed by the flat, inarticulate dialogue of the teenage leads. In response he'd created the Stingrays. And he had so far surpassed my wishes that their music now inundated every scene in waves of euphoria, charging the mundane environment, transforming the most mediocre moment into florid cinematic art. The bland Spanish high school overlooking the Pacific was now an ecstatic CinemaScope set, the sea a brilliant painted blue, the lush hills a shimmering iridescent green. The reds were so searing they'd have to be dipped in black; otherwise they'd bleed across the Technicolor screen.

That film begins, always, with a monumental tracking shot. The camera sweeps up the full length of the classroom, closing in on the female star as she comes through the door on the first day of class in September of 1963. She enters breathlessly, late, books held tightly to her breasts, books which are shiny with fresh Palos Verdes High School covers. Breasts which are high under a tight pink blouse. A charcoal skirt stretches tautly over Kim Novak thighs. But her eyes and her skin are what cause the cameraman to gasp, always, and ruin the take.

Eyes of a pale metallic blue, a brilliant artificial Detroit color GM would call a phosphorescent blue, a seductive chemical blue, an instantly addictive blue that must begin with stolen bliss and end with paralyzing overdose and death. An illicit, profane blue, an elating, destroying blue matched to a skin that can only be perceived with stunned awe.

A cream white skin blushed lightly with pink. A pure, flawless, achingly luminescent skin, movie-star skin, skin of the imagination, of fixation, of unspeakable, lonely erotic longing. Skin that courts rage and envy by daring to exist in the natural world.

Her eyes, her skin, the astonishing clear sweet beauty of her face. Only her hair is common and cheap. Brunette, it is perhaps soft and lustrous in its natural state. But it's ratted up now, stiff and mean, in a fierce fuck-off beehive. No Breck Girl, this lacquered angel from the flatland tracts.

"Your name?" says the froglike biology teacher.

"Cheryl Rampton," she says shyly with her cherry-red mouth. With her complex, intelligent mouth. With her low-life white-trash mouth. With her elegant patrician mouth. With her hot, foul little Ann-Margret mouth. With her ethereal love-me-forever mouth.

Some guy behind me snickers. I think it's just because she's come in late. My heart is buzzing against the windows like a trapped hummingbird.

The sockhop two weeks later. Guys on one side, girls on the other. Old-maid chaperon eyeing both with folded arms. Chiffons singing "One Fine Day" as I pad across the gym to ask her to dance. She has her back to me, talking with some girlfriends. Slowly she turns as they tell her I'm approaching. Slowly she turns and takes my breath away. Apparently I manage to get out the word "Dance."

Because the next thing I know we are moving slowly to the Ronettes' "Baby, I Love You." I'm floating, the bleachers giving way to glistering sunlight. Unbearable raptures as her breasts press against my chest, my chin brushes her soft white neck. Yellow butterflies explode from my solar plexus, flutter through my heart like flames. Her hips brush mine. My cock is a granite donkey dick pulsing through white denim. My madras shirttail is out, just in case of this, so nobody sees. I come hard with a poker face before the song ends. If she knows, she doesn't let on. I smile nervously and thank her for the dance.

I go back to the guys as the bell shrieks, meaning lunch-time is over. I'm disoriented, a little punchy. It takes me a second to realize several of the guys are snickering at me. I don't get it at first.

"Hey, man. She try to cop your joint?"

"Shit, you better hose yourself off, man. And get a shot of penicillin."

"What are you talking about?" I say, really not knowing.

A guy I will come to know and hate as Bill Holtner leers in my face. "Don't you know, rube?" His crooked teeth are stained with nicotine. His hair is kinky, blond, and greasy. "She's the biggest fuckin' pig in Southern California. Shit man, she'll fuck anything that can stand up on its hind legs and shoot."

I consider ripping his tongue out, but I am surrounded by a chorus of cackling hyenas who are all on his side, so I implode with rage and embarrassment instead. At least no one notices the splotch on my pants.

I hear the rest in the days to come. Cheryl Rampton is notorious. A real whore, a real nympho. She blows niggers behind the gym. She beats off guys under the table in home-room. She let Larry Fast fingerbang her during a health-ed film. She likes to spread her legs on a park bench every Saturday night and take on all the guys who couldn't get dates. She's insatiable, a constantly wet and eager pussy, dying for it, dying for it, Jack, twenty-four hours a day.

I decide they're all full of shit. It's wishful thinking. They wish *somebody* was putting out. Because the right girls, the good girls, aren't. Our snooty blond PV horse-show girls are all saving it for future counsels to the President, for after the wedding in the glass chapel-by-the-sea. Surely, things must be different on the other side of the tracks—or more precisely, on the other side of the Pacific Coast Highway. Cheryl is part of that minority, which, although it includes a few blacks, is economic rather than racial: a hundred or so kids bused in every day from Lomita, a crummy blue-collar suburb a few critical miles to the east. The Lomita guys are all dark and hoody. They're ignorant and talk like morons and will all end up inhaling fumes at Dow Chemical. While *we* will end up sitting on the board. And the Lomita girls— well, let's be blunt. They're trash. They'll suck your rich cock in a phone booth for a dime and cherry Coke. But there's always a best at everything, isn't there? If Becky Cheeseborough, with her pristine Princess Grace beauty, is a shoo-in for Homecoming Queen and First Lady of the 1990's, then Cheryl Rampton is now and forever the quintessential Class Pig.

But it's a bum rap—no, worse, it's blatant character assassination bred of jealousy and stifled desire. Because she is more beautiful than all those finicky spoiled PV blond bitches combined. And it isn't just a physical beauty either. I watch her around campus, in the quad before class, on the benches at lunch, sneaking off to smoke a cigarette with several Lomita girlfriends behind the music bungalow, and she radiates something no one else has. More than anything it's in her laugh, a crazy, elated, roller-coaster laugh—loud, abandoned, infectious—the antithesis of the smug snicker that seems to be a PV-girl trademark. It's a laugh that says all rules are arbitrary, all boundaries crossable, a laugh that suggests joys and adventures that are at this time only barely perceived. It is a laugh that includes sex but is not just sexual in any vapid *Playboy* sense. You sense that with her, sex is

just one of many ways you can break out of dull, bland
expectations. At least it seems that way to me when I hear
her laugh and try not to look but inevitably do.

And when I do, I never see her sleazing off with any black
guys for a blow-job party behind the gym. I find out who
Larry Fast is, a buck-toothed dork whose entire face is one
huge zit, and I cannot imagine him fingerbanging Cheryl in
health ed or anywhere else. In fact I never see her with any
guys, not even the hoody Lomita guys. She is always just
with her girlfriends, several of whom are genuinely tough
and forbidding. It's as though she has bodyguards and no
male dares approach.

Of course, I'm obsessed with her. I call it being in love,
though, and in 1963 there is generally less of a distinction
made between love and obsession. I am painfully aware that
it's one-sided, that she has seemingly forgotten our one brief
moment of physical contact, that it meant nothing special
to her at all. I'm sitting too far away from her in Biology to
carry on any illicit communication, even if I were loose
enough to do so. Which I'm not. When I do happen to run
into her in a way that might call for at least a smile, I immediately look at the floor.

Finally, though, I can't stand it any longer and one night
I call her on the telephone; that is, I dial her number, which
I have had for some time. This is a critical juncture for me,
perhaps symptomatic of forces that are changing my entire
life at his time. For one thing, I have begun to smoke marijuana, then a felony, a serious business, tantamount to taking a dump on Ozzie and Harriet's dining-room carpet. I've
also taken to reading certain books that will never be con-
densed by *Reader's Digest*, books by Kerouac, Henry Miller,
William Burroughs; books that seem to propose a version of
reality that doen't include merit badges and Ike pins. I am
beginning to realize that being happy and being accepted by
my PV peers are not the same thing. It takes guts to make
this distinction and act on it—guts I don't quite have that

night. I chicken out as soon as I hear Cheryl's voice. I'm very drunk, having just come from an abysmal Rolling Hills birthday party. I might slur my words, but I want to speak, I want to say so many things I will regret in the morning. But I can't say a word. "Hello? Hello?" Neither can I hang up. A Beehives' record is playing on my RCA player, the flip side of "Angel on the Highway," called "Baby, Please." It's a slow, pulsating, romantic song, an early Contrelle prototype of the Stingrays, surprisingly tender considering the aggressive nasal harshness of the hit side. I've never heard it played on the radio but it's my favorite song of the moment, a song that always makes me think of Cheryl, and that it's playing now while she's on the phone seems wholly appropriate, so I turn up the volume and hold the receiver close to the speaker and let Dennis and the Beehives say everything to Cheryl that I myself am too chickenshit to say.

Apparently I pass out, because the next thing I know, it's dawn and my head is exploding and I'm still holding the phone in my hand, and the record is still playing, having repeated it seems for hours. I snap to, put the phone to my ear. At the other end I hear the morning sounds of the Rampton house, pots and pans in a distant kitchen. Cringing with embarrassment, I slam down the phone.

I see Cheryl in class the next Monday, look away guiltily, certain she knows somehow that I was the asshole who called her. Jesus, maybe I actually said something too, I was so drunk I might not remember. I sneak a glance as she walks past my desk, but she ignores me as always.

The coming Friday turns out to be an eventful day. My parents and brother have gone back to Ohio to spend an extended Thanksgiving period with relatives. I am supposed to stay home and study hard. I'm a dunderhead in math and some dork is tutoring me in algebra so I won't fail. Fine. At least I'll be alone for a while. I can get out the scalp massager and jack off in the dining-room mirror.

I pull out that Friday morning in late November 1963, in

my new car, a '54 Nash Metropolitan, white and pale green, a demeaningly nerdy transportation car (though some people might consider it cool now, it was a Wally Cox automobile then), which I will trade in the following year for a bitchin' Chevy Bel-Air. One thing it has, though, is an eight-track with Vibra-Sonic, so I can drown out the smirks and snickers with an avalanche of glistering metallic sound. Which is what I'm doing as I tool up PV South that morning, the sea glistening under a clear sky, a soft breeze rustling the lush greenery, unaware that I'm driving along the edge of an era that in less than three hours will pass into history, when I see Cheryl Rampton standing with her thumb out up ahead on the curbless road.

I'm tempted to pretend suddenly to notice something interesting off to my left as I roar by, but somehow know I will hate myself forever if I do. Also, the Beehives are snarling on the eight-track, which she will think is cool even though she might be secretly guffawing at the car, and I am insulated in the raucous Contrelle melodrama for the few seconds it takes me to pull to a stop. My heart is pounding as she opens the door and immediately starts talking a mile a minute.

"Hi. Thanks. I'm late. Jeez, I missed the bus and this guy offered me a ride. He seemed cool, a suit and tie, like some businessman on his way to work. Then he took a right off Hawthorne and guess what he did?"

She's talking to me like we're old friends. "I don't know. What?"

"He pulled out his cock. I mean, Christ." She sounds more exasperated than traumatized. "I mean, I'm just trying to get to school on time."

"So what happened?"

"Nothing." She shrugged. "When he pulled up to a red light, I jumped out. He was still beating his meat as he drove away."

The way she says this astonishes me, because she sounds

amused and oddly compassionate. It's as if she doesn't know that sex is supposed to be disgusting or that nice girls shouldn't talk this way.

"Well, don't worry about me," I say, and instantly cringe when I realize I've just evoked an image of *me* feverishly pounding my pud.

"Huh?"

"Nothing." I must be turning red.

She suddenly reaches for the volume. With cold horror I realize it's the Beehives' "Baby, Please," the song I played to her over the phone.

"I love this song," she says, seemingly making no connection. Then she's digging in her purse, for her cigarettes I think, when a joint falls out in her lap. She lets out a little shocked gasp, knowing I've seen it.

"It's cool," I say quickly, knowing she must think I'm a total square. "As a matter of fact, I've been known to partake of the evil weed myself on occasion."

"Are you serious?" She's clutching the joint in her fist now, as though she expects me to pry it away from her and drag her straight to the principal or Jack Webb.

"Yeah, on occasion." I am astonishing myself at how cool I suddenly am. It's a performance bred of terror. I am on now. This may be my only chance with her.

"You don't seem like the type."

"Looks can be deceiving."

"Can they?" I feel her checking me out. Then she starts doing a mock Mashed Potato to the Beehives, still holding the joint, as if unsure what to do with it. I take the turn toward school. The red tile roof and the chain-link fence appear up ahead.

"God, it's a great day," she says.

"Yeah, it is."

"Can I ask you something, Scott?"

Oh Lord, she knows my name. "Sure, what?"

"Are you really into going to school today?"

I slam on the brakes in the middle of the street, grind into reverse, back into somebody's driveway, then chug back up the street with my dream girl beside me at last.

A few hours later we are at my house, on the sofa in the rumpus room, a haze of marijuana smoke obscuring the Norman Rockwell Thanksgiving print above us. A rerun of *Bachelor Father* plays silently on the Magnavox TV as James Brown screams "Lost Someone," from *Live at the Apollo* on the cabinet hi-fi. We have been making out for what seems like days and we're now in a mesmerized stupor of love.

I open her blouse. She removes her bra, showing high firm breasts with pink nipples. She unbuttons my madras shirt. Her skirt is already up around her waist. I lift her legs, pull her black lace panties down, and bury my wholesome face in her glossy brown muff. She's as sweet as Hawaiian Punch with just the right tang of passion fruit. I can't stand it. My cock feels like Godzilla. I raise up and she guides me into her. She is not a virgin. Neither am I—now. Deep inside her, I kiss her sweet pink mouth where no more cherry-red lipstick remains.

On the silent TV, *Bachelor Father* has been replaced by a live shot of Chet Huntley. But this means nothing to me now.

In a hot staggering sweat, James Brown sings hypnotically. In a hot stupefied daze, we pump on the sofa, Cheryl Rampton crying out as the black girls in the Apollo audience *scream*.

The roar of morning traffic came through my open windows at the Tropicana. I punched off the stereo and slipped the Stingrays' record back in its sleeve. As I did, I looked at the cover again and remembered the first time I'd seen it: on a display rack in Wallach's Music City, in September of 1964. Six months after I'd lost Cheryl.

Looking at Sharlene's picture on that album cover twenty years ago, I'd thought I'd found her again.

That two girls could look so much alike was almost not to be believed. Sharlene and Cheryl could have been twins. I thought it *was* Cheryl at first. I really thought it was her. I'd had to read the liner notes and study the candid studio shots on the back—where the resemblance was less than total—to convince myself it wasn't Cheryl, but just one more instance of my grief-distorted mind involuntarily searching for her, as it had been all that summer.

I'd seen her everywhere: across crowded shopping centers, in cars going in the opposite direction on the freeway, through an impenetrable horde of screaming girls at the Beatles concert at the Hollywood Bowl. The times I'd pursued these phantoms had always turned into dark *Twilight Zone* jokes.

The girl with Cheryl's hair, with her creamy baby skin, would turn out to have buckteeth and glasses. "Excuse me, I thought you were someone else."

It almost *had* to be someone else. Because even then, though there wasn't any proof, I was almost totally convinced that Cheryl was dead.

There was still no proof twenty years later. But how could it possibly matter now? Trying to figure out *now* what had happened to Cheryl would be as futile and obsessive as poring over photographs of President Kennedy's wounds.

I covered my head with the pillow and fell asleep.

2

A brutal knocking woke me up around noon. The last time anyone had knocked on my door like that, it had been the cops when I stole a car at fifteen. No, it had been the FBI when I was dodging the draft in '66. No, it had been my dad when I'd been in the bathroom masturbating with the scalp massager.

I sprung out of bed, my heart going into a manic biphetamine jerk, and peered through the drapes. It wasn't the cops or the FBI or my dad. He was big and black, Idi Amin in a linty navy-blue warm-up suit that didn't hide his piece or his schlong.

"Yeah, what do you want?" I asked through the closed door after hooking the chain.

"Open the door. I want to talk to you."

"What about?"

His reddish eyes caught me peeking at him through the drapes. "What's the matter? You scared, just 'cause I'm black? Afraid I'm gonna steal your stereo and butt-fuck your wife?"

"I'm afraid the stereo isn't worth much," I said, and wished I knew Lynn's current address. I opened the door a crack, chain in place. "So what is it?"

He checked me out, smirked disparagingly. "Mr. Contrelle would like to have a word with you."

My brains went into shock. "Mr. who?" I said, about as convincingly as a Nazi doctor at the Nuremberg trials.

"Dennis Contrelle," he said, a little bored, a little pissed off.

"You mean, uh, the record producer?" I fumbled for time.

"He called you last night."

"He did?"

"He wants me to tell you he's sorry. It was a rough night."

I saw that he had his foot in the door. "Well, look, pal, I really don't know what you're talking about. We get a lot of kooky calls in the wee hours of the morning, but whatever it was, I'm sure it's over and done with. Now, excuse me while I get back to sleep, okay?"

He pushed the door with his fingertips. The chain snapped. The door banged against the wall, the knob knocking a hole in the plaster. "Get dressed," he said softly. "I got orders to take you back to the house."

I considered screaming, but it struck me as somehow unmasculine. I considered lunging for the phone, but believed if he grabbed me, and we fell, and he was on top of me, I would die.

"This is outrageous," I said indignantly.

"Looky here," he said, as if addressing a retarded child. "The man is waiting to see you. You bein' given a big opportunity. He ain't talked to no one in a long, long time."

That was true. And I was curious.

"Don't worry." He put his hand on my shoulder. "He *likes* you. He listens to you all the time. He just wants to talk, that's all. Just talk."

I was still apprehensive, but my curiosity was growing. "Okay," I said finally. "But let me pull on my pants. Or you want me to go like this?"

He snorted, and stepped back out on the balcony, sweat trickling down his face as he dug out a cigarette, lit it, and watched me get dressed.

I followed his shiny black '66 Fleetwood out Sunset to PCH, then north. It was hot and my air conditioner needed Freon.

By the time we reached Point Dume my red-and-yellow
Clash T-shirt was soaked with sweat.

Near Decker Canyon he took a sudden left to an un-
marked road that curved through a thick grove of eucalyptus
trees. You went up a slight rise, came out of the trees, and
there it was, bolted into a high cliff overlooking the ocean: a
glass-and-concrete Egyptoid mausoleum burning sick and
hot in the glaring sun.

It was a chunky two-story building, an Eighteenth Dynasty–inspired travesty of Frank Lloyd Wright's Mayan de-
signs, by way of C. B. De Mille circa Jacqueline Susann. It
was faced with cast-concrete hieroglyphic panels inter-
spersed with plate-glass windows over which the faded
drapes were drawn. Horus steles framed the front door,
huge slanting slabs, waiting for Charlton Heston to point
the way to the Promised Land. On a more jarring note, I
saw as I drove closer, security bars covered every window.
But they weren't Egyptoid security bars; they were fussy
French Quarter ironwork, added perhaps on a paranoid Desoxyn whim in the wake of the Manson murders.

I followed the Cadillac through the electric gate, noting
the rusted signs attached to the chain-link and razor-wire
fence that surrounded the property. They stated that as the
fence was electrified, the owners bore no liability if you
touched it and died, and also that the grounds were patrolled
by armed dogs and vicious guards (though it might have
been the other way around; I read it pretty fast). The
grounds were overgrown with tropical shrubbery and palms
so you didn't see the Romanoid parking court until you
pulled into it. This was hard-core Vegas dementia, bad
early-sixties glitz. Columns and decorator plaster statues,
like an early *Playboy* pictorial set. You could imagine toga-
clad businessmen chasing bunnies with dripping blond hair-
dos and huge bazooms back toward the two-story Ramses
garage.

He pulled up to the Luxor front door and got out. I pulled

up behind him and was getting out too when he shouted at me, "No! Get back in the car!"

I didn't understand at first. Then I caught movement on the lawn. Two German shepherds were loping toward me as if I were a spilled sack of Gravy Train.

A second later they were spraying saliva against my window as I frantically rolled it up. They pawed the glass and scratched my paint job, their teeth bared ferociously as they snarled—except they weren't making a sound. No growling, no barking, nothing came from their throats: they were mute. Just pawing and scratching to the pop of spittle and heave of panting breath, like the thing in *Alien*, pressed an inch from my face, maiming slick death. I fumbled out my ignition key

He called the dogs. "Buddy! Chuck! Heel!"

They broke and went to him. He slapped Buddy across the muzzle. Buddy shook his head, dazed, but didn't whimper. "Sit, you fuck! *Sit!*"

Both dogs sat now, panting hard. He grabbed both by their collars and called to me. "It's all right, it's okay now. Go on in the house. Go on in the music room. Straight back."

I got out cautiously, trembling with my second adrenaline rush of the day. He held on to the dogs as I walked to the door. Buddy strained, and appeared to snarl, but still he made no sound.

I entered the house.

It was worse than anything Liberace could have imagined. Next to it, Graceland looked like a Zen teahouse. It was as though he'd hired a hundred shopping-cart packrats and given them carte blanche to go out and collect the cheapest, most stomach-turning kitsch from the far corners of the globe. For starters one of them had cleaned out the local Pic 'N' Save. Everywhere you looked were cabinets and shelves filled with intricate bric-a-brac, figurines and tacky crap, with a special emphasis on celebrity death memorabilia.

There were Elvis ashtrays, John Lennon goblets, Jimi Hendrix belt buckles, Jim Morrison tumblers, Joplin coasters, a Karen Carpenter toothpick dispenser, enough JFK and RFK china to serve a Holiday Inn full of OD'ed guitarists. Against the chartreuse flocked wallpaper in the living room, overlooking the *Valley of the Dolls* French Provincial furniture, was a copper-relief portrait of Ritchie Valens, jellyroll tarnished, and a garish oil painting of a red-eyed, terminal Brian Jones. In another room, against baby-blue flocked wallpaper was a dim black velvet painting of James Dean with an erection in a tree. Everywhere there were angel figurines, angels and cherubs, insipid kissing cherubs, vacuous Christmas-tree angels, praying angels, harsh crypto-expressionist angels, lurid plaster Mexican angels, Day-Glo Hong Kong angels, refined bone china cupids. The smell of patchouli—or was it formaldehyde?—wafted through the air as I crossed the beige-shag-covered foyer to the corridor straight ahead.

It was a long vaginal corridor, upholstered in crushed red velvet. At the end of it was the music room, dim and cavernous, a sea of dirty pink shag. To one side by the plate-glass windows there was a sunken conversation pit where you could imagine a young Hef joking woodenly with Dino while somebody fingerbanged a smiling Miss July. Beyond the aluminum foil that covered the plate-glass windows there was no doubt a stupendous ocean view from this Berchtesgaden-by-the-sea. Scattered around the room was a half-ton of stereo equipment, top-of-the-line circa 1968, amps, preamps, tape decks, a board, all of which looked as though it had been hurriedly set up fifteen years ago and not moved since. The four speakers were big enough to hold several crouching Vandellas apiece.

The one wall that wasn't glass held his gold records, about a dozen of them. The first I looked at was for his last hit, "Tidal Wave of Flame," Louise Wright, 1969. That song had been his Götterdämmerung, his masterwork, his last ten days in the bunker. The glass was cracked in the frame, a chunk missing, the rest about to fall out.

A collection of photographs traced his career. In '62, with a blond chrome-finned flat-top, twenty-three years old but looking about fourteen, glad-handing several smarmy shark-skin-suit Brill Building types who despite their grins appeared eager to stub their cigars out in his eyes at the first opportunity. Then a series with his various creations, '63 through '67: the Beehives, dumped after "Angel on the Highway" like a cheap date at a gas station after quick sex. The Stingrays, of course, receiving their various gold records. The same with the Vectors, his male surf duo. The trademark Balorama shades came in '64 and stayed. So did the paisley shirts and Edwardian collars, replacing the narrow ties and lapels of his early kiss-ass days. The glowing tan went too, as perhaps did a few of the teeth, and didn't come back. Mid-sixties, with Jagger, Dylan, the Byrds. Posing ecstatically in a new studio before a board that seems to contain about five hundred tracks; shades off in this one, a mistake, showing eyes like those of a wolf ten years without sleep. At various Hollywood psychedelic Mod Squad–era parties, with a pudgy Sonny Bono, a dowdy Cher, various minor pop lights who were either dead now or out to pasture in Petaluma. His boyish features are blasted in these, insipidness blowtorched away. His small body, beneath the black silk blouse, is skeletal. In Morocco, about '68, a cadaver in shades. Finally, in 1969, from the infamous last sessions (early on, apparently; they're still smiling). Louise Wright beaming like a klieglight, yet cringing involuntarily, as Dennis places a kiss on her black cheek with chapped lips.

In a small space by the door hung his private life, what he cared to reveal of it. His pleasant, dumpy Mom and Dad, before a tiny stucco postwar tract house, squinting, smiling. A few years later before the Vegasoid monstrosity he built for them, looking puzzled, distracted. A wedding picture, Dennis and Sharlene cutting the cake. She looks about fourteen, pouty, red-eyed, as though she's been crying. Have they just had their first fight? He's showing her how to cut the cake, his manner slightly irritated, indulgent, as though she has to be shown everything. On her finger glistens a diamond as big as a sperm whale's clitoris.

The door swung open, and Dennis Contrelle entered like a thing from outer space destined to burn up in this atmosphere.

"Hello, good morning, glad you could make it. Would you like some coffee? Some dope? A Pepsi? Some blow?"

He hadn't even looked at me yet. He was all over the room, checking through papers on the table, sheet music on the piano, as if searching for a piece of vital information while somebody hung on the phone long distance from Hong Kong; though nothing was really going on, of course, and hadn't for years. It was clearly just his way of avoiding eye contact.

"Maybe some coffee."

"Big Willy!" His voice broke with exhaustion. "Bring Mr. Cochran some coffee."

He let his eyes flit over me. A condor could have swooped through those pupils dragging a blimp and still have made it.

"Any relation to Eddie Cochran?"

"No, I'm adopted. But I did some checking a while back. And it turns out—you'd better get ready for this—my *real* parents were Screamin' Jay Hawkins and Kate Smith."

"Well, you've got her hair," he said in a dry, frayed voice. It took me a second to realize he was joking too. He smiled, or tried to. It looked more like a samurai grimacing over a painful shit. "Yes, Eddie Cochran. 'Summertime Blues.' Still a classic. I remember where I was when I heard he'd been killed."

I waited for the rest of it but there wasn't any. He wandered back among the speakers, momentarily withdrawn in thought.

Sunlight cut through tears in the window foil, exaggerating the sockets of his charred blue eyes. His skin was powdery white and lifeless, his once boyish features a mask of parched lines, as if a kind of mummification had set in, arresting the rapid destruction documented in the wall photos. At forty-five, he was the world's oldest living teenager. You could still see how the girls of the early sixties would have swooned over his adorable face had he been a teen idol himself rather than a producer. They would have wanted to sneak him into their satin bedrooms at night and fall asleep cuddling him like a stuffed toy. There was still something toylike about him; perhaps a damaged, moldering, neglected toy. His blond hair was still tossed across his forehead but it looked set and dusty now, like a mannequin's wig. His anorexic Tutankhamen frame was wrapped in tapered *Dr. No* slacks and a bright Mod blouse of a kind not seen since the cover of *Highway 61 Revisited.* Inside the elbow of the left sleeve, no bigger than a spindle hole, was a dot of fresh blood.

He stepped back to me as Big Willy entered to hand me the coffee in a chipped turquoise cup. I thanked Big Willy and Dennis dismissed him with a nod. Big Willy lumbered out, his warm-up pants showing the crack of his fat butt.

"I'm sorry about last night," Dennis said almost cordially, though barely below the surface there was a great screeching pain.

I lifted the coffee and saw a bright red lipstick print on the rim. Specks of blue mold and undissolved crystals floated on the surface of the tepid brown water. I set it down. "That's okay. I didn't mean anything by it, I assure you. I'm a big fan of yours."

"Yes, I know." He sat down on the piano bench, then immediatey jumped up, like a man with an untreatable rash. "I listen to you a lot. When I'm up. And not working."

"I thought you were retired."

I saw instantly that I'd said the wrong thing. He drilled me with a wall-crumbling Mansonian glare.

"I'm not retired. I'm advanced."

"Advanced?" I cleared my throat.

"Ahead of my time. That's why I listen to you. I want to know what people are doing now. Can I tell you something?"

"What's that?"

"It's all shit. Everything that's out now. All of it. They're still living off me. Everything they're doing now, I did it all fifteen years ago. Do you know that?"

Now that he was finally looking at me I almost wished he weren't. If he'd ordered me to go scrawl "Pig" in bloody letters on somebody's front door I probably would have been compelled to obey.

"You've got a point," I said, looking at the crud in my coffee cup. "A lot of the things people are doing now are derived from your earlier work."

"Derived?" He reeled into Führerbunker shtick. "*Derived? Stolen* is more like it! If it weren't for me they'd still be recording Gogi Grant in a shower! Running mikes like Dixie cups on string! If it weren't for me, you'd still be listening to Perry Como and Pat Boone!"

"Actually, I just heard a new Pat Boone single the other night. A really raunchy hard-core punk cover of 'Whole Lotta Love.' Not bad. Didn't think he had it in him."

He stared at me, a vein beating in his temple. "That's funny," he said, though he didn't laugh or smile. "That's pretty fucking hilarious. You've quite a sense of humor. I like that. Humor's important."

"I couldn't agree more. In fact, I honestly believe that if we could get Henry Kissinger and the late Totie Fields to trade places, even for a day, we could—"

He waved me to be quiet. "Fuck all that, I don't care about politics. Look, Scott, there's a reason I asked you up here—"

"I'm sure there is, but before you say anything I should tell you I look lousy in a mini-skirt and go-go boots."

He exploded. "Goddammit, shut up, you stupid ignorant fuck! How dare you make a joke about this! I'm about to share something with you that's so incredible and astonishing no words can even describe it. And you're making glib, stupid jokes!"

This more or less wiped the smirk off my face. I stood, shaken. "I'm sorry, I didn't mean—"

"No, no, no, no, I'm sorry, I'm sorry, it's me, it's me." He touched my arm, forlorn and desperate now. "Please, I'm just not used to . . . anything anymore. My nerves are shot. Shot. It's not you, it's me. I'm sorry. Please say you forgive me. Please. Please."

He held my arm, his eyes imploring, abject. There was something horrendously unwholesome and studied about this performance, as if it were a game he was used to playing with someone else. But the pleading Bambi look still got to me.

"Forget it, it's no big deal. But I think we're both tired, so I'm gonna take off—"

"Wait." He hurried back to the table, looking frantically through the junk that was piled there.

"Here it is." He held up an audio cassette. "I want you to hear this." He pressed it into my hand as though it contained the secret to cheap solar energy.

"What is it?"

"It's the end product of fifteen years of accelerated pain," he said reverently.

"No kidding," I said, then braced myself for another explosion.

But he continued on the same solemn tack. "This cassette holds the music of the future. It's going to render every other form of music obsolete. There's never been anything even remotely like it. Never."

"I'll give it a listen," I said as neutrally as I could.

But now there was a flash of rage. "Don't humor me."

"I'm not humoring you, Dennis," I said as gently as I knew how.

"I don't need to be patronized. Just because I'm a genius doesn't mean I can't tell when people are laughing at me."

"I would never laugh at you, Dennis. I've practically worshiped you since I was fifteen." I was exaggerating only slightly. "Your records were the soundtrack to some of the key events of my life—"

"I'm not interested in your life," he interrupted, but the anger was leaving his voice now. "Or mine. The past is a trap. Believe me, I know." He attempted a laugh; it sounded more like a dry, embalmed cough. "That's what a lot of people think, isn't it? That I'm trapped in the past. That that's all I've been doing for the last fifteen years, just sitting around the house listening to my old records and reliving my glory days. Well, they're wrong. Nothing could be further from the truth. While they've been sucking my blood like the parasites and leeches they are, I've been surpassing them all. I'm light-years ahead of them. And this cassette is the proof."

"I take it this isn't the only copy." A little joke.

No smile from him. No explosion either. "I warn you, you may not understand it."

That was what I was afrad of. If his current state of mind were any indication, I'd be better off listening to chalk screech.

"I don't care what you think of it. If you laugh, or if it makes you sick, it doesn't matter. I expect to be misunderstood. I don't care about people's opinions anymore. People are vermin, they're all idiots."

"Yeah, I know what you mean." I moved toward the door.

He followed, slipping his hand over my shoulder. "But I like you, Scott. I don't know why, but I do. You seem decent, and that's rare. This is a city of scumbags. Rich powerful scumbags, poor desperate scumbags, it doesn't matter, they all have one thing in common. They'll cut out your heart and sell it to you for lunch when you're starving."

"Yeah, I know. That may be why I generally brown-bag it."

"But you seem different. I've been listening to your voice for a long time now, and there's something genuinely good and innocent about you. Frankly, I thought you were much younger, just from your voice."

"Well, I'm really only nineteen. But I did a lot of speed in elementary school."

"Didn't we all, didn't we all." Another dry laugh. "But I can't touch that stuff anymore myself, which is a shame, in a way. But I can't."

I considered suggesting that he might have used up all his allotted cocaine thrills as well.

"But you listen to this tape and you will know, you will see, why it's taken me so long. How long did Einstein work on the theory of relativity? Does that sound egocentric? I know some people consider me a megalomaniac. I've heard all the stories. I have people who tell me things. But this tape is going to destroy everyone who's against me. It's going to bring them to their knees. They'll be left holding . . . nothing. It'll be like the Great Depression. They'll be jumping out windows once this music hits the streets. No one will ever want to listen to anything else again, there'll be no need to. I've said it all here, I've summed up everything. After this there's nothing more to say."

He was walking me up the red velvet corridor, continuing to hype the tape in the same disturbingly abstract way—"a new music, a new *form* of music"—when I heard her. She was somewhere far back in the house, singing "Angel Baby," accompanying herself on piano.

The song was very clear by the time we reached the foyer, echoing plaintively from a distant upstairs room. I stopped following what he was saying completely. I was stunned. Her voice had not changed. It blew through me like a wet wind, like a wet sob, like a tough teenage girl sobbing in an empty house. Even the song, the penultimate lowrider anthem I might ordinarily have laughed at as so much camp romanticism, gave me chills up the back of my legs and my spine. She was transforming it, beyond all possibility of ridicule, into something harrowingly poignant and sad. When I realized he was still talking to me about the tape, I was astonished. How could he ignore her, ignore what was happening now, this moment?

"What's *she* doing these days?" I said, trying to make it sound like simple curiosity as I glanced to the top of the stairs.

"Nothing. She's finished," he said, vaguely irritated.

I almost laughed, thinking he was being facetious. Then Big Willy was opening the door and the sun and heat were beating in. I felt funny, slightly light-headed. Dennis and I exchanged a few final words, a handshake, then I was climbing into my car. I looked up at the room her voice was coming from. The window was dark, and like all the others, barred. I sat in the car for a moment, sweaty again, increasingly light-headed. Her voice broke as she sang the chorus, then abruptly stopped. I heard Dennis, his voice echoing, distorted, angry. She responded softly and his anger became more emphatic. Although I tried, I couldn't make out their words.

Then I looked over at the front door, which was still open. Big Willy was leaning against the frame, glaring at me.

"The gate's open," he said.

I started my engine.

3

I drove in silence for quite a while, Sharlene's voice still in my mind. There'd been nothing from her, musically or otherwise, since the Stingays were terminated mid-tour in 1967, for reasons known only to Dennis. She'd married him shortly after that. In oldies' books she was officially listed as "retired."

When I'd thought of her over the years—and I had—I'd always reluctantly concluded that she must be a mess. If she hadn't been initially, she would be by now, locked up in that asylum with him for fifteen years. I usually pictured her as a whacked-out rock-and-roll casualty, like an "after" shot of Anita Pallenberg, fat and blasted, lurching through the corridors in a filthy muumuu, stepping over hypodermic needles stuck in the shag. Rock hell.

Now I wasn't so sure. The voice I'd just heard didn't go with those pictures. It was a clear, pure voice. Though it was steeped in loneliness, the emotion was clean, not muddied with the self-pity and narcissism of drugs.

But then, what could you tell from a voice? It was her instrument, after all; it might well be the last thing to go. She was probably a zombie, a complacent cow ploppd in front of soap operas, stuffing herself with gothics and Haägen-Dazs, waddling over to the piano once in a while. Maybe she was an alcoholic, slurping up vermouth, and I'd caught her early in the day before she started slurring. There had to be *something* wrong with her, something serious, if she was still with him.

But that voice, so emotionally direct and uncontrived. So young. If I hadn't known who it was, that it was a woman in her mid-thirties, I would have thought he was keeping a teenage girl prisoner in one of the upstairs rooms.

I flipped on the radio, about to play Dennis' cassette, and heard that voice again. Though I knew it was just a coincidental collision with my thoughts, it still jolted me that they should be playing a Stingrays song on the oldies station just now.

"When We Kiss" surged from the speakers in glistering waves of romantic euphoria as shimmering as the blue-green ocean off to my right.

> When we kiss
> Baby, under the boardwalk
> When we kiss
> Baby, down on the strand
> When we kiss,
> Baby, in your Sting Ray
> When we kiss
> Baby, on the sand

I was quickly gone to the present, drawn back into the Cheryl Rampton film, to where we . . .

. . . kiss on the sofa, drenched with sweat, the TV flickering through the haze of marijuana smoke, the James Brown record clicking in the groove.

"Scott?" Cheryl whispers as we move togther. "Are you wearing anything?"

"Just my socks. Shall I take those off too?"

"You know what I mean."

Yeah, I know, and I'm not. But I'm prepared. I've got one

in my chest of drawers, hidden under my merit badges. I withdraw with a sense of poignance.

"Maybe we should go into my bedroom," I say.

"What about your parents?"

I explain that they're gone for the whole weekend, and catch another glimpse of Chet Huntley on the silent TV before Cheryl blocks the screen with her sweet perfect ass as she hits the off switch. She's coming back to me now, her wet glossy brown muff level with my face.

We go into the bedroom and don't come out for hours. When we do come out, we're starving. I've invited her to stay over and she calls her mother, prepared with a story. But her mother doesn't answer. This worries her until she sees that it's after ten; her mother has invariably passed out drunk by now, she tells me.

We go out to the local Jack-in-the-Box, ordering through the plastic clown. When we pull up to get our orders and pay, I'm startled for a second because it looks like the girl at the window is crying. Then I realize she must just have a cold. Cheryl and I eat ravenously in the car.

Saturday morning we smoke a joint with our coffee and end up slipping and sliding off the slick plastic breakfast-booth seats in fits of giddy laughter. Around noon we decide to head down to the beach, swinging by Cheryl's house in Lomita so she can get her suit. I park a block away and wait while she goes to get her bikini, and a lid of grass. She comes back looking worried. Her mother has been gone all night, she says, and she obviously left in a hurry the previous day; as her lunch was still uneaten on the table and the door had been left wide open.

Cheryl's still worried as we reach the beach, which is oddly deserted, considering that it's Saturday and fairly warm.

"If she isn't back by tomorrow, we can call the jails to see if she's been arrested," I say, which is a valid suggestion, since her mother has been picked up for drunkenness a number of times before.

Then we do our best not to let what we can't control spoil the weekend, and with more dope, and my eight-track blasting, we succeed.

That night we make love for hours again. I'm already addicted to her, totally strung out. And as we lie there later, holding each other on the bed, the real jolt hits, because as I look in her eyes I can see that she's in love with me too. And it hasn't just happened. I can see that she has been as aware of me through the months since our first encounter as I have been of her. But now there's no more need to be cool.

"You called me that night, didn't you," she says, "and played that Beehives' song all night long. That was you, wasn't it?"

She looks amused. I shrug, amused myself, only slightly embarrassed. "What can I say? I was very drunk."

"My mom was very pissed off." She kisses my chest.

"It could have been worse. I could have played Pat Boone records all night long." We both laugh.

"My mom would've liked that."

"What about you?"

She kisses my stomach, my cock brushing her cheek. "I don't think I'd be here right now if you had."

The next morning, I'm frying eggs in the kitchen when she flips on the TV in the rumpus room. "There's nothing on but religious shows," I call out.

"What the hell is this?"

I look and see a live shot of a bunch of people in a crowded corridor, a big guy in a light suit and cowboy hat, and a bunch of uniformed cops. Then a guy is being led through the crowd, a rabbity, nondescript guy, and then there's this firecracker pop. Somebody says, "He's been shot. He's been shot. Lee Oswald's been shot." And then there's total chaos and we're both shocked because it's obviously real, it's not a

TV show, it's really happening, we've obviously been missing out on something pretty major, and the eggs are burning on the stove but I'm too stunned to move. "Who the hell is Lee Oswald?" Cheryl says. "What the hell is going on?"

We find out. Cheryl gets hysterical, crying in disbelief, especially devastated because all this has been going on for two days without us even knowing about it.

"I should have known there was something wrong when there was nobody at the beach, yesterday," she says through her tears.

I don't cry. More stunned than anything, I do my best to comfort her. We learn that her mother went out and got so drunk she ended up in the Harbor General Psych Unit, where she will remain for another week, leaving Cheryl to fend for herself.

I drop her off at her house late that afternoon, since my parents are due back that evening. I know she's going to be alone at least for several days. She promises to call. I promise to come by, but secretly I'm apprehensive. It isn't logical, but then neither is Catholic guilt. That's what worries me: her Catholic background and the possibility she may feel some sort of bizarre guilt over the fact that we were fucking while the President died. Of course that's absurd. What we were doing didn't *cause* the President's death; only a true religious psychotic would believe that. But I'm worried. I don't want to lose her. I don't want what's begun to be tainted in any way.

My fears prove groundless. On Monday I go over to her house and we watch the funeral together, and I realize that our sharing of the national ordeal has only brought us closer together. "I'm glad I was with you when I found out," she says.

"I'm glad I was with you," I say, and realize how much I really mean it. The picture of Kennedy above the TV, his face and the simulated frame stamped in plastic relief like a map, has been draped with dark blue ribbons.

So our romance begins in tragedy. But in the weeks and then months to come, we're as inseparable as two teenagers in love but still living at home can be.

On weekends we often have my house to ourselves. My parents are headed toward a divorce, my mom spending more and more time in San Diego on an archaeology project, my dad losing himself in compulsive Boy Scout activities. My little brother, Joey, can be a problem if dad hasn't taken him along. In our family it's my mother who's doing the cheating with another archaeologist, and my father who's the martyred prude. And Joe is a twelve-year-old replica of dad. Most of the time, I can palm him off on his best friend's parents. But one Saturday he comes back unexpectedly and nearly catches Cheryl and me in the act. She hides behind my bedroom door, naked and trying not to laugh, as Joey glares at me suspiciously and asks if I've see his snake-bite kit.

One Friday evening Cheryl and I are doing it on the living-room carpet in front of the fireplace when we hear a key in the front-door lock. We grab our clothes and duck into the hall just as my mom steps through the door, humming the theme from *Mondo Cane* under her breath. She stops humming when she sees the fire.

"Scott?"

I cringe, pulling on my pants, my cock jutting the fabric, and no shirttail to hide it. I can't let my mom see me like this. Cheryl zips up her skirt, hastily tucking in her blouse as she tries not to giggle.

"Scottie?" my mom calls, striding toward the hall.

Cheryl suddenly turns sober. "I'll handle it," she says.

I lunge into my bedroom, leaving Cheryl to intercept my mom at the door.

Pulling on a Pendleton to cover my persistent bulge, I expect to hear an explosion at any moment. Instead I hear low voices.

Finally, I step into the living room. As I do, Cheryl and my mom erupt in a gale of laughter over something one or the other has just said. They turn to look at me from the rattan bar where they're both nursing beers. My mom is smiling, a bit too brightly. Casually, as if no one will notice, Cheryl is buttoning her blouse. But it's cool, it seems cool. I get a beer from the bar refrigerator, finishing half of it in several gulps.

Cheryl and my mom continue their feverish talk (the subject is archaeology, but I suspect a more profound spiritual communion) until I finally mention that we'd better get going if we're going to make the movie. This is a pointless discretion since my mom clearly knows she's interrupted our weekend, but Cheryl picks up the cue, and her overnight bag (which my mom makes a point of ignoring). As we're walking out the door, my mom's lover arrives. After a four-way exchange of blinding bright smiles, Cheryl and I drive off into the night.

We're less discreet at school. We walk along with our arms around each other and I am only occasionally aware of the looks of envy and hate—in the eyes of my PV peers she might as well be black. If I'd just fucked her at the drive-in, then told all the guys about it later, it would be no big deal. But this is much more; this is love, and that's wrong.

But I don't care what they think anymore and they know it. I'm not playing by the old rules, or any rules at all. With Cheryl I have a new bearing. Whatever people are thinking, no one dares to say anything to my face.

We're happy. Though Cheryl and I are together for only five months the time seems stretched out, the days seem to last forever. The dope we're smoking constantly makes a three-minute song seem to play for an hour. "Don't Worry, Baby" is a euphoric rock symphony as we stream down the coast in my souped-up '57 Chevy Bel-Air.

I'm the deejay at the sockhops now, my first gig. I like to play what they want—Leslie Gore, Connie Francis, Paul and Paula—then slip in, say, "Please, Please, Please" or "Little Red Rooster" and watch the Breck Girls making barf faces while their boyfriends blow their Goldwater crewcuts. I dance with Cheryl to "Hold Me Tight," insulated in the ecstatic glow of the music, protected from the mean-spirited world.

We make plans for the future, inventing adventurous scenarios as we loll naked on my single bed, the sunlight flickering through the eucalyptus trees outside the plate-glass window. We talk about taking off when summer comes, going to Mexico or Greece or Morocco, wherever fate takes us, not coming back at all. Of course we don't have any money. We also talk about getting our own place when we graduate, a beach apartment in Hermosa where we can shimmy in the sunshine and let the sea breeze dry our sweaty loins. But graduation is an eternal two years away.

We have fun. Going anywhere with Cheryl is always a scene. She turns heads with her beauty and her laugh. That uncouth, thrill-crazy, roller-coaster laugh coming from such a sweet angel face.

We're thrill-crazy all right, with a love that's hard to hide. We go out to an International House of Pancakes one Sunday morning, covered with hickeys, reeking all-night sex. It's a church crowd. We're cuddling in a booth, minding our own business, when Cheryl apparently says "fuck" too loud. A family is offended and we're asked to leave. I piss on a Rambler in the parking lot and we drive away laughing.

One evening in Wallach's Music City, we're spinning a Beehives platter in one of the listening booths when the manager walks past and catches Cheryl and me making out, my hand in the V of her capris, hers squeezing my cock through my Levi's. "There'll be none of that in here." We leave in a daze and pick up where we left off in the car.

It's the quiet times that are the best though. The lingering walks along the beach. Like the time at Redondo, the twilight sky filled with pink clouds, when she tells me about her father.

"He's a cowboy. In Arizona. He's great."

"Do you see him very often?"

"No, not too often. He's got another family and everything. But he said I could come stay with him if things ever got too bad with Mom."

This disturbs me. I know things are bad with her mom, but I don't want her to move to Arizona. Something else disturbs me too, a sense that she may be coloring the truth.

"He's a *cowboy*?"

"Well, he's retired now. But he lives on a ranch. He's rich, too. See, he never really married my mom. But he used to send money. And gifts. I know he loves me."

"I love you too." I kiss her cheek as we walk.

"I know," she says lightly, as if it were a joke. "That's why I'm still here."

There's a lightness to everything between us, which sometimes amazes me. We can talk about anything. I don't have to watch myself, and neither does she. Without even trying to, we seem to have moved beyond the more insipid aspects of romance. We have no need for games of jealousy and possessiveness. We're one of those few lucky couples who've found each other early in life. We know we love each other and always will. We can afford to relax.

Then one Friday evening I'm waiting for her in my Chevy at a Norm's Restaurant near her house. I always meet her here rather than risk a scene with her mom. She's late. It starts to rain. Finally through the spattered windshield I see a Ford Woody pull up. It belongs to Bill Holtner, the prick who bad-mouthed Cheryl worse than anybody, and so I am more than a little amazed when the Woody door opens and she gets out. Bill guns his engine in deliberate provocation and peels out as she ducks over through the rain and gets in. I'm boiling. Though I know it's crazy, stupid, I can't control myself.

"What the fuck's going on?"

She opens her bag as though she hasn't even noticed my irrational anger. Inside is a lid of grass. "Didn't you want me to score?"

I remember that we discussed it. I usually score but my connection had been busted. She said she knew someone, but not that it was Bill. All very logical, but my adrenaline is still going berserk. I'm thinking cheap evil thoughts, like: Oh yeah? What did you have to do, suck his cock for it? All the while she's beaming like Heidi, which I take as a tip-off in itself. Finally she starts talking about where we can go during Easter break, and I can't understand why she isn't picking up on my foul vibrations—unless she just doesn't want to. I try to relax and let it go. And mostly do.

For her seventeenth birthday, I give her a silver anklet. Naked on my bed, she stetches out her right leg, the anklet glimmering in the sunlight. I look up her leg to where a blade of sunlight glistens in her muff.

"I think I'll wear it on the left side," she says, fumbling with the clasp. "Damn, I can't get this thing off."

"That's the idea," I say, trying to open it for her. "It's a slave anklet."

"Then you should be wearing one too," she says softly. "You're my slave, aren't you?"

"Yeah, I guess I am at that. I should've listened to my father. He sat me down and warned me."

"Did he?"

I finally get the clasp open, using my teeth. "Yeah, he told me not to do certain things with a woman or she could make me her slave for life."

I drape the chain around her left ankle, but now I can't get the clasp closed. She doesn't seem to care.

"What things?"

"Oh, he told me . . ." I set the anklet aside. "He said, no

matter how much a woman begs you to . . ." I spread her legs. "You should never, ever, under any circumstances, do this." I bury my face in her glistening muff.

That night a storm bludgeons the PV house. We see floods on TV, hear about roads washing out. From the patio we can see Cal Trans crews trying to save houses down at Portuguese Bend. Safe on high ground, we joke about it when I'm in her, kissing her as we move together slowly.

"What would you do right now," she says, "if the house started to come down?"

"Nothing," I say, knowing it's the only possible response. "What would be the point? Everything after this is all gonna be downhill anyway."

We both laugh, thinking this is fairly neat and clever, wondering if by any chance it may be true.

That reel ended as I pulled up to the Tropicana. It had always been my favorite reel, and it was a good place to stop. I knew what was on the next one.

It wasn't as if I'd been watching the Cheryl Rampton film every night for the last twenty years. Life had gone on. There'd been three marriages, enough affairs to fill a thick country-western songbook, meaningful relationships, meaningless relationships, a few Mann Act violations, and maybe three or four one-night stands. I'd been in love, in hate, I'd been infatuated, bedazzled, obsessed, satisfied, tricked, fucked blind, and fooled again. I'd been with redheads, brunettes, honey blonds, and punkettes with violet hair. I'd been with Sharon Tate and Linda Kasabian types, Debra Harry and Debby Boone types, Pat Benatar and Patty Hearst types, Bianca Jagger types and types that needed Binaca, Diana Ross and Big Mama Thornton types, China girls and girls strung out on China White, Latino spitfires and German Messerschmitts, girls with smiling Irish eyes and laughing Italian elbows. I'd gone home with models and movie stars, secretaries and psychopaths, telephone linewomen, comediennes, authoresses, masseuses, rock songstresses, female mud wrestlers, housewives from the Simi Valley, widows in Bel-Air, Avon ladies, hit ladies, former First Ladies, Seven-Eleven checkers, Ph.D.'s and retardees, chemists and cocktail waitresses, Garbo look-alikes and good-natured geeks, at least one nun, a fifty-two-year-old virgin and a twelve-year-old Campfire Girl who'd turned out to be a whore. I'd been with short ones, tall ones, fat ones, skinny ones, ones with big tits, small tits, no tits, one tit, three tits. I'd been with some of the world's most intelligent, beautiful women and some of the stupidest, ugliest broads alive. And I'd loved 'em all. I had a memory bank full of good fucks, bad fucks, so-so fucks, wild fucks, listless fucks, unforgettable, lacerating, mind-bending fucks, fucks I still drank to forget, other fucks I drank to remember, fucks that were over too soon, or not soon enough, fucks interrupted by a husband or boyfriend or father or lesbian lover pulling into the driveway, headlights shining on the wall.

I hadn't just sat around for two decades grieving over Cheryl Rampton. My grief had been confined to a three-year period, '64 to '67, the duration of the Stingrays' career. Even then it wasn't constant, but a sporadic, low-level grief. And it was private. None of the new friends I made in college knew anything about Cheryl. But when a Stingrays song came on the radio, when I heard Sharlene's voice, I was instantly drawn back into the Cheryl Rampton film.

I'd had a girlfriend during that time who made a face whenever I turned up a Stingrays song. She considered them dated, anachronistic greaser music, from the dead plastic age of the early sixties. Heather preferred the timeless now sounds of the Strawberry Alarmclock and Moby Grape.

It was a kind of blessing when the Stingrays made their final pit stop in early '67. Their music was so inexorably bound up with my memories of Cheryl that as long as they were coming out with new songs I would have never been able to let go of her. When they stopped I did—and the break was clean. The Stingrays vanished from the airwaves overnight, washed away in the wave of psychedelia, of Jimi Hendrix, *Sgt. Pepper*, and Cream. They were relegated to the oldies stations, where "Love Me Tonight" remained a favorite. Only when I heard them in passing did I still see clips from the Cheryl Rampton film. I didn't play them myself for many years.

I was playing them again now. Up in my room at the Tropicana I put on side two of *Fuel-Injected Dreams*.

Why was I doing this to myself now?

Some of it had to be because of Lynn. All kidding aside, I'd had high hopes for Lynn. She was schizoid, to be sure, ideas and emotions pulling in opposite directions. But we did have fun. It was really good in the beginning. And I did love her. I'm not sure I was *in love* with her. We discussed that once, both of us agreeing that the concept of "being in love" was a "puerile, oppressive construct" (these were her words, actually), something people did back in high school when they didn't know any better. What we had, according to Lynn, was a "mature, supportive relationship." Until the night she accused me of trying to rape her in her sleep.

Side two concluded with "Paradise in the Rearview Mirror," a voluptuously dreamy, cyclical reverie. After the churning, ecstatic anthems of romantic utopia that filled the rest of the album, it provided a soft sense of closure, Sharlene alone again in her pastel suburban bedroom yearning for the summer just passed:

> Those long hot afternoons
> when the sun seemed to never set.
> Laughing softly on the beach,
> Baby, I'll never forget.
> But the night finally came,
> and you drove me home,
> and I saw in your eyes so clear:

    Paradise fading away
    with the light in the rearview mirror.

Colored angels swooned behind her, triangles tinkling like tears.

Rumbling down Sunset in the Lincoln later that night, I stuck Dennis' cassette in the deck. I'd delayed listening to it as long as possible. It began with a long empty hiss—no Dolby here—increasing my apprehension. I didn't really know what to expect. Some sort of dissonant avant garde crap probably, judging from his "new-*form*-of-music" talk. Ersatz John Cage, something like that. Or maybe something truly psychotic—ambient sound recorded with rooftop microphones. Birds chirping, a distant dog, jets—though it was difficult to imagine a Contrelle sound, no matter how unhinged, without a pulsating onslaught of percussion, like the entire population of South America on marimbas and glockenspiel. I suppose what I feared more than anything was some sort of competent but lifeless rehash of what he'd already done.

No music came. Instead I heard a voice. Dennis, speaking low and throatily, close to the mike. "Oh, angel. My sweet little angel. You're my precious little angel. That's all you are."

I figured it had to be a joke. A parody of a Barry White disco rap. I waited in vain for the thumping bass line to start.

Instead, there were scuffling sounds, the rustle of clothing or sheets.

Then Sharlene: "Dennis, stop. You're hurting me."

"Am I?" He laughed dryly.

"Oh, baby, no. Not like that." Her voice had a pouty, baby-doll quality, though there seemed to be a tinge of panic.

A loud slap. Dennis: "Shut up."

"But, baby, I can't take it—"

"You're *going* to take it, though. Because you're still my angel. My little fucking angel. That's all you are."

"Dennis, stop! Oh my God, baby, you're killing me!"

Dennis grunted. Bedsprings squeaked. "You cunt."

Sharlene cried out. "Oh, Dennis! Oh no!"

I pressed Eject.

Whoa. What the hell was *that*?

For starters it had to be a mistake. He'd given me the wrong cassette. This was certainly no music of the future. He couldn't be that demented, could he?

Then what? They couldn't be serious, could they? It had to be a game, a depressing little sex game. It turned him on if she pretended to be hurt. It flattered his ego, which probably needed a lot of flattering. That had to be it. It was there in her voice, the stylized baby-doll quality, not unlike the attitude she struck in some of the Stingrays' more tearful songs.

And what about his voice? He sounded exhausted. And fixated. From adoration to contempt in less than fifteen seconds. Why? Had she done something wrong? Or was the transition itself part of the game?

I really didn't know, I really wasn't sure. It was like hearing a couple having sex in the next apartment. The sound alone could be deceiving. Their grunts and moans might sound like a parody of lust, when they weren't at all. You might think they were fighting, hurting each other, when the opposite was true.

I considered playing more of the cassette, but I decided I'd already heard too much. It was probably a game. But even if it wasn't, it was none of my business what they did, was it? I slipped the cassette back in its case.

At five after midnight the phone lit up.

"KRUF. This is not John Lennon speaking, but an incredibly obscene simulation—"

'I gave you the wrong tape. Have you listened to it?"

"Not yet. I was going to—"

"Don't. The contents of that tape are extremely private."
He was calm, matter-of-fact. "If you listen to so much as a
minute of that cassette, I'll be forced to have you killed."

I laughed. "Dennis, there's no reason to be melodramatic.
I haven't listened to it and I certainly won't now. Whatever
your reason, it's fine with—"

"Where is it now?"

"Right here. I've been swamped with new releases. I just
haven't had a chance to—"

"Don't touch it. I'll send someone by for it. And listen,
friend—" He said *friend* the way Jim Jones had on the last
day of his life. "—I know tape. I've got sophisticated elec-
tronic equipment. If you play that cassette even once, I'll be
able to tell. And I'll kill you, my friend. I don't lie. I'll have
my bodyguard doing rope tricks with your intestines." He
hung up.

So. I examined the cassette. I hadn't bothered to rewind
it in the car. I did now. He was crazy, of course. You
couldn't tell how many times a tape had been played. Could
you? I ejected the rewound cassette and examined it again.
There was a slight ridge where I'd stopped it in the car. I
tapped the housing, trying to level the tape. That didn't
work. I considered unscrewing the housing, tapping the tape
down by hand. Then I thought: Wait, what is this shit? Am
I going to allow myself to be reduced to a sniveling state of
terror by the gibbered threats of some burnt-out brain-dam-
aged geek? Jesus, come on! He wasn't going to have me
killed, for Christ's sake, just because I happened to listen to
thirty seconds of him balling his wife. Balling, jeez, what a
sixties word. Probably the word *he* would use. Come on,
baby, let's ball. Turn on your lava lamp. Hit the black lights.

I spun a B-52's side, and went out and put the cassette on
the table in the lobby. That way when Big Willy came to get
it, I could buzz him into the lobby from the safe sanctuary
of my glass vault. Just in case he was in a rope-trick mood.

Hours passed and he didn't come. I half-expected another

call, but all I got were the usual romantic dedication requests; a buff wanting something by a group called the Fucks
—this was either a joke or a local punk group I hadn't heard
of yet; a graphic overture from a lonely male nurse; a sultry
request for "Misty" ("No way, baby, crawl back in your
cage"); and a Latino girl who'd just had a fight with her
boyfriend and taken thirty 'ludes. I got her address and re-
layed it to paramedics in Pico Rivera. My good deed for the
night.

Finally it was almost six and he still had not come. Eddie,
the morning man, breezed in, grinning harshly, reminding
me why I preferred the graveyard shift. "Hey, look what I
found in the lobby." He had the cassette.

I took it. "Yeah, that's mine." I didn't bother to explain.

"Good morning, Los Angeles," he was screeching into the
mike as I cringed out the door. "Up and at 'em, kids. Let's
start things off with the J. Geils Band!"

I ran for the elevator and its soothing Muzak version of
Neil Young's "Like a Hurricane."

In the car I decided to be done with it. I hadn't slept in
two days and didn't want Big Willy coming around again
pounding on my door at noon. I shot out Sunset to PCH
opposite the rush-hour traffic, my top down, radio blasting
Randy Newman, the air already charged with a broiling fur-
nace heat. I reached the Contrelle place a little after seven.

Because of the hour I assumed they were either still asleep
or still awake. Not wanting to disturb them in either case, or
risk a second encounter with their pets, I pulled up to the
mailbox by the gate and opened the slot. I was about to drop
in the cassette when the intercom emitted a staticky female
voice.

"Yeah, what do you want?"

It was Mrs. Contrelle. I looked at the house and could
just make out her silhouette in the barred upstairs window.

"Delivery, ma'am. Got a case of Coppertone here for
Gidget."

"You've got the wrong house." She had a cheap biker-mama voice. I imagined her fat and blasted again.

"Just a joke, Mrs. Contrelle. This is Scott Cochran. I've got a tape for your husband. He was going to send somebody by to pick it up, but—"

"A tape? What kind of tape?" She sounded vaguely paranoid now. Was she a Preludin banshee, with a brain like a piece of coral?

"A cassette. Your husband gave it to me by mistake."

"Yeah, well, he's not here right now."

"That's okay. I'll just stick it in the mailbox."

"No, you better not do that." The gate began to hum open. "He thinks people steal things from the mailbox. You'd better bring it up to the house."

I stubbed out my cigarette and drove up to the house, where one of the Luxor front doors stood open. "Come on in," she called in the same trashy voice.

I stepped quickly from the car into the foyer (still no dogs in sight). From the empty foyer I saw a light go on back in the kitchen, where coffee was brewing.

"I'll just leave it here on the table," I called, when she stepped through the door behind me.

"I'll take it."

I turned to look at her and my brains blew up. I smiled so hard my teeth turned to chrome, my eyes turned to headlights that exploded. My head went through the windshield, the wheel crushed my lungs. For what seemed like minutes I was certain I was looking at a ghost.

My sense of her based on her singing voice had been insanely correct: she'd barely changed. If Dennis was mummified, Sharlene appeared suspended, as if she'd been frozen in '67 and only revived this morning. She could have stepped from the Stingrays' first album cover: her hair ratted up in a mean brown beehive, her mouth cherry red, her pale skin, so like Cheryl's, blushed with youthful luminescence, even in this hard morning light. Her eyes—I'd never

understood this before, print photos failed to capture it—
were the exact same shade as Cheryl's, an addictive phosphorescent blue.

She broke my heart; her sweet mouth edging toward a
sarcastic smile so like Cheryl's. A sheer red-and-blue Japanese silk kimono stuck to her high, jutting '58 Cadillac
breasts; rubber-tipped and ready for a head-on collison, they
made me want to jump behind her wheel like Hud, burning
rubber up the coast till I dropped a rod and blew her
engine.

"So you're the deejay," she said like an angel with the
voice of a gum-chewing slut.

"So you're my teenage dream," I heard myself say with
rattled elan, like Belmondo OD'ing on Dexatrim.

"I doubt that." Her eyes took in my body. "We were big
with greasers and lowriders. You look more like the Beach
Boys type to me."

"You're right, I was. But every once in a while I'd drive
over to the wrong side of town, score some reefer, and listen
to the Stingrays in Vibra-Sonic till I got hard."

She laughed, thank God. "Sounds lonely."

"I usually had company."

"Yeah, I'll bet. Some guy with buckteeth and zits."

"More like the homecoming queen." Her smile made me
feel cool, audacious. "Or a Breck Girl on Spanish fly."

"Yeah? I'll bet you came home with lipstick on your
Bermudas."

"That's right. And anchovies on my breath."

She winced. "You should save lines like that for your radio
show."

"We stopped for pizza," I explained.

"Is that what you told Ozzie and Harriet?"

"Ward and June."

"And how'd you explain the lipstick on your Bermudas?"

"No napkins. She had to blot her lips on my crotch."

"Did they believe you?"

"They told me to can the horny talk and go to my room and beat off."

"Sounds like good advice." She held out her hand for the cassette. "And don't tell me, you've been there ever since."

"Not quite." I put the cassette in her hand, her fat diamond wedding ring sparkling like a grinning Zulu's teeth.

"I'll see that he gets this," she said, smiling broadly, dismissively.

She slipped the cassette in her kimono pocket and brushed past me, going to the stairs. As she did I caught a whiff of cheap tropical perfume, a sweet Juicy Fruit scent Cheryl had also worn; perhaps many girls had. Two bucks an ounce at Thrifty's, as vulgar and galvanizing as a luscious fuck.

She started up the stairs, her silver anklet catching the sunlight.

"I expected him to send someone by," I said, knowing I was just trying to prolong the encounter.

"Yeah, well—" She turned on the stairs and I saw the reddish-purple mark on her neck. It was either a hickey or a bruise. "—he's at the studio. It must have slipped his mind." She continued up the stairs, adding, offhand, "What's left of it."

I stood there watching her go all the way up the stairs. The kimono was short. She wasn't wearing any panties. At the top she turned abruptly and looked back down.

"You know," she said, "you're not what· I expected. I mean, just from your voice."

"I didn't realize you were a fan."

"I'm not. I think you're tasteless."

"But you're forced to listen. Because your husband does."

She sniffed. "We sleep in separate rooms."

Whoa. "And what did you expect, Mrs. Contrelle?"

"I don't know. Prince Charming or somebody maybe." She was being sardonic, but something told me I shouldn't dismiss it.

"What does that make you, Sleeping Beauty?"

"Yeah. Letting my hair grow out the window."

In the sunlight her beehive looked as stiff as steel wool. "I'd try to climb it," I said. "But I'm afraid I might cut my hands."

"So use the stairs." She grinned.

And I reeled. Was she inviting me up right now?

But she laughed lightly, with a kind of bland wholesomeness, to show it was just an idle flirtation. To show she was just being a tease. "You'd better get out of here," she said, almost graciously. "He gets mad if the gate's left open."

She disappeared along the upstairs corridor, laughing merrily to herself when perhaps she thought I'd finally gone. I heard a door close. Then I left.

Back at the Tropicana I went straight to bed. As I lay there drifting off, I absently pulled my pud, thinking about Sharlene. But it was a futile dream. Not only was she married, she was married to a notorious psychopath, a man clearly capable of extreme violence. Further, though she appeared normal enough on the face of it, living with him, she had to be, ipso facto, as warped as a record left in a hot car. Oh well, in a better world . . .

It seemed like a waste, though. Her voice, that plaintive, heartrending wail. "She's finished." How could he say that? Did he just decide one day to put her in mothballs? Yes, apparently.

How could she have let him?

I felt for the ringing phone a few hours later. "Yeah?"

"What were you doing at the house? Why didn't you wait?" Dennis, brittle with rage.

"Nobody came. It was on my way, so I just—"

"It's not on your way. It's way out of your way."

"Look, Dennis, I'm not even awake yet. You got the tape, what's the problem?"

"I understand you talked to Shar."

"Yeah, briefly. I—"

"What did she tell you?" His voice slashed through the phone.

"I don't know what you mean—"

"Listen, listen, you've got to understand something." He was on the edge of hysteria, struggling not to go over. "Shar's very sick, she's a very sick lady, she's very fucked up. She's a pathological liar. She has severe emotional problems."

So would I if I were living with you, I thought. "I'm sorry to hear that."

"But nothing happened then? Nothing at all?"

I felt an obscure twinge of guilt over the lust in my heart. "No," I said, trying too hard to sound innocent. "I just gave her the cassette and—"

"Okay, fine, fine, fuck her, I believe you," he rattled on, as if suddenly bored with the subject. "Scott, listen, you've *got* to come down here right now. I'm doing some really astonishing things. Moments never to be repeated—"

"Dennis, I appreciate the invitation, but I'm really exhausted—"

"That means you're not coming down?" He was breathless with frenzy.

"Not today, I really—"

"Then fuck you, you simple shit! Who needs you, you mediocre moron. If sleep is more important than being privy to a key moment in the history of music and sound, then get fucked in the ass and the face." He hung up.

I laughed wearily, unplugged the phone, rolled over, and pulled up the sheet. For a moment I thought I caught a whiff of sweet perfume on my fingers. But it was just my imagination.

4

I told Neal all about it a few days later. We laughed over beers at his place in Ocean Park, a Victorian house he was restoring. He'd been my best friend since junior high, which I guess was fairly rare in a time when people come and go like trends. We had an easy friendship that had changed little over the years. We still talked about the same things we had as kids in Palos Verdes, ostensibly with a bit more sophistication: cars, music, girls.

He was a criminal attorney with a high-powered firm in the Century City Towers. In college his wavy brown hair had run down past his shoulder blades and his nickname had been "Aura." These days he was balding, his neat beard turning gray, his suits and bronzer featured in GQ, and his nickname "Shark." From *Siddhartha* to *Winning Through Intimidation*, from Melanie to Romeo Void. If I really wanted to drive him up the wall, all I had to do was call the "Sharktank" and ask to speak to "Aura."

He laughed incredulously as I described Dennis' schizoid mood shifts. But when it came to the business of the cassette, I found myself telling him, as I had Dennis, that I hadn't had a chance to listen to it. I guess I just wanted to spare Sharlene.

"He threatened to *kill* you?" Neal said.

"Yeah, but I don't think he was serious. His mind's completely gone. It's sad. I mean, he really was a genius."

He mourned this appropriately, then, with a sly look, said far too casually, "But she's still hot?"

"Sharlene? Yeah. Yeah, I'd say so." I gave him my best Jack Nicholson leer, hoping to convince him that simple lust had been my only response. "And if you ask me, she's *dying* for it. I mean, I don't think she's been getting it much from him."

He was supposed to take it as a joke, but he didn't. He studied his Lowenbrau bottle. "Well, a word of advice, Scott. If I were you, I'd look elsewhere."

"I don't know if I can *restrain* myself," I said, rubbing my crotch and refusing to get serious. "I'll tell you, when I went up there to drop off that tape, she was smoking. It was all I could do to get out of there with my dick in my pants."

"You take it out with her, it might be the last time you ever take it out," he said mirthlessly. "I'm serious, Scott. Guys like Contrelle . . . I mean, he sounds very paranoid—"

"Oh, just a tad maybe. But it's good, clean paranoia."

"It doesn't sound too clean to me. So what's her story? Is she a junkie too?"

I felt a flash of anger, imagining for a moment that he was deliberately baiting me. "I don't think so," I said. "She didn't look that way to me."

"What do you mean? No tracks? Junkies can be very clever about that. They shoot up between their toes—"

"No, I don't think she even does drugs. She looks too good. Anyway, I'm not exactly a babe in the woods when it comes to that sort of thing." If we were going to be in a court of law then I would be the key witness in her defense. "I would state unequivocally, basing my judgment on years of experience with numerous rock-and-roll dope fiends, that she does not do drugs of any kind."

"Then what's she doing with him?" He laughed.

"He's her husband." Inadequate answer. "He's got bars on the windows. Maybe she can't leave."

"What do you mean? What's stopping her? Is she a prisoner?"

"I'm not sure." This answer puzzled *me*, though it didn't seem to bother him.

"You said there was a scar on her neck?"

"A bruise. I'm not even sure it was a bruise. It could have been a hickey."

"A hickey!" He laughed. "A hickey! How sweet! They're still out there after twenty years giving each other hickeys!"

"You're a cynical man, Neal."

He laughed and went over to the shelves that held his video cassettes. "What was that song? 'He Hit Me—' "

" '—and It Felt Like a Kiss.' The Crystals."

"Maybe that's their trip. Fight and fuck. 'I knew he really loved me when he knocked out my teeth.' Jesus, how sick. But it's funny. I remember when all that was considered very cool."

"So do I." I thought about the cassette. Sharlene's pouty voice: "Dennis, stop. You're hurting me." "Am I?" His dry laugh.

"Times change though," Neal said as he shoved a tape into the VCR. "Or do they?" He laughed.

James Brown screamed "Please, Please, Please" for a moment, till Neal fast-shuttled through the vintage black-and-white performance, and we watched the hardest-working man in show business collapsing several times onstage.

"What's this?"

"History of Rock and Roll." He slowed the tape to normal speed when he came to a Stingrays performance. "Here we are."

It was "Love Me Tonight," live in an arena, circa 1966—you could tell because the guys now sported Beatles cuts and fruit boots, the flashbulbs were incessant, the screams deafening; probably one of their openers for the Stones. Although the instrumentation was rough and tinny, a pale sketch of the dense Contrell studio sound, Sharlene's voice cut through the din like a switchblade through fat. "Love me, baby. Love me now!"

The picture cut to a grainy close-up of Sharlene, a few strands of her beehive wilted with sweat, matted to her forehead, her eyes glistening, insane with crowd energy or amphetamine or both. She was possessed, transported, at the absolute peak of her form—singing more for herself really, or something beyond the arena, than for the thousands of screaming girls who could barely hear her anyway, and were finally only revving up for the Stones.

"You know who she always reminded me of?" Neal said at the exact moment I didn't want to hear it.

"Yeah, I know." I tried to sound casual.

An awkward moment followed. Neal broke it, speaking boisterously to change the mood. "Say, speaking of the past, I got a call from Gale Spivey, remember her?"

"Love me now, baby, *now*," Sharlene wailed into the mike, "because tomorrow may not come!"

"Can't say I do. Who the fuck is Gale Spivey?"

"Jesus, Scott. She must be in the damaged part of your brain. You were practically engaged to her. Drama class—"

She came back. A pudgy blond, sweet but square. "Oh, right. But we were hardly engaged. I think we did a couple of scenes together from *Streetcar*. She accused me of trying to dry-hump her during the rape scene."

"Maybe *that's* why she remembers you so well. Anyway, she's on the committee for the reunion, and she was wondering if you would help out—"

"Help out?"

"Yeah, you know, bring some records, some oldies. I told her, sure, he's kept everything he ever bought back to the 'The Ballad of Davy Crockett.' I gave her your number."

"Thanks. But I really don't know if I'm up to a reunion."

"Oh, come on, Scott. It'll be fun. Aren't you curious about people?"

"No." I stood. "Hey, look, I'm late for my mambo lesson. I'll catch you later, okay?"

I looked at the screen a last time. The song was over and hordes of teenage boys were storming the stage, pushed back by beefy security men, as Sharlene disappeared in a flash of sweaty chiffon.

I drove down to Redondo Beach and cruised along the broad Esplanade. The red sun was just touching the water. Surfers were out, a few waiting for waves, most standing around the VW's and Datsuns, sharing joints, radios and tape decks pumping out competing blasts of rock. In many ways the beach scene had changed little in twenty years, though you would have seen more Fords and Chevies then, you would have heard the Animals and the Dave Clark Five instead of Men at Work and ZZ Top.

I swept past a '65 Mustang convertible, top down to reveal two blond girls who could have passed for *Shindig* dancers, snapping their fingers to a nouveau rock remake of "He's a Rebel." I pulled into the lot and cut the engine.

The lot, the infamous beach lot. The rally point for the car culture of twenty years ago, for summer nights of endless cruising, quarts of Coors, and sex. I sat there watching the sunset, the sky so clear Catalina stood out in painful relief on the shimmering horizon.

Inevitably I looked to the spot by the powder-blue snack-bar building, under the grove of seedy palms, where I'd seen Cheryl Rampton for the last time on a hot April day in 1964.

That fateful Saturday begins around nine, as Cheryl taps on my bedroom window and wakes me up. My parents are gone—Mom ostensibly to visit her sister, Dad and my brother out with the Scouts—and this is a big day for us. It's the start of Easter vacation and we're going to sneak off to Catalina for the entire week. My dad has a small ranch house over there, not far from Avalon, but private, and this is the first time we've had a chance to use it. My dad thinks I'm going over by myself to do some work around the house. Yeah, I'm gonna lay some pipe, all right. Whip out my Black and Decker and drill a hole, drill it deep. Putty up a crack till it drips caulk. Then take a break and eat a box lunch. Smash a peach in my face and let it dribble down my chin.

So I'm excited; this will be the longest time we've ever spent together, and for once we won't have to worry about parents or school or my little brother walking in on us or anything at all.

I pad naked to the kitchen door and let Cheryl in, my erection roaring. In the bedroom, I playfully pull her down to the bed and unzip her tight aqua capris. She says, "Scott, not now," but I think she's joking, that it's just a game. Then she says, "Really, there's something I have to talk to you about." I still don't stop until she tells me what it is. Then my muscles lock like gears, my erection stops roaring, and I start to sweat.

"Are you sure?"

"Of course I'm sure. I saw the doctor yesterday."

This is about a month and a half after I saw her with Bill Holtner. In my stunned state I say what I'm thinking: "Well, it wasn't me."

I'm sorry as soon as I've said the words, but it's too late. "Well, who else could it have been?"

"You tell me."

She's hurt again, and now I'm not sorry, I'm mad.

"I haven't been with anybody else."

I light a Tareyton and try to speak carefully, reasonably. "I just don't see how it could have been me. We've always been careful." What I mean is I always wear a condom.

"Well, sometimes accidents happen."

I consider this doubtful. "In that case, maybe we should sue the Trojan company."

She gets up now, buttoning her pink blouse. "Oh, that's funny, that's hilarious. I'm pregnant and you're a comedian."

I sigh heavily. "Cheryl, look. This isn't the first time something like this ever happened to somebody—"

"To somebody? It didn't happen to somebody, it happened to me. Are you pregnant? No, I'm the one who's pregnant."

I sigh heavily again as she tucks in her blouse. "Well, what do you want to do?"

"What do *I* want to do?"

I'm thinking more and more about Bill Holtner, not that I suspect her of a juggling act. Seeing Bill Holtner wouldn't qualify as an affair. It would qualify as a fast fuck. And if she's been doing it with him, there may have been others. I mean, let's face it, she may not be the all-time slut of legend, but she's not exactly one of the Lennon Sisters either.

I get up and walk to the window, looking out at the dry backyard, at the bright blue swing on which we fucked one night a while back, while the neighbors had a barbecue just beyond the hedge. How we tried not to giggle when the springs squeaked.

I wore a rubber that time; she brought it to me herself when she came back from using the bathroom. She knew where I kept them, hidden behind my radio. She knows how careful I always am.

Still, I did feel something different that time when I came. The blast was hard, full, unimpeded. It was so good I just didn't question it. Or examine the rubber afterward to see if it was broken.

"What do you want *us* to do?" I say.

She's sitting on the bed now, looking numb and petulant. "There's only one thing we can do," she says in a Bambi voice. "Get married."

"Married?" She might as well have said leukemia.

"Yeah, you know," she says with breezy innocence. "Chapel bells, wedding cakes, honeymoons. Worse things could happen."

"Oh yeah?" I force a wry laugh. "Like what? Nuclear war?"

She starts to cry, plaintive little-girl sobs, breast-heaving Elizabeth Taylor sobs. I go to her and hold her in my arms but I'm practically hyperventilating. I hear a baby screaming in the dim back bedroom of a shitty housing project near San Pedro where a friend had to move when he knocked up a girl and married her. I see myself there, Cheryl fat, in curlers, dirty diapers in the tub, unpaid bills on the kitchen table, a lunchbox with my name on it.

"Cheryl, we can't get married now."

"Why not? It wouldn't be so bad. We could get a place in Miraleste Heights." Yuhhhh! The very same housing project! "Those places are pretty cheap."

"I can't," I run on, hating myself for sounding so selfish, but totally freaked out. "I don't even know what I want to do with my life yet. I don't know anything about raising a family. Shit, I'm only six-fucking-teen! I've never even written a goddamn check."

She pulls away from me now, fixing me with an evil, squinty-eyed glare that is such a parody of malice I almost laugh, thinking she's putting me on. "Well, let me tell you something, buster. You'd better learn."

I laugh, hoping it will dissipate her anger, but it only infuriates her more.

"If you think you can wriggle out of this, you've got another think coming."

I feel a little sick, the breath knocked out of me. "Cheryl, come *on*—"

But she's on an evil roll. "Let me tell you something, Mr. PV spoiled blond Republican, Mr. *Beach Boy*. If you think you can have all the fun and not have to pay the price, you're in for a big surprise."

"What's that supposed to mean?"

She looks at herself in the mirror, patting her beehive. I half wonder if she's reaching for a hidden razor blade. "It means you don't *fuck* with me."

I'm pissed now. "Yeah, well, if I don't, I'll be the only one who doesn't."

She cinches her white plastic belt like she's trying to strangle me with it. Hate-filled silence as she grabs her bag, spills it, scoops up the junk.

I watch from the bed, consider a number of remarks, both shitty and apologetic, but say nothing. The air is too charged. If I open my mouth again, she'll explode.

When she has scooped up eveything, she starts for the door, then does a dramatic Lana Turner whirlaround and fires point-blank. "Mark my words. You are going to regret this day for the rest of your life," she says with an icy, trembling voice, and stalks out.

I hear her slam the front door. I race to the living room and peer through the drapes, watching her stride angrily down the driveway to the street. How the fuck is she going to get home? There aren't any buses up here. I race back to my room, pull on my Levi's and huarachi sandals.

It takes me maybe five minutes to find my car keys; then I rush out to the Chevy, squeal out of the driveway, and roar down Conqueror Drive. She can't even have reached PV South yet on foot. But I don't see her. I reach PV South and she's not there either. Could she have hitched a ride this fast? Well, apparently. I drive north toward Redondo but she's gone. Probably sharing a joint with a carload of lowriders by now. "Hey, sweet thing. How far you goin'?"

Fuck her, I say, though I'm still worried.

I drive back to the house. When I pull up I see the station wagon in the driveway. This is unexpected. I get out and hear Boy Scouts in the house. Perhaps this disagreement was a blessing in disguise. Then I think about the evidence. I stroll in casually, trying to keep down the trembling, hoping to see my dad in the rumpus room with the Scouts. But he's not there. They quit talking and stare at me, then start whispering to each other as I cut toward the hall. Whispering? Why? Has my own father already cited me as an example of what they must never become?

He's not in the master bedroom loosening his kerchief, nor is he in the john taking a scoutmasterly whizz. I step to my bedroom door and stop cold.

He's at my desk. A few inches fom his dangling left hand are two foil-wrapped rolls of bennies. Barely hidden by the ashtray I made in junior high are six neatly rolled joints. But he isn't looking at the drugs, he's looking at me with a slapped, stunned expression as though he's just discovered proof that I'm a cocksucker working for the KGB. In his right hand he holds a playing card which I know he has taken from the pages of my old Boy Scout manual. I know this playing card is the jack of diamonds, but that's not what's upsetting him. It is also a grainy, poorly printed photo of a nun—or let us pray merely a wanton Mexican whore of yesteryear blasphemously garbed in nun's attire—a grinning naked gentleman poised behind her. Her mouth forms an O of delight. His large cock is buried in her ass.

"What are you doing in my room?" I say, moving to the plate-glass window and turning so he'll turn his back to the pills and joints. Through the glass I notice Joey and several other Scouts are chasing something through the bushes with a stick.

He's trembling now, Jim Anderson having caught Bud with a Polaroid of Betty's muff. "I was looking for your old Scout manual . . . when I came across this filth."

"Liar. You were snooping," I say, and laugh when I realize what I've said. I never talk to him this way, but right now it doesn't seem to matter. This scene is petty and unimportant. I'm worried about Cheryl.

"Don't you talk to me like that, young man. Don't you *ever* talk to me like that."

"Give me that." I point to the playing card. "I went through a lot to get that."

He sticks the playing card in his green shirt pocket and looks out the window. Joey has a twitching frog impaled on the end of a stick.

"We'll discuss this later," he says, and walks angrily past me.

Not if I can help it. I scoop up the joints and pills, shove them in my pockets, and head out the door.

I go over to Neal's, a Spanish split-level house overlooking Abalone Cove. He's mowing the lawn, but I hang around, telling him how Cheryl and I had a fight, but not over what. He's sympathetic right up to the end, when he says, "I guess it was inevitable." Meaning of course it wouldn't last, we were too different. I realize even Neal probaby thinks the whole thing's just sex.

Around four I call Cheryl, Neal's twin brother Larry's record player blasting a Bartok violin concerto in the background. I'm not going to say, "I'm sorry, Cheryl, let's elope." But I can't stand the idea of losing her, either. Her mother answers the phone, slurred voice. No, she's not there, bang.

Now I'm really worried. What if the lowriders rape her and kill her and throw her body off a cliff? How will I feel for the rest of my life then?

Neal has to get ready for a date so I leave his place around six. Definitely do not want to go home and face *Father Knows Best*. I drive down to the beach lot at Redondo. It's jammed because of the heat, tops down, radios blasting "She Loves You." A horrendous orange sunset. I'm cruising along, overcome with tender feelings for Cheryl, compassion both cheap and profound, seeing some sort of truth in the whole thing, realizing that of course whoever got her pregnant, it's me she wants to marry. It's me she loves. She's probably home right now crying her eyes out on a satin pillow, just had her mom say she wasn't there. You cad.

Drive over there right now, barge through that screen door, push past her mom, and take that girl in your arms. Walk like a man, for Christ's sake. Show her that you love her, drive on over there and show her right now

I see her dead ahead by the snack bar. Leaning against Bill Holtner's Woody, Bill Holtner's arm around her, Bill Holtner's fingers crawling over her breast. I screech to a halt. This is a real teen-pic tableau. Scuzzy Bill and his surf dork buddies, everybody drunk, including several ratty white-trash girls I've never seen before, who look like they just blew in from Fontana or Corona or someplace equally scabby "for a good time." And he is treating Cheryl just like that, openly mauling her tit now. Naturally they are all laughing. At me. And I'm not being paranoid. But they are all finally just a blur of teeth because I am drilling her. And she is drilling me right back, with the same evil glare she had at the house, only now it's even fiercer, drunk, don't give a fuck anymore. And she's telling me: See? Isn't this what you expected? Isn't this what you always believed? I'm just a whore, a nympho, a sleazy pig like everybody always said, so go on, get the fuck out of here, I don't need you, fuck you. Now, as though I didn't get it, she shoots me the finger as her mouth forms a bad-ass beaver-toothed: "Fuuuu!"

I reverse, grinding gears, then shoot out of there. In the rearview mirror I catch some action that looks like Bill Holtner cramming his tongue down her throat.

End of reel. It was twilight now and the beach-lot lights snapped on, throwing palm shadows on the snack-bar wall. Right there, where he jammed his tongue down her throat. Right there, where a couple of young surfers were now laughing and sharing a joint.

The rest of that night was a mystery. Some people said she'd gone out to a party on the beach. There'd been a campfire, more drinking, things got rowdy. Other people said she'd gone off with some guy to the decrepit bohemian apartment building up on the Esplanade. That was gone now. There were cheap condos where people had once watched the material world dissolve.

Some people even said she'd left with me, the one story I knew for certain wasn't true. Of course the people who said that were generally the same ones who thought that if anybody killed her it was probably me.

Catalina was a soft purple mass now, fading into the blue night. A light twinkled at its shoreline. It could have been Avalon, or it might just have been some lonely swinger's yacht.

5

A week passed, then two weeks, and I heard nothing from Dennis. No apologies left on my answering machine, no demented threats on the request line. Nobody came pounding on my door in the early-morning hours. It was over.

Until I came up with a way to get it going again.

I stopped by the station one afternoon and cornered Hank, our program director.

"What would you say if I told you I thought I could get an interview with Dennis Contrelle?"

Hank looked at me as if I'd said I'd just discovered the whereabouts of a fifty-three-year-old, horribly disfigured James Dean.

Then he became elated. Dennis hadn't given an interview in over fifteen years, not since "Tidal Wave of Flame." Talk about coups. This would be tantamount to getting Martin Bormann on *Sixty Minutes* or landing Jesus for a Barbara Walters special. And the timing couldn't be better. In the fickle rock world the Contrelle Sound was classic, permanently cool. The last few years had seen a number of covers of the old hits. He was overdue for a major revival, and we could be in on the ground floor.

Hank had only one reservation: the rumors of Dennis' emotional instability. I reassured him. Dennis might be a little moody, but then, who wasn't? Eccentric, to be sure, but that was part of his charm. Coked out? No more than anybody else, I winked. In any event, I was sure he would be at his best for me. We were friends. Pals. Mutual fans.

I recalled Dennis' last words of effusive idolatry: "Then get fucked in the ass and the face."

What was I doing? Was I out of my mind?

But Hank was rolling, the commercial possibilities clicking through his mind. Why not bring in all the Contrelle artists? A reunion—that was it!—with the Vectors, the Beehives, Louise Wright. I nodded and grinned, unable to tell him how impossible that was, how there was no one Dennis had ever worked with whom he didn't now hate.

"And the Stingrays," he said. "Sharlene whatever-her-name-was. He married her, didn't he?"

"Yeah, I think he did."

"Get her too—"

"Right-o. That shouldn't be a problem."

I called Dennis that night from the station. Big Willy answered. After a long wait, Dennis came on the line. "How did you get this number?"

"I called Information."

"Information? It's supposed to be unlisted. That fucking phone company. I'm gonna kill those fucking assholes."

See, I told myself, he threatens people all the time, it doesn't mean a thing.

"So what do you want?" he said.

"Well, I'll tell you, I got to thinking. You know, I've done interviews with a number of the really key, pivotal people in the history of rock. In fact, I've talked to just about everybody of any importance who's still alive—except you. It'd be no big deal, really. No pressure. We'd just sit around and play a few sides. You know, reminisce about the sessions, that sort of thing."

"You must be kidding."

"Obviously, with your body of work, there's a great deal to talk about—"

"You've got to be out of your fucking mind. What do you think I'm going to do, talk about how I make my records? These fucking idiots have been trying to figure that out for twenty years. You think I'm going to give it all away?"

"Well, naturally, we wouldn't get into anything too technical. It could be whatever you want, really. A lot of people are still very interested in you."

"You're an idiot!" he screamed at me. "A piece of opportunistic subhuman filth! You don't care about me anyway, you probably hate my music. You strike me as the kind of guy who used to beat his meat to Connie Francis records. Don't you think I know the real reason you're calling me? You're just like every other horny dork in this town who ever came into a pink Kleenex. You just want to fuck Sharlene, don't you? That's it, isn't it? Well, I'm sorry to disappoint you, tuffy, but the bitch is quarantined. You raise your leg against our fence, you're gonna get your nuts burned off."

He ended the call. I felt stung, deeply affronted. The stupid megalomaniac prick, I was doing him a favor, giving him a chance at a second life. Furthermore, I had never, ever jacked off to a Connie Francis record, Jesus Christ, give me a break. Furthermore, I worshiped him creatively, what did he expect me to do, lick his Beatle boots? It was a horrendous insult to everything I was about as a human being to suggest that all I really wanted to do was kiss his wife's cherry-red mouth. That I only wanted to lick every square inch of her soft vanilla skin. That I just wanted to spread her ivory legs and bury my face in her bursting pomegranate, then punch in a slick chrome rod till she screamed like Tina Turner in a blood-red Ferrari careening toward a concrete wall. When in truth I wanted to do all that and oh so much more.

Neal was right, of course. I should drop it. Forget I'd ever seen her. To do anything else was just flirting with a death wish, a game that didn't really play now. I was too old to die young. I'd waited too long to leave a fresh-faced corpse.

But I couldn't quit thinking about her.

That night around two I did a Stingrays set: "Love Me Tonight," "Endless Kiss," "Storm of Love," "In Your Car," "When We Kiss," "I Never Meant to Hurt You," "Baby, When We Fight," "Kiss Me Again"—I was wallowing in it.

Jack, one of the day jocks, stopped by around two-thirty with a party of trendy friends. As far as I could tell, they were laughing and taking trendy drugs in one of the offices, when he addressed me over the PA. "You've got visitors."

I was dreaming through "Every Night (I Cry Myself to Sleep)" and looked up too late. Big Willy was already coming through the door, Dennis right behind him. I winced, expecting an ebony fist in the face. Instead, I felt Dennis' hand slide smoothly across my shoulder as he laughed ingratiatingly.

He smiled, showing off a set of rebuilt teeth at least as good as Keith Richards'. Movie-star incisors now gleamed where there'd once been rotted brown Methedrine stumps. I'd never seen him smile like that, or any way, before. I'd never seen his eyes like that before, either. Pinholes. He chuckled like a blitzed terminal-cancer patient.

"Hey, Scottie. I hope you don't mind me dropping in on you like this. You don't mind, do you?"

"No, I guess not. It's a bit of a surprise though."

He slid into the chair next to me. Big Willy stood in the door, arms crossed, towering over us.

"I'm sorry," Dennis said. His face was covered with a film of sweat. "I was an asshole on the phone. You caught me at a bad time. Do you forgive me?"

"Sure. It's okay. Forget it."

He rubbed my shoulder, squeezed my neck. He was looking dead at me, his face closer than I wanted, and I couldn't meet his eyes. The intimacy made me anxious, not that there was anything sexual about it. It was much creepier than that.

"I like you," he said. "You're one of the few people I've met in a long time I genuinely like."

"I like you too." I pulled away, indicating the record was about to end.

"What I said about you wanting to fuck Shar— I was way off the beam. I knew it even as I said it. It's just that—" He did his constipated-samurai grimace. "—you don't know what that bitch has put me through. You have no idea. It's a long story."

"Excuse me a second, will you?" I segued into a Pretenders side, feeling a rush of anger I didn't totally understand.

"I want to talk," he said, close enough for me to smell his Polident. "I want to do that interview. I want to do it now."

His face was still too close to mine. I sensed he could flip over to violence at any time. "Well, gee, I'm not really too prepared at the moment, but—"

"We can wing it." He pulled the mike to his face. "Is this thing on?" It wasn't, but he switched it on.

I spoke before he had a chance to, fading the Pretenders. "Hey, boys and girls, you'll never guess who just dropped into the sumptuous KRUF studios, taking me and our svelte legions of crotchless-pantied secretaries by total surprise. I find myself sitting this very moment much too close to one of the true living legends of rock. A genius who, to those of you over thirty streaming down La Cienega in your cheap toupees and oxidized Datsun Z's, needs no introduction . . . though to you painfully hip young post-new-wave trendies and trendesses, he may. The Beehives, the Vectors, Louise Wright, and last but not least, the immortal Stingrays. I could go on, but as my idol Arthur Godfrey used to say: 'Nuf said?' I refer of course to the timeless titan of twenty-four-track production, the eccentric and enchanting king of teen, the original Wagner of vinyl, the one-man surfing Luftwaffe of car-crash romance. May I present, simply, Dennis Contrelle."

He opened his mouth but he didn't speak. His eyes rolled

back in his head, showing the whites. His face was about to hit what was left of my Chicken McNuggets when Big Willy grabbed him by his paisley collar and stopped his fall. I switched off the mike.

"Jesus—"

He was semiconscious as Big Willy lifted him from the chair. He flailed. Big Willy restrained him expertly. "You got a john?"

"End of the hall. Listen—" I imagined his lips turning blue, the paramedics, the oxygen mask, the funeral.

Big Willy glared at me. "Yeah, what?"

"You think he's gonna be all right? I mean—"

"Yeah," Big Willy said with weary petulance. "He'll be fine. Don't worry about it, okay?"

I watched him lead Dennis up the hall, and switched on the mike.

"Hiya, kids. Hey, sorry about that dead air space, but we had a slight technical problem here in the vast computerized studios of KRUF. Seems a pregnant, naked, angel-dusted nun took a shortcut through our control room, foaming at the mouth and wielding a machete, the LAPD SWAT team in hot pursuit. There *was* an exchange of automatic-weapons fire, but thank God nobody was hurt. As for Dennis Contrelle, it seems my introduction was a bit premature. I could have sworn I felt him rubbing up against me here in the cavernous candlelit interior of my customized Playboy broadcasting suite. Turns out it was just the drooling mongoloid niece of our parent company's chairman of the board. As I guess you can tell, things are pretty darn chaotic around here tonight. I'm going to try to straighten things out. In the meantime, here is a true Contrelle classic, the Vectors' 'Rincon.' "

The song began with the sound of crashing surf, giving way to a throbbing, glistering percussion, the dreamy voices of the Vectors sounding like beach boys from Watts.

The song built through a series of crescendos, each verse

adding new layers of sound as the perfect wave formed. The release came in the final verse, as they went over the edge of audial orgasm, hurtling through a tube of pure bliss. It was then that Dennis stepped back into the booth. If his sweat had been a sheer film before, it now stuck to his face like Karo syrup. His breath was short; he looked close to a heart attack. He dropped to the chair, still enjoying the rush —though "enjoy" was an inadequate word. He appeared totally incapable of speech. The song went into fade. His eyes caught mine and read my apprehension. I then witnessed the most spectacular show-must-go-on routine since Bette Midler gathered her strength and sang three grating pseudo-rock songs before dropping dead at the end of *The Rose*. "Five seconds, Mr. Contrelle."

It couldn't have been any longer than that. Precisely as the song ended, he addressed the mike in total, if sweat-drenched, control. "Hello, Scott," he said in a bouncy, healthful voice. "It's a pleasure to be able to drop in on you like this. I've been a big fan of yours for a very long time."

I pressed the record button on the cassette deck, claiming my footnote in the history of rock.

"Well, that's very flattering, Dennis. Of course, I've been a fan of yours since before I was born. As most of my listeners know, I'm only sixteen and look a lot like Matt Dillon."

"More like Richard Gere, I'd say."

"Yes, I do have his mouth. I've been meaning to return it but I keep forgetting." We both laughed, Dennis with a disconcerting wholesomeness. Big Willy was standing outside the door now, arranging the contents of a leather manicure case.

"Dennis, 'Love Me Tonight' was really *the* breakthrough song for you, wasn't it?"

"Yes, it was, Scott. Prior to that I'd done mostly junk."

"With the exception of 'Angel on the Highway'—"

"No, that song was crap too, Scott. Not the song itself,

but that particular production. The Beehives—they were nothing. Three tramps, scuzzy pus buckets from La Habra or someplace. They couldn't even sing. It's not generally known, but I did most of the vocals on that record myself, using my God-given falsetto, imitating a girl. I left the lead in on certain parts, I can't even remember her name now. She was disgusting. A real sow. Someday I'll do that song again, and do it right."

He said all this with such charm you almost didn't realize what he'd said. I hoped none of the original Beehives were listening, from their posts as matrons in women's prisons or whatever it was they were doing these days.

"I understand you've been back in the studio lately?"

"Yes, I have. In fact, contrary to rumor and vicious myth, I never left. However, I have become a bit of a perfectionist." Again the wholesome quiz-show-host laugh. "I've been working on one track for over fifteen years now."

"It must be quite a track."

"It is. In fact, I can honestly tell you, it's going to be the best thing I've ever done."

I sensed I should change the subject. "The sessions that produced 'Love Me Tonight' are legendary—"

"Yes, they are, Scott. And rightfully so. Everything came in one tremendous rush. We went in with nothing. Just a case of Busch Bavarian beer and a couple of rolls of whites, as I recall." Wholesome laugh. "Six days later we emerged with everything the Stingrays ever did. It all came at once, all of it. We couldn't repeat it. We tried, but we couldn't. It was gone."

He stared into a black hole.

"But of course not really gone. Because you captured everything on vinyl," I said.

"That's true, that's true." He smiled wistfully. I felt a rush of sadness and compassion for him.

"And there were even greater triumphs to come. The Vectors, one of the seminal surf groups of the sixties."

"Yes. I made them what they were," he said, without irony.

"And of course the true apex of the Contrelle Sound, Louise Wright's 'Tidal Wave of Flame.' "

"Yes," he said cheerfully, "that record destroyed me. I was nothing but a piece of charred gristle when I stepped out of that."

"I understand those sessions were quite extraordinary in their own right."

"Yes, they certainly were, Scott. I believe I spent three days trying to fly in the Mormon Tabernacle Choir—"

I laughed. He didn't.

"You had people coming and going in shifts, most of the top musicians in town."

"Yes, I felt like Adolf Hitler in the bunker, trying to organize the defense of Berlin. You may recall how it ended for him." Good-natured laugh. "There were explosions going off . . . in people's heads. Blood on the walls . . . squirted from syringes. Blood streaming down a muscular guitarist's arms. The drummer fixed in his dick—"

Although you can get away with a lot at three A.M., I felt obliged to interrupt. "Why don't we spin that historic side right now?"

It began with a dense roar, like an ocean being sucked from a shoreline. Then it lurched, as if drained through a fissure, the record badly warped. When Louise Wright came on, her voice teasing, coaxing—that slipped too, as though she were singing on a gallows as the trapdoor snapped. It was unlistenable. I lifted the needle.

"Sorry about that, kids. Slight mix-up. I believe that was the autistic children's choir—a hell of a cause, but not much of a record."

Dennis laughed—as though he had no idea what was funny, or supposed to be, but was merely being polite. "Probably the reissue, Scott. Cheap vinyl. That's half of what's wrong with the record industry today."

"What's the other half?"

"The fact that I've been . . . preoccupied."

We both laughed. We kept going like that the rest of the night, playing everything I could come up with—from the Contrelle *Golden Years* anthology album, from *The Stingrays' Greatest Hits*, a few obscure early tracks he'd contributed something to, marimbas here, vocals there. Between cuts, I asked him everything I could think of, and he responded with the same odd cordiality that probably sounded totally credible to the listeners. You had to be there to see him sweat, to see those pinpoint eyes, to know how close he was to flying apart.

I guess I knew it wouldn't end at six. Whatever exotic stimulant-narcotic combination he had coursing through his blood, he faced the sunrise like a vampire immune to light.

"Let's go back to the beach," he said after I signed off. "Breakfast." He smiled and his chapped lower lip split.

I grabbed some cassettes and my Sony recorder.

We soared up PCH, Big Willy at the wheel of the Fleetwood, Dennis and I in the maroon leather backseat. We made small talk for a while, Dennis amiable and pleasant.

"You listened to the cassette, didn't you?" he said finally with a wry, cajoling air that caught me off guard.

"Yeah, I started to. Until I realized it was a mistake."

He smiled. "I know. I could tell exactly how long you listened. Fifty-six-point-three seconds." The sunrise glanced off his shades. "That's when I knew you were all right."

He laughed his wholesome laugh. "Shar and I making love. If you want to know the truth, the last time we ever did it. Nineteen sixty-nine. I shit you not. Right before 'Tidal Wave.' I fucked her in the ass. The biggest mistake of my life. You know how finicky some of these bitches are about getting fucked in the ass. Mama said they shouldn't or something. But what could I do? Her cunt wasn't any good anymore. Fucking her cunt was like fucking air. Anyway, she completely freaked out, though I could tell she liked it. But she wasn't *supposed* to like it. Catholic guilt or something, you know. But that was it—1969. She hasn't put out since." He paused for a moment of studied sadness. "That cassette is my only souvenir." He smiled. "But you had the decency to stop listening to it after fifty-six-point-three seconds, when you realized you were listening to a guy fucking his wife in the ass. I like that. Most guys would have listened to the whole thing and probably even jerked off to it." He was a shark with dentures now. "It *was* pretty hot, wasn't it?"

Make allowances, I told myself. This guy has a shriveled fig where there once was a brain. But a tremendous rage was coming up. "I really didn't hear enough of it to form an opinion," I said.

"Oh, I'll tell you, Scott, she was a hot fuck," he said nostalgically. "A hot, *hot* fuck. Talk about snatch? Shit, they coined that word to describe her juicy little cunt. If you want to know the truth, I think that's the only reason I married her. Because of that hot little velvet gash."

I felt a sudden urge to smash his fucking face in, and I knew why now. It was only partially about Sharlene. This was the same way the guys used to talk about Cheryl.

"I mean, to be blunt, she had a really tight, an ultratight, pussy. Like an Oriental girl. Like a gook. Guys in the war used to tell me how tight those little Vietnamese pussies were, and I used to feel like saying: 'Oh yeah? You think they're tight, you oughta fuck my wife.'" He laughed grimly. "Apparently I didn't have to say anything, because a lot of them already had."

I was imploding now. He was a moron in the locker room bad-mouthing Cheryl. Bill Holtner! "Dennis, I don't want to hear this," I said.

He ignored me. "You have no idea what she's put me through, Scott. No idea. I just don't know what to do with

her, I really don't. I've given her everything any woman
could possibly want. Fame, stardom, a Malibu dreamhouse,
wealth—more money than she could ever hope to spend. I
rescued her from nothingness. From being a waitress or a
dime-store clerk. From growing old and fat and being a nobody. I gave her more than she ever deserved, if you want
to know the truth."

We shot past Zuma, tanned young bodies reflected in his
shades.

"Too much too soon, that's what it was. I spoiled her. I
turned her into a spoiled-rotten princess. She had too much
attention, too many fans, too much impersonal love. When
it all stopped, she couldn't handle it. She went a little crazy.
There were no more waves of love washing over her from
crowds in huge arenas. It left a void, I guess. And she filled
it, yeah, she filled it all right. With an endless procession of
hot, pulsating cocks."

This was shit. I snorted disgustedly and stared out the
window. Christ, couldn't he see how I was taking this? Apparently not. He continued as if we were in total rapport.

"It took me several years to realize what she was up to.
You see, I left her alone for a while. After I killed off the
Stingrays, before 'Tidal Wave.' It was a confusing period. I
was heavily addicted to speed, which is a very bad drug. I
was always at the studio, always. When I did come home,
she wouldn't be there. She'd be gone for days on end. That's
when I began to realize she was a nymphomaniac. No, that's
too weak a word. She was sexually insane, and it was self-
destructive fucking, self-destructive. I mean she'd go after
these total scumbags: Filipino busboys, Mexican parking-lot
attendants, scummy low-life petty criminal types trying to
pass themselves off as hippies. And of course they all knew
who she was. They were fucking the Stingray. I hired detec-
tives, that's how I know all this. They brought me evidence,
photos, tape recordings. It was sickening. My own wife.
Jesus, she could have been killed or blackmailed. That's why

I confined her to the house, for her own protection. She
denied it all, of course, which was totally ridiculous, because
I'd caught her red-handed. And then she sulked. For years
she sulked. And then the hypochondria began. I didn't realize that's what it was at first. Jesus, I spent a fortune on
doctors. Then I realized it was all bullshit. She wasn't so sick
she couldn't get out of bed and answer the door in the nude.
That's her favorite trick; she's an exhibitionist. Every time
somebody comes around, it doesn't matter who. The gardener, this sixty-year-old Jap. The water man, the gas-meter
reader. The guy who used to come to clean the pool, a
young blond stud. I walked out one day and there she was,
straddling the lawn chair, flashing her gash at him like one
of those dirty pictures in *Hustler*. Really stomach-turning.
This guy had an obvious erection—his last, I might add. I
taught her a lesson too, after that."

Big Willy braked as our turn came up. This was bullshit,
an impotent junkie's paranoid delusions of sexual disgust. I
didn't believe a word of it.

"After that I made sure she was locked in her room before
I even so much as opened the gate. Of course she reacted
by not coming out even when she could. It was totally absurd. We had to send her meals up to her. You would have
thought she was an invalid. I finally started sending her to
this therapist. At first Big Willy had to drive her there, she
wouldn't even drive anymore. She wouldn't settle for anything short of being waited on hand and foot. But seeing
this guy seemed to help."

We swept through the eucalyptus trees and the house
came into view, looking dead, abandoned.

"Pretty soon she was driving again, and she seemed to be
back on the straight and narrow. I had high hopes for her."
His voice took on a hammy, ominous tone. "Then I realized
what was *really* going on. You see, one night I tried to fuck
her, I thought she might be well enough that I could fuck
her again, that maybe her pussy had tightened up through a

period of disuse. So I went to her room, and she said no, she didn't want to. But I smelled cooked carrots."

"Cooked carrots?" This had to be a demented non sequitur.

"On her skin. The smell of cooked carrots. See, she'd been to see the therapist that afternoon and hadn't bathed since. She saw him three times a week. No wonder she was smiling! I tried to kiss her neck but his smell was all over her and I practically vomited right then. I hate the smell of cooked carrots."

Big Willy pressed the remote. The gate hummed open ahead of us.

"You think she was having an affair with her therapist?"

"Not think, *know*. It was nauseating. She has no taste. He's just this fat sack of sixty-year-old Polish shit, one of these Northern California types who goes around preying on fucked-up celebrities. Maybe he was a father image or something. But I'm paying him three hundred a pop so he could stick his warty nose up Sharlene's cunt?"

We drove through the grounds.

"This just came to light. I haven't confronted her with the evidence yet." He smiled bleakly. "But this Polish scum bag . . . has been dealt with."

This had to be a joke, a depressing Richard Conte impression. "Dealt with? What do you mean?"

The car stopped. Big Willy got out and opened the door for Dennis. He had no intention of answering my question. Instead he put his hand on my knee and leaned closer for a few intimate words before we got out of the car.

"But you know something, Scott? In spite of everything she's put me through, I still love her. No, 'love' is too weak a word. I worship that woman, I adore her, I cannot imagine what my life would be like without her. I suppose in every life there is only one great love and I consider myself very fortunate to still have the only woman I've ever loved by my side." He smiled like Robert DeNiro. "It hasn't always been easy. It's not like the storybooks. In some ways the cost has been great. But my advice to you, Scott, if you should ever find a woman you love above all others, is to never let her go, no matter what."

He squeezed my knee, gave me a virile buddy pat, and laughed lightly, as if to dissipate the serious mood. "Come on."

We settled into the music room and continued the interview. Big Willy brought Jack Daniel's and ice for me, canned Cokes for Dennis.

Though the air conditioning was frigid, I began to sweat. At first I thought it was just from exhaustion, or suppressed anger leaking through my pores. But as time passed, I felt feverish. I got drunk so I wouldn't notice, pushing on with the interview, just wanting to get it over with.

"What about the Spector influence in your work, Dennis?"

"Oh, that's crap. People have been saying that for years. If anything, it was the other way around. He was influenced by me. Brian Wilson too. Though I don't begrudge either man. They're both geniuses in their own right. Or were."

"That seems unusually magnanimous of you."

"Just reality. We're the triad of the great age of rock. Spector, Wilson, and me. Of course, as I say, I'm at the top of the pyramid. A thousand years from now, they'll be footnotes, but I'll be a god."

I waited for a smile. None came.

"Speaking of surf music, why don't you tell us how you discovered the Vectors?"

"We went to the same high school. In Hermosa. They used to laugh at me in gym class."

"Laugh at you?"

"Yeah. They thought I had a small dick. Actually, it's not that small. It's the kind that gets a lot bigger when it gets hard, you know what I mean? But in the locker room it looked small."

"I see." We'll have to cut this, I thought. I checked the tape, feeling queasy.

"So anyway, they were these big guys, big blond surfers, with big blond surfer dicks, and they *used* to laugh at *me*. Which was funny. Because they turned out to be the homos, not me."

"You think they were gay?" I said by rote, knowing we couldn't use it.

"Not think, know. They used to butt-fuck each other every chance they got. I caught 'em at it once in a hotel room in Milwaukee. 'Okay, fellas,' I said, 'this is it.' "

"But they were surfers too. I mean, they actually surfed?"

"That's right. They were surfing homos. They used to come up out of the water with their dicks hanging out."

I poured myself another stiff drink. "Their first hit, 'Come With Me,' was fairly bold for its day. In terms of the sexual meaning."

"What are you talking about?"

"Well, the double meaning of the title. And the kind of orgasmic crescendo—"

"What do you mean, double meaning? There are no double meanings! I don't write songs like that, with double or triple meanings. I make it a point never to do that. I write songs with only one meaning, that's why it takes me so long."

He was on his feet now, gulping Coke to ease his dry mouth. "That's what's wrong with music today. All these rancid fucks know how to do is shake their dicks at the audience. We live in a diseased culture. People's minds are like giant sickening pornography shops. They waddle down the freeways like giant Rodans and Godzillas with their pricks and cunts in giant wheelbarrows! They don't know what love is anymore! Love? What's that? It's all: Come on, baby, let's fuck! These kids today are nothing but dick-headed morons with their heavy metal garbage and MTV. Ever watch it? I feel sorry for these kids today, they've got nothing to live for. They're nothing but robots with hairy fuckholes where their hearts should be. You and I are lucky, Scott. We grew up in the last searing glow of an aching, yearning, hopeless, unrequited love—before the world turned to shit forever!"

He stood there trembling, red and rigid like a penis about to explode. I really thought: This is it, he's just going to die right now, he's going to have a massive simultaneous heart attack/stroke, and I will be interviewed tonight on the news.

Instead, his head jerked to the door and his feet made tracks. "I'll be right back," he said furtively. "I gotta hit the john."

I was sure he did. An opulent Osiris bathroom with a Horus tub and an Isis bidet, where his obese Nubian valet would be waiting to serve him, a tie over one arm instead of a small white towel, a syringe in his hand instead of a whisk broom.

I stood abruptly and nearly passed out. Jesus, I was worse off than I'd thought. I felt my brow; I was burning up. The flu probably. Shit, I just wanted to go. Why hadn't I driven my own car? I felt trapped, miles from the nearest bus stop. But I'd had it. As soon as Dennis came back, I'd tell him the score. In the meantime, air.

I pulled back the sliding glass door, wincing as the bright light hit me. It was a hot, dead, cloudless day, no breeze, the ocean looking fake, like a blue cellophane horizon in a forties movie. Even the slapping of the waves below sounded strangely metallic and artificial, like an isolated sound effect.

I stepped onto the patio, which overlooked the empty, cracked Nefertiti swimming pool. The heat was erotic. It was a Coppertone sex day, a shirtless convertible day, a bikini-clad Lolita at the Alpha Beta day, exactly the kind of atmosphere that had driven generations of Midwestern rubes sexually insane. Too hot, too thick, to do anything but sweat, drink beer, and slowly fuck.

Then I saw Sharlene. She was on the far side of the pool basin, lying facedown on a canvas mat in a cherry-red bikini, the top undone. Her head was resting on her arm, facing the ocean, so she didn't see me. Her pale, luminescent skin, so like Cheryl's, was slick with lotion, gleaming in the sun like chrome. Like Cheryl's, it was skin that seemed to glow in another dimension, edges blooming like a brilliant figure on nitrate film. Next to it, tanned skin seemed like leather, surfer girls looked like garish billboard models. Skin such as this should be protected in the filtered light of a mythological English glen, not exposed to the harsh cancerous glare of this aerosol sky.

I was staring, long enough that if she'd been awake she would have felt my presence, when I saw a line of smoke rising from her hair. I was drunk enough that I thought she was on fire.

"Hey, hey!" I ran out to her.

As she stirred I saw that it was just her cigarette, held in the hand by her head, burning down to the filter.

"What?" She came awake fast when she saw me.

"Your cigarette."

She stubbed it out on the tile, pulling on her top—not with modesty exactly, but as if she were wondering how long I'd been looking at her. Her nipples were an eloquent, succulent pink.

"I thought your beehive was on fire," I said, immediately aware she might question this.

"Don't worry. It's flame-proof."

"Yes, I can see that now. You use plenty of Asbestos VO5."

She smirked, the way Cheryl used to. "I appreciate your concern."

"Well, it's fire season."

"Yeah, we've been lax this year. The summer's almost over and we still haven't cleared our brush."

"All it takes is one careless butt."

"We're usually very careful about our butts." She turned back on her stomach.

"I can see that," I said, too drunk to care. "Yours is in mint condition."

"It should be," she said blandly. "It's been on blocks for fifteen years."

This startled me, if what I thought she meant was true. "That's a pity. A butt like yours should really be driven."

"Oh, look." She sat up abruptly, more exasperated than mad. "No more car metaphors, okay?"

I grinned. "I guess you've heard them all."

"You bet I have. Every one. Wouldn't you like to ease it down into my bucket seat and shove your key in my ignition?" she said sarcastically.

"It's a nice day for a drive, now that you mention it."

"Or maybe give me a lube job?"

"I've got a grease pit at my place."

"Or ride my clutch?"

"I'd never do that."

"Or rev me up and blow me out?"

"Not until I check your oil, ma'am, 'cause I can tell from here you're runnin' hot."

She smiled and reached for her cigarettes. "Actually, I'm not running at all. I think my battery is dead."

"Probably just needs a jump," I said gently. "I've got some cables in my trunk."

She snorted and lit her cigarette. "I like your Lincoln. What is it, about a '63?"

"Yeah. Wanna go for a spin through Dealey Plaza?"

"That's not funny."

"Yes it is."

"So is that why you got it? 'Cause it's like the one he got shot in?"

"I can't tell you. That information's classified until the year 2063." I reeled, steadying myself against a palm trunk.

"You're drunk, aren't you?"

"Yes. And dying. I think I just contracted hepatitis from a dirty phonograph needle."

She smiled. She didn't want me to go. It suddenly struck me how lonely she really was.

"So where were you when he got it?" she said.

"Kennedy? Gee, you know, I don't really remember."

"Oh, come on. Everybody knows where they were when that happened."

"I try to live in the present—"

"Come *on*," she said with amused irritation.

"Wait a second. I think it's coming back. Oh yeah, right, I remember now. I was in Dallas actually. I was eating a box lunch on the Grassy Knoll. In fact, I'm still a little deaf in my right ear. Where were you?"

"Gym class. At Arcadia Junior High. We were playing volleyball when we saw Miss Pierce, this lesbian coach, running to her office, sobbing."

"I know. I was a lesbian myself then. And I sobbed."

"I think you're still a lesbian."

"I am. But I'm the exotic, sensuous kind. Eurasian, actually." I did a breathy French nymphet voice: "Maybe you see me in *Emmanuelle?* Oh! I've got a naughty idea! Why don't you and I lick one another on the breast while your husband watches? You think he would be into that? Watching two beautiful girls, eh?"

"My husband isn't into anything," she said, turning grim. "And I should warn you, Mr. Cochran, the last man who even *panted* over me got his tongue lopped off."

"Why are you so formal?" I said with the French accent.

"You're panting, Mr. Cochran."

"It's the heat, Mrs. Contrelle," I said in my own voice.

"Then get out of it."

I didn't understand the sudden shift. But then I was too punchy to understand much at all. She had a point, though. This was not smart. I tried to back off gracefully.

"What I'd really like to do is go for a dip. Too bad the pool's cracked—"

"Scott!" Dennis yelled. Sharlene cringed.

I whirled around, expecting to see him in the music-room door, but he was still back inside.

When I looked at Sharlene again, she was grabbing up her things.

"Go in," she said, and ducked behind the shrubs a second before he stepped to the door.

"Oh, there you are." He came out. "What are you doing?" He was still breathless and sweating from his latest injection.

"Just getting some air."

The yellow canvas mat was damp with her sweat. And she'd dropped her sunblock lotion.

"Air? What's wrong with the air conditioning?"

"Nothing. Not a thing."

I came around to him, to draw his attention away from the mat. "This is a really incredible place you've got here. Talk about a view."

"Are you kidding? It's fucked." He stared off toward the mat. "See that wall? It's crumbling." He ignored the mat. "They told me there was solid rock under here. You know what it is? Dirt, that's all. Dirt. Christ, I poured my heart into this place because they said it would last a thousand years. It'll be gone by the end of the century. I've already begun making other plans."

"It's good to think ahead," I said as we walked back to the music room. "I'm toying with the idea of moving to France sometime in early 2150."

I looked back as we stepped through the door and caught a glimpse of Sharlene darting through the shrubs.

Inside I dropped to the sofa in the conversation pit, pouring sweat. Dennis could not have been more concerned. Big Willy appeared momentarily with a couple of pills alleged to be aspirin. I washed them down with whiskey without examining them. Then I waited alone for Big Willy to bring the car around to take me home. The last thing I remember was passing out.

When I came to it was night and I was in a strange room. A very strange room. The walls were pale blue with phosphorescent stars and crescent moons painted on the ceiling. A playpen and children's toys gathered dust. A crib hung from the ceiling beside the single bed on which I lay. Naked. I sat up, drenched with sweat, feeling slugged with the fever and force of the Quaalude they'd given me. The real moon shone through the barred windows. I was on the second floor.

The room was both eerie and sad. A nursery for a child they'd never had. Why not? Had she miscarried, or had the child been born prematurely and died? How long ago?

On the table by the bed there was a faded catalog of baby clothes dated October 1969.

The hanging crib disturbed me. I stood, steadying myself against the wall, half-thinking that when I looked in the crib I might find something black and shriveled. But there were only cobwebs.

I had to take a leak. Where the hell were my clothes? I stumbled around the room, stepping on tinkertoys, and found my pants tossed over a low child's chair. I pulled them on, nearly losing my balance, and stepped into the upstairs hall.

A light glowed down in the foyer, throwing railing shadows on the orange flocked walls, but the house was quiet. I padded up the hall looking for the john.

Then I heard faint music coming from the room at the end. A crack of light showed that the door was slightly ajar. Very quietly I approached, already suspecting whose room it was.

I looked through the crack, wider now than I'd thought. I saw that the TV, an old cabinet model, was the source of the music: a Cars video playing on MTV.

The room itself was decorated in soft pastels: pink walls, blue velvets, violet chiffons. A vanity overflowed with perfumes and cosmetics. Plaster cupids swooned above an upright piano. Rock-star photos—some recent, but most dating back twenty years—were pinned to the walls, including an early portrait of Bobby, a glossy fan-magazine shot, his fruity red lips and blond pompadour glistening, his zits airbrushed away. The room was a frilly dream refuge of a pampered fifties teenage girl.

Sharlene was on the pink bed, curled up against the pillows, her back to me, ignoring the TV. At first I thought she was reading, holding a paperback. Then I saw where her hand really was.

I was jolted, both embarrassed and galvanized. Abruptly she turned on her back, one hand running up under her black T-shirt to her breasts as she stared at the ceiling, the other hand moving between her legs.

Then she winced and arched her back, her eyes closing as she uttered a single muffled syllable. I was stunned. Was I losing my mind or had she just said my name?

Carefully I stepped away from the door, terrified that I might make a sound. A floorboard might creak and give me away, and she would start screaming.

Then again . . . I hesitated. What would happen—what would really happen—if I just pushed open the door and said: Baby, here I am. Had she really said my name, or had I just imagined it? I wanted so badly to believe that I was the object of her fantasy. But if I was wrong . . . or even if I was right . . . She might prefer her immaculate version of me to the flawed and sweaty reality.

I was still pondering the matter when I saw a shadow on the orange flocked wall and my heart flew out of my throat. The shadow of an evil dog. Chuck—I was pretty sure it was Chuck. His teeth were bared, though as before he seemed incapable of growling or barking. There was nothing but the hellish whisper of his breath.

Very carefully I backed up the hall to Sharlene's door, clearing my throat loudly, finally calling out, "Hello? Hello?"

She opened the door, her black T-shirt—it had a vintage picture of James Brown on it—falling just below her crotch.

"I think I may have a slight problem with your pooch," I said, and she immediately called to him. "Chuck!" She clapped her hands. "Downstairs! Downstairs! Bad dog!" She was emphatic, but kept her voice to a hoarse whisper. "Chuck, you get downstairs!"

She came out after him, chasing him back to the stairs. At one point he turned and snarled at her, silently. This infuriated her and she jumped at him. He broke and loped down the landing, where he turned again and seemed to glare at her before arrogantly sauntering on down the stairs.

She brushed past me in a wave of sweet perfume and lather, turning in her door. "Are you all right?"

"Yeah. I was looking for the john."

"Back there." She looked off up the hall. "How do you feel?"

"Like shit."

"Yeah, you look like shit."

"Thanks. So do you."

She smiled. "You're sweet." She drummed her fingers on the door fame.

"So is your perfume. Does it have a name?"

"Yeah. It's called Skip it." She started to close the door. I ran my finger under her sleeve.

"I like your shirt too."

"Thanks." She removed my hand. "You want it?"

"Yeah."

"It might be a little tight for you."

"Only one way to tell. Slip if off."

"I think I chased off the wrong dog."

"I can't help it, I'm a James Brown fan. He played a big part in my personal mythology."

"Don't tell me. 'Night Train' was on the radio the first time you got laid."

"I was listening to the Go-Gos."

"Why do I believe you?"

"Actually, I'm still a virgin."

"You're feverish. Go back to bed."

"I'm not sleepy."

"Yes you are."

"Not in the nursery."

This rattled her. "He put you in the nursery?"

I swung in the door toward her pink satin bed. "That bed looks comfy."

She blocked my way. "It wouldn't be with your brains all over the headboard."

I swung back. "Where *is* your husband?"

She indicated a door halfway down the hall. "He crashed."

"Crashed? I haven't heard that term since Altamont."

"Well, I'm a disillusioned flowerchild, you know how it is."

"You were never a flowerchild."

"You're right, I wasn't. I was too busy fending off horny young guys like you."

"I'm not young anymore."

"I can tell. Neither am I."

"So why don't we crack open a bottle of Geritol and have a party?"

"You really have a death wish, don't you?"

"That's right. I'm the Charles Bronson of rock and roll."

"Yeah, well, right now I'm the Greta Garbo. So why don't you do us both a favor and leave me the fuck alone?"

"Garbo never talked like that."

She smiled. "Your fly's open."

No way was I going to look down. "My fly's always open."

"I know." She closed her door.

I looked down at my fly, open wide, my crank in full view.

Just as well I hadn't known. It might have interfered with my display of élan. I strolled coolly off down the hall, not bothering to zip up, imagining I was Yves Montand.

A minute later I was standing before the commode, hands on hips, urinating with panache, when I heard their voices.

"You fucking shitbag cunt."

"No, Dennis. Baby, please—"

A loud, bludgeoning slap.

A door opened, its knob hitting the wall. Running footsteps in the hall. Dennis: "I'll fix *him*."

My panache dissolved as my heart reeled into a crazed hucklebuck. Stuffing my tool back in my pants, I peered into the hall.

It was empty, but Dennis' bedroom door was open. He was in there pulling out drawers, frantically searching for something.

I stepped out and saw Sharlene in her room, steadying herself against the TV, holding her jaw. When she saw me she gestured frantically for me to get back.

I heard the chamber of a gun click, looked back, and saw Dennis standing in his bedroom door.

He held a nickel-plated .357 Magnum in both trembling hands, looking like an angry little kid in his baggy Jockey shorts—a little kid with relief ridges of hypodermic scar tissue running up both arms like the Andes through Chile. The gun was aimed at me, though his vision seemed distracted by things that weren't there.

"What did she tell you?" he said.

I was breathless with terror.

Sharlene screamed, "Dennis, no! Oh, Christ—"

I dived for the nursery as he fired. Six bone-jarring blasts went off as I hit the floor. Above me the bullet-riddled crib swung wildly on its chains. A window had been shattered, setting off the alarm. It rang shrilly as I cringed on the floor, finally looking for blood. There was none.

I heard heavy footsteps and saw Big Willy bounding up the stairs, his huge gut hanging over his red bikini briefs.

Dennis was laughing now, the gun hanging limp at his side, though it was the most agonized laugh I'd ever heard. Big Willy slipped up behind him and expertly relieved him of the gun, as though he'd dealt with this sort of thing many times before.

Sharlene stood frozen in her doorway, both hands over her mouth.

Big Willy said something comforting to Dennis, his words lost under the deafening alarm. Dennis' lips were moving now, but he was talking to himself, or responding to inner voices, not to Big Willy.

"He's very tired," Big Willy shouted to me over the alarm. "You should go now."

Yeah, right. Sounds good.

I watched him lead a muttering, enfeebled Dennis into the bedroom. Then I looked at Sharlene. Her eyes appeared permanently startled with shock. I got up. As soon as she seemed convinced I was all right, she stepped back into her room and closed the door.

The alarm was still ringing as I grabbed my shoes and shirt and the interview cassettes and stumbled through the electric gate to freedom. It was still dark as I stuck out my thumb on PCH, catching a ride with a couple of El Salvador death-squad refugees in a gutted Fiesta.

6

I was in bed with the flu for two days. Norrine brought me chicken soup from Canter's, the deli on Fairfax. I had the interview cassettes on the bedside table, but I felt too rotten to listen to them. Frankly, I wasn't sure I ever wanted to listen to them. I was just biding my time till I felt clear-headed enough to talk to Neal and decide whether or not to press charges for attempted murder.

I felt well enough by the third day to make it down the stairs to Duke's for a late breakfast. I was working on a chili-and-avocado omelet, packed in at one of the long tables between a beefy roadie and a ducktailed rockabilly girl, when a hand tapped my shoulder. I looked up. It was Sharlene.

"Hello, Scott."

She was alone and extremely anxious, doing everything but wringing her hands. Actually her left hand was squeezing the strap of her bag so tightly her knuckles were white. Her lollipop shades covered her eyes but her red mouth was distorted with stress and she cringed when someone laughed by the register. As usual the place was a madhouse, packed, people clogging the doorway, milling outside.

"Good morning," I said.

"Listen, I have to talk to you—"

She took off her dark glasses, her eyes darting fearfully about the room. I addressed the rockabilly girl. "Would you mind moving down a little?"

Locked in a conversation with a handsome young actor,

she shot me an irritated look, but complied. I made room for Sharlene, but when I looked up she was gone.

I saw her pushing through the crowd, frantic, bumping people, in a panic to get out the door. I went after her.

I expected to see her running up the sidewalk, but she had stopped a few yards from the door. With her back to me, she was digging in her bag as I approached. "Are you all right?"

She jumped when I touched her shoulder, dropping a silver pillbox. Yellow Valiums scattered on the sidewalk. "Oh shit. Oh Christ, no."

We both bent down to pick up the pills. The first one she got she popped in her mouth, swallowing it dry.

"What is it, what's the matter? You want a drink of water?" I started back toward Duke's.

"No." She waved me to stop. "Forget it. It's all right now. I'm all right."

In fact she was calming down, as if by magic. She steadied herself against the flagstone facade and took a deep breath, the pressure falling from fever pitch back to normal in nothing flat.

"How can you be all right? You just took the pill."

"It's just a cue," she said, a little irritably, as if there were so much I didn't understand. She was right.

"What is it? You had an anxiety attack?"

She took another deep breath. "No, it's agoraphobia. I'm agoraphobic."

I knew what she meant, but couldn't stop myself from joking. "Yeah, I hate Agoura too. It's not as bad as Calabasas, though."

She smiled twistedly, making me feel as if I'd just told a spastic joke at a muscular dystrophy dinner.

"I'm sorry if I embarrassed you," she said, looking back at the crowd by Duke's. A few people watched us discreetly.

"You didn't embarrass me. Are you sure you're all right?"

"Yeah, I'm fine now. Once I take the Valium, I know the attack will pass. And it does."

"Does this happen to you often?"

"Only when I leave the house." She snorted. "Actually, that's not true, I'm a lot better. For a long time I couldn't leave the house at all, let alone drive. Then I got so I could drive again, at least as far as Point Dume. To see Leo."

"Leo?"

"My therapist. He's desensitizing me. Santa Monica was a big victory, to go that far. I can even go to Inglewood now, to get my hair done." She stared up the wide boulevard. "This is the farthest I've ever come. I still can't get on a freeway. PCH is bad enough." She indicated Duke's. "Mostly, it's crowds though. I can't take being packed in with a lot of people. It's like claustrophobia, I guess, only worse. I should never have gone in there. It's a perfect setup." She scowled self-reproachfully. "I'm sorry. You were eating. I didn't mean to interrupt you—"

"Don't worry about it. Listen, have you eaten yet? There's a drive-in up on Sunset. We could stay in the car. Would Tiny Naylor's freak you out?"

"Looks like this place is doomed." I indicated the "For Lease" sign stuck in the dirty palms outside Tiny Naylor's. "It's a pity too. Some of the memories. Picked up a little hippie chick here once. Late summer of sixty-nine. She took me back to her commune, some old movie ranch out by Chatsworth. We dropped acid, and then she and some guy named Tex, and a couple other girls, went off to crash some party in Bel Air. I stayed behind, tripping to the *White Album*. Just as well, as it turned out."

Sharlene snorted. "You are so full of shit."

I shrugged.

"So you were a hippie?" she said.

"Me? Ha, don't make me puke blood. I never fell for any of that *love* shit. Hell, if anything, I was proto-punk. Shit, I had a Mohawk in sixty-seven. Lou Reed was *my* man. I wore black hobnail boots and stomped babies at love-ins. I drenched Melanie with spit at a concert once."

"Oh, bullshit," she said, "I'll bet you were into the Moody Blues."

"Never."

"And Donovan."

"Give me a break."

"I'll bet you knew every Dylan song by heart."

"No way. The Doors, Captain Beefheart, and Nancy Sinatra, that was it."

Sharlene laughed. The carhop fixed our tray to the window.

The sweeping glass and brown stucco drive-in seemed poised on the edge of converging speedways as cars roared past on Sunset and La Brea. With the stifling, windless heat amplifying sound, it felt like twenty years ago: the streets full of muscle cars, rumbling at the stoplights, burning rubber when they peeled out, shredding old ladies' nerves a half-mile away.

When a battered Barracuda full of skinhead off-duty marines squealed in next to us, Sharlene barely reacted. The Valium had kicked in. She turned her back to the marines and took off her shades. "I want to leave Dennis," she said.

I dipped french fries in ketchup. "Gee, I can't understand why."

"The thing is, I'm not sure I know how."

She seemed to mean it in some abstract, metaphysical sense, but I took it literally.

"Well, if you want a divorce, you should see an attorney."

"I know." She was irritated, then bleak. "The thing is, I don't even know anybody. Dennis has always taken care of everything. I can't go to *his* attorney."

"I can refer you to the guy I used, if that would help. He's okay. I mean, he's not a *total* scumbag. Which in *this* town," I said with mock cynicism, "is about the highest recommendation you can give."

She stared off down Sunset at the tropical motels. "I don't know." Her voice took on a heavy tone similar to grief. "I'm thirty-four years old. But in a lot of ways I still feel like I'm fourteen. That's how old I was when I met Dennis. He's been taking care of me ever since. Not like all these liberated women . . ." The marines laughed raucously behind her. "I just feel so out of it. I've never done anything for myself. Nothing. I've never filed a tax return or paid a bill. I've never even written a goddamn check. I've never had a job—"

"I wouldn't say that."

"Sure. Unemployed rock singer. I'll put that down on my work application. Last job held: Stingray, 1964–67. Christ. They'll probably think I was a fuckin' fish."

"I doubt that you're going to be applying for a clerk's job at Zody's. Not when you walk away with half of what he's worth."

She laughed. "You think that's going to happen? You don't know Dennis."

"I'm getting to."

She snorted. "So has he called you yet?"

"No. Is he going to?"

"Yeah. He's really sorry about what happened."

"Good. I guess that means I can call off the DA."

"You're kidding, aren't you?" She looked scared.

"For the moment."

She touched my arm. "Listen, you really don't want to fuck with Dennis. Don't think the law will protect you. If he wants to get somebody, he does."

I thought about her therapist, whom Dennis claimed to have "dealt with." I wasn't so certain that was bullshit anymore.

"I just don't want you to get hurt," she said, still touching my arm. Her intensity disturbed me. It was almost as if we were already involved in a passionate affair. She seemed to sense this herself, and laughed to dissipate the mood, as she reached for a cigarette.

"Why have you waited this long, if you don't mind me asking?" I said.

"Scared, I guess." She lit her cigarette. "He's told me that if I ever try to leave him, he'll kill me."

Behind her one of the marines said something in a lisping voice and the others guffawed.

"Why does he want to keep you if he doesn't—"

"Fuck me anymore?" She shrugged. "He's afraid of me. I know too much."

"About what?"

"About everything." She tried to dismiss it. "You know, he thinks I'll write a book or something. Tell all his secrets. He's a man with a lot of secrets. Listen," she rushed on before I could say anything, "I'm really sorry to bother you with all this. I've talked to Louise. I know what *she* thinks I should do. I guess I just wanted another opinion."

"I think you kids can still work it out," I said in a nerdy marriage-counselor voice. "But I'd like to see you both at the next session." She smiled. "But if I can be objective for a moment, I think the only sane thing for you to do is leave him and spend the rest of your life with me."

I was glad that she laughed. "Oh yeah?" she said. "Where? At the Tropicana?"

"Hey, I'm only a deejay. I couldn't promise to keep you in the style to which you've grown accustomed."

"That's okay. Being kept, period, has grown a little thin." She seemed depressed for a moment, lost in thought. "I *would* like to sing again."

"I don't know why you shouldn't. You're still incredible. I heard you the first day I came out to the house."

"Dennis says I'm no good anymore."

"He's full of shit."

"He says I was never anything to begin with. That he made me. With his production. He says without him I'll fail."

"Sharlene, he's out of touch."

She looked through the windshield and groaned. "Oh, shit, I've been made."

I looked up and saw the Latino dishwasher inside Tiny Naylor's grinning, and pointing her out to the Asian busboy. I looked around for the carhop to take our tray as the dishwasher came out.

"Oh Christ, I don't need this," Sharlene said, covering her brow with her hand.

He came up to her side of the car, grinning with soft-headed adoration. About forty, he had a teardrop tattoo below one eye. "Sharlene? Oh, man, I don't even believe it. Sharlene Contrelle, man. This is too much."

Sharlene smiled at him like a stewardess and shot me a look of desperation.

"I been a fan of yours practically forever, man. I got 'Love Me Tonight' on my tape deck right now."

I finally caught the carhop's attention.

"Thanks," Sharlene said.

He rolled up his sleeve to reveal a heart-shaped tattoo strategically placed to hide the tracks inside his elbow. Inside the heart was the word "Char."

"My first wife, man. She looked just like you, I shit you not. Everybody said so. Hey, whatever happened to the other Stingrays, man? How come you guys don't ever do no revival shows?"

Sharlene spoke flatly, as if by rote. "Well, Bobby OD'ed back in sixty-nine, and Frank got stabbed to death in seventy-two. Billy got killed in a motorcycle accident in seventy-five, and Jimmy found Jesus in seventy-nine."

"Jeez, what a bummer, man," he said, a bit dumb-founded. "I remember about Bobby, but all the others . . . I was in the joint all through the seventies. I guess I lost touch."

The carhop removed our tray. I started the engine.

"Look, thanks for remembering me," Sharlene said.

"Remember you? Shit, man, how could I forget? I still call

up KRLA every Saturday night and dedicate 'Love Me To-night' to my first wife. She's dead, man. In a car crash. Fifteen years ago. Fuckin' convertible, man. Sixty-seven Ca-maro. Flipped over on the freeway, man. Ground off her head."

I backed out.

"Thanks," Sharlene said. "Thanks again."

"Hey, drive carefully, man," he called as we pulled away. "Don't flip over!"

Back at the Tropicana I walked her to her car, a white '65 Mustang convertible—not restored, you could tell from the hairline cracks in the paint, but hardly ever driven. The red pony interior was as bright as fresh blood.

I wrote my divorce attorney's name on a Duke's match-book. "Are you sure you're okay to drive?"

"Yeah, I'm fine now, really. Going back's always easier."

I still didn't know quite what to make of this agoraphobia business—it struck me as one of those trendy psychological disorders—but I had no doubt it was real to her.

"Look, thanks for everything," she said. "I guess I really just needed to talk to somebody."

"I'm glad you chose me." I saw her as she'd looked on her pink satin bed. "I have a tendency to become self-obsessed. It helps me to talk to someone else who has problems."

Impulsively she hugged me. And as I held her, I felt a hesitancy, a kind of paralyzing desire that I hadn't felt in years. She drew away, a little embarrassed, and got in her car.

She steadied herself behind the wheel for a moment, then pulled into traffic without checking her mirror. Horns blew and a Buick nearly smashed her tail as she waved at me and gunned away.

Climbing the steps to my room, I ran into a young woman on her way down. "Are you Scott Cochran?" she said, beam-ing with strained television charm.

"Possibly."

She took a deep breath and belted out the first plaintively apologetic verse of Brenda Lee's "I'm Sorry," drawing a few laughs from people around the pool.

As she handed me a small padded envelope, I forced a smile. "Thanks. That was great." Inside, my phone was ringing. I tipped her a buck and unlocked my door.

I let the machine take the call, opening the envelope as the outgoing message played. I dug out a fat little packet of cocaine. The machine beeped:

"Scott—presume you've received my little peace offering by now, and if that dumb singing messenger bitch did what she was supposed to, I guess you know how I feel. You should be canonized, pal, for putting up with me. I was a prime A-one asshole, and would be a complete jerk if I didn't admit it. Scottie, I'm groveling on the floor, pleading, whimpering, drooling all over your filthy shoes. Please call me back and let me know I haven't lost my one true friend." Buzz.

I laughed disgustedly and erased the message.

I was getting ready to go back to work that night when Hank paid me a visit. I had made the mistake of leaving the over-the-air interview cassettes at the station. Hank had listened to them, and he was ecstatic. Dennis was everyting I'd promised: verbal, articulate, outrageous. A little twisted, maybe, but that was part of his mystique.

Hank leaned in the bathroom door while I shaved, talking about the video possibilities. Our parent company owned a cable network that featured a popular rock video and interview show on the weekends. At the very least, Dennis Contrelle and his stable of artists could be a two-hour special edition. Of course, it would be my show. With my good looks, I was a natural for the small screen. And the cassette potential, needless to say, was literally limitless.

And that wasn't all. Hank had spoken with a writer, a

respected rock journalist who'd done a lot of stuff for *Rolling Stone*. A true Contrelle fanatic, this fellow had been trying to get an interview with Dennis for over ten years. When he'd heard that Dennis and I were palling around, he'd flipped. If I could help him in any way—well, to be blunt, I might be looking at a shared book credit. This could be as big as the Morrison biography a few years ago.

Exciting stuff, I told Hank as I stepped from the bathroom, casually tossing a pair of dirty Jockey shorts over the remaining interview cassettes before he noticed them.

As he walked me down to my car, he asked when I was going to see Dennis again.

"Next Monday, I think. In Criminal Courts."

"Huh?"

"Nothing."

Hank was still talking excitedly as I got in the Lincoln. "Just stay on his good side," was the last thing he said.

If there'd been a way to let a machine answer the request line that night, my life might have turned out quite differently. Because, inevitably, the call came.

"Didn't you get my message?"

"Yeah, I got it."

"But you still hate me? Is that it?"

I sighed. "I don't hate you, Dennis."

"Then meet me at the Whisky tomorrow at three. Neutral ground, okay? I don't blame you for being leery of me. I was a bad boy, a very bad boy. But all that's over now, you'll see. The Whisky, all right?"

"I don't know, Dennis. I really don't know."

"Scott, I have to go now, I'm at the studio. But I'll see you tomorrow. I know you won't fail me. You know, I love you, Scott. I really do. I love you like the brother I never had."

The Whisky has been closed and boarded up for some time; I wondered if Dennis knew that as I walked up the glaring sidewalk to the gutted landmark on the Strip. The black walls were plastered with Police and Pia Zadora posters, but the door was open. As I approached I heard music: a piano and singing.

I stepped in, my eyes having trouble adjusting to the dark. On the dim stage I saw the source of the music: Big Willy at an upright, knocking out a Fats Dominio–style "My Blue Heaven." He wasn't bad. In fact . . . it suddenly hit me who Big Willy was, or rather had been, briefly, twenty years before. I was still reflecting on this when a barstool slid on the floor off to my right, and Dennis said, "Over here, Scott."

I saw a dark form and a cigarette ember and started over, bumping my shins on a chair.

"Careful, Scottie." He laughed good-naturedly.

I saw him more clearly as I approached. He was smiling serenely, a beatific Ray Milland smile. He held open his David Cassidy–era black velvet jacket. "You want to frisk me?"

"Not especially."

He laughed wholesomely. He was smoother than I'd ever seen him, not even a hint of underlying violence. If he was on a combination of drugs, it was, at least for the moment, the precisely right combination. I noticed a nasty gouge mark on his forehead—from a fingernail?—as he gestured about the cavernous room. The place was a mess, as if punks had trashed the last show, strewn with broken tables, chairs, glass on the floor.

"Ah, the Whisky," he said with hammy nostalgia.

"Ah, yes." I matched his tone. "Yes, indeed. Otis in his red suit, sweating up a storm right there. Love. Remember Arthur Lee and Love? And the Byrds and Buffalo Springfield, of course. Hey, 'Mr. Spaceman!' Hello, 'Mr. Soul.' God, that was a horrible period for me. I was still in college and somebody sold me some uppers that turned out to be estrogen. I had big tits for a whole semester. Let's see, who else? Ah, yes, Sky Saxon and the Seeds. 'You're Pushin' Too

Hard.' I could never get enough of that song. But, of course, there was only one real debut here, wasn't there? Jim! The Lizard King! Can you believe it, I was here the first night, the very first night, man, that he ever sang 'The End' in public. There was a glass booth right up there suspended from the ceiling with a go-go girl in it. She became famous a few years later, I think, as a terrorist. Anyway, when Jim got to the line about wanting to *you-know-what* his mother —and the word he used wasn't *thank*—this go-go girl was so blown out she *urinated* right up there in the booth! But that's not all. Guess who was standing directly under it? John Wayne, man. The Duke himself, I shit you not. Don't ask me what *he* was doing here. Maybe his Eldorado broke down and he stepped in to use the pay phone. But that's not the worst part. The worst part is . . . *the booth leaked.*"

"Oh, that's horseshit," he said mildly.

"Horseshit? What do you mean, man? I was here. I saw it with my own two eyes. Okay, granted, I was floating on about two thousand mics of Sandoz blue, and I'd skin-popped ten Tuinals a few minutes before in the john, but the eyes don't lie! If that dude *wasn't* John Wayne, man, then I must be Dale Evans! Stuffed! And mounted! Beside Trigger on an Apple Valley ranch!"

He sighed. "Scottie, listen. Relax, I'm not going to hurt you. Big Willy's not going to hurt you. You're making taste-less jokes because you're nervous. There's no need to be." He slipped his arm around my shoulder. I caught a whiff of patchouli. "Scottie, please believe me when I tell you I didn't even know what happened till Big Willy told me the next day. You cannot even begin to imagine the remorse I've experienced. My God, to think I very nearly harmed the one person who's shown me any basic human decency and affection in . . ." His voice caught. ". . . in God only knows how long." He was Olivier now, mugging Jewish angst. "I wouldn't have been able to live with myself if I'd . . . Oh God, no. I don't even want to imagine it. Cocaine is not a bad drug, in and of itself. But woe be unto he who mixes it with Dilaudid"—he cast a fierce Othello glare at Big Willy—"or whatever it was that evil nigger slipped into my medication. It's just like mixing gasoline with nitroglycerin and starting up your car. Someday that fat sack of black shit is going to *kill me*." He did a booming, diabolical Orson Welles laugh. Then, in hushed, religious tones, he went on, "But I've learned my lesson this time. I'm giving up all drugs. *All* drugs. Everything, even aspirin. This time I mean it. I'm going to Switzerland next week. For a blood change. It's expensive, but it's worth it."

I took the packet of cocaine from my pocket and tried to put it in his hand. "Here. Why don't you get your money back and make a donation to Cocaine Anonymous?"

He held up his hands, refusing to take it. "No, no, no, you keep that. A week's a long time. I don't want to be tempted. You'll be doing me a favor."

Big Willy segued into a plaintive, excruciatingly soulful Otis Redding–style "Try a Little Tenderness." I slipped the packet in the breast pocket of Dennis' jacket. "I really don't want this shit, Dennis. For all I know, it's rat poison."

"It's not rat poison," he said, affronted, and for the first time I caught a whiff of violence. But he returned to smooth charm. "Big Willy scores nothing but the best. You can say what you want about him, but believe me, there are two things he knows. Drugs. And how to fix a fat Polack therapist so he never sticks his nose in Sharlene's twat again." He grinned, showing his brilliant false teeth.

Big Willy's voice soared into the grating falsetto stratosphere, caressing the lyrics with a dementedly genteel preciousness, the way a psychopathic murderer might fuss with a strangled ballerina's tutu.

I'd had it. "Look, I'm late for my jazzercise class. I'll see you around, okay?"

I started for the door. He took my arm. "Scott."

Big Willy stopped playing. I froze. Dennis gripped my

arm. "Please," he said, almost tenderly. "Don't treat me like this. I've apologized so many times already I just don't know what else to do." He let go of my arm.

"I accept your apology, Dennis."

"Then please come back to the house with me. There's something I want to show you. Something I want to share with you, Scott. That I sense you and only you may understand."

"What?"

"I'm not going to say. I don't want to spoil it. But please trust me, Scott. I'm not going to hurt you. You can see that I'm in a better mood today. Jesus Christ, I'd rather hurt myself than do anything bad to you. This is just a gesture of friendship. Please say yes. Please."

He smiled a frail ET-like smile, as harmless as a eunuch from a distant world.

"You're my only friend," he said an hour later as we walked up the driveway to the Egyptoid garage. Egyptoid garage, indeed. What would be inside? A 1948—B.C., of course—Chrysler Cheops? Or a cheesy '74 Dodge Tut? Perhaps a '58 Cadillac Ramses with a locust-smeared windshield.

"My only friend. Do you know that? I've never had a male friend before, not really. Or a female friend, for that matter." Despite what he was saying, his manner was still light. He walked with a bounce. "I never had a buddy when I was a kid. I always played by myself. I guess I was a loner. But I liked your voice the minute I heard it. You sounded like a guy I could have been friends with."

He opened the padlock and lifted the garage door. I guess on some level I knew what it had to be, but actually seeing the thing was still a jolt. It was a 1963 Corvette Sting Ray split-window coupé, an immaculate, gleaming phosphorescent blue, as fresh and perfect as it had been on the Stingrays' album cover twenty years before.

"My first real set of wheels," he said proudly, adding dismissively, "Oh, there were a few others before it, but they didn't count. An old Ford, a Buick. Dogshit." He beamed. "I paid cash for this. Five grand in November 1962. It's worth at least five times that now. Though, of course, it's priceless to anyone who cares."

It was astonishing, polished beyond endurance, not a scratch in the sea of addictive blue. It was tempting to imagine it was literally phosphorescent. Passing under a streetlamp it would pick up the light, snaking off down the highway in a smear of neon blue. Cooling off back in the garage, it would continue to glow for hours. It seemed to glow now, unnaturally bright in the shade.

He popped the hood. The fuel-injected 327 engine sparkled, factory fresh.

"I'm drooling," I said, only half-kidding. "You take it out much?" The cast-aluminum knock-off wheels were spotless.

"Only at night." He closed the hood. "The sun does bad things to a car like this. And the smog's a disaster. Check it out as closely as you want. There's isn't a speck of rust anywhere. Not a speck."

It had to be the ultimate Sting Ray, the purity of its lines unequaled before or since. None of the fussy chrome or cute little coves of the fifties models, none of the grossly phallic Coke-bottle imagery of the seventies Corvettes. It was a sleek, wet fuel-injected dream, as poignant as remembered love.

I peered through the window. The interior was mint. A Borg-Warner four-speed, factory air. The black leather bucket seats were custom, as rich and glistening as living skin.

The only slight flaw was a ridge on the back of the passenger seat, where you could see he'd wedged a surfboard, its tail slanting out the window.

"You used to surf?"

"Watch your hands," he said sharply.

I was touching the chrome door handle. He used his
sleeve to wipe off my fingerprints. "Sorry." He laughed
good-naturedly. "But I'm a bit of a fanatic when it comes to
this car." I saw that he was trembling slightly with excite-
ment. "Yeah, I used to surf," he said boyishly. "Not many
people knew how much. I went by myself. Up the coast.
Rincon. I was good, too. I didn't like the other guys, though.
Most surfers are pricks. That's why I gave it up, finally.
Because, thanks to the Beach Boys, the water was soon full
of pricks. Guys like the Vectors, Mark and Gary. Did I tell
you about them?"

"Yeah, you did."

"But I was good, Scott. Really good. Man, I used to get
out there before dawn, just to avoid the pricks. I froze my
ass off more than once. Even with a wetsuit. One morning
I was alone and almost drowned. Sometimes I could feel the
sharks moving around me, see their fins. But they never
attacked me, I still don't know why. Maybe because I'm so
cold-blooded they couldn't even tell I was there." He
laughed as if he'd told a great joke. Then he indicated a door
in the back of the garage. "Come on. There's something else
I want to show you."

The door led to a narrow interior stairway. Sunlight cut
through the dust from a dirty window at the top. He led the
way up.

Halfway to the top an old surfboard rested against the
wall, its resin yellowed, a mummy surfboard from a dead
age.

"This was yours?"

He came back down. "Yeah. I made it." He turned it over,
blowing off dust. "My own design. I worked in a shop in
Hermosa one summer. Of course, the design was ripped off
later—like everything else. I could have made a fortune and
retired to Hawaii—if I hadn't gone into music instead. I was
an engineering genius. See this fin?" He ran his finger down

the blade. "This shape came to me in one instantaneous Benzedrine rush in July of 1962." He smiled wistfully. "I can still remember that crazy, ecstatic night." He looked pained for a moment, then laughed to show he wasn't taking himself too seriously. We went on up the stairs.

The room at the top was dark, its windows shuttered. I caught a faint whiff of Sharlene's sweet perfume and felt a chill. He snapped open the shutters on one window, letting in a block of light. I knew what the room was before he said it.

"My old bedroom. Where I grew up."

It was a boy's room, from an L.A. suburban house, circa 1960: a colonial bunk bed, like David and Ricky might have shared. Surfing pictures cut from magazines, faded pink, were held to the powder-blue walls with yellowed Scotch tape. A neat colonial chest of drawers, on which rings, a wristwatch, and a yellowed handkerchief were laid out. A turquoise plastic pole lamp stood beside an aqua metal black-and-white portable TV. On the bedside table was an RCA 45 player, the Stingrays' "Storm of Love" resting on its spindle. It was like standing in a moldering historical shrine, one nobody visited anymore.

I touched the globe on the corner desk. It had mountain relief ridges and a pink block in Africa labeled the Belgian Congo. I'd had one just like it. In fact, the entire room was a lot like my own. I looked at the chest of drawers, wondering if there was a set of Tijuana playing cards stashed under the Boy Scout memorabilia in the bottom drawer.

"The Beach Boys really said it all, didn't they?" Dennis said. "Credit where it's due."

"How's that?"

"With 'In My Room.' " He smiled gently, calmer now than I'd ever seen him, serene really, as if this room somehow contained his ultimate peace. He opened the closet door. "All my clothes."

There were windbreakers, searing red and navy blue, Pendletons, short-sleeved madras shirts, white Levi's, a single gray suit. On the floor were Clark desert boots, huarachi sandals, crumbling blue go-aheads, disintegrating Keds. He fingered the narrow lapels of the gray suit coat. "This has come back into style. I should start wearing these things again."

The closet smelled of mothballs, but when he closed the door, Sharlene's perfume scent returned. It seemed to be centered around the bunk beds. I touched the banister. "My brother and I had a bunk bed like this once," I said. "When we tried to share a room. It didn't work out."

The scent was definitely coming from the lower bed. There were rust spots on the cactus-motif bedspread. No, not rust. Blood.

"I was an only child," he said.

"You were lucky."

On the wall by the bed was a framed photo of a very young Sharlene. It looked like a blowup of a Polaroid. She was standing at the *Rebel* knife-fight location behind the Griffith Park Observatory, scowling in the sunlight, trying hard to look hard. "Dennis, this is forever. Angel," she'd written below a lipstick print that was now brown.

"She looks very young here," I said.

"Yes, she does. One of our first dates. I took that myself." He laughed wholesomely, but his eyes were nervous.

There was another door leading to a second room. "What's in there?" I said. "Your old elementary school?"

He laughed good-naturedly. "No, just storage. Sharlene's old go-go boots." Smiling broadly, he slipped his hand over my shoulder, guiding me toward the stairs. "Come on. There's something else I'd like to share with you."

I was glad we were going. The room disturbed me in a way I didn't completely understand. It had something to do with its similarity to my own old bedroom. It had a lot to do with the perfume and the bloodstains on the bedspread. And with Sharlene's voice on the cassette.

I excused myself in the foyer to go use the john as Dennis continued on to the music room.

I was taking a leak when the door opened suddenly. Sharlene. I went pee-shy. She stepped in, closing the door behind her.

"I talked to Mike," she said, meaning the divorce attorney.

"Great." I zipped up. "Glad to hear it."

"I'm going out tonight. Meet me in the thirteenth row of the Century Drive-In."

"I've got to tell you, I'm not too crazy about drive-ins. My car battery always runs down when I use the radio for a speaker."

"I need to talk to you," she said adamantly, just as Big Willy yanked open the door.

Sharlene and I froze like animals caught in headlights. Big Willy glared at us. She glared at him. I think I glared at the floor. Sharlene shot me a meaningful look, then pushed past Big Willy and headed toward the stairs.

"Hey, do you mind?" I said to Big Willy, taking the doorknob. "I was just about to change my Kotex."

Still glaring at me, he held the opposite knob so I couldn't close the door, a test of wills. Then—I should have expected this—he released the knob, letting the door smash my knee.

In pain, I leaned against the door for a moment, trying to decide what to do. I gimped out after him.

"Hey, I finally figured out who you were," I said, catching up to him in the foyer. I knew I was just delaying the inevitable. But maybe if I got a chuckle or two out of him his report to Dennis wouldn't be so bad. "You were Little Willy Wheeler, the ten-year-old piano-playing dynamo. I was a big fan of yours."

"*Shit*," he said disgustedly, and kept walking.

"What was your big hit? 'Chopsticks Parts One and Two,' that was it, wasn't it? But hey, wait a minute." I took his arm, stopping him. "Weren't you blind? I mean, you were like Stevie Wonder, right? With the dark glasses and the big smile—"

"*Fuck* you, Jim," he said, and knocked my hand away. "Just *fuck* you in yo' white ass."

He drilled me with a look of total hate, and then hiked his warm-up pants and sauntered arrogantly off toward the kitchen.

I went into the music room. Dennis wasn't there. Then I heard his loud, incredulous voice from the kitchen. "She *what?* When?"

I heard feet running on the shag carpet—just like the morning he'd gone for the gun. I dived for the sliding glass door. Fumbled with the latch. Shit, it was locked. Locked! Dennis burst into the room. "What happened?" he shouted.

I looked back, expecting death. He wasn't armed. But his face was as red as cheap veal.

"What do you mean?"

"Right now. With Shar. Big Willy just told me."

My heart was lurching into a manic Watusi. "Nothing. I was just using the bathroom—"

"That cunt. What did she do? Did she expose herself?"

"No." Of course. He was blaming her.

"Go on, tell me. She showed you her tits, right?"

"No."

"Did she show you her pussy? Did she open her robe and spread her legs and finger the lips of her dripping gash?"

"She wasn't wearing a robe. It was just an innocent mistake. She didn't know I was in there—"

"She knew. Big Willy saw the whole thing. She watched you go in, and waited till you had your cock out. Did she grab it? What did she want to do? Wrap her whore lips around your rod—?"

"This is crazy. Nothing happened."

"Don't protect her—"

"*I'm not protecting her!*" I shouted with a sudden un-hinged rage that frightened even me, that I realized a second later from his look of shock must have given it all away.

But I was wrong. He grinned, a little cockily, pleased, like a dad whose favorite son had finally shown some spunk. "You're a gentleman," he said. "I appreciate that. You're only trying to make the best of a foul, depraved situation. My hat's off to you, Scottie."

He went to the stereo equipment, where a two-inch tape was set to roll. He turned on the power, adjusted knobs on several amps.

"The time has come to lower the boom on that bitch once and for all," he said, almost to himself.

I was trembling now with clogged adrenal energy. Why didn't I just ram his sick brain through one of those linty speakers?

He flipped a switch and the speakers gave out a huge rumble. He lowered the volume. "You know why her cunt's so big?"

"Shut up," I said, just as one of the speakers popped, as if fate meant to drown me out.

He turned to me. "I figured it out just the other day. It wasn't the therapist. You know how I know that?"

Jesus, couldn't he see the look on my face?

"Because he had a dick like a thimble. That's what Big Willy says. And Big Willy doesn't lie—not about things like that. I'll tell you why her cunt's so big. She's getting fucked by niggers."

A sense of *déjà vu* swept over me. Circuits blew. I was OD'ing on my own rage. I'd waited too long. I should have ripped his tongue out the first time we ever met.

"Louise Wright! That depraved black bitch! That's what *that's* all about. Shar isn't going over there to listen to oldies. She's going over there to get fucked by a bunch of horny buck niggers with schlongs like rancid sausages. That bitch

ruined me anyway. I should put a contract out on her tooth-
less head. She's got no teeth, did you know that? Pyorrhea
as a teenage girl. Probably got it licking smegma off all those
clap-ridden donkey dicks she chomped on to make it in
rhythm and blues. She destroyed me, that evil black cooze!
She walked out of the studio with my brains stuffed in her
snatch!"

"It was the best thing you've ever done," I heard myself
say, and felt totally disembodied. I was giving myself cancer,
I was sure of it. I would have a tumor by the weekend if I
didn't kill him now.

"Of course it was. It was a fucking masterpiece! I re-
molded that dogshit nigger into a throbbing monster of pure
and timeless chrome. But 'Tidal Wave of Flame' was nothing, it was just a cheap piece of disposable crap, compared
to *this!*" He rolled the tape. "Scott, *this* is what I was planning to share with you on the cassette, but that was just a
shitty dub. This . . . is the original. Fifteen years of accelerated pain!"

It began in cacophony, shrill and unbearable. For thirty
or forty seconds what sounded like the Mantovani Orches-
tra, the Mormon Tabernacle Choir, the Sex Pistols, James
Brown's Fabulous Flames, the E Street Band, Roxy Music,
the Clash, and the Crystals collided midair with the entire
howling population of South America. Then, at exactly the
most excruciating limit . . . it all fell into perfect place,
knocking my breath out. I felt a cold rush up the back of my
legs, my spine. The horrendous, grating dementia of the first
forty seconds, giving way to this, somehow, in a way I was
helpless to stop, exorcized and wiped away my rage. What
followed was a driving, glistering, pulsing, and melodious
onslaught of pure music, rushing like hot lava through an
infinity of mirrors, all of it with a depth and presence, a
digital perfection, that made even "Tidal Wave of Flame"
sound like an old 45.

Each massed army of sound moved across the landscape

in perfect isolated detail, yet flowed with the whole as if connected by invisible laws to the core of the universe itself. The final tone was overwhelmingly poignant, yet celebratory, euphoric. A transcendent romanticism, a lyrical rock equivalent of Rachmaninoff, preposterous yet shattering. He was right. It was beyond all doubt the best thing he'd ever done, perhaps that anyone had ever done. You knew that even though it still lacked the most important element. The lead vocal.

It built, until it was almost unendurable, until euphoria was nearly pain. Then it dropped again, with shuddering suddenness, a simultaneous orgasm-disembowelment, and ended with a soft rush of dark cellos as dense and massive as a night sea.

"Jesus," I finally said, and looked up at him.

There were tears in his eyes. And in mine.

7

The Century Drive-In protruded from a flat, desolate vista like a surrealistic shrine to lost teenage dreams. Pristine in the days of *The Blob,* it was mean and seedy now, duplexed, the tall plastic curtains that had been meant to hide the screens from the nearby residential neighborhood now shredded like rotted sails.

I drove past the snack bar to the nearest thirteenth row. Why had she said thirteenth row? That was always where you agreed to meet people, the row where all the action supposedly was, all the fucking. If everyone who'd wanted to had parked in the thirteenth row, the cars would have been stacked in wrecking-yard heaps, the rest of the lot deserted.

Of course that was in the days when there was only one thirteenth row. I waited several minutes, watching a summer-camp decapitation on the screen ahead of me and a silent rape in the rearview mirror, hoping Sharlene would find me. She did, startling me as she opened the door on the passenger side.

"It's all right," she said as she got in. "He thinks I went to visit Louise."

I laughed. "Great. A good, innocuous ruse."

"What do you mean?"

"He thinks you're going over there and getting—how can I put this tastefully?—getting jumped on by Afro-American gentlemen with large—"

"Oh look, I don't want to hear this."

I couldn't blame her.

She lit a cigarette, glancing around at the other cars. She seemed nervous—not like she was going to have one of her attacks exactly, but anxious.

"This is where we met," she said.

"You and Dennis? I thought he was driving through Arcadia and heard you rehearsing in a garage—"

"No, that's crap. It was here. In August of 1964. They were showing *A Hard Day's Night*. I was with Bobby. He recognized Dennis and went over and started hitting on him to listen to our demo. Dennis wasn't going for it at all. Until he saw me."

"You were going with Bobby then?"

"No. We were just friends, like brother and sister. All that stuff in the magazines about a triangle—that was all crap." She stared at the screen. "He had a crush on me, I guess. But I never felt that way about him."

"Yeah, I remember when he died," I said, aware that I was gauging her response. I'd leafed through some of those magazines. "They found him in his car—"

"Yeah. Out by some refinery in Carson. In a shiny new sixty-nine Camaro. He'd just bought it. He had the sticker on the windshield, *Let It Bleed* on the tape deck, and the needle in his arm. He'd been dead for over a week when they found him."

"Heroin—"

"I guess." I could see that she had loved him, though I believed her that it hadn't been romantic. "It was such a waste. He sang originally, too, when we were the Darts. A lot of people don't know that. He was good too. He could have been another Jagger. But, of course, Dennis had this concept of the Stingrays, and he wouldn't let Bobby sing. He kept promising he would. After the Stingrays broke up, he did some solo stuff with Bobby but nothing was ever released. They had a falling-out." Her eyes caught the movie light. "Bobby was so excited the night we met Dennis. It seemed like the ultimate break." She snorted. "I guess I was pretty excited too. Who wouldn't be? Here was this genius who wanted to make me a star. He was young, rich, handsome, powerful, creative. Every girl's dream. The car didn't hurt either. He was driving this sixty-three Sting Ray that was not to be believed—"

"Yeah, I saw it. It's quite a car."

"What?"

"This afternoon. In the garage."

"He let you in the garage?" Amazed laugh.

"Yeah. Showed me the car. And the room."

"The room?" She looked puzzled.

I thought about her perfume scent on the bunk bed. "Upstairs. His little bedroom shrine. You know."

She shook her head. "I've never been up there. The garage is off limits. It's his private retreat."

She looked off out the window, as if she knew I could tell she was lying. Why was she? I thought about the cassette, and the bloodstains on the bed. Jesus, what was he doing to her up there?

I covered for her. "It's just his old bedroom. You know, where he grew up." She wouldn't look at me. "A little creepy in a way. I mean . . ." How could I get out of this? "It's the kind of thing you usually don't see until after somebody's dead. Like Walt Disney's birthplace or something."

She seemed to have stopped breathing. The ash fell off her cigarette.

"Sharlene, are you okay?"

No reply.

"Oh Christ, are you having one of those attacks?"

"No." She snapped out of it. "And please don't ever ask me that. Sometimes just asking that question can bring one on."

"Sorry."

She brushed the ash off her slacks. "No, I'm just a little ragged tonight. It's been a bad day. We had a fight this afternoon. After you left."

"Did he hit you?"

"No," she said defensively. "No, it was just verbal. He wanted the keys to the car."

"But he has hit you?"

"Oh sure. Once or twice." Her voice was hard. "But it's cool, you know. Because it always . . . whenever Dennis hits me, it always feels like a kiss."

She turned to the window again, her shoulders shaking. I thought she was laughing at first. But she was crying.

"Scott, would you do me a favor and hold me, please—"

Oh Christ, yes. I put my arms around her and she wept against my chest, her stiff hair brushing my cheek.

"It's okay. You're gonna be okay."

I caught a whiff of her sweet perfume and felt a terrible rush of tenderness for her. If only there'd been some way to instantly erase what he had done to her.

I held her for a long time. I couldn't believe what it did to me. I'd never thought anything so simple could ever thrill me so much again.

"I had a long talk with Mike yesterday," she said finally, digging a pink Kleenex out of her bag. "You were right. He's not a total scumbag." She blew her nose.

"Wait till you get the bill."

"Anyway, he's going ahead. But he thinks I should get out of the house before he puts things in motion."

"Sounds like a good idea."

"I'm not sure where to go. Dennis knows about Louise's."

"You have any other girlfriends?"

She shook her head. "Louise is my only friend, period." She blotted her eyes. "There's some facility for battered wives. In Azuza or someplace. It's supposed to be secret, but I don't know. If Dennis finds out where I've gone, he'll come after me."

"Forget it. You don't have to sleep on a cot in some crummy halfway house—you're a star. I know a place."

"I think he knows about the Tropicana."

"He doesn't know about my mom's in PV."

Slight pause. "Would she mind?"

"She won't know. She's in Guatemala."

"Guatemala? What's she doing there?"

"Promise you won't hold it against me?"

"What?"

"She's supposedly just an archaeologist. But she's really a Marxist guerrilla. She's down there teaching children how to fire an AK-47—"

She laughed. "Give me a break. There aren't any Marxists from Palos Verdes. That's Reagan country."

"Shows how much you know. It was hell growing up in the fifties with a Red in the house. Most kids had den mothers. Mine was a cell captain."

She swatted me. "You're so full of shit."

"Ouch. I think you just nicked me with your ring." I took her hand, looking at the gleaming rock set in silver. "Jesus, Sharlene, you really shouldn't be wearing this here. It's not safe."

"Most people think it's fake."

"Just don't go to the ladies' room. You might come back without a finger."

She tried to remove the ring, but couldn't.

"Hold on, I'll go get some buttered popcorn."

She smiled at my suggestion, and quit struggling with the ring. She looked at me, her mouth glistening in the movie light. "So anyway . . ." She took my hand, lowering her eyes. "Is there something special I have to do . . . to get you to kiss me, or what—"

I kissed her. Gently at first, then deeply. I guess we both went a little crazy for a while, as though it had been years for both of us since we'd really kissed. I believed it had been for her. If I had ever given any credence to Dennis' demented accusations, they were dispelled now. Kissing Sharlene was like making out with a teenage girl twenty years ago, when a kiss still meant something. She gave herself to me with a passion too many women I'd been with had faked. I was as starved for it as she was.

I loved kissing her so much. She was so sweet and pretty. How could he hit her, what could make him want to do that? How could he not want to just love her? Her cherry-red mouth. Her hot little tract house back bedroom mouth. Her intelligent, patrician, ethereal mouth.

I kissed her neck and squeezed her breasts through her cream silk blouse, undoing the pearl buttons. She wore a delicate black lace bra. My cock was concrete in my blue Levi cords; when she squeezed it, I died.

Eventually she whispered, "Scott, I should really go." We both laughed: it was so classic. We were both so hot we were half-crazy with the pent-up urge to fuck and now she had to be in by eleven.

"He might check to see if I'm at Louise's," she explained.

I wanted to take her back to the Tropicana and eat her tangerine pussy till my tongue fell out, make up for fifteen years in one endless night, fuck her till we sweated to death and went to hell.

But no, not at the Tropicana, where he could find us. Not in that dingy room, on that lumpy bed. With Sharlene everything should be fresh and pretty.

"Are you sure it's all right for you to go back there tonight?" I said.

"Yeah, it's cool. He's at the studio by now. And he's going to Switzerland at the end of the week."

We lit cigarettes. I kept my arm round her, gently rubbing the curve of her breast through her black lace bra, as we made the plans for her escape.

8

It would go like this. Dennis was leaving for Switzerland Friday morning, Big Willy with him. That evening Sharlene would be alone in the house. The fences would be charged with electricity, the alarms set, and she wouldn't even be able to open the front gate. But there was a breach: the gate to the steps leading down to the beach, locked with a dead-bolt. Sharlene had the key. No alarm would sound.

A short way down the beach she could climb another stairway to a small gravel public parking area up on the bluff. I'd meet her there at nine, as Dennis and Big Willy were coming in over the Alps. Sharlene's attorney would begin proceedings on Monday, by which time Dennis would be under sedation. By the time he came to and found out what had happened and got back to L.A., Sharlene's trail would be cold.

Still, as the week progressed, I had feelings of impending doom.

On Wednesday I met Neal for lunch at a noisy place in Century City and made the mistake of telling him what was going on. He sat there staring at me as if I'd gone completely insane.

"But she's got someplace she can hide for a while?" he said finally.

"Yeah, that's been worked out," I said, not sure why I didn't want to tell him where.

"You'd better go with her," he said.

The next day I met Hank for lunch at a diner on Melrose. He wanted to know if I had mentioned the cable deal to Dennis yet. He became upset when I told him I hadn't.

Dennis was definitely up to something in the studio, Hank said; he'd been calling in some of the top musicians in town. A reemergence seemed imminent. If we didn't act fast, we might lose him.

He also mentioned the rock journalist again, who was now definitely envisioning a major book. The fellow was already exploring other avenues of approach. If Dennis should suddenly turn gregarious—without me—I could easily be left out in the cold.

"That's not going to happen, Dennis trusts me," I said, keeping the irony to myself. "He's shared things with me he's never shared with anyone else."

Hank gave me a funny look. I felt a rush of desolation, guilt over my betrayal. Then I thought about the bruise on Sharlene's neck the first day we'd met, the way he'd hit her the morning he'd tried to kill me, and my doubts fled.

Thursday night at the station, zero hour minus eighteen. Dennis called. "Scott, listen, I'm at the studio, you've got to come down here, get somebody to fill in for you. Magical things are happening, moments never to be repeated, and I need one sane man as a witness."

This worried me. If he was really into something, would he cancel the trip tomorrow? "Dennis, I can't. I've been off so much lately, they're threatening to replace me with a tape of Art Laboe."

"Afterward then. I'll still be here."

"I thought you were going to Switzerland . . ." I stopped myself, aware *he* hadn't told me the exact day of his departure. There was a pause.

"I am," he finally said. "At ten tomorrow. That's why I'm in a race against time. Oh, Scottie, I haven't felt like this in years! I'm nineteen again! Bursting with a spastic energy I can barely control! But I have *my mind!* My mature, experienced, razor-sharp mind! Scottie, I've waited so long for just these precious few moments."

He believed what he was saying, of course. And in a strange way I was happy for him. In fact, I was willing to come down and solder the doors shut so he could stay in there and be a genius forever.

"Come to me, Scottie. After work."

"Dennis, I can't. I've got another commitment."

"Hey. I understand." A dirty snicker. "You rub a little of that stuff I gave you on your pecker, and you'll be able to go *all* night long." He yowled like James Brown.

"An idea worth considering." He'd forgotten that I had put the cocaine in his jacket pocket.

Then: "Hey, bring her along! We've got a lounge down here, a posh lounge. People fuck in there all the time. You can lower the lights and listen to the playback, and fuck that hot little twat till the cows come home."

"She's a born-again Christian, Dennis."

"Yeah? That's what I'm gonna be when I get back from Gstaad. Not a Christian, but born-again. You wait and see, Scottie. I'll be a new man. What happened with you and me was a blessing in disguise. It forced me to come to my senses. And believe me, I haven't finished making it up to you."

I could hear a playback of his mastertape in the background—an unauthorized playback, it seemed. He covered the mouthpiece and screamed at someone. Then he came back on. "Scott, these morons are trying to destroy me, I've got to go. Fuck her one time for me, okay, sport?"

"Right-o."

He hung up.

I didn't sleep much Friday morning. Around ten, when Dennis should have been boarding his plane, I called in sick, saying I'd had a relapse of the flu. I stayed in the rest of the day, wanting to be near the phone in case something went wrong. I considered calling the studio, employing a ruse to find out if Dennis was still there. I considered calling Sharlene too, but that was far too risky. It was better to wait and proceed as planned.

I left around eight that night. An hour later I pulled into the designated lot on the bluff. She wasn't there. I could see the house across the ravine, illuminated in yellow security lights like an Egyptoid women's prison. I waited several minutes, smoking a cigarette, then went down the steps to the beach.

The moon was full, so bright it gave the skimpy beach a day-for-night feeling. I trudged up the sand, climbing over some rocks, till I saw the wooden steps coming down from the house. No wonder the gate hadn't been used in years; the steps were crumbling. They looked far too rickety to climb. At least I thought so until I heard panting and looked back and saw the German shepherd charging me.

I lunged for the steps, scrambling up as the wood creaked. I stopped when I came to Sharlene's shapely calves.

"What are you doing!" she said.

I looked back down. The dog was at the foot of the steps, barking. *Barking*. A figure on the beach called: "Rolf! Come here!"

"It's all right," Sharlene said as I got up. "It's just one of the neighbors."

My heart was still pounding as I looked in her eyes. She held a pink Samsonite suitcase. The wind blew her aqua silk dress flush against her body, revealing every luscious curve.

"Well, this is it," she said softly. "I guess I'm free."

We soared up PCH, the top down under the full yellow moon. It was a florid Technicolor night, the air as warm as breath. The wind tossed Sharlene's hair, which for the first time wasn't set or sprayed. She moved in her seat, snapping her fingers to "My Boyfriend's Back" on the oldies station. As she sang along, she aimed the words at me with a mock-inflammatory air, till I had to laugh. Impulsively I kissed her as we barreled through an intersection, the light turning red, her mouth as red as the light.

As we streamed past the Malibu Colony I asked about her last conversation with Dennis.

"Don't worry," she said, "I played sick. Said I had the flu. He expects me to be bedridden for a week." The Crystals' "Da Doo Ron Ron" came on, and she turned it up. "Of course he thinks it's psychosomatic. He thinks everything I ever get is psychosomatic. But then, it doesn't really matter what he thinks, does it?"

"Not now."

She sang along to the Crystals' song—a little manically perhaps, but who could blame her?

"Hey, what's the story with those dogs, anyway?" I said.

"What do you mean?"

"Well, am I crazy or do they not bark?"

She gave me a blank look. "Of course they don't bark. How could they? *You* try barking with your vocal cords ripped out."

"*What?*"

"Yeah, he had it done about six years ago." She stared straight ahead. Something besides the dogs was bothering her. "They barked all the time. There were three of them originally. Chuck, Buddy, and Gene. Gene was the worst. He whimpered. Constantly. You know how your nerves get when you've been up a few days on speed? It drove Dennis right through the ceiling. Anyway, Big Willy tried to fix Gene, but he screwed it up. Severed his windpipe or something. It was awful. I saw it from my window. It took him a long time to die. He staggered all over the lawn, trailing blood."

"Oh, hey, listen, I don't want to hear this. I've got a thing about animals."

"You asked me." Her elation gone, she scowled, digging out a cigarette.

"What's the matter?"

"Nothing. I'm just not going to worry about it all weekend."

"What?"

She sighed. "Oh, the guy that fixed Buddy and Chuck. A security guy. A sick geek, I hate him. He was gonna put a closed-circuit camera in my bedroom once." She blew smoke. "He'll be coming by tomorrow to feed the dogs. When I'm not there . . . *Fuck*. I never even thought about those fucking dogs."

"Sharlene, it doesn't matter. You're already free. It's too late to stop you. Nobody can do anything. You're not an escaped convict, for Christ's sake. They're not going to send out the bloodhounds."

"Yeah, I know." She tried to smile. "This is just a little strange, that's all. I mean, this is the biggest thing I've ever done." She took my hand on the seat.

"I know."

"I'm glad I'm not doing it alone," she said. "I don't think I *could* do it alone."

I put my arm around her, her fresh hair against my cheek.

As we approached the tunnel in Santa Monica where PCH turned into the freeway, I said, "You know what this is, don't you? You want me to get off?"

I felt her tense. I didn't really understand her fear of the freeways. It seemed irrational, as if it was the word itself that scared her more than anything. The traffic on PCH was just as fast, and far more dangerous.

She squeezed my hand. Hers was cold. "No, go ahead," she said as we passed the last turnoff. "It's okay. As long as you're driving."

We roared through the tunnel, merging smoothly with the flow. She released her tight grip on my hand, giving in, as we surged through the balmy night.

As we swept through the interchange to the San Diego Freeway, she took off her wedding ring. She held it for a moment, weighing it. Then she rolled down her window.

She couldn't. That tasteless rock had to be worth at least three hundred grand. But before I could say anything, she dropped it into her bag as if it were a stale roll of Certs.

For a long time after that it almost felt as if we'd left the past behind, as if the past were an evil little town we'd driven through a few miles back but would never have to see again. It was just the two of us, right now in the present, streaming through this warm, immediate, sexual night, "Eight Miles High" on the radio, then "Don't Worry, Baby," "You Can't Catch Me," and "No Particular Place to Go."

Then we came back down to the surface streets and my own past rose up dead ahead. The Hill. Palos Verdes, spotted with lights, like candles on tombstones in a cemetery of bad trips. A Boot Hill full of ghosts: old dates buried alive in ranch-house kitchens, old enemies embalmed in Cutty Sark in the den. Pipe-smoking scoutmaster specters—the spirit of my father still roamed those ravines, calling out a disembodied: "Val-da-ree, val-da-raa . . ." Canasta-playing cadavers still cackled from the fifties living rooms. Of course for me there was only one ultimate tomb of memory. Too soon we took a right on Palos Verdes South and swept up the hill to the glass-and-redwood sarcophagus at 914 Conqueror Drive.

Trouble started right away. My key wouldn't open the front door. "Shit, she changed the locks."

We cut through the illuminated shrubs to the kitchen door. Every dog in the neighborhood started barking when I broke the window.

I reached in, unlocked the door, and caught a whiff of something unbelievably foul.

"Jesus, what's *that?*" Sharlene made a nauseated face.

I felt a sick rush as the rot burned my sinuses. Oh Christ, my mom wasn't in Guatemala. She'd come back. And had a heart attack. We were going to find her in the other room, dead. Dead for days. Please, no.

Then I saw what it was. Leftovers on the counter, loosely covered with aluminum foil, intended for the refrigerator, but forgotten in the typical haste of my mom's departure. I pulled back the foil to reveal a small fuming chunk of putrified meat.

"Oh, Jesus. What is it?" Sharlene said.

"A human heart, from the looks of it. I'm afraid my mom gets a bit carried away with all this Mesoamerican stuff."

"Yuk."

It was a pot roast. I picked up the platter, and squinching my nostrils shut, took it out to the trash, where I dumped it, platter and all. When I got back, Sharlene was spraying Wizard air freshener around and I almost gagged. It was a draw which was worse, the stench of the rancid meat or that sickening floral odor.

"Stop it, I'm allergic to that stuff," I said, and opened the kitchen windows to air out the room.

We went into the living room, the Wizard reek already permeating the rest of the house. I flipped the wall switch and a light came on in the empty aquarium. The room was even more desolate than I remembered from my last visit, the Danish furniture threadbare and beaten, books and papers stacked on the hardwood floors. There were also signs of an intimate farewell party. Dirty glasses, stale peanuts and, tossed over the sofa, Mom's bra.

"What's this?" Sharlene smiled, indicating the bra.

"Aztec, I'd say. Fourteenth-century cross-your-heart."

Sharlene snorted. "Looks more like late American to me. Republican dynasty. Pre-nuclear war. Probably Maidenform."

I laughed and stepped behind the bar.

"You were kidding about your mom being a Commie, weren't you?"

"Yeah, she's completely apolitical. The present is of no interest to her. She only cares about the past. I think the last time she bothered to vote she wrote in Quetzalcoatl." There was only one bottle behind the bar, a fifth of Jim Beam with an inch of whiskey in it. "Want a drink?"

Sharlene nodded.

"Never mind." There was a cigarette butt in the bottle.

We laughed dismally, then I went to the john. When I came back, Sharlene wasn't at the bar where I had left her. The sliding glass door to the patio was open. I heard a squeaking sound and saw Sharlene outside sitting on the blue swing. It was less blue than gray now, faded from the sun, but it was the same swing on which Cheryl and I had made love twenty years before. Sharlene was even sitting on it the same way Cheryl had, legs crossed, one arm across the back, rocking gently, waiting for me to come join her. The rusty springs creaked like chains. She was smiling. "It's nice out here."

I went out. "I wouldn't sit on that if I were you."

"Why not?"

"It's fucked up. The chain could break anytime."

She rocked a little harder. "It seems okay."

"Really. Come on." I took her hand, tried to pull her up.

"Come on where? I like it out here. It's pleasant. You can see the stars."

"Fuck the stars." I pulled her to her feet. She laughed, not understanding my tenacity.

"Scott—"

I slid my arms around her. We kissed. Gently at first, then passionately. Behind her, the swing was still squeaking.

"Let's go in the rumpus room," I said.

She laughed. "I'll bet that used to be your favorite line."

"Not really. You're the first girl I've ever brought home."

She smiled. "I'm not exactly a girl, Scott."

"This isn't exactly home."

As we stepped to the door I looked over my shoulder and saw a flashback from twenty years before: my little brother standing there, holding up a used rubber—sun-baked now, with twigs stuck to it—the rubber I wore when Cheryl and I had sex on the swing. You can see where Cheryl neatly snipped off the end. "Hey, Dad, what's this?" Billy calls to my father.

The swing was still squeaking, long after it should have stopped, as Sharlene and I stepped inside. I slid shut the sliding glass door.

In the warm glow of an amber-shaded lamp the rumpus room seemed relatively inviting. We settled in on the plaid sofa where I'd lost my virginity. I was afraid it might still be there, buried under the cushions with the loose change and black Fritos—but to hell with it. The whole house was crawling with sexual nostalgia; there was practically nowhere Cheryl and I hadn't made love.

I tuned the old Magnavox on which Oswald had been shot to MTV. At least that was contemporary. There were some beers in the refrigerator. For the next hour we drank and talked, MTV in the background.

I talked about my mom, about the freak accident that had killed my dad at a Scout jamboree in '69. She talked about

her dim childhood in Arcadia, "a real armpit," how Dennis
had rescued her from a dull, grinding life.

She stopped talking when a Stevie Nicks video came on,
watching as Stevie rushed breathlessly through Victorian
fairytale rooms, showing off her voluptuous throat.

"How old do you think she is?" Sharlene said.

"I don't know. Fifty?"

She swatted me playfully. "I'm serious."

"How old do *you* think she is! In her mid-thirties, something like that. Looks pretty good, doesn't she? I understand
she watches her diet and dematerializes regularly."

She smiled politely, watching Stevie sing at the camera. It
wasn't hard to read her thoughts. "And she's still popular,
isn't she? She's still on top."

"Yeah, I guess she is. A little dated, if you ask me. Her
crystal-fairytale shtick's getting a bit tired."

Sharlene reached for her cigarettes. "Tell me something,
and be honest. Do you think I'm any good? As a singer, I
mean?"

"Yes!"

"You're not just bullshitting me?"

"Jesus, no. Shar, you've really got to start developing
some self-confidence. You must know how good you are—"

"But do you think I could still be a hit today?" She glanced
at the TV, where the Go-Gos were singing in a Mustang
convertible now.

"Yes."

"You don't think I'm dated? Or too old?"

"You're not that old. Look at Chrissie Hynde of the Pretenders. If she can still shake it, you sure as hell can."

She smiled, not so much at what I'd said as at me in
general. The way Cheryl used to smile.

"Not only is your voice incredible, you're visually compelling. If you're presented properly, with a certain lewd
dignity—"

"With what?"

"Sharlene, you've got to understand something. You're more than a singer. You're an icon."

"A what?"

Her blue eyes caught the light from the kitchen. She had never looked more like Cheryl.

"You *mean* something to people. Because of your past. Because of the very fact that you've been on ice for fifteen years. You're a living metaphor."

She scoffed.

I became more intent. "You represent something people lost a long time ago. A part of people that's been shut up in a satin room for the last fifteen years."

She looked uneasy now, and finally lit her cigarette.

"The Stingrays were the epitome of the last great age of rock romanticism," I said. "The last searing glow of an aching, yearning love. Before the world turned to shit forever."

This startled her. I realized I had been paraphrasing Dennis. And she had heard it before.

"But your gig can't be nostalgia," I added quickly. "That would be a gross miscalculation. The Stingrays are like a previous movie role, a connotation you'll bring with you. The middle-of-the-road route would be just as disastrous, singing easy-listening pop tunes on the assumption that all your former fans are middle-aged rock burn-outs. But nobody really wants to hear you sing 'Feelings,' no matter how stodgy they've become. You should go back to what you were in the beginning, when the Stingrays were still the Darts. A basic, tight, raunchy R & B sound, like the early Rolling Stones. No trendy shit, no homogenized synthesizer crap. Just good simple rock and roll. Your voice is timeless; your backing should be too. You could be a true mythic rocker, Sharlene. The territory's yours, just claim it. The West Coast is waiting. The American dream's just as fucked up out here as it is back in Asbury Park."

She laughed. "Maybe you should manage my career. It sounds like you know more about it than I do."

I lay back on the sofa. "Hey, I'm just giving you my opinion. I could be wrong. Maybe you should do Christian music exclusively. Follow your muse."

She got up. "I thought only guys had muses." She turned in the kitchen door. "I'm just not sure if I want to be an icon. It sounds like it might be kind of a burden."

"We don't always have a choice in these matters, Sharlene."

"Yeah? Well, we'll see."

She went back through the kitchen to the bathroom. I leaned back and watched three stylized sluts in a ZZ Top video, moving to the beat. I liked some rock videos, but the phenomena worried me at times. When I listened to older music, like the Stingrays, I entered my own private CinemaScope dream. But when I heard songs from the last few years, all I could see in my mind was the video, no matter how vapid or lame. I was mulling this over when I heard Sharlene scream.

I ran to her in the hall, the shag carpet wet under my bare feet. She was cringing at my old bedroom door.

"What is it?"

"I was looking for the bathroom . . ." She indicated the bedroom door.

I started to open it.

"No!" She stopped my hand.

"Why? What is it?"

Jesus, there was terror in her eyes. What had she seen in there? An ectoplasmic specter in aqua capris?

"A rat," she said.

"A rat?" Again I started to open the door.

"Scott, no for God's sake!" She grabbed my arm.

"It's all right," I said, turning the knob. "As long as it doesn't lunge directly for my face."

She cringed, backing away as I opened the door a crack.

I reached in and flipped on the light. The room wasn't blue, as it was in my memory, but a bright disgusting orange.

A divorcee friend of my mom's had stayed there a while, redecorating the room. I heard a rustling sound. There, by the ruffles that trimmed the twin bed—the bed on which Cheryl and I had fucked all day and talked all night, and finally fought—I saw its tail. Christ, it was as big as a tabby. The rest of the room assaulted me, the wicker furniture spray-painted orange like the walls, the dusty stuffed toys on the bed. This was where I'd planned for us to sleep tonight. The rat skittered under the bed.

"Jesus, shut the door!" Sharlene said.

I shut it as Sharlene let out a groan of disgust. I looked down at the wet carpet and saw why. The toilet had overflowed the last time I had flushed it.

I covered Sharlene's eyes. "Don't look," I said.

A short time later we were airborne, veering in over Avalon Bay. This was where we should have come in the first place, where there were no squeaking blue swings, no plaid sofas, no rats under the ruffles.

The chopper flight didn't seem to bother her. I reminded myself it was basically crowds she couldn't handle, lots of people packed in a tight place. Except for an old guy with a Sterling Hayden beard who talked to himself the whole flight, we were the only passengers.

We took the bus into Avalon, and from there we had to walk about a mile along a dark gravel road. The moon shimmered through the eucalyptus trees; the waves lapped against the shore below. Finally we saw the house, nestled on an otherwise empty cove, the white board walls reflecting the moonlight. We hiked down the path, I found the key under the steps, unlocked the door, and switched on the light. It was a cowboy's retreat, circa 1940: leather sofas and chairs, antlers and a rifle over the stone fireplace, brass rodeo statuettes, Remington prints on the knotty-pine walls, my dad's collection of Zane Grey books. An abandoned, defunct mythology—as musty as Hopalong Cassidy's wink.

"Here we are," I said. "Paradise at last." Then I went out back for some wood to build a fire.

A while later we took separate showers. I lay on the brass bed while she took hers first. When she stepped from the bathroom she had a towel wrapped modestly around her, as if intent on preserving a PG rating. I got up, still wearing my Jockey shorts, and went into the steamy bathroom. I got in the shower, feeling strangely awkward. Why did I feel so hesitant and unsure of myself? Certainly we'd broken the ice the other night at the drive-in. Yet she'd been abused so badly: extra care was called for not to do anything that might remind her of Dennis. But what the hell, she wasn't made of glass; she wasn't going to break the second I touched her.

I saw her through the translucent shower curtain as she stepped back into the bathroom to brush her hair at the mirror. She was wearing a diaphanous black negligee now, a little cheap—a little mouth-watering. I was running out of hot water. I shut off the faucet, pulled back the curtain, and grabbed a towel. The bathroom was narrow, and I wouldn't be able to step out of the tub unless she moved. Still brushing her hair, she watched me in the mirror. I couldn't help looking down at her ass, which the negligee barely covered. It was a perfect, flawless ass, perfect. Too perfect.

"Quite an improvement," she said softly.

She meant the house.

"Yeah, it is." I saw her breasts in the mirror. Those jutting pink Cadillac breasts.

"It's a perfect hideout," she said. "I'll bet you used to bring a lot of girls out here."

" 'Fraid not. Not unless I wanted a troop of Boy Scouts watching. This was my dad's place."

"I figured. It seems so masculine. Like a cowboy lived here or something."

Yes, ma'am. I reckon so. My cock was jerking up like Billy the Kid awakened by a rifle crack.

The air was thick with steam and the delicate smell of her toilet water as I stepped out and removed her saloon-whore negligee from behind. I kissed her soft schoolmarm neck, and she gasped when she felt my hot steel Colt press against her bare Belle Star ass. I kissed her brothel-red mouth, squeezing her Annie Oakley tits, the nipples as hard as bullets. I burnt her face with my stubble, running my outlaw hand down her cowgirl stomach to the treasure of Sierra Madre. Then I took her to the brass bed and shot the lock off her strongbox. I found a vein of silver and followed it, as deep as I could go, digging all night, till I was slick with sweat, my face glazed with a mist of silver. I yowled as the mine caved in around me, pulled out fast, then sank another shaft. I took a nugget into Frisco, and when I bit it with my teeth, the ground began to shake. Chandeliers fell like teardrops and a crevice split the street. Then the whole city came down around me as Sharlene exploded like a detonated Nob Hill mansion, and all the gas lines blew at once.

Afterwards I wandered the rubble-filled streets, dazed in a torn black tuxedo, till I found her, singing "Because the Night" high on a sun-drenched hill.

"It's funny," she said later, as I held her under the patch quilt. "You're only the second guy I've ever been with. I'm practically a virgin. And he thinks I'm such a slut."

I kissed her shoulder, and noticed for the first time a small pearlescent scar. I kissed that too.

In the morning we walked into Avalon and ate breakfast at a sidewalk café overlooking the bay. It was Saturday so there were a few families wandering around with cameras, but Catalina was no longer high on anybody's list of tourist priorities. It had probably peaked out in the early fifties. I remembered hordes of Hawaiian-shirted tourists when I was a kid. But Disneyland had sucked them away with its wholesome plastic thrills. Though there was nothing unwholesome about Catalina, it was far from state-of-the-art in terms of thrills. Most of the wood-frame bungalows and hotels dated back to the twenties, and hadn't been painted since Tinkerbell hexed the island. There were no Holiday Inns or Pizza Huts, few colors much brighter than palm-frond green and adobe. William Wrigley, the chewing-gum tycoon who'd originally owned the island, had kept out development, which was the only reason it hadn't long ago been turned into the Santa Catalina Estates.

It was soft and peaceful, seedy and nostalgic, like the faded location of a fifties Riviera romance. You could imagine Grace Kelly gunning a red MG through the hills overlooking the Spanish/Moorish casino where the big bands had once played. You might find Cary Grant's rusted Dunhill lighter washed up on the pebbly beach. Or you might see John Huston loping around on his cane, tending his horses or plotting water-district power plays under a stuffed swordfish in a private club overlooking the bay. You might see Lloyd Bridges snorkel past Amelia Earhart's Lockheed Electra as you looked through the glass-bottom boat.

"You know, last night was really something," Sharlene said. The breeze tossed her hair. She looked so good this morning, her pale skin luminous in the shade, her eyes their most addictive phosphorescent blue. I was already strung out, like a chump, after just one hit.

"Yeah, I had a good time too. Beats MTV."

We were sitting close together against the adobe wall. She ran her hand up my leg, the tablecloth hiding us from view. "What I mean is, I think I'd like to have you fuck me a lot."

"See here, young lady," I joked, but I was getting a hard-on. "You know how I feel about that kind of talk at the breakfast table."

She smiled. "You're really good in bed. How'd you get to be so good?"

"I read a lot of Mickey Spillane novels as a kid."

She squeezed my cock through my Levi's. "Is this a turn-off?"

"Yeah, I hate it." My cock was chrome. I ran my hand up under her skirt to her panties.

"I hear some guys don't like forward women."

"I used to be like that. I always chloroformed my first wife. I couldn't get it up if she was conscious."

"What about your second wife?" She unbuttoned my Levi's.

"She was a sumo wrestler. She liked to pin me to the mat and sit on my face." I rubbed her through her panties.

"I can see why. You've got a nice face."

"Is that all I am to you, Sharlene? Just a visual object?"

She reached into my Levi's. I winced, and glanced at the tab, as her hand closed over my bare cock.

"No. But I'd rather be with you than Quasimodo."

"Are you sure? I hear he's good in bed. I mean, you haven't really been humped until—"

I jumped when I felt a hard tap on my shoulder, and looked up to see the manager. He was scowling.

"I'm afraid I'm going to have to ask you to leave."

"Oh yeah? Why's that?" I said, pulling out my shirttail, stuffing my cock back in under the table.

He glanced at a family across the patio, mom and dad and two teenage boys. Mom and dad were glaring at us. The boys were grinning furtively.

I looked over the table and saw how the breeze was billowing the tablecloth.

Once out on Crescent Avenue we both started laughing, but I could see that Sharlene was embarrassed.

"I really didn't know they could see," she said.

"Yes, you did. I know your type. Shock the middle class. Anything to be offensive."

"I wasn't thinking."

"I'm sure those kids are damaged for life."

"Why didn't you stop me?"

"I wanted to. I knew it was wrong. Jiminy Crickets was telling me no. But Robert Plant kept going: 'oohh!' "

She laughed and swatted me.

I put my arm around her as we walked along the beachfront toward the casino. We were quiet for a while, listening to the slapping of the waves.

"You know, I've been thinking," she said finally. "I think you're right about my doing something basic, a classic R & B sound. In fact, a lot of what I've already written is kind of in that vein."

"You've written songs?"

"Sure—I mean, you can only do your nails so many times. Nobody's ever heard them though, except Dennis. And the one time I played something for him, he laughed at me. He told me I was—" She pushed the memory away. "Fuck him. I know some of them are good. That's what I want to do, get my own band. Horns and stuff. You know, a Stax/Volt sound. There are some young guys in L.A. that do that real well. Shit, I can play clubs now, just think. You don't know what I'd give for a smoky, smelly little club with black walls. No more arenas, fuck that. I want to get down in it and work up a sweat. And I can do that now. I can go into a packed club and not freak out. Now that I've graduated."

"Graduated?" I had a bad feeling.

"Oh Christ," she continued in the same elated tone. "I didn't tell you, did I? I graduated my therapy. Leo cut me loose last week."

"No kidding?" We had never gotten around to discussing how Dennis might have "dealt with" her therapist.

"Yeah. It was a total surprise. *That's* what made me decide it was time to finally make my move. He called me from the hospital—"

"Where he works?"

"No, no, he works out of his house at Pt. Dume. He was in for some minor surgery. Hemorrhoids or something. But, Scott, he said I didn't need to see him again. Because I'd crossed the invisible line."

"The invisible line?"

"Yeah. See, he was slowly desensitizing me so I could do more things without having an attack. But once you cross the invisible line, the whole process just continues on a subconscious level until you're totally free. He said he didn't tell me sooner because then I would've been constantly watching for the line. But I've crossed it! Isn't that terrific?"

"Yeah." I hadn't smiled so painfully in a long time. "That's great."

"It is. It really is. It means I can do anything! I can stand in a checkout line or get in a crowded elevator. Or sing in a club. Everything that used to terrify me. Do you realize what this means to me?"

There were tears in her eyes.

"Yeah, I do." I put my arms around her. "I can't think of anything better." I felt horrible knowing her joy was based on a lie, but no way was I going to tell her. What the hell. If she believed she was better, maybe she would be.

"Of course, 'cured' is too strong a word. I can't try to do everything at once, he warned me about that. But if I take small steps . . ."

"It's good news."

That didn't come out quite right; I was afraid she saw what I really thought. Maybe she suspected the truth herself. Her reaction was more than joyous; it was becoming manic.

"I mean, he cut me loose, can you believe it? He was so great, he really was. When's the last time you ever heard of a therapist cutting you loose? Usually they go on bilking you for years. Of course, Dennis was picking up the tab, but still . . ."

We were at the casino now, and she broke away. "Oh God, this building is so great. I just love old buildings like this. Can we get in some way?"

She went up one of the ramps to the grilled glass doors and peered into the lobby.

"I don't think so. It's closed up this time of year."

"Wait, there's the janitor." She rapped on the glass. "Hey!"

Back in the art-deco lobby I saw a black guy with a mop. "Shar." I felt oddly self-conscious, a little embarrassed by her manic mood.

"Oh, come on," she said to me. "Don't be such a tight-ass. He'll let us in. Here he comes."

This guy was about fifty and didn't look like he gave a shit about too much. He dug out a wad of keys and unlocked the door.

Before he could open his mouth, Shar pleaded, in the worst French accent I'd ever heard, "Oh please, monsieur, we know you are closed but won't you make an exception? We have come all the way from France just to see this marvelous casino."

He looked at me as if to say: Is she on something or what? "France, huh? Sounds more like Pico Rivera to me."

"Oui, oui," she said. "The Pico Riviera. Oh please."

I looked down, embarrassed, but laughed.

"Aw, shit, yeah, I guess it's all right," he said, waving us in as he went back to his mop and pail. "But just don't do nothin' funky," he called as an afterthought, his voice echoing. "The ghost of Guy Lombardo don't go in for that shit."

"Thank you, monsieur. You are a true gentleman."

I took her hand and led the way up to the second floor. "Come on, it's up here."

The vast ballroom was dark and barren and smelled vaguely of mildewed cummerbunds. I pulled back a set of art-deco drapes that covered the windows lining the walls. Dust sparked in the sunlight. I did the same with several more windows until the room was drenched with light, the sea gleaming all around us. The parquet floor was lustrous.

"God, this is great," Sharlene said. "It's too bad shit like this had to die, you know?"

I laughed. "Yeah, it is."

She was radiant. The sunlight glimmered through her

hair and caught the curve of her breasts, her nipples, under the blue silk blouse she wore, a blue that did not match, but complemented, her eyes. She smiled at me again, the same way she had at breakfast, a warm, sly, suggestive smile, suggestive of only one thing, a subtly bemused Dietrich smile, and I was her fixated professor, her groveling slave of love.

Drooling, I crawled over the the band shell—okay, I'm exaggerating slightly, I strolled—where the janitor's Panasonic was resting on the floor. I flipped it on. Michael Jackson boomed out. Not quite right. I rolled the dial till I came to Roxy Music's lanquidly romantic "Avalon." Fate.

"Wanna dance?"

"Sure," she said easily, and slipped her arms around me. As she did, I felt a rush of tenderness, a butterfly explosion from the pit of my stomach, or perhaps it was my heart, a physical elation I hadn't known in so long.

"You're wearing a new perfume today," I said. Not the cheap tropical scent, but something softer, more delicate. Not a lot. Just enough to make me bite my lip so I wouldn't whimper like a dog.

"Yeah. Do you like it?"

"Yeah." The music reverberated through the ballroom as we began to sway.

We swayed for quite a while, the music blowing through us like a cool salt breeze. Then I kissed her in the soft glow of the sunlight, and knew I would never be able to get enough of her, never. Oh Christ, she was so fine. Worth waiting for, worth waiting all my life. I kissed her neck, her sweet pink mouth. My cock was pressing hard against her as we moved. I undid the top buttons of her blouse and kissed her breasts, and she made that sound in the back of her throat that would have been cheap and fake coming from anyone but her. Her hand went down to my pants and squeezed my cock through the denim. I kissed her hot mouth.

I was sure the janitor was right, that Guy Lombardo was watching. But I knew he was smiling upon us, with soft-headed syrupy approval, as we passed into a stupor of love.

That evening I made a stew for dinner, the first time I'd cooked in months. As I worked in the kitchen, Sharlene sat down at the upright piano in the living room and began to play. It was an old piano, badly tuned, and I was amazed at what she was able to get out of it. She was much more versatile than I had gathered from the one other time I had heard her play. After a run of boogie, she began to sing: "Whatever happened to . . . the boy that I once knew . . ."

I laughed, recognizing the old Shangri Las' hit, "Remember (Walking in the Sand)." She did it perfectly straight in a powerful, compelling voice.

Then she went into "The Night Before," the early Beatles song, which had always been one of my favorites. With an oddly ominous, even bitter edge, it still held up, unlike some of the more cloying Beatles love songs that seemed so dated now. She went from that to a loping, offhand version of Mary Wells' "Beat Me to the Punch," her voice affecting a sleepy black drawl until she forgot the words in the second verse and we both disintegrated in laughter.

"And here's one from New Jersey," she said, and I braced myself, fearing a Four Seasons screecher, but it was Springsteen's "Point Blank," and it ripped my heart out. Her voice gave me goose bumps. It was the perfect song for her. If it had been a single it would have reestablished her career overnight. As always, the last verse did me in. As always, the recounting of a chance meeting of former lovers reminded me of Cheryl, and Sharlene's version was almost unbearable. It was like hearing Cheryl sing it herself. I was projecting into it so heavily I barely considered why it also meant so much to Sharlene.

Then she went back a couple of decades to "You Don't

Own Me," from Leslie Gore, and I grinned, certain she'd
dug up this chestnut as a joke to lighten the mood. A black
joke perhaps. It was hard not to notice that on a serious level
the words applied almost as much to her marriage as they
had to Leslie's imaginary predicament.

I found her next selection disturbing. Timi Yuro's "Hurt,"
perhaps the quintessential suffering romantic's song of all
time. This *had* to be a joke, right? But I watched her closely
as I added more wine to the stew and realized with horror
that real tears were glistening in her eyes. She came to the
line: "I'm hurt . . . much more than you'll . . ever know—"
and, oh Christ, a tear actually shot down her cheek.

"I'm so hurt," she wailed, "because . . . I still love you
so."

No. This wasn't happening. She wasn't thinking of him,
couldn't be, no. But then again, what if she were? They'd
had something together at the beginning, hadn't they?
Maybe all that was flooding back now that it was finally over.
That made sense, didn't it? I had to give her the right to go
through whatever she had to go through. Still, it scared me.
Women's emotions could be unpredictable sometimes.

Finally "Hurt" was over, and she paused for a moment. If
this had been a set, I would definitely have punched in
something upbeat at this point, say, "Brown Sugar" or a
peppy tune by Doris Day, before the listeners all slit their
wrists. But she was on a heavy down roll and not about to
stop.

"Childhood living . . . it's easy to do . . ."

Oh Jesus, "Wild Horses." At least seven minutes of romantic dirge. Order another triple and toss back a handful
of reds.

It was exquisite, though. It was aimed at Dennis, there
could be no doubt. She was exorcising him. She seemed
transported, singing for herself as she must have done so
many times over the last fifteen years, oblivious to my pres-

ence. The fading sunlight filtered through the eucalyptus trees out the window behind her, illuminating her in its soft glow. She had never looked more beautiful.

Her voice broke on the wrenching last verse. I thought for a moment that she was going to break down sobbing. But she continued on a harrowing wave of poignance and finished the song.

Then she was silent. I thought she might sing one of her own songs now, but perhaps she had nothing that wouldn't be jarring after what she'd just done.

"That was great," I said finally, aware that it sounded too casual, almost insensitive.

"Thanks," she said, and laughed to dissipate the heavy emotion of the song. "Dennis cut a version of that once. With Louise. Right before 'Tidal Wave.' "

"Doesn't seem like her kind of song."

"It wasn't. It was horrible. He sped it up till it sounded like a bump-and-grind routine. Threw in everything he could think of: calypso drums, mariachis, a jillion backward violins."

I laughed. "Sounds like his tape."

She stared at me. "What tape's that?"

I immediately sensed it was a subject I should back out of. "Just a tape he played for me. The last time I was up at the house."

"What do you mean? The stuff he's been working on?"

"Yeah, I guess." My voice was as tight as Gary Cooper's. "Haven't you heard any of it?"

She laughed. "Are you kidding? He thinks I'm a jinx. He's afraid if I even *looked* at one of his precious tapes it would automatically erase or something. I'm surprised he'd even play it for *you*."

"Well, he likes me."

"Yeah, I guess so." Her fingers drummed the edge of the piano. She seemed suspicious, as if anticipating lies.

"So how was it?"

I shrugged. "Not as bad as I'd expected."

"You mean, it's good?"

"No, I wouldn't say good. It's still got a long way to go. There's no vocal yet, for one thing."

"No vocal?"

"Not yet."

She hesitated. "But it's a song? I mean, a regular song, not just a bunch of noise—"

"Well, it starts out as a bunch of noise and then it becomes a regular song."

She seemed vaguely amazed, as though I were describing an unreleased James Dean film.

"Did he say who he's planning to get for the vocal?" Though the question was perfectly casual, it set off a bomb in the back of my mind.

"I think he's going to patch things up with Louise—"

She snorted. "Come on."

"He mentioned Karen Carpenter at one point—"

"I'm serious."

"I think he was too. He also mentioned Joplin. Or possibly Mama Cass. I think Minnie Riperton's high on his list—"

"Scott—"

"I really don't know. It's a long way off, anyway. He hasn't even written the lyrics yet. That could take another ten years."

Jesus, I felt like an idiot. Why was I afraid to tell her how good it really was? Did I think she was going to go rushing back to him, begging to be allowed to sing? Was I that insecure? Did I think she was that stupid?

"Well, you can be sure of one thing." She got up and came into the kitchen. "No matter how good it is now, he'll keep futzing around with it until he's completely fucked it up. That's half his problem, you know. He just doesn't know when to stop."

She went to the stove and checked the stew.

"Well, there's always the chance he'll drop dead before he ruins it," I said. "Then it'll be released as his posthumous masterpiece."

She sniffed the stew. "It's that good, huh?"

"If you like Edsels." I hugged her from behind.

"They're worth quite a lot now, aren't they? As collector's items."

"Yeah, I guess. But getting parts is a problem."

I kissed her neck. She put her hand on mine as if to stop me from ending the conversation.

"Scott, you know that cassette you dropped off at the house?"

"Yeah." My throat went tight again.

"Did you listen to that?" There was fear in her voice.

"No, I never got a chance to," I said smoothly. "It was a mix-up. It was supposed to be a dub of his music. But he called me at the station and told me not to listen to it."

"Did he say why?"

"No. Not really. Just that it was something else."

I felt a nervous trembling in her body. She slipped out of my arms, looked around anxiously for something to do and settled on opening the wine.

"I'm glad you didn't listen to it," she said, her back to me as she peeled off the bottle foil.

"Why's that?"

"Oh, because it was some really embarrassing stuff I did a long time ago. Back in sixty-nine. Outtakes, really horrible stuff. For a solo album that never got off the ground."

"No kidding. I wish I'd listened to it then. I can't imagine you doing anything that wouldn't be at least marginally overwhelming."

"Yeah, well, there's a lot you don't know."

Was there? Did I *want* to know?

"He used to send me off on some pretty bizarre tangents."

Used to? Back in '69? Had the perfume on the bunk bed been lingering since '69? "Yeah, I'll bet," I said as breezily as

I could, and lifted the lid on the stew. The burgundy aroma rose.

"Um, that smells good," she said, and hugged me from behind, squeezing me, leaning into me, as if she wanted to take shelter in the present and stop her mind.

"Yeah, it does," I said. Then I kissed her.

After dinner we settled in on the leather sofa and watched *Gidget* on TV. We laughed all through it, both of us doing voices, adding dumb lines to the dialogue. "Oh, Moondoggie," she'd say in a perky Sandra Dee voice, "I don't give a darn about surfing. I just wanna ride your face." "Come on, Gidg," I'd say in James Darren's voice during a dull two-shot, "it's hard as a rock and nobody's looking." We ended up rolling around on the sofa till our stomachs hurt. I hadn't had so much stupid good fun in years.

In a way that evening was the best time of all. It was like the times I'd spent with Cheryl when we were just laughing and having fun, though I didn't even think of Cheryl that evening, which was part of what made it so great. It was just Sharlene and me, free of ghosts, free of reflections, free of the past. Just the two of us in that room, on that sofa, the Remington prints on the knotty-pine walls, an amber lamp glowing softly, a stupid movie on TV. Just us, entertaining ourselves, happy and content. The way we could be for the rest of our lives.

When the movie was over I switched off the lamp and she switched off the TV. Then we went surfing, riding murderous waves through most of the night.

Sunday was a perfect day, crisp and clear, not a cloud in the sky. I hiked into town to pick up some more food. As I got close to the house on my way back, I could hear Sharlene playing the piano. I didn't recognize the tune, but it was beautiful. It was romantic but with an edge that kept it from being cloying. I suspected it was one of her own songs.

She stopped playing when she heard me on the porch, as she must have stopped so many times when she heard Dennis in the house. She met me at the door. We kissed.

That afternoon the island was as uncrowded as I'd ever seen it. We rented horses near Avalon and set out along the trail. The only riders we encountered were a weathered, elderly couple, the guy an agile white-haired cowboy, his wife spry in faded Levi's and denim vest. They had a contented air, as though they were one of those rare couples who had fallen in love forty or fifty years ago and remained that way. We exchanged smiles; long after we passed them, we could hear the woman's jolly laughter echoing up from the trail below.

That night in bed Sharlene leaned over to me. "You know," she said, "this may sound strange, but you're kind of a fantasy come true for me."

"Yeah, you're kind of a fantasy for me too." I stroked the soft curve of her breast, gently squeezing her nipple.

"I'm serious," she said.

"So am I."

"No, you're not. But I am. I mean, when I was at my worst point, I used to imagine how things might be different. I'd fantasize this whole other life, where I'd be free of Dennis, out on my own. Taking care of myself. Like a modern woman and everything. It was insane because this was at a time when I couldn't even leave my room. But I think that holding on to that fantasy, no matter how absurd, was all that kept me going."

"I don't think it's absurd."

"Of course, I always figured that eventually I'd want to meet a guy. Somebody who was nothing like Dennis. Somebody like you."

She took my hand. I watched her eyes in the soft light. Her voice was a whisper now, as if she were thinking out loud.

"Somebody who wouldn't treat me like a precious little doll one second, then punch me out the next."

I kissed her forehead, her cheek. I loved her so much.

"But I'm not going to fall in love with you," she said.

This didn't affect me; I was sure she already had.

"Why not?"

"Because . . ."

"Because why?" I kissed her neck.

"Because I can't right now. I need time."

"That's all right."

"I need time to heal."

"I know." I thought I did, too.

"Because the thing is . . ."

"What?" I slid my hand between her legs.

"I'm a lot more fucked up than you know." Her tone chilled me.

"So am I," I said lightly. "We're both fucked up. Maybe that's why we deserve each other."

She laughed softly, then winced with pleasure as my Roy Rogers finger rode her lathered-up trigger. Then she kissed me, and we galloped off over the hill.

"Goodnight, angel," I whispered later, as we were about to drift off.

"Please don't ever call me that."

What? Oh, angel: *his* nickname for her. The way she'd signed the old photograph. His voice on the cassette. The cassette. No, don't want to think about that. Not now.

"All right," I said and kissed her shoulder. Then I fell asleep.

10

I got up early Monday morning to catch the chopper back to San Pedro. Sharlene walked into Avalon with me to get a few things from the grocery. The sky was depressingly overcast, the kind of atmosphere that made you want to go back to bed till noon, when it burned off. Sharlene seemed a bit off, or preoccupied, but it was early; maybe she wasn't fully awake yet.

"I'll call you this afternoon," I said when we reached Metropole Street. The day was just starting, the locals opening their shops, fishermen, a few natty yachtsman types. Everyone walked in the street, as if Metropole were the main street of an old Western town. A sheriff passed us, checking out Sharlene. I decided it was most likely just lust; he was too young to know who she was.

"You're probably safer over here anyway," I said.

She looked at me, confused for a second. "What do you mean?" She spoke too carefully. "Why do you say that?"

Jesus, she was loaded. Valium? "I mean, if he tries to look for you, the chances of him finding out about this place over here are fairly remote."

Her eyes were flitting all over the place. If she had taken the Valium to calm herself down, it wasn't working. Were all the people making her paranoid, was that it?

"Why would he look for me?" she said.

"Shar, are you all right?"

"Yeah. Why shouldn't I be?" She forced a laugh. "I guess

I'm nervous, if you want to know the truth. I'll be glad when today's over. I still have the feeling something's going to go wrong."

"You want me to stay? I can call the station—"

"No, no, it's all right, really." She tried for good-natured charm. "Believe me, I'm not as helpless as you think. I can take care of myself. Really."

Her smile was not convincing. When a couple of guys laughed harshly as they crossed the street behind her, she cringed. I put my arms around her.

"I love you, Shar," I said, hoping it would sound breezy. It didn't.

"I know." She broke away. "Look, I better get back to the house. Mike might call back."

"Yeah, right." I looked at my watch. "Shit, I gotta hurry." I took off toward the bus to the chopper pad. When I looked back, she'd already disappeared around the corner on her way to the store.

By the time I got back to the Tropicana the overcast was gone and the dirty blue sky was burning with a harsh desert heat. With my return to the fallen world—the parched streets of Sodom after a luscious idyll in Eden—the worries I'd suppressed for most of the weekend came back. I had a meeting at the station at five. Hank would be there and he was sure to bring up the Contrelle interview again. Stalling him would be pointless. I'd be better off just saying it fell through and ending it there. He'd want to know what happened. I'd make up something. But that was the least of my worries.

The real problem was Dennis and how I was going to stay alive once he found out I had helped Sharlene escape. And he would find out; the only question was how soon. He had enough evidence to put it together immediately. He'd already accused me once, after all; even though he'd retracted it. But Big Willy's interruption of our bathroom meeting still seemed like a bust to me. Though Dennis had given that his own demented interpretation at the time, I was fairly certain Big Willy would put it together in a saner and more accurate light.

Still, the possibility remained—and in a way this made me even more uncomfortable—that at least initially, far from suspecting me of having conspired against him, I might be the very one he would come to for solace. Hadn't he told me, ad infinitum, that I was his only true friend? I pictured him coming to me, teary, abject: Scott, I don't know what I'm going to do, my brains are on fire, my heart's twitching like a skinned toad, the only woman I've ever loved has left me, and I feel like burning my guts out with a blowtorch, tell me, Scott, what should I do?

I also pictured myself floating facedown in a red-tinged Tropicana pool, people peering at me through draped windows, once he did discover my betrayal. Oh well. I had been talking about getting a real apartment for months. A security place in Duarte, maybe. No name on the mailbox and a shotgun by the door.

I also considered just leveling with him, being a man about it. Being honest, forthright. Yes, I helped your wife get away, Dennis, but that in no way impinges upon my massive and genuine respect for your errant genius, though I must tell you for your own good that you are beyond any doubt the most totally deranged and fucked-up human being I have thus far encountered on this planet, and I say as your friend that your only recourse is a complete brain transplant and twenty years of inpatient psychotherapy and a thousand milligrams of Thorazine three times a day for life. I imagined saying this to him if I were in Buenos Aires and he were shackled and caged in, say, Hong Kong.

In any event, I had a few days to mull it over. He wasn't due back till Friday. If I got really paranoid I could always go stay at Neal's.

At least Sharlene was safe on Catalina. A detective could have easily traced my mom's place in Palos Verdes, but the existence of the island house was obscured. Some rich guy my mom had been going with for a while had picked up the lease about ten years ago. It was sad in a way. Their affair had been brief, but he'd remained in love with her. He was in a stroke coma now up in Montecito, but his trust continued to pay the Catalina rent. And as long as he was alive, Sharlene would have a virtually untraceable place to hide.

I cut past the Tropicana pool and climbed the stairs to my room, the Count Five's scrap-metal "Psychotic Reaction" blistering from an open door down the balcony as if the entire room were a giant mono speaker. I gauged the time in Switzerland. Evening. He was probably unconscious, floating in a timeless Pentothal limbo somewhere between the old Dennis and the new. When he came around, there'd be a message waiting for him from his attorney marked "urgent." Big Willy, standing dutifully by, would already know. Dennis would see the look in those mean red eyes and know too.

I unlocked my door and stepped in. Hot stagnant air. I left the door open, raised the windows, and peeled off my shirt as I crossed the room. I had to take a crap. Picking up the latest issue of *Rolling Stone*, I went into the john, keeping the door open for ventilation. I turned to an article on the Talking Heads. "Angel Baby" swooned from the room down the balcony.

A blade of light cut through the crack of the bathroom door. I moved the paper to see the print, but suddenly something blocked the light. I looked up. If I hadn't just shit, I would've then. Big Willy was standing in the door.

I stood, starting to pull up my pants. (You forget hygiene at moments like this.) Big Willy grabbed my arm, my pants slipping down around my knees as he yanked me from the john. I stumbled and hit the carpet. Now I saw another set of feet. Petite suede Beatle boots under high where's-the-flood black pipestem pants. Dennis stepped around me, so Big Willy could quietly close the door. I didn't move.

Dennis had a slapped look as though he'd recently shot up some very good junk while simultaneously being informed of his mother's death. He didn't seem mad at all. He seemed destroyed.

Big Willy locked the door and began closing the windows.

"Scott?" Dennis whined. "Scottie?"

"Dennis," I said calmly, "let me get up and talk to you, okay?"

I began to sit up, but Big Willy nudged me back down with the toe of his boxing shoe.

"*How could you?*" Dennis said, like Marlon Brando playing an English fop near tears. It was both absurd and grotesquely sad. He really saw himself as a Dauphin betrayed.

"You're a very disturbed man, Dennis," I said. What the fuck, I was going to get it anyway. "She had to get away from you."

"But I trusted you!" He was pouting now, his face squinched up as if he were about to cry. "I really liked you. I really did. I showed you things no one else has ever seen."

I tried to sit up again. Again Big Willy pushed me back with his foot. It was hard to be cool with my crank on the carpet, but I tried.

"All I ever wanted was a friend," Dennis bellowed, then started to cry.

He leaned against one of the milk crates that held my record collection and sobbed. Good. A nice bloodless catharsis.

Abruptly he stopped sobbing. Shit. His nose was an inch from the first album in the crate: *Fuel-Injected Dreams*. He was staring at Sharlene's picture.

"Did she tell you?" he said in a dry, embalmed voice.

"Tell me what? I don't know what you mean—"

In a sudden rage he knocked over the top milk crate. It

hit the floor with a room-shaking thud. Surely Norrine
downstairs must have heart it—if she were home.

"Did she tell you?"

Tell me *what*, for Christ's sake? That he beat her up? That
he did something else to her, even sicker? Up in the garage
bedroom? "Dennis, really. I don't see why—"

I sat up. Big Willy kicked me hard in the chest.

"Get down!" he shouted.

I fell back, certain the kick had broken my breast bone.
That fuck! He could have kicked in my heart.

Nauseated with pain, I watched Dennis pick up a foot-
high plastic spindle of the most valuable 45's I owned. He
took off the first record and studied the label. "How many
times did you fuck her?" he said.

"Dennis, don't fuck with those records, okay?"

He threw the record at me like a knife, hard. It cut my
thigh.

"Jesus."

"I asked you a question. How many times did you fuck
her?"

"Dennis, come on—"

He took off the next record and spun it on his finger. With
horror I recognized the yellow label. It was my Elvis Sun
recording of "Baby, Let's Play House." Priceless.

"Dennis, put that back, please."

He spun it on his finger but he was looking at my cock. At
my cock! Was he thinking of the old circle jerk game of
slipping a 45 over your cock? Jesus, I'd almost razored myself
that way once with, I think, "Judy's Turn to Cry." Was he
thinking of that? Had he done that too? Quit staring at my
cock, you homo, I wanted to shout.

"I just don't know what to do," he said to Big Willy.

Leave. Walk out the door.

He seemed suddenly drained, confused. He put the Pres-
ley record back on the spindle and carefully returned the
spindle to the crate. "I just don't know what to do with a guy

who would fuck his best friend's wife. I really just don't know." He started for the door—good, good good—and said to Big Willy as a dismissive afterthought: "Cut off his cock."

What? My mind must be playing tricks. "Angel Baby" was still so loud.

"Are you sure?" Big Willy said.

"Yeah." Dennis whirled around. "Yeah." He laughed sharply, as though the more he thought about it, the better he liked it. "Yeah! Cut that fucking cock off and flush it down the toilet." Then to me: "Let's see how you fuck my wife without a cock. You think you can fuck her without a cock? You think you can do that? Huh? Huh?"

Big Willy yanked me up with one hand. With the other he drew a switchblade knife. "Angel Baby" swooned as he pressed the release and the steel blade gleamed in the sunlight. He seemed to be trying to pull me to the john, perhaps not wanting to stain the carpet. I screamed like a terrified girl and dived through the door.

The door, as it happened, was closed. It was a cheap door —I guess I knew that subconsciously—a hollow door, the kind that always slams at the wrong time, like when you're mad at someone but trying not to show it. I don't think it would have mattered though if it had been solid oak, I would have given it a shot. The fact of the matter was, I had derived considerable pleasure from my peter over the years, and I was convinced the quality of life would deteriorate markedly without it. Stumbling toward the stairs, my pants down around my ankles, I was vaguely aware of people below around the pool. I saw blood on my chest, dripping from my head, but I didn't feel any pain, there wasn't time. I saw Dennis and Big Willy coming out after me. Then I saw the stairs, the Astroturf-covered concrete below, and I knew I was going to fall. Then I fell.

Jack Lord was moving his hard jaw on the TV suspended from the ceiling at the foot of my bed. Neal was leaning against the window with a pitying expression. Behind him I could see the Hollywood Hills and knew I was at Cedars.

My mind was packed in a cotton candy of Demerol, but I felt a dull ache in my shoulder and chest. Then a twinge of panic. I reached for my crotch, nearly tearing out the IV. Pulled back the sheet with my pledge-of-allegiance hand. Saw the bulge. Proof through my gown that my cock was still there.

"How am I?" I asked Neal.

"You're going to live. You got a concussion when you fell down the stairs."

"Did they arrest him?"

Neal hesitated, choosing his words. "No. They couldn't."

"They couldn't? What do you mean, they couldn't? Jesus Christ, Neal. They were going to cut off my cock!"

"Nobody saw anything like that, Scott. You bashed through the door and fell down the stairs. That's all anybody saw."

"Oh sure, I do that all the time. I get sick of opening doors, I mean, it's a real hassle. Especially if you're in a hurry." I howled. "Neal! He was gonna cut off my crank and flush it down the toilet!"

I heard the guy in the next bed cough wetly through his tracheotomy. I didn't look.

"My advice to you is to let it go," Neal said calmly.

"Fuck that. I'm suing him. I'm gonna send him to Folsom. Let him get butt-fucked by black guys with twelve-inch dicks. He can do a new version of 'Back Door Man' when he gets out."

The anger made me sweat and feel light-headed. Something pulled my scalp. I touched the spot. Stitches. I felt above my left eye. Stitches there too. I saw the beige phone on the swivel tray, out of reach.

"Hand me the phone, will you? Gotta call Shar."

"She won't be there."

"What do you mean?"

"She went back to him, Scott."

"What? Are you nuts? Are you out of your mind? Give me the phone."

"Look, I talked to Mike just a little while ago. I was going to have him call her and tell her what happened to you." He paused momentously. "But he said she called him this morning and told him to stop proceedings."

"You're full of shit."

"She said she was going home . . . from wherever it was you two spent the weekend. Apparently she thought she could get back in the house and just act like nothing had happened. She had no way of knowing it was already too late."

"Too late? Why?"

He shrugged. "Well, obviously somebody tipped Dennis off that she'd split. He must have gotten word sometime Saturday and caught the next flight back."

The guy who came to feed the dogs. Shit.

"I'm sorry," Neal said.

"Don't be sorry. Fuck that. How did Dennis know about me?"

"I'm sure she must have told him everything. Don't you imagine? As part of the process of making up."

As that moment I didn't doubt that version at all. I stared at Jack Lord's hard jaw. "Fuck her," I said.

11

"Forget her," Neal said more than once in the days that followed. I stayed at his place in Ocean Park for about a week after I got out of the hospital. I was supposed to rest and take it easy, which gave me far too much time to sit around and think. I took Empirin codeine for my chest and shoulder, and Jack Daniel's for my heart, a combination that tended to warp my mind. But even totally sober, I would have been bitter.

"Be glad you got off this easily," Neal said.

"What do you mean? Before he sawed off my crank?"

"Scott, you knew going in she was damaged goods. She told you that herself."

"I just can't believe she willingly went back to him. It defies every precept of logic."

"Maybe she likes to get knocked around."

"I don't believe that. That's bullshit. Nobody likes to get punched out."

"Then why didn't she leave him years ago?"

I picked at my chest bandage. "She was scared."

"Of course, women *are* different from men."

"That's a pretty daring observation."

"No, I mean, there are certain biological differences in how the sexes respond to threats. I read a magazine article about it once. When men are threatened they'll either fight or take flight. But women are like cats."

"Cats?"

"Yeah. They'll withdraw. Find a place to hide."

"That's crap. Cats fight. Haven't you ever heard of a cat-fight?"

"Yeah, but they hide too. Haven't you ever seen a cringing, frightened cat?"

"Where did you read this article anyway? *Veterinarian Digest?*"

Neal sighed. "Scott, be realistic. You spent one weekend with her. One weekend! Do you think one weekend is going to erase twenty years? She's never known anything else—"

"She has now."

"Look, sometimes people would just rather stay with what's familiar, no matter how oppressive it is, because the unknown is even more terrifying."

"You make a lousy Joyce Brothers, Neal. Maybe if you put on a little white blouse with a bunch of ruffles at the throat—"

"I'm telling you the way it is." And he wasn't finished. "Look, I can see why you were attracted to her. I mean, if she's still as foxy as you say—"

"Foxy? That word went out with Jimi Hendrix. Where are you, 1970? Anyway, it wasn't just sex."

"I didn't say it was. Let's be honest, she set off certain psychological reverberations."

"Psychological reverberations? What is this shit? Are you my shrink now or what?"

"You know what I mean."

Yeah, I did, but if he said much more, I was going to rip his tongue out and feed it down his Cuisinart.

"Scottie, you're still too young to be trying to recapture the past. You should wait another twenty or thirty years, when you're *really* old and softheaded. When you've got pee stains on your khakis—"

"I'm not trying to recapture the past. The past was fucked, everybody knows that. What I saw in her had nothing to do with the past."

"Are you sure? Nostalgia can be a powerful erotic force. Memory distorts. We forget how mundane and tedious people actually were. We have a tendency to romanticize them—"

"I really think you should have your own radio talk show, Neal. It wasn't nostalgia. It was *her*, Shar, the way she is right now, thirty-four and fucked up—*that's* who I fell in love with. I had no illusions."

"Didn't you?"

I picked at the tape on my chest. "No more than anybody else."

He gave me a pat on the back. "Anyway, it's all over now. End of chapter. Turn the page."

"Yeah." I took a big swallow of Jack Daniel's and felt bile burn the back of my throat. Did that ever happen to Mick or Keith? "That's what I'm doing. Turning the page."

But the pages were stuck together—with my tears. There were tracks across my sheets and pillows. Every night I shed hot tears over the sweet pornography of the heart.

I moved back to the Tropicana in late September. Neal had spoken to Dennis' attorney, accepting his offer to pay my hospital bill without consulting me. I was furious when I found out, because I still relished the image of Dennis pinned to the wall of a Folsom shower. Then Neal explained to me what trying to bring that about would actually entail, and how futile the effort would ultimately be. The cops had arrived well after the event. No one had seen Dennis or Big Willy trying to harm me. In court his attorney might actually contend they were trying to help me, as I was clearly berserk on PCP; why else would I smash my way through a closed door?

I had a new door, federal blue like all the others, but brighter, and a new deadbolt lock, and a three-hundred-dollar charge tacked onto my bill. But I felt safe; I believed it was over. They wouldn't be back as long as I left her alone.

He had what he wanted: his trembling thrush back in her electrified cage.

Norrine was great, the perfect rock-and-roll Jewish cowgirl nurse. She brought me more chicken soup, and tongue sandwiches, from Canter's. She gave me backrubs and Percodan, and we spent a couple of nights together listening to old Spade Cooley records and fooling around— such as I could, given my injuries. Thing were always light and uncomplicated with Norrine. Neither of us took the other that seriously. She was primarily obsessed with her career, with no time for a "draining relationship." But she was beautiful, if incongruously so—like Charlotte Rampling dressed up for a square dance in a Gene Autry movie—and she was smart and funny with a warped sense of humor. As the days passed we kept each other company more and more.

One night we were sitting out by the lighted pool as hot gusts of Santa Ana wind began rustling the palm trees, and I told her the Cheryl Rampton story. It took a while to tell it. As I talked, the wind grew more intense, buffeting the blue umbrellas, until the desk clerk—a young guy with a scruffy beard he hoped would cause nubile young guests to mistake him for Tom Waits—came out to take the umbrellas down. I excused myself then to go up to my room and take a leak; we'd polished off a six-pack of Carta Blanca. I was glad Norrine was still there when I came back down.

I wasn't quite sure how she was taking the story. She had a serious expression, what I could see of it. Much of the time she kept her hand over her mouth as she listened. It always bothers me when people keep their hands over their mouths while I'm talking. The most paranoid possibility of course is that they're trying not to laugh in your face. I sat back down, as a year's worth of cigarette wrappers gusted across the Astroturf, and concluded the story with the not-so-tidy last scene.

"So I burned rubber out of the beach lot, watching Cheryl recede in my rearview mirror. Hating her. Loving her. Feeling a thousand different emotions all at once. All of them fucked." I paused. A dead palm frond dropped into the pool. Norrine studied me with her serious brown eyes. "And the rest, as they say, is silence. No one ever saw her again after that night."

Norrine took her hand away from her mouth. She wasn't smiling. She looked irritated, a little pissed off, as though the film had broken five minutes before the end of the picture.

"What do you mean? She moved away?"

I blew into my empty bottle. "No. She just . . . disappeared. Vanished . . . into the misty salt air."

"Vanished? What do you mean? What happened to her?"

"A provocative question, my dear." I was doing Robert Morley now. "There were a number of theories, a veritable *Rashomon*-like plethora of conflicting stories as to what happened later that night."

"*Rasho*-what?"

"An ancient Japanese art film, my dear. Before your time."

"So what happened?"

I cleared my throat and continued in a hard-boiled Fred MacMurray *Double Indemnity* voice—an average Joe who'd been around the block one too many times.

"Well, supposedly she went on out to the beach with Bill Holtner. The zit with the Woody? So it's not exactly your typical *Gidget* scene, if you catch my drift. There's a campfire, a few beach towels, and they're sticky all right, but not with Sea and Ski. This is a balls-out rowdy get-down Friday night. I mean, Moondoggie's pissing in the fire through a hard-on, and the Great Kahuna's out to fuck some face, you dig? So Cheryl gets pretty liquored up, and she and Holtner have a spat. So out of spite she sleazes up to some Mexican dudes, maybe one in particular, some totally greased-out chino-clad cholo, and starts eating the wax out of his ear for surfer boy's benefit. But instead of getting jealous and starting a fight like she hopes, he just says fuck her, who cares, she's a pig. So, really mad now, she goes off with these *vatos*, and ends up getting zoot-suited to death in the backseat of a '63 Impala to the strains of 'La Bamba.' "

Upstairs somebody slammed a window shut. Was my voice carrying on the wind?

"On the other hand, maybe she loses the Mexicans in the parking lot. Maybe they're almost to the car and she makes an off-color remark about Trini Lopez, and they say, later for you, bitch, and leave her standing there, laying out a scent . . . when a gang of bikers, who are loitering downwind, catch a whiff and roar up on their hogs. Now, maybe they're not exactly Hell's Angels, but the local version— Heck's Pussies maybe—but then let's face it, she's no Nancy Sinatra either. So the last *this* group of anonymous witnesses sees of her, she's got her mitts jammed into Moose's pocketless Levi's, a nut in each, as they scream off into the ozone. So who knows, maybe they ravage her en masse to 'Twist and Shout' all night, then throw her body in an oil sump. Or maybe it's true love between her and Moose, and they live happily ever after for three months in Fontana till they collide with a tank truck one rainy night in San Berdoo."

On the third match I lit a cigarette. "Or maybe it was surfers."

"The guy with the Woody?" she asked.

I felt my guts lock. "Yeah, right. Maybe it's Bill Holtner and his buddies. Maybe there never *are* any Mexicans or bikers. Maybe it's just *Gidget Gets Butt-fucked*, starring Cheryl Rampton in the part made famous by Sandra Dee. Maybe they lay her out in the Woody, where in the frenzy of the moment a surfboard slips and accidentally impales her between the shoulder blades. So they're all totally blown

out and devastated with remorse and terror, but rather than
risk not getting into SC, they bury her in somebody's flow-
erbed, where to this day a concrete pagoda serves as her
gravestone."

I was trembling now. I sat up so Norrine wouldn't see my
knees shaking.

"That seems, I don't know, unlikely," she said.

I moved on quickly. "Or maybe this beach party's really a
drag, just a bunch of simps making out to Shelley Fabares
records, so after five seconds she splits. Crossing the parking
lot alone, she says to herself, 'Shit, it's the mid-sixties, isn't
there a cultural revolution going on someplace or something? Why am I still hanging out with these regressive fifties
dorks who treat me like a pig just 'cause I _enjoy sex?_ Where
are all the advanced, cool, hip Now Generation people?'
When suddenly she collides with this sinewy young Nordic
Apollo with wavy blond hair down to his ankles and eyes like
wind tunnels, tripping on a thousand mics of Sandoz blue,
which is not even illegal yet. He tells her she's a beautiful
child of the universe and starts to take off her clothes. Not
here, she protests, so they go back up to the run-down apartment building on the bluff, where twenty different stereos
are playing at once, and three hundred people are writhing
and grinning at the same time under the strobe lights. So
Kid Galahad takes her into a closet that's been converted to
a bedroom, and they drop acid together and listen to Donovan and make slow beautiful love, but it isn't acid, it's strychnine, and they've almost reached the rainbow when
suddenly she goes stiff as a bat."

Norrine shielded her eyes against a gust of grit. "What did
her parents think happened?"

"She only had one. A mother."

"What did her mother think?"

"That I killed her."

Norrine squinted at me a long time. "Did you?"

No way could I give her a straight answer. "Would it add a certain provocative element of danger to my persona if I said yes?"

She didn't smile as I had hoped. "No. I think it would make me never want to see you again."

Leaves skittered across the Astroturf. "Stay where you are. I'm innocent."

"Then why did they suspect you?"

"Not they. She. Just her mother. The police never took the charge seriously."

"Why did she suspect you?"

"Because I was one of the few people with a real motive."

"What motive?"

I flicked my cigarette away. "I loved her," I said.

I stopped by the station the next afternoon, my good looks still marred with bruises and a permanent scar over my left eye. I could tell by the way people treated me, offering pats on the back and flustered condolences—but not asking questions—that they knew what had happened and, like Neal, considered it just a botched affair of the heart. I mean, if I'd been mugged they would have been all over me with questions: when did it happen, what did the police say? But this was considered the price you pay when you try to steal another man's wife. Sometimes I wanted to grab people and try to make them understand, but I knew I'd end up sounding like a moron with a cleft palate trying to recite one of Shakespeare's sonnets. Mostly, though, I just wanted to forget her.

But I couldn't. The Contrelle requests kept coming—my own fault, since I'd been playing them so heavily before. I was drinking quite a bit, on the job as well as off, which may have contributed to my attitude problem.

"KRUF. Ernest Hemmorhoid speaking."

"Yeah, Scott. This is Fred. Could you play that old Vectors tune, 'Rincon'—"

"Oh, hey. I'm sorry, Fred, but no can do. I guess you haven't heard, pal, there's been a format change. We're playing nothing but foreign covers now. How about a Filipino techno-pop version of Kenny Rogers' 'Lady'? Or, let's see, how about the Cambodian Children's Choir doing 'Little Red Corvette'—" Click, buzz.

Closer to dawn I grew a bit short on charm. "Yeah, Scott, could you play the Stingrays' 'Love M—' "

"No way! I don't play that sick fuck's garbage anymore. You want to wallow in that deranged treacle, call Dr. Demento. Fuck you, too, you *ass*hole!" Bang.

One afternoon in a nerve-shredding hangover I read an item in *Billboard* as I choked down a peanut-butter-and-kiwi omelete at Duke's.

> Legendary record producer Dennis Contrelle announced plans to cut a new single with his wife, Sharlene, best remembered as lead singer of sixties rock group the Stingrays. "I've been working on the instrumental tracks for some time," said the reclusive Contrelle. "But I wasn't sure who was going to do the vocal till one day it just hit me. Of course! Who has the greatest voice of this or any era? Sometimes you can't see what's right in front of you until you've wandered far from home."

I laughed like a dad who'd just backed over his deformed little girl with a brand-new car. There was no one in Duke's who didn't stare.

I got ready for work early that night, washing down a couple of black beauties with a pint of tequila, smoking several joints of stiff Bangkok dope. I shaved, took a crap and a shower, all the while listening to practically everything Mary Wells ever recorded. "My Guy," "You Beat Me to the Punch," "Two Lovers," et al., until by the time I was ready to leave—but fell back on the bed and grabbed the phone instead—I had virtually *become* Mary Wells, which right then was exactly who I wanted to be.

"Hello," I said in a soft black-woman voice. "Is this the Sunrise Studio? Yes, I'd like to speak to Miss Sharlene Contrelle, please. Yes, just tell her it's Mary, Mary Wells."

Long pause, the real Mary singing "You Beat Me to the Punch" on my stereo, the walls starting to spin.

Finally Sharlene came on, her voice flat and dull. "Hello."

"Hello, Sharlene? This is Mary Wells. You remember me, don't you? I had a big hit about twenty years ago called 'My Guy.' "

Pause. "Who is this?"

"I told you. Mary, Mary Wells. Can't you hear one of my other hits playing in the background right now? Anyhow, listen, girl, here's why I called. I was pulling a one-nighter in Orange County last week, doing a revival show with Martha Reeves and several other legendary ladies of rock, when I saw a familiar face in the first row. He stepped into my dressing room after the show and said, 'Mary Wells, I'm in deep psychic pain. Would you like to go for a long drive with me in my hotrod Lincoln so I can cry on your shoulder and tell you all about my botched love affair with Sharlene Contrelle?' Well, girl, I guess you know who I'm talkin' 'bout now."

She said nothing for a moment. Dennis' tape was playing in the background.

"Are you out of your mind?" Her tongue was thick. She was blitzed on something.

"Well, I don't think so," I said in the same soft drawl. "But I *am* more than a little puzzled and dismayed. I just can't understand, girl, why you'd choose to go back to a psychopath, instead of stayin' with the one who really loves you."

Long pause. The playback stopped. Male voices. Was she in the control room?

"Maybe I just decided I love my husband," she said with a mouth full of cotton.

"Frankly, girl, I find that hard to swallow. After all that man has put you through—"

"Maybe"—her voice rose sarcastically—"I just decided I'd rather be with a real man."

"Excuse me," I said in my own voice, "while I reach for my vomit bag."

"You *are* a vomit bag."

I should've hung up then. "Well, look, I'm glad there are no hard feelings. Just thought I'd check in. Let's get together for coffee sometime."

"You make me sick."

"You *are* sick, you fuckin' bitch," I said, losing my sense of humor.

"You're nothing, a zero. You're just a glorified fan. I'm married to a genius and he's making me a star again—"

"You're married to a burned-out speed freak who beats you up, you stupid twat."

"You don't know anything about women, you know that? That's why you're such a failure. That's why women always leave you. Because you're a wimp."

"Yeah, I guess you're right. I guess if I'd knocked your teeth out, you'd still be with me."

"No, I wouldn't. Because you know what?"

"I'm a lousy lay?"

"That's right. You can't fuck for shit."

I laughed. She was so pathetic. "In that case you should win an Oscar for the best performance since Jane Fonda in *Klute*."

"Why don't you eat my shit?"

"That's delightful. Didn't Loretta Young say that in *Ramona*? Why don't you eat mine, you scuzzy pus-bag pig—"

Suddenly I could hear Dennis' voice in the background, loud, manic: "What are you doing? Who are you talking to?"

"M-M-Mary Wells," she stuttered in fear as he grabbed the phone.

"Hello!" he barked.

I hung up.

12

That did it. It was over. I didn't have to take shit like that from anybody. She could go fuck herself with a lava lamp.

I pushed her from my mind. For almost a week I thought I was over her.

In truth I was manic, working up bullshit projects, making jillions of bullshit phone calls, anything so I wouldn't have to think. I hit a pickup bar in Beverly Hills, brought home a script call on Wednesday, went home with an agent on Thursday. Friday I stayed in, jacking off three times.

I couldn't sleep and my nerves were shot. Sounds began to bother me. Music I liked was suddenly shrill and grating, like Bruce Springsteen on a cheap radio. I was beginning to feel like a nerve-damaged speed freak, jumping every time somebody coughed in the next room. Like Dennis.

I began avoiding Neal, my voice of reason. I certainly wasn't going to tell him I'd called Shar. I knew what he'd say about that. I wasn't going to tell him that after a week of grace, the obsession was back; I wouldn't have to. He knew me well enough to see it for himself.

When I thought about the phone call I still hated her. But when I thought about everything else, I still felt so many other things.

I was thinking about everything else one afternoon at the Tropicana when Neal called. He was in a light, joking mood, grating against my leaden depression. Eventually he mentioned the reunion, which I had completely forgotten. Just the word—reunion—and the flash of what I imagined it would be like filled me with existential nausea.

"I think I'm gonna pass on that, Neal."

"Pass? What do you mean? You said you'd bring some records."

This disturbed me. "I never said that."

"Didn't Gale Spivey call you yet?"

"No. Fuck Gale Spivey," I said bleakly.

"I tried. God knows I tried." He did a quick Vegas-comedian laugh, then took a deep but-seriously-folks breath. "Scott, what's the matter with you? Ever since this thing with what's-her-face—"

"Neal, I don't want to be rude, but I'm right in the middle of my Jane Fonda workout, you know what I mean? You're making me lose the beat."

I imagined him smiling indulgently. "All right, kiddo. But come to the reunion. That's half your problem anyway. You don't get out enough. It'll be a hoot. Life goes on, pal. 'Bye."

Gale Spivey called me the next afternoon. I recognized her voice immediately, as though no time had passed: a border-line hysterical Mouseketeer voice. I remembered her as a cute pixie in a pink party dress, an image I connected for some reason with a cheesy smell of pizza vomit in a station-wagon backseat. Had she perhaps upchucked once on a double date? Some things are lost forever.

"I've been meaning to call you, Scottie." She ran on in a rush of strained enthusiasm about the reunion, about several people who were blanks to me now, whose dull histories drove me to pick dirt out from under my nails as she talked. All in all, it sounded like the worst, stodgiest, most stifling evening imaginable. But when she asked me if I could bring some records, I said, in the same fake enthusiastic voice, as though I were working the Top Forty drive-time slot on KRLA circa '65, "Hey! Sounds groovy, Gale. I'd love to, doll. Count me in."

"Oh, wonderful!" she squealed, like a game-show winner. "I just knew you'd have plenty of old records, being a deejay and all. Perry and I both listen to you every chance we get."

Why, Gale, you little fibber, you. I'll bet my left nut that every button on your Volvo radio is set to the soothing sounds of Christopher Cross.

"Yeah, I've got lots of stuff from that era," I said. "Lots of girl-group stuff. The Marvelettes, the Ronettes. The Ette-ettes. And of course the Beehives . . . and the B.J.'s. Cathy and the Coke Bottles. Now, *there* was a hot group."

She cringed audibly. "I'm sure whatever you bring will be fine. Well, I'll look forward to seeing you. Oh yes, I almost forgot. I'll need your wife's name for the name stickers—"

"I won't be coming with my wife, Gale. Mrs. Cochran was cut down by a speeding school bus only last week."

"Oh God."

"Yes, it was pretty horrible. But she had it coming." I felt a jolt of desolation. "Gale? Just kidding. Actually, the missus and I had a fistfight a while back. But I'm being a man about it and suing her for every cent she's got. But seriously. I was toying with the idea of asking Cheryl Rampton. You remember Cheryl, don't you? Got her current address by any chance?"

The pause that followed was so long she had time to call her shrink on another line and get his advice, meditate, pour a drink, take a crap, and write Ann Landers. I quit trying to imagine her reaction. When it came it was TV-movie grief, and ludicrously wrong. "It was so sad, wasn't it? She had so much to live for."

Yeah? Like getting fucked by nine thousand more guys? Were we talking about the same person? Perhaps she'd perceived something I hadn't, like Cheryl's obvious future as a Supreme Court justice, a nuclear physicist, an astronaut. The first slut in outer space.

"Yes, yes, she did," I said, matching her phony grief. "She

could have been a superb Manson girl, had she taken too
much acid and survived another five or six years."

"I suppose in a way it's a relief to finally know what happened," she said, ignoring my humor. "It's like those MIA's
in Vietnam. At least now people can quit wondering."

My heart lurched into a Dexedrine duckwalk. "Come
again?"

"I mean when they found her remains."

"They what? When?

"Oh dear. I just assumed you knew. It must be almost two
years now."

"Where?"

"Scott, I have a million calls to make. Maybe we can talk
about it at the reunion—"

"Gale, don't hang up this phone. If you don't tell me
everything you know right now, I'm going to come over
there and shove your collie down the garbage disposal one
paw at a time. Now, spit it out, liebschen."

I imagined her middle-aged Mouseketeer breasts vibrating
with terror. "They found her body, that's all," she said
breathlessly. "A skeleton. When they put up those condos. I
think she was wearing an anklet. That's how they identified
her."

"The condos on the Esplanade?"

"Yes. Remember those old apartment buildings? She was
buried in the backyard of one of those. They found her
when they were digging the foundaton."

"How did she die?"

"I don't recall. It was just a skeleton—"

"Come on, Gale. Don't withhold vital information. I'm
sure you talked about nothing else for the next six months."

"Scott, I really don't remember. Why don't you talk to
Mrs. Rampton, if you really want to know?"

"She's still alive?"

"Yes. She's in the same house. Scott, I really have to go."

I couldn't believe Mrs. Rampton was still alive. The last

time I'd seen her she'd been a wild-haired alcoholic banshee, a leather-faced demon with jaundiced eyes. That was at the Vons' a week after Cheryl disappeared, when she threw a jar of Tang at me and called me a murderer.

I looked up her number and called her right away, while I was still reeling, otherwise I knew I wouldn't. I identified myself. There was a pause. I expected either a hang-up or a shrill drunken Baby Jane Hudson assault. But when she spoke it was all pleasant, melodious Blanche. "Scott Cochran? Why, of course I remember you."

She invited me out to the house.

It was a pale yellow stucco tract house in Lomita, still a working-class suburb, the kind where guys parked their pickups on the skimpy front lawns. She unlatched the screen and let me in, shooing back a white cat. The place was early-sixties modern, severe vinyl space-age furniture, pole lamps, a starburst clock—though I knew better than to compliment her on her wacky sense of kitsch. I was amazed at how good she looked. Though in her mid-fifties, her face was smooth —too smooth really, the ceramic look of a chemical peel. Maybe the alcohol had taken its toll there, but her slim body seemed quite young. She had Cheryl's dark brown hair and luminous skin, the same startling blue eyes. I followed her into the den, our voices reverberating off the linoleum as she offered me a Tab. When she came back with it she said, "I can't tell you how glad I am you called. I've been aware for some time that I owe you an amend."

"An amend?"

I sat down on the edge of a green Naugahyde recliner.

"Yes. For the way I behaved after Cheryl disappeared. I know it was a long time ago. I don't want to open old wounds, but—"

"That's okay. I've been thinking about those days a lot lately. In fact—"

"It was toward the end of my drinking," she said, inter-

rupting me in a pleasant voice. "I quit not long after that."
She smiled and took a sip of her Fresca. "Just in time."

"That's good." I wasn't quite sure what to say. "I guess
back then it always sounded to me like it might have been
kind of a problem."

"It was more than a problem." She laughed heartily and
reached for a pack of Virginia Slims. "Anyway, I'm sorry."

"That's all right. I guess it was a difficult time. For everybody—" I stopped myself from saying: "—who loved
Cheryl," realizing, with a clarity I did not want, that it was
probably just her and me.

"Yes, it was."

I had already drained my plastic glass of Tab, out of nervousness. There was more in the can. I poured it, and repeated somewhat awkwardly what Gale Spivey had told me,
adding that I'd just recently heard about it. While I spoke,
Mrs. Rampton walked to the sliding glass door and looked
out at the skimpy backyard. Her blouse and slacks were
tight, exaggerating her shapely figure. When she turned and
looked back at me, the bright backlight hid her features and
more than ever she reminded me of Cheryl—standing in
front of the plate-glass window in my bedroom on a similar
afternoon. I drifted out for a moment, imagining Cheryl and
me growing old together, paunchy and saggy in our sixties,
but still in love. When I finished, Mrs. Rampton was silent
for a moment.

"I guess I always knew in my heart she was dead," she said
finally. "I tried to tell myself she'd just run off. God knows,
she had every reason to. I was a pretty lousy mother."

I saw a scene from twenty years before, from the summer
of '64, when I'd pursued the one explanation of where
Cheryl might have gone that seemed most plausible:

It's sunset in the Arizona desert as I drive into the trailer
park and find Cheryl's father's address. I park and walk up
to the dull aluminum trailer, my heart pounding. I'm jolted
when I notice a pair of aqua capris hanging from the clothes-

line out back. I approach the screen door, my adrenaline surging, certain I've found her. She's come here to be with her father, as she had once said she would, "if things got too bad." I knock on the door.

An old woman with a leathery face appears. "Yes?"

"Is this the Horton residence?"

She hesitates. "Well, we're the Bryers now. You're referring to my late husband. He passed away some time back."

Stunned, I explain that I'm really looking for the late Mr. Horton's daughter, Cheryl.

"You know, I think the last time I saw Cheryl was at her father's funeral. That's been almost six years."

On the way to my car, I take another look at the aqua capris. They're for a fat girl.

I stream back through Monument Valley with tears in my eyes, thinking: Yeah, she's gone to be with her father all right, on his big fucking ranch in the sky.

Mrs. Rampton's voice pulled me back to the present. "It was tough when they found the remains," she said. "I couldn't pretend any longer. There was a kind of delayed grief."

I forced myself to wait a moment before I asked, "Could they tell how she died?"

"Yes." She went into the kitchen. I could see her over the serving counter as she opened the refrigerator. "She'd been raped. With an instrument. Would you like another Tab?"

No, but how about some head cheese and chili con carne? I almost laughed, out of nervousness. "No, thanks," I said.

"Are you sure?"

I walked into the kitchen. "How do they know she was raped?"

"They found the flashlight. Her pelvic bone was broken a certain way. I guess they're experts at figuring out that sort of thing."

"I'm sorry to ask you about this."

"I've got Fresca—"

"No, I'm fine."

"You loved her, didn't you?" She finally looked at me.

"Yeah, I did."

She closed the refrigerator door. "That wasn't very smart. She was no good." She started to cry. There was a moment when I could have put my arms around her, but I didn't.

"How could they be sure it was her?"

"They found her little chain," she said, and I assumed she meant the anklet. "That little silver chain she wore."

She tore off a paper towel and used it to wipe her cheeks.

A gentleman would have left then, I suppose. But her crying angered me. I saw it as evasion. "Who do you think did it?"

"I don't know."

"You must have some idea."

She shook her head. "You know what she was like. It could have been anybody."

"What do the police think?"

"They don't care. It was twenty years ago." She looked at me, her eyes red. "And you know something else? I don't care either. Not now. I can't afford to. My daughter died a long, long time ago. I have to live today."

"I can't believe you don't want to see justice done," I said feeling square and strident, like Charles Bronson in some schlocky revenge movie.

"I'm sure whoever did it has already paid. I have to believe that."

My heart was pounding, I was still angry, but not at her really. "Look, I'm sorry I've upset you." I moved toward the door.

"You've got to understand," she said, "I've had to live with these people for the last twenty years."

"What people?"

"The guys," she said, as though she were referring to an informal club.

"Which guys?"

"You know." She wouldn't look at me. "The ones who were probably with her that night at the beach."

"*Who?*"

Suddenly she fired on me. "You're as responsible for what happened to her as anyone. If you want to start pointing fingers, point one at yourself."

"Bullshit," I said, but I was shaken.

"Don't you think I know what happened? Why do you think she let herself get pregnant? Because she thought that was the only way she'd ever get you to marry her. But you still rejected her. She wasn't good enough for you, was she? You could have saved her—"

"That's crap. I offered to help her—"

"Help her? What do you mean, to get an abortion? She didn't want an abortion! *She loved you!* She wanted to spend the rest of her life with you!"

Her smooth face was pink with rage. In my opinion she owed me another amend.

"There's only one way you could know what we talked about," I said quietly. "She came back here that afternoon, after she left me." I saw by her expression that it was true. "She came back here and told you she was pregnant and you threw her out."

She forced herself to look at me. "I've had to forgive myself for that."

"Great, that's fine. I'm glad. That sounds very therapeutic. And you've forgiven her killers too. Boys will be boys and all that. But they're a great bunch of guys now, so no hard feelings. So nobody's to blame for what happened but me? Let me tell you something, lady. You're full of shit. You need an enema for your brain."

Her white cat ran as I kicked open the screen door.

I drove down to the Esplanade and parked. The beach was deserted because of the wind. Gusts of sand hissed across the sidewalk. I kept the windows rolled up even though I was sweating.

I watched a silver Mercedes pull up to the condo building across the street that marked Cheryl's old grave. A gray-haired man was at the wheel, the woman beside him young and blond. She was laughing harshly as the subterranean garage gate opened to receive them.

Down on the beach the blue snack-bar building stood against the drifting sand, shut up tight like a defunct shrine. What was inside? Perhaps an old calendar with JFK's picture. Rusty lipstick cases and a pair of panties stiff with age . . . when suddenly the cobweb-covered griddle sizzles! The smell of hot dogs and french fries wafts through the air. A ghost radio throbs with the Stingrays' "Down by the Ocean":

> Down by the ocean,
> Baby, where we met.
> Those long, hot summer nights,
> Baby, I'll never forget.
> The look in your blue eyes that night,
> against the sky so black.
> Baby, I loved you so much then.
> Why can't we go back?

Sharlene's aching wail.

Cheryl's roller-coaster laugh.

I turned on the radio, punching KRUF. A Culture Club song was fading. It took me a second to recognize what followed. I thought it was a joke at first. A burst of chaotic noise that would give way to a Jack Webb line, or a Reagan line; the day jocks went in for that a lot. But it wasn't a joke. It was Dennis' tape: a new single.

He'd cut it down to fifteen seconds of grating, screaming cacophony, but when it all fell into place the effect was just as stunning. A few seconds after that, Sharlene entered wailing as though a blowtorch were aimed at her crotch.

The words were classic Contrelle junk, but as always they hardly mattered. The execution was everything—and that's what it was: *her* execution, that's what he had captured. Death by drowning, bludgeoned in a flash flood of strings, slammed in the face by a monster wave of brass, sucked under by a riptide of seething percussion. "I've loved you for a long time, since I can't remember when," she sang fearfully, her voice unintentionally subverting the lush romanticism of the melody, revealing it for what it was: stupendous kitsch, rapturous Nazi sentimentality. He wasn't known as the Wagner of rock for nothing. "And when night comes I wonder . . ." she sang, "when will it end?"

The rest was lost until she reached the chorus, which was like an earthquake in Monument Valley, an aural snuff film by John Ford. Everything literally caved in around her, chunks of sound coming down like Cadillacs, as she wailed, ecstatic, terrified, only seconds to live:

> My love is a burden
> I can barely survive.
> Kill me if you have to
> But oh please God don't bury me alive!

The sound dropped in orgasm/disembowelment and that was it. Or so you thought. Until a tough-talking bridge jumped out, with a beat like chewing gum and syncopated snatch.

> I hear the dirt hit the coffin lid,
> I hear the minister's prayer.
> I feel the smooth satin lining—
> But oh God! THERE'S NO AIR!

Now she screamed for release as the music built again, punctuating her panic with fussy crescendos. It was simultaneously the most absurd, histrionically demented record

I'd ever heard—and the most harrowingly real. At least to me, knowing what I knew. Her voice dug through the smothering strings like fingernails shredding satin. The ohmming cathedral choir poured through every crack like loose dirt. Groaning cellos broke above her like boards. Her voice was naked terror now—beyond melodrama, beyond acting. Jesus Christ, how could they play it, couldn't they tell?

The terror built to a white peak of total unhinged insanity —then dropped again . . . to a perfect serene valley of release. The coda.

She sang softly now in a wispy Dusty Springfield voice, pink cotton candy amid the clouds. Something about heaven. Synthesized cherubs swooned behind her like ten thousand castrated hummingbirds. Heaven. She was dead.

13

"Have you heard 'Premature Burial'?" Neal said.

I was already drunk a few nights later in a Melrose bar when he walked in and spotted me.

"Yeah, I heard it."

"Not bad."

"No, it's not bad."

"I mean, it's horrible. It's the most idiotic piece of dreck since 'Leader of the Pack.' and yet . . . it's strangely affecting."

"Yeah. So were the Nuremberg rallies."

He put his hand on my shoulder. "Are you okay, Scott?"

"Yeah, I'm fine." Except for my Adolf Hitler eyes. "I haven't been sleeping well lately. They're tearing up the street behind the Tropicana. You know, jackhammers all day."

"You've been drinking a lot."

"It blots out the cirrhosis pain."

"You seem, I don't know, a little manic."

"I'm on a new MAO inhibitor, that's all. It may not be working out."

"I talked to Gale Spivey."

"So did I."

"I know. She was concerned."

"About what? I said I'd do it."

"You asked her about Cheryl Rampton."

I fixed him with a point-blank psychopathic stare. "Did you know?"

He looked at himself in the mirror behind the bar. "Yeah, I knew."

"Why didn't you tell me?"

"I thought you knew."

"Bull-fucking-shit, Neal. How would I know? You're my only contact with any of those people."

He looked at me with a TV reporter's pity. "I just didn't want to upset you, that's all. I didn't want to set off exactly what's happening right now."

"You should have told me." I tossed back my Jack Daniel's. "I consider it a serious breach of our friendship."

He spoke with infuriating gentleness now. "I really don't like what's happening to you, Scott. Maybe you should take some time off."

"I just did."

"I mean, really go somewhere. Get out of L.A."

"And miss the reunion?"

He chose his words carefully. "Are you sure you're all right for that?"

"All right for it? In just what way do you mean, Neal? Why are you looking at me like that? What do you think I'm going to do, walk in giggling and pull out a sawed-off shotgun?"

He didn't smile.

"Lace the punch with paint stripper?"

He still didn't smile.

"Squirt lighter fluid in Bill Holtner's hair and toss a match at him?"

"You've obviously been giving it a lot of thought."

"It beats counting sheep. Hey! But seriously, Neal. I'm as sane as I've ever been."

"That's what worries me."

"Look, the past is over. What's done is done. You forgive, you forget. To just *be* here in the ever-present *now*, that's what's important."

"Who said that? Baba Ram Dass?"
"No. I think it was Adolf Eichmann."

The next afternoon I went through my 45's and made a four-hour tape of the best and worst of early-sixties rock. On the plus side I stuck mainly to early Motown and the girl groups, on the minus I tossed in Fabian and Bobby Rydell, knowing "Volare," for example, would set more than one pair of chunky thighs aquiver. I included nothing from Dennis Contrelle, which was like trying to write the New Testament without mentioning Jesus: a lot of whores and cripples and greedy moneychangers wandering around the desert toward no particular end.

I made other preparations, hitting a store on Melrose that sold vintage clothing from the sixties—supposedly never worn. That I couldn't figure, unless they raided a lot of dead servicemen's closets, but everything seemed authentic enough. I bought a pair of 1965-issue white Levi's, a short-sleeved madras shirt, and a pair of wraparound shades. Then I went to a barbershop and read about topless Amazon death squads in Central America while Erich Von Stroheim gave me a flat-top.

I asked Norrine to be my date for the reunion. She said yes and laughed a lot when I described how I wanted her to dress and fix her hair. I encouraged the idea that it would just be a campy, hilarious good time—like the previous Halloween, when I'd put on a striped tie and Ivy League suit, and she'd worn a pink Dior-style dress and matching pillbox hat, and we'd gone out trick-or-treating in my presidential Lincoln. If she suspected what I was really up to, she didn't let on.

The night of the reunion, the sun went down around seven, but an hour later the sky was still glowing orange. It seemed as if every canyon, every mountain range and shake roof, anything in L.A. County that could possibly

catch fire, had. The TV news was a steady stream of reports
on firefighting efforts in Bel-Air and Topanga, Laurel and
Mandeville canyons, the Angeles National Forest, every
place you could think of, including the dry brush hills of
Malibu/Agoura. Because of the Santa Ana winds, most
of the fires were raging out of control. A sudden gust could
carry sparks over the containment line, starting new fires
a mile downwind. The force of the wind blew burning
embers against the sides of wooden houses, holding them
there until the structures ignited. By dawn, three-million-
dollar dream homes would be charred chimneys with
views.

"Are you sure we can get there?" Norrine said as we got
ready. She was from New York and didn't understand the
seasonal disasters that were part of L.A.'s charm.

"Yeah, sure. It's in Redondo Beach. There's nothing to
burn there, except a few Burger Kings. But I don't think
they burn, they just melt. It's the fumes that kill you."

I watched her behind me in the mirror as I waxed the fins
of my flat-top, and smiled. She was perfect. It was almost
chilling. She'd fixed her hair into a fierce-looking beehive
that was lopsided, already crushed in the back. She'd pinned
the orchid corsage I'd given her to her pink cotton blouse,
which was nearly identical with the one Cheryl Rampton
had been wearing the night she disappeared. The aqua capris were the same too, and she filled them out voluptuously, her waist cinched tightly with a shiny white plastic
belt. She stepped up next to me at the mirror, her starched
blouse crinkling, and checked her cherry-red lipstick. "So is
everybody going sixties or what?"

"No, baby. Just us. Everybody else is going knit suits and
expandomatic slacks."

I wiped Butch-Wax off my forehead, still shocked at how
much my hairline had receded. I'd wanted to look like early
Ricky Nelson; instead I looked more like early George
Gobel. "By the way," I said as casually as possible, still

checking myself in the mirror, "if anyone should ask you tonight, I'd appreciate it if you said your name was Cheryl."

"Yeah, I know," she said, and I saw that she'd known what I was up to from the start. Her mood turned dark. "What is it, do I look like her?"

"You do now," I said as lightly as I could, and tried to hug her from behind.

But she pulled away from me and tore off the corsage. "I don't think I want to do this."

"Why not?" I said, trying too hard to sound innocent.

"It's too sick."

"Sick? It's not sick. It's like last Halloween."

"That was sick too."

"The bloodstains on your pink dress, *that* was sick maybe. But that was *your* idea, Norrine."

"Well, the cow's brains on the trunk wasn't my idea. That was *really* sick."

"Nobody forced you to crawl back after them, Norrine. You did that repeatedly along Hollywood Boulevard, as I recall. Turning more than a few heads."

"You got me drunk."

The phone rang. I grabbed it. "Oswald residence."

"Scott?"

It was Shar. I couldn't speak.

"Scott, listen, I need your help." Her voice was clear, undrugged, her tone absurdly casual, as if I were the auto club and she needed a jump.

"Yeah, well, you picked kind of a bad time," I said in my coldest Clint Eastwood voice.

"The thing is, I'm trapped," she said giddily. "I'm locked in my bedroom and the fire's coming real close. Will you come and let me out, please? I just need someone to open the door."

I laughed incredulously and tried to gather my thoughts. Was this bullshit or what? I was still so pissed off at her. I still loved her so much.

"Scott? I'm not kidding. If the fire jumps the highway, the house is gonna go."

Then hose down your beehive, bitch, I thought. "All right, okay," I said. "I'm coming."

An hour later I reached the sheriff's roadblock on PCH at Trancas, Norrine beside me. She didn't want to be there, but I needed her. I knew she had a fake California driver's license with the Malibu address. I passed it to the deputy.

"I have to get my cats!" she cried convincingly, giving me a dirty look.

"Okay," the deputy said. "But you see those flames coming, you get the hell out."

We roared on up the empty highway, the sky lit up ahead as if an armored division were pulverizing Oxnard. A few residents were out hosing down their rooftops. A Rolls-Royce stuffed with pets and paintings shot past us, heading back toward Trancas.

We came over a rise and saw it.

"Oh my God, shit," Norrine said.

The hills were a sea of fire. Sparks gusted in the wind. It had already jumped the highway in several places. The heat was so intense we both shielded our faces as I bore down toward the house through clouds of smoke.

"Scott, turn back."

"We're almost there," I said as we shot past the wall of flame. "It's cool."

Ahead of us on the ocean side a palm tree ignited.

"Cool? *Cool?* Are you out of your fucking mind?"

She said something else, but the whomp of a chopper drowned her out as it veered in over the hills, making a water dump.

I turned up the road to the house, a gust of embers raining down on the open car. Norrine screamed, swatting sparks from her hair.

"Norrine, don't get hysterical."

"You asshole! If I die, I swear, my parents are gonna sue you."

We reached the gate. It was open. I parked and got out. "I'll be right back."

"*Fuck* you."

I jogged through the gate, my eyes watering from the smoke. I thought about the dogs, but figured if they were loose, they'd have taken off through the gate by now.

I stopped when I came to the driveway. The Cadillac was there, its lights on, engine running, driver's door open, "Hello, Stranger" wafting from the Vibra-Sonic. My heart was pounding out of my chest as I stepped to the open front door.

The foyer was empty. I started for the stairs. Then I heard a crash in the kitchen, and footsteps on the tile. I ducked up the side corridor across from the stairs, stepping into the first room, so I couldn't be seen from the foyer.

I watched the foyer through the crack of the door, but no one came. I looked around and realized I was in Big Willy's bedroom.

It was a mess. A double bed with filthy red sheets, dated posters peeling from the red walls: Hendrix, Eldridge Cleaver, Isaac Hayes. There were stacks of soul and R&B albums amid the disposable plastic syringes that littered the tabletops like butts overflowing from ashtrays. But most disturbing was the S&M paraphernalia. There were bullwhips, a muzzle, a black leather executioner's mask, studded dog collars and leather wrist restraints, tit clamps and a steel bit, and a two-foot-long black dildo that was either a joke or a murder weapon. There were handcuffs, chains, a makeshift stock, there were ropes on each of the four bedposts. There were glossy porn mags of women in bondage, blond girls appearing to cry out in pain as black men in ski masks sodomized them. There were detective magazines, illustrated girls on the covers, tied to chairs, breasts popping buttons.

BLOND RAPED, TORTURED. Grisly black-and-white murder-victim photos inside. There were gun and muscle magazines too, glistening barrels and veiny balloon biceps. How to shoot through an engine block and get twenty-two-inch arms.

What a guy.

I heard a door slam in the kitchen. Then Sharlene called from upstairs. "Scott, hurry! He's out back!" She must've seen me coming up to the house.

I sprinted up the stairs, which were strewn with two-inch recording tape, ripped from its reel, tangled in snarls. At the top of the stairs I saw the new door installed halfway down the hall, a black steel-grid gatelike security door. Sharlene stood behind it, her eyes panicky. I reached out for the knob.

"No, Christ! It's electrified!"

I stopped my hand just in time.

"There's a switch in his room. In the closet."

I went into his bedroom. There was a round Playboy bed with black satin sheets, and the walls were black too, all the windows blocked out. The room gave off a stink of tobacco tar and stale semen, like a porno theater. Under a single track light, illuminated like a little display, was an antique silver tray holding a variety of needles, syringes, and bent antique spoons, all neatly arranged. I found my way to the closet, and the control box. I flipped a switch and a red light went out.

I was stepping out of the closet when Sharlene called, "Scott, he's coming up. He's got the dogs!"

I couldn't see the stairs but I saw her. She was still behind the security grille; she didn't know I'd already hit the switch. I heard the dogs loping up the stairs, panting wildly, and slammed Dennis' bedroom door just in time. A second later they were scratching frantically at the wood. Even through the door I could hear the wet gummy sound of flesh sliding

back over teeth. I saw a wet nose at the crack under the
door.

Then a shadow. Dennis. He spoke to Shar, as if thinking
out loud. "Cunt. Cunt. No-good cunt."

I braced myself against the door as he tried to push it
open. There was no way for me to lock it. It had a deadbolt
that required a key from both sides.

Keys jingled. "All right," he said to himself. "You can both
burn up. Fine. Great."

The deadbolt clicked over and I was locked in.

The door was too thick to smash through. The windows,
I knew, would be barred. I was trapped in a vault. I was
going to die at the foot of his Playboy bed, watching the
black satin sheets ignite around me as I suffocated on the
fumes of his burning cum stains.

I pulled the knob and pounded the door. "Dennis. Dennis!"

I heard a shot. A pause, then another shot. Then two
more in quick succession. I was certain he'd killed her. I
listened. But there was nothing. There seemed to be nothing
for hours.

"Scott?" It was Sharlene's voice.

"Yes."

"There's a switch in the closet—"

"It's off," I called to her. "I turned it off."

A moment later the deadbolt clicked back and Sharlene
opened the door.

She was shaking. I saw for the first time the red bruise on
her cheek, the choke-marks on her neck. The gun was still
in her hand, the .357 Magnum he'd fired at me, hanging at
her side.

Dennis was sprawled on the carpet, next to Buddy and
Chuck, his blond hair soaked with blood. The dogs were
dead too, blood glistening in their fur. There was blood
everywhere, on the door, on the orange flocked walls. There

was gray matter too, on the dogs and the carpet, blown out the back of his head. I nearly puked.

"Where's Big Willy?" I said.

She shook her head. "He's gone. He took the Sting Ray."

Smoke was rising from the foyer. I took the gun from her, sticking it in my pants waist.

"Let's get the fuck out of here," I said.

We made it down the stairs and out past the Cadillac, "Be My Baby" on the Vibra-Sonic now, the Ronettes sliding a corkscrew to hell. As we ran to the gate I glanced back at the garage. The door was up, the Sting Ray gone, the lights on in the room upstairs. Maybe Dennis had come back for his old 45's. I noticed Sharlene's Mustang still under the carport, and wondered if Big Willy might be coming back for that.

We reached the Lincoln but Norrine wasn't there. "Shit."

We caught up with her a few minutes later on PCH. She ignored us and kept walking. I pulled up ahead, got out, and opened the rear door. "Norrine, come on."

"You're crazy," she said, but got in. "I could've been incinerated."

"You're all right, aren't you?" I pulled out again.

I caught glimpses of Sharlene and Norrine checking each other out as I drove. Sharlene seemed puzzled by Norrine's appearance, her sixties attire, especially her hair, and seemed to consider for the fist time how I looked as well, but she didn't say anything. I saw that Norrine wanted to say something too, but she restrained herself.

Sharlene turned her face to the window. For a moment I thought she was crying. But her eyes were dry.

An hour later we pulled up to a club on Sunset Boulevard in Hollywood, where Norrine wanted to be dropped off. I got out of the car and drew her aside.

"Listen, I know you don't want to get involved in any trouble," I said. "Especially something involving pornography and the Mafia and Salvadoran death squads. Am I right?"

"Scott, what the hell happened out there?"

"Norrine—"

"Okay, okay." She glanced at Sharlene's silhouette in the car, another question forming.

"I'm sorry you had to get drawn into this," I said, before she could speak. "This evening hasn't gone as I'd planned."

"Yeah, well—" Her eyes were still on Sharlene. "I'm sure it's just as well."

"You're a good sport, Norrine," I said, and hugged her.

"Yeah, well, fuck that," she said, and kissed me hard on the mouth. Then she turned and strode into the club, a pissed-off phantom in aqua capris.

"What now?" Sharlene said as I took a left on Highland, heading for the freeway.

"I think we should discuss this with Neal."

"Do you have any cigarettes? I forgot my bag."

I gave her my Camels and dug out some matches, but they were soggy with sweat.

She used the car lighter. "He destroyed the tapes," she said calmly. "All the work from the sessions. It's all gone."

A fire engine roared past us.

"I liked the single."

"Did you?"

"Yeah. It's visceral."

"Yeah."

"Majestic."

"Yeah. Majesty. That's what we were aiming for."

"A little cluttered at times—"

"Yeah, well, you know how he gets."

"But a classic, all things considered. Disturbing, but a classic."

"Yeah. That's what I said to him when we finished. I said, 'Dennis, I think we've just made a disturbing classic.' "

"Why did you go back to him, Shar?"

She didn't say anything for a while. A gust of wind buffeted the car as we shot across Melrose. The bruise on her cheek looked even nastier under the yellow streetlights. "I don't know," she finally said. "I really don't know."

More silence.

"I guess I just lost my nerve. All that Sunday on Catalina I kept thinking, Jesus, this is never going to work, he's never going to let go of me. It won't matter what the law says, or the courts, he'll never let me get away. He'll pay somebody to kill me, to have us both killed, that's the way he is." I felt her looking at me. "I thought if I got back in time he'd never know I'd taken off. I know you won't believe this, but I was thinking of you too. That's why I was so shitty to you on the phone. So you'd see how useless it was and leave me alone. Because he said if you ever—"

"Save it, baby. No sale. That plotline hasn't worked since 'My Little Margie.' "

"I just didn't want you to end up like Bobby—"

"Shar—" I cut her off, not sure what she meant, but sensing an evasion. "—you told him all about me as soon as you got back."

"What?"

"I almost lost my peter 'cause you shot your mouth off."

"What are you talking about?"

"Come on, baby. I'm talking about Big Willy's switchblade and my cock."

"Oh Jesus." Her surprise seemed genuine. "He didn't—"

"No. He missed it by a millimeter. Then I smashed through a closed door and got away."

"Is that how this happened?" She touched the scar above my eye. "Oh, baby—"

"Fuck the 'oh, baby' shit." I knocked her hand away. "You dumped on me, Shar. You sold me out. Don't play naive."

"I didn't, I swear. I never mentioned your name. Scott, he already knew—"

"How?"

"We weren't very cool. Big Willy saw us together—"

She was right, of course. "I don't know, Shar. I really don't know."

"Are you calling me a liar? Jesus Christ, I just saved your fuckin' life, didn't I? What do I have to do now, tell you how stupid I was?"

"I already know that."

"Why don't you get fucked?"

"Why don't you blow me?"

A tense silence followed, neither of us able to come up with any further witty Noël Coward rejoinders. She stared out the side window. I knew I couldn't take it if she started to cry.

"Shar, I'm sorry."

"You're right," she said morosely. "I *was* stupid."

"No, you weren't." I took her hand. "Come on. It's okay."

"I'm sorry too." She moved over next to me. I put my arm around her. "I'm sorry about everything. Involving you in this."

"It's okay." I kissed her cheek.

"I had my chance with you and I blew it. You should let me out. Up at that bus stop."

I laughed. "Shar, come on."

"No, I mean it."

"Shar, it's all right. It's over now. It's over. You're going to be okay."

"Like hell. I'm going to end up in prison."

"No way. It was self-defense. You were saving yoursef and me."

"I'll be in some cell with a Manson girl."

"It'll never happen."

"I don't think I could handle prison, I really don't. I think I'd have one giant agoraphobic attack and just die."

"Sharlene, you are *not* going to go to prison. You're innocent. Shit, if anything, you're going to be a fucking cause célèbre. Times have changed. Wife-beating is no longer considered cool. Look at that woman who set her husband on fire—"

"What?"

"Some woman. Her husband terrorized her for twenty years till she finally dumped gasoline on him in his sleep and tossed a match at him. She became a feminist icon."

"Really?"

"Really."

"Yeah, *I* should've done something like that. On our honeymoon." She laughed. It was not the most cheerful laugh I had ever heard.

"How'd you get the gun?"

She lit another cigarette. "I snuck into his room one morning. Right after he put in the door. That was the last straw, that door." She blew smoke, and seemed tough now. "It's funny, though. He really did change for a while. That Monday when I got back to the house and he was there waiting, I almost died. I thought he was going to kill me. But he didn't even get mad. He was just stunned, totally wiped out, that I'd actually left him. I'd never seen him like that, ever. He said, 'Look, I'm not going to make any promises, I've broken too many in the past. But this is a turning point in both our lives.' Then he detoxed. For the first time in years he got completely clean. It was kind of a miracle. A rebirth. He seemed young again. I began to wonder if maybe it *was* just the drugs that made him crazy. The sessions for the single were great." She rushed on now, a little manic. "It was just like the early days. He was calm—well, calm for Dennis. In control. Confident. He seemed to have found it again. Then after the single took off he agreed to come up with a whole album, and that's where the trouble started. I mean, he couldn't spend fifteen years on each cut. He couldn't take the pressure, he went dry. It was horrible. All these people eating up studio time and he didn't have a clue as to what to do. So he had Big Willy score some speed.

Methedrine. He thought that might help since all the big hits were done on speed. But he flipped out almost immediately. I mean, he went psychotic. It was 'Tidal Wave' all over again. Everybody was betraying him. He was firing people right and left, accusing me of sucking off the drummer in the bathroom, fucking the engineer. I started popping Valium; it was the only way I could survive. He put in the door last week. We came home one morning and there it was. For my own protection, of course. I didn't argue. I've had the gun since last Tuesday. I was just trying to decide which one of us to use it on."

"I think you made the right choice."

"Yeah?" Faint smile. "Maybe so. I just wish I didn't have to tell a bunch of cops about everything."

"You may not have to. They'll find his body in the ashes. It's probably going to look like he got caught in the fire. Assuming it's possible for that house to burn down."

"It is. It's a lot cheaper than it looks. A lot of it's stucco and plaster. Wood. It's like a movie set." The tough air returned. "Too bad the fire won't get everything. That Sting Ray. That stupid fucking Sting Ray. I hate that car. I hate that fucking house. All that *crap*. It makes me sick, it always has. I hope it's all gone. I hope it all burned to the fucking ground."

14

The fires were a distant glow, orange veins in the Santa Monica Mountains, as we pulled up to the Surfrider Inn in Redondo Beach. It was a sprawling early-sixties futuristic complex, a cross between a Sambo's Coffee Shop and a Tomorrowland pavilion. Metal spires jutted from the corners, chunks of translucent plastic mosaic smeared around the windows like brains. The wind bludgeoned the spindly palm trees as I parked in the vast lot behind my former classmates' German cars.

"I'll go get him. Why don't you wait here?"

She cracked her door. "I have to use the little girls' room."

"Sharlene, I think it might be wise if we weren't seen together."

"Why?"

Good question. "Just because."

Stalemate. I sighed irritably, and it wasn't an act. My nerves were shot. It was the heat, the wind. What had happened. What I knew I was going to confront inside.

"What do you want me to do? Pee in the ashtray?"

"All right, come on."

We ducked across the lot, the wind pounding us. As soon as we stepped through the doors in the lobby, I could hear the band playing in the Orbit Room, a girl group doing a cover of "Our Lips Are Sealed." The lobby was glaringly lit, bright orange and yellow vinyl everywhere.

"Look, the coffee shop's down there. I'm sure they have a

ladies' room." I gestured down the corridor opposite the
Orbit Room. "I'll get Neal and we'll meet you. Just wait
there."

She nodded and took off.

I braced myself and started toward the Orbit Room. Halfway there I passed a mirrored column and caught a glimpse
of myself and cringed. My shirt was partially unbuttoned,
revealing the stock of the gun jammed in my pants. Jesus,
I'd forgotten I still had it. I must have been more out of it
than I'd thought. I quickly buttoned my shirt—Christ,
somebody could have seen the gun in the lobby—and noticed the blood on my desert boots. My eyes were glassy,
wax from my flat-top glistened on my forehead, sweat was
trickling down my arms. I was a mess; I looked like a goddamn psychopath. I couldn't go in there like this. What
would people think?

Christ, had it really come back to that? Fuck *that* shit.

I went on toward the door.

The room was dimly lit, like a bar. I could see a few couples dancing on the spacious floor as I stepped up to the
greeting table, which was no longer attended. There were
only a few name tags left. My own. And Neal's. Shit shit
shit.

"Scott? Is that you?"

I looked up and saw Gale Spivey coming at me. She
looked better than I'd imagined during our phone conversation. She was slim, made-up to the teeth tonight, of
course, but you could see she wouldn't look too shabby in
the morning either.

"Hi, Gale. How's it going?"

Her expression of phony exuberance changed rapidly to
genuine apprehension the closer she got to me. She lurched
into nervous bubbly overdrive.

"Scott, I'm so glad you made it, but to be honest I just
wasn't sure you were going to. So we got Becky Morton's
daughter's band at the last minute. You remember Becky.

She was in Drama with us, remember? She played Emily in
Our Town and then she married Bob Stubner. You remember Bob, don't you? That didn't last, of course, but—"

"Gale, listen. Neal isn't here by any chance, is he?" Grasp-
ing at straws.

"No, but I spoke with him last week." Nervous laugh. Yes,
I know you did, Gale. About me. "I'm sure he's coming.
Here"—she picked up the name tag, undid the pin—"let me
pin on your tag—"

"No, that's okay—" I pushed her hand away, afraid she
might detect the gun, and caused her to drop the name tag.
She jumped back a little, flustered, scared. This was horrible, excruciating. I had to get out of there.

I felt a hand on my shoulder and whirled around. It was
Steve, one of my old buddies, with a big florid Frans Hals
face I found painful to look at.

"Jesus Christ, I don't believe it. You haven't changed a
bit, man." His voice was charged with exaggerated joy but I
could feel his eyes clicking over me, registering my mood,
the look in my eyes. He made like he was going to give me a
bear hug, but I couldn't allow that, he'd feel the gun for
sure, so I stuck out my hand. He squeezed it hard, but I saw
he took my formality as rejection and immediately cooled.

"How are you, Steve?"

"Great, I'm great, never better. Shit, Betty and I flew in
from Tulsa just for tonight." He waved to a stacked blond in
a tight jumpsuit the way you would beckon a distracted but-
ler for more drinks. "Went back in seventy-four to visit my
brother and haven't left since."

"Seems like I heard something about that," I said, looking
over the crowd. It was too dark to make out most people
unless they came right up to me. A light over the dance
floor, a weird revolving sputnik fixture, threw a glare in my
eyes.

"The greatest place in the country, Scott. A land of opportunity. L.A. is overrated, believe me."

"I do, Steve. I'm sure you're right."

"You still a deejay?"

"Yeah, that's right." *Still* a deejay, what the fuck was that supposed to mean? What the fuck was wrong with being a deejay? It was better than selling ratburger franchises or whatever the fuck it was he did in Tulsa. "It's a living, Steve."

Betty wriggled up now, undulating like a sex kitten who'd blown a fuse. "Honey," he said, "this is my old war buddy" —figuratively speaking of course, ha ha—"Scott Cochran. I'm sure I've told you about Scott—"

"Oh yes," she said in a squeaky Betty Boop voice, and I almost guffawed in her face. I mean, I almost couldn't stop myself from laughing in a way that would have wounded her instantly, I was almost that out of control.

I heard a squeal and saw Mary Ann James stalking at me like an irate giraffe in high heels. I felt like squealing right back if only to demonstrate what she'd just done to my nerves.

She came at me with her lips puckered and her arms spread and before I knew what was happening we were hugging and she was squealing again right against my ear. "Scott, yuuuuh! I can't stand it!"

Neither could I. I stood slightly away from her so she wouldn't feel the gun against her stomach. She'd been my date for the prom. I had attempted seduction later, after the graduation party, but she'd thrown up apricot brandy all over my tuck-and-roll.

"Scott, you look too good, too good, I can't stand it!" You must be looped, Mary Ann. "Where's Charlie?" she said. "Where's my husband? I want to make an exchange!" She laughed boisterously but I suspected she was only half joking. She'd been in love with me, but of course back then I was still getting over Cheryl.

"You look good too, Mary Ann." She did. She just needed a little Thorazine.

"Life's good," she said, beaming harshly in my face. "Life's been very good." But her eyes were crying: Save me, I'm dying inside.

Then Jeff Menton, the all-time eunuch nice guy, stepped up, sticking his hand out with a choked, taciturn "Hey, buddy," as though afraid to show too much emotion toward another guy lest somebody get the wrong idea.

"How's it going, Jeff?"

"Can't complain." He laughed sheepishly. Golf moron. Sad.

"Well, well, well."

I recognized the sarcastic voice immediately, a voice I remembered from gym class, where his locker had been right next to mine, where he'd pull down his jock while I was untying my sneakers, knowing that his uncircumcised cock would be practically in my face. It was the voice that had warned me that Cheryl would fuck anything that could stand on its hind legs and shoot. It was the voice of the man who had jammed his tongue down her throat in my rearview mirror on the day she died.

"Hi, Bill."

He was drunk, fuming whiskey at me, and you could tell from his face that he drank a lot. The blond hair was still kinky, greasy-looking, but the body had changed. Gone was the skinny twerp; he was a gym-built mastodon now, in a tight polyester bodyshirt and gray Dacron slacks that were just as tight.

He shook my hand slowly, as though acknowledging that we had once been mortal enemies, but that that was all behind us now, like an old football game, the final score all but forgotten in the musty annals of sports.

"Man, you must be doing something right," he said. " 'Cause you don't look a day over forty-five." Guffaw. Still a wit.

"Well, you know how it is, Bill. I try to watch what I eat.

Get plenty of exercise. Never stay up for more than four days in a row."

"Yeah?" He seemed vaguely confused. "That's what I hear. The fast lane, living in the fast lane. Rock-and-roll." He laughed again. Jagged patterns of light passed over his face from the sputnik fixture above. "Is that what this is?" He ran his hand over my flat-top. I cringed. "What do they call this? Is this some of that new-wave horseshit or what?"

"It's nostalgia, Bill," I said calmly. In fact, I felt lethally calm.

"Nostalgia? Shit, I thought it was new wave." He guffawed and looked around for support, but people were drifting off. Only Mary Ann was staying around, talking to somebody else now, but looking eager to get back to me.

"So what are you doing with yourself these days?" I said, though I knew.

He didn't take my cue. "Just trying to stay sober, but not having much luck." Honk. "Third marriage just went kaput, you know how it is—"

"Yeah, I do, Bill, I do. Are you still working at that surf-board shop?"

"Are you kidding? Hell, no. Jesus, that was fifteen years ago. Boy, you must not keep in touch." Instinctively he tried to tone himself down, but was so drunk he only turned stealthy. "I'm a police officer, Scott. I'm a cop."

"No shit? Where?"

"Right here in good old Redondo Beach. Yessir. And a fine city it is too. Glad to be of service."

"No fucking kidding. Well, if this isn't one for the books. I mean, I gotta tell you—and I hope you won't take this the wrong way—but you're one of the last guys I would ever have figured to become a cop."

He seemed oblivious to my sarcasm, too drunk to perceive it. "Well, people change."

"Yeah, I guess they do."

"I had my wild period—"

"Well, let's face it, we all did, Bill."

"Which is not to say I'm exactly domesticated now—" He winked.

"Hey. Know just what you mean, pal."

"I'll bet you make out pretty well yourself. You get those little rock fans all excited—"

"And how. I'll tell you, sometimes there's so much hot young pussy around I just don't know where to start."

"Yeah, well, next time you have a problem like that, you give me a call—"

"Hey, I just might do that, pal. Say, while we're on the subject of hot teenage snatch, tell me, what's the inside scoop on the Cheryl Rampton murder? I hear they finally found her twat buried under a condo."

I watched every gear in his body strip. His eyes seemed locked in place, staring a hole in the blond girls on the stage, never to move again. Finally his hand lifted his glass up to his mouth. He tried to drink but there was nothing left but ice. "Who told you that?" he said, still not looking at me.

"They ran a segment about it on 'Eye on L.A.'" I stared at the sweat popping out on his forehead. "About a haunted beachfront condo . . ." I let my voice drop to a dead Dirty Harry monotone, ". . . filled with screams and grunting sounds." I smiled. I doubt that it was a pleasant smile.

"It wasn't murder," he said. "She wasn't murdered."

I became aware of the cold gun against my stomach. "What was it then?"

"It was an accident."

"Yeah, right. She slipped on a jellyfish and fell cunt-first on a Boy Scout flashlight. Stranger things have happened, I guess. Gee, I wonder whose flashlight it was. Say, you were a Boy Scout, come to think of it—"

"We were all Boy Scouts." His eyes flitted back to me for a second. "That was the problem."

"Hey, you're being cryptic now, Bill. Come on, it drives me nuts when people get cryptic—"

"Look." He raised his voice now. "I don't care what *you* think. It was an accident. Anyway"—he looked at his glass —"it wasn't Cheryl they found."

He started past me toward the bar. I grabbed his arm. "What the fuck are you talking about?"

"Just what I said. It wasn't Cheryl they dug up down there." He was talking quite loudly and suddenly realized it. "It was somebody else," he said quietly, looking around to see if anybody had overheard.

"Who?"

"Nobody you knew."

I still had a hold of his arm. He seemed weakened, unsure of himself. I stepped around so he had to look at me. "Bill, I want to know what happened that night."

I knew he saw what it meant to me, and at first his mood seemed to match my own. Then he smirked and shrugged as if to say: What the hell, why not, you can't pin anything on me. "All right, I'll tell you," he said. "But I'm going to get a drink first."

We both got drinks and stepped over by the glass door leading to the veranda, some distance from the main body of the crowd. We would have stepped outside for more privacy, but the wind was still intense, buffeting the palms that lined the veranda.

My calm was gone now, I was trembling with adrenaline, but his seemed to be returning. He sipped his drink and watched the palms, as if staring into the past. If this had been a movie the camera would have tracked in on him, and dissolved into a florid Technicolor flashback.

"As I'm sure you remember, I was with Cheryl for a while that last afternoon. Down at the beach lot. I believe you came by in your car at one point, that old Chevy, and saw us together."

Ah yes, memories, misty sunlight of the mind. Get on with it, you fuck.

"Well, as you may recall, it was a hot evening and there was a lot of drinking. That night the lot was jammed, people coming from all over to get down by the beach and cool off. Eventually Cheryl and I had an argument and she left my company in favor of some other guys she appeared to know, some guys I'd never seen before. I was not unduly upset by this, inasmuch as my relationship with Cheryl had always been what you might describe as casual. I certainly didn't feel I had a hold on her or anything." His eyes went to me, then quickly back to the veranda. "In any event, I left not long after that, so when I tell you what happened next I should qualify it by pointing out that it is secondhand. Though I have every reason to believe that this sequence of events is true."

Sure, Bill.

"So apparently Cheryl is with these new guys now, a carload or two. They're from out of the area, like I say. More your lowlife greaser types, perhaps more Cheryl's kind of people, if you follow. Certainly not your average suburban PV types. So there's more drinking, maybe some fooling around. Things are getting pretty rowdy. Now, this is where the other girl enters the picture."

I studied him closely for any hint that he was making this up. I saw none. What I saw was that he was describing his own memories. He hadn't left. He'd still been there.

"Now, like the guys, she's from out of the area, and is clearly your cheaper type of girl. There is some concern later that she may have come down there looking for some action with a girlfriend or two, someone who would be able to place her there that night, but nothing ever develops from this. In any event, what happens essentially is that these greaser types pick up both Cheryl and this other girl. So now Cheryl is with one guy, okay? But at a certain point a bunch of his friends take this other girl out to the beach. Now, it's willing on her part. She understands that she's going to be taking on several guys, four, five, something like that. But once they get down there, word spreads about what's going on. More guys start coming out, at first just to watch, but pretty soon they want in on the act. Some kind of strange thing happens to everyone, some kind of animal thing. You know, even those clean-cut PV types have their cocks out. It's like a test maybe. If you don't fuck her, you're not a man. Maybe it's something like that, who knows? But at some point this girl starts to freak out. She wants to stop but the guys won't let her. I suppose in a way it turns into rape at this point"—he snorted—"though I would hate to be the prosecutor who got her case."

I suddenly realized the girl group was doing "Love Me Tonight," and had been for a while. Jesus, how long had I been here? Sharlene was probably having a panic attack in the coffee shop, hyperventilating in one of the booths. But I had to know the rest of this. The song swelled rapturously, the girl copying Sharlene's vocal nuance for nuance.

"So meanwhile Cheryl is in the car with this other guy, this greaser guy she's with. They're going at it in the backseat when they hear the other girl screaming out on the beach. Cheryl immediately climbs out to go see what's happening. But when she gets down there, it's like a small mob scene. And this other girl has passed out, although some guy is still fucking her. Now, maybe at this point Cheryl starts screaming at them to stop or something, but the second they see her, you know, the rest is inevitable. This is like a golden opportunity, you know, because everybody's always secretly wanted her, and now all the rules are broken, there's nothing to stop them. This is their chance to get back at her for not being the big whore they always said she was. Because, you know, she wasn't really. She was just something they didn't understand. But this is their chance to show her, and they do. She doesn't fight when it's clear she can't get away, and this they hate even more. Then when she tries to talk to them, they hit her to make her shut up. She knows most of these guys, she's in classes with them, but they can't stand to hear her say their names, or anything at all. So they fuck her, one after the other, everybody standing around, shouting constantly about what a whore she is, what a pig. The only thing that saves her is that the other girl dies."

His mouth was dry. He took another swallow of booze. Maybe he'd thought he could tell it without feeling anything again, but it was clear now that wasn't possible.

"See, when they turned their attention to Cheryl, they just ignored the other girl, but some time has passed now and she's still not moving. It's hard to say exactly what killed her. She was drunk, there could have been pills, it could have been an OD. Or an internal hemorrhage, that sort of thing. Nobody really knew who did that with the flashlight."

"It probably happened while your backs were turned," I said. He didn't contradict me.

"But at some point, a kind of vibe just passes over the crowd that says: Hey, this girl is dead. Now, nobody actually says anything. I mean, they really don't want to know, and they all start leaving. You know, still acting like it was just a good rowdy time, but secretly scared now. I mean, it's like for sure nobody wants to be the last to leave this party. So at some point Cheryl gets away. Now, for sure she knows that this other girl is dead. I mean, they're only a few yards apart, so this causes some concern later too. But the last anyone sees of her, she's hightailing it down the beach, still half-naked, till she disappears into the night."

The group finished "Love Me Tonight" to scattered applause. In the lull that followed, the din of chatter seemed to rise. I stared at the crowd as the jagged light washed over them, wondering how many of those guys were furtively checking me out right now, thinking I'm the only one who really cares about what they did.

"Who buried the body?" I said, mostly just to keep him talking.

"I really don't know the answer to that one, Scott. My guess is a few of your more straight-arrow types got nervous and came back before dawn. It was a shallow grave. Somebody threw up a workshed on the spot not long after. That's the only reason they didn't find her sooner."

"This greaser"—his eyes went to the floor—"the guy Cheryl was with in the car. Why didn't he try to stop the other guys?"

"What could *he* do?"

"There wasn't any greaser, was there, Bill? That was you."

"No." He couldn't look at me. Jesus, there were tears in his eyes.

"You loved her too. Didn't you?"

"No, she didn't mean anything to me. She was just a good lay, that's all. A hot piece of tail."

"You rotten fuck."

"She was nothing." He forced a sarcastic laugh. "She was a pig. Only a stupid pussy like you would fall in love with the class pig."

I came so close to killing him then. He was everything I hated—about myself, about every smirking locker-room creep who'd ever put Cheryl down. He was every fucking moron who deserved to die. I took a step back so I would have room to pull out the gun, and I was just about to do it, when he looked beyond me and said, "I'll tell you who *I* loved. And I don't believe it, but she just walked through the door."

There was an instant where I really thought I would turn and see Cheryl Rampton entering the room, women gasping, guys popping sweat, the music grinding to a halt.

Of course it was Sharlene, looking around for me, and there were a few gasps as people recognized *her*—though I couldn't have been the only one who had noticed the resemblance between Cheryl and the Stingrays' singer.

She scanned the crowd anxiously, spotted me, and started

over. Although I was still revved up for attack, I forced myself to turn from Bill and intercept her on the dance floor.

"Jesus Christ, what the hell is going on?" she said." I've
been waiting forever. Is he here?"

"No. Let's split," I said, guiding her toward the door, de-
termined not to look back at Bill. If I just didn't have to see
his face again, I was sure I could walk out of there.

But he slid up behind me and took Sharlene's arm.

"I just don't believe it," he said with evil facetiousness.
"Sharlene Contrelle. Christ, you haven't changed a bit. I'd
know that face anywhere. Wouldn't you, Scott?"

He held on to her arm, grinning like a florid drunk who
didn't know what he was saying. But he knew.

"I just can't tell you how much joy you've brought me
over the years," he said, and now Sharlene began to look
panicked. "You know, I'm quite the oldies fan. And while
there are some songs you eventually get sick of, I never get
sick of you."

"Thanks," Sharlene said, but it sounded more like "Fuck
off." She looked to me for help.

"Bill, let go of her," I said evenly.

He ignored me—the fuck ignored me!—never taking his
eyes off Sharlene. "You know, I'd hate myself if I let you get
away without at least one dance."

I hit his shoulder, rage blasting through me. "Let her go,
you fuck!"

He came at me. We grappled awkwardly, flailing at each
other. He tried to trip me, but I finally smashed his face.
The gun slipped out of my pants. I felt a new surge of adrenaline rip through him as the weapon clattered across the
dance floor. I was trying to smash his face again when he
caught me with a pulverizing gut punch. As I doubled over,
he dived for the gun. Just as he reached it, Sharlene slid in
out of nowhere, jumping on his back like a cat. He grimaced
and howled as her fingernails shredded his bodyshirt. In
agony he tried in vain to peel her off. Finally he elbowed

her hard in the face and she fell back flat on the floor. Bleeding and enraged, he rocked back with the gun in both hands to take aim at Sharlene. That was when I grabbed him again.

We fought for the gun, rolling on the floor, the weapon between our faces. I could taste his breath as he grunted like a wrestler and pressed the muzzle of the gun into the socket of my right eye. My fingers dug at his grip on the gun. I felt his finger press the trigger.

Cringing, I forced his hands down as the gun went off.

The blast was excruciating. I rolled away from him reflexively, certain I'd been shot in the head, though I felt nothing yet. Then a spray of warm blood came down on my face. Opening my eyes, I saw Bill sitting on the floor a few feet away, jerking his head as if he were stunned or befuddled from a powerhouse punch. But it was much worse than a punch. He had shot himself under the chin. His jaw was gone. His face was a gorge pouring blood.

Through the ringing in my ears I heard a few high, keening screams. I saw the looks of horror and incredulity on the gallery of tanned faces behind Bill. Amazingly, it was only now that the girl group quit playing, their rendition of "Yesterday" thumping to a messy halt as they strained to see what had happened beyond the lights.

Bill tried to get up, but he couldn't. He also seemed to try to speak. He would probably never do that again. Finally, to more screams and cries of disbelief, he quietly lay back down in the growing pool of his blood.

The next thing I knew, I was standing, aware that the gun was in my hand, though I didn't remember picking it up. I looked down at my body, and it seemed small and remote, as if viewed through the wrong end of a pair of binoculars. I saw Sharlene's small hand touch my arm.

Then Glenn Mead and Jack Killingsworth started coming toward me, cautiously, gently trying to talk me into giving up the gun. But I raised it. They stepped back, holding up their hands. I felt Sharlene pulling me back toward the veranda exit door.

I looked down and saw that we were leaving footprints on the dance floor in Bill Holtner's blood. I felt the hot wind on the back of my head as Sharlene opened the door.

15

We ran along the veranda and climbed a set of wooden stairs that led back up to the parking lot. We reached the Lincoln and got out of the lot okay. As we crossed PCH we heard the first sirens of the cop cars converging on the Surfrider.

I stayed on the residential side streets, heading toward the freeway. Everything was cool till I cut back to Hawthorne Boulevard. We'd gone less than a block when a black-and-white spotted us and made a skidding U-turn.

"Baby, I know you don't like freeways," I said. "So you'd better not look."

I shot through a yellow light and made a hard, skidding right onto the San Diego Freeway heading north, the cop car yelping behind us.

"Scott—" she said as I roared up the ramp, watching the red and blue lights in my rearview mirror.

"What?" Headlights blinded me. Something didn't seem right.

"We're going the wrong way."

"Whoa." She was right.

A horn blared and a set of headlight careened back onto the freeway to avoid a head-on collision with us. Another car right behind it did the same, jumping the divider curb, skidding back into the right lane, other cars veering out of its path, other cars veering out of theirs.

Then I saw the tank truck bearing down on us and nearly

shit in my pants. Sharlene screamed as the driver blasted his
horn. His brakes squealed. I reached the freeway shoulder a
second before he reached us.

Sharlene was still covering her face as I plowed along the
shoulder doing sixty. The cop siren was still yelping, the
lights flashing in my rearview mirror. The stupid fuck was
coming after us.

I was beyond terror, certain we were going to die. Horns
blew, cars veering from the right lane as they saw us coming.
The shoulder was barely wide enough for the Lincoln, and
it was bumpy. One wrong move would send us into the
oncoming lane.

I pushed it past seventy as we went around a curve, a
canyon of headlights washing over us. The flashing lights in
the rearview mirror left spots on my eyes. Sharlene
scrunched down in the seat, covering her head, braced for
the imminent crash.

Then I saw it, dead ahead parked on the shoulder, a
Honda, its yellow emergency lights flashing. I braked. Sharlene looked up, too wiped out to scream. I heard the cops'
brakes squeal behind us.

I wasn't going to be able to stop in time. I was going to
smash into the Honda. Less than fifteen feet from impact, I
swerved into the oncoming lane, skidding cars veering out
of my path. Sharlene threw her arms over her face.

I swerved back onto the shoulder just as the cop car
smashed into the Honda. The lights quit flashing and the
yelping stopped. Conditioned by movies, I expected a fiery
explosion, but none came.

I saw an off-ramp coming up and slowed. My nerves so
shot I felt like a spastic, I made a hard U over the divider
curb and headed down the off-ramp, a Pontiac nearly plow-
ing into my rear.

I drove a few blocks once we got off the freeway, the
temperature gauge far into the red, then turned up a dark
tract-house side street and cut the engine. As soon as I did,

I wished I hadn't. I could hear the radiator hissing. But I had to catch my breath.

"Are you okay?" I said to Sharlene.

She was a ghost in the moonlight. "Oh, yeah, sure. I'm fine."

She looked like a rape victim—bruised, blouse torn, hair askew. I didn't look so hot myself. In the rearview mirror I saw that my face and hair were caked with dried blood. It was all over my shirt.

"I need some air," Sharlene said, and got out.

I joined her. We leaned against the hood of the Lincoln, smoking my last two cigarettes. The street was dark and dead, the tract-house windows barred. Leaves blew across the asphalt.

"So who was that guy?" she said.

"A former clasmate."

"I figured that."

"Also a cop."

"A cop?" She shook her head and snorted disgustedly. "Yeah, well, he started it."

"Yeah, he was drunk."

"I mean, it was self-defense."

"Actually, he shot himself."

"Yeah? Well, that figures. What an asshole." She stared off down the street. "You think he's gonna live?"

"Yeah. But his spit-swapping days are over."

"Christ." She hugged herself.

I put my arm around her. "Look, I'm sorry this had to come down on top of everything else. It was an old conflict. It didn't really have anything to do with you."

"Didn't it?" Her cheek was red and swollen where Bill had hit her.

I avoided her eyes. I just wasn't up to telling her the Cheryl Rampton story, not right then. "Anyway, thanks for jumping him when you did. You'd have made a great female wrestler."

She smiled wearily. "Yeah, well, I've had some practice."

I kissed her forehead. "We'd better get moving."

Just as I'd expected, the Lincoln wouldn't start. The freeway jaunt had been too much for its brittle nerves. It had had a heart attack and died. I put the gun in the trunk. There was only one round left in the chamber, and I didn't feel like giving the cops a retroactive excuse for blowing me away. We set out on foot.

When we reached Rosecrans Avenue we walked east for several blocks until we came to a dark do-it-yourself car wash. I stuck a quarter in the slot and washed the blood off my face. I used my shirt to dry off, then tossed it in a dumpster.

The night was warm enough to plausibly go without a shirt, but I still felt conspicuous as we got on the bus. After minimal discussion we'd agreed on our destination, a good place to safely regroup—provided we could get there alive.

I had some doubts. We were the only white people on the bus. I dreaded the new arrivals: janitors, nurses, groups of young girls, young guys with boom boxes coming up the aisle, doing stunned double-takes at the sight of my lily-white torso. Sharlene stared out the window at the orange-lit housing projects while I tried to ignore the turned heads and glares.

We got off at Avalon and 103rd Street and started walking fast. The last whites seen on these streets had been National Guardsmen in 1965. We passed liquor stores where old black men drank in the parking lot, we passed fast-food stands where young blacks stopped mid-bite and stared in shock. The element of surprise was probably what saved us. They just couldn't believe we were actually there, that a white couple could be so stupid. By the time they thought to hassle us, we'd already passed.

Until a car began following us, an old Riviera, Lionel Richie crooning on the radio.

"How much farther?" I said.

"Right up here." She turned the corner. I did too. So did the Riviera.

At the end of the short block was a high-walled crypto-Moorish fortress, like a tire plant from the twenties with fake minarets at the corners and a thick arched gate. The stucco facade was cracked and covered with spray-paint graffiti.

"*This* is it?" I said.

"Yeah." Sharlene pressed a button on the intercom by the gate.

I looked back. The Riviera had stopped, its occupants watching us.

A female voice came through the intercom. "I hope it's important."

"Louise? It's me."

The gate hummed open. The Riviera backed into a drive-way, then pulled away.

The run-down exterior was a deliberate deception. Inside the walls, the grounds were immaculate—though the wind, which had abated now, had taken its toll. Brown palm fronds littered the driveway, dead leaves were packed against the marble steps leading up to the house, a Jazz Age tycoon's Ali Baba dream. Sharlene led the way along the central por-tico, where red and blue lights threw palm shadows on the intricately tiled walls.

We entered a large den furnished in Persian rugs and glitzy Arabian fabric couches with dozens of pillows. There was a hookah and a huge brass bowl filled with marijuana. A used-car commercial played silently on the big-screen TV, a narcotic Al Green song drifting through the air from deep in the house.

Stiletto heels clicked on the tile as Louise Wright made her entrance. Except for the heels, all she wore was a diaph-anous black babydoll negligee, and she had a body that was not to be believed. She might have stepped from a vintage Frederick's of Hollywood illustration, her breasts were so high and firm and befuddlingly pointy. Below her narrow waist her caramel legs were smoothly muscled, powerful enough to snap Rudyard Kipling's neck with a single contraction. And from the dark humid region of her crotch there emanated a musky perfume scent laced wth a pungent Congo aroma.

She strode into the room, but stopped when she saw Sharlene's condition. A scowl disrupted the smooth ebony perfection of her face. "Oh, shit, not again," she said with a soft Mississippi drawl.

"It's over," Sharlene said. "I shot him tonight. He's dead."

Louise didn't blink. Instead she took a drag off her fuchsia Sherman. "I'll dedicate my next show to his memory," she said, as if she'd rehearsed her response. "I'll sing an *a cappella* version of 'Tidal Wave of Flame.' "

"Oh, Louise."

The women hugged, Louise murmuring words of comfort as Sharlene told her in a rush about everything that had happened—about the fire, the security door, how I'd come to save her. Louise checked me out over Sharlene's shoulder.

"Don't I get a hug too?" I said.

Louise stepped over and checked me out, making no attempt to keep her eyes on my face. "Sharlene, who is this man?" she said sardonically. She knew who I was. "And why is he all stinky with sweat"—she stuck her finger under the damp exposed band of my Jockey shorts—"right down to his underpants?"

"Hey, baby"—I removed her finger—"if you'd gone the wrong way on the 405, your panties would be stinky with more than sweat."

"I don't wear panties," she drawled.

"Yeah, I noticed."

"I'm sure you did." She stared off into space, blowing smoke through her broad nostrils.

I sighed. "I could use a shower."

"You tellin' me. Up the hall and to the left. Drop your

soiled clothing by the door. I'll send along the manservant to pick it up."

"Thanks," I said, and took off.

Walking up the hall, I passed Louise's bedroom. A young man lay naked on her canopied bed, smoking a cigarette, snapping his fingers as he sang along to "Wang Dang Doodle" on the stereo. About twenty, he had dirty blond hair, tattoos on his biceps, and the biggest, greasiest dick I'd ever seen. He was staring at the ceiling, lost in the song, and didn't see me as I passed.

I found the bathroom, took off my pants, and left them by the door.

Under the shower I replayed the reunion fight. Sharlene was right, Bill had started it by hassling her. When the gun had slipped out he'd gone for it. If Sharlene hadn't jumped him, he would have shot me then, I was sure of that. And if I hadn't grabbed him again, he would have shot her. As it was, he'd come quite close to blowing my brains out. That had clearly been his intention when he pulled the trigger, accidentally shooting himself.

But what had my former classmates seen? Was it clear to them he was going to shoot Sharlene? Or just cover her? Did they know he'd been hassling her, or did they just see me hit him, apparently provoking the fight? They would certainly know the gun had been mine. But did they see that he had intended to kill me with it? Were they sorry he hadn't?

The whole thing was exceedingly fucked. I had to talk to Neal. That was what I should be doing.

But I leaned against the tile and let the hot water pound my body awhile longer. There were still so many things to figure out. For so long I'd blamed Bill for what I had assumed had happened to Cheryl. Even if his story were true that there'd been two girls, he was still responsible for what had happened to Cheryl, by default. He could have tried to stop it, but he hadn't. Any way you looked at it, he was guilty. I wanted to believe he'd finally got what was coming

to him. But as I saw him again sitting on the dance floor
with his face pouring blood, I felt a cringe up the back of my
legs, the same sort of impersonal but visceral empathy you
might feel catching a glimpse of a maimed traffic accident
victim. Even though I'd come so close to shooting him minutes before, what had actually happened seemed so much
worse than the clean sudden death of imagined revenge.

Had there really been two girls? I'd believed him as he was
saying it and I still couldn't see why, at this late date, he
would want to make up something that baroque.

Of course, what it meant was that Cheryl was probably
still alive. Where? Was she a trashy housewife in Bakersfield
with a shitkicker husband and four screaming kids? Did she
spend her days spreading Jif on Wonder Bread, watching
General Hospital, going shopping at the Food Barn in a '72
Monte Carlo with a peeling vinyl roof, popping a can of
Schlitz malt liquor while she read her horoscope in the *Star*?

Or had she gone up-scale, marrying a doctor or attorney
twice her age? Was she a svelte Montecito matron with a
billfold full of charge cards, driving a silver Mercedes
500SEL to her French cooking lessons and her exercise
class?

How could it matter anymore?

If she was alive and had lived twenty years without me,
then she was dead to me in a way she hadn't been when I
thought she'd died still loving me. If she was alive, she'd be
nothing like my memory of her. Even if I knew where she
was, I had no right to disturb her. In a way I didn't completely understand, thinking she was alive made it easier to
let go of her. Maybe it was really my memory of her that I
loved, not the real Cheryl, however she would be now.

Drying off, I made the mistake of looking at myself in the
mirror. That was when I realized how deranged I still was.
My image went through permutations, as if I'd taken bad
acid. I saw myself at sixteen, smooth and bland, then aged
abruptly to a weathered thirty-six-year-old man. Then I

looked handsome, virile, like a raunchy, unshaven outlaw.
Then I saw terror and a lifetime of agony. It was pain that
killed people eventually, psychic pain. I looked away.

I tried to collect myself. Cheryl didn't matter, twenty years
ago didn't matter. Nothing mattered but tonight and Sharlene.

I wrapped a towel around my waist and went out and
found a phone. I could hear Sharlene in the den telling
Louise about the reunion as I punched Neal's number. I
was expecting his machine—he was undoubtedly at the Surfrider by now, watching the cops draw chalk marks on the
dance floor—but a woman answered.

"Hello."

"Karen?" His date for the reunion, a young studio story
editor he'd been seeing a lot of lately. "This is Scott. Is Neal
there?"

"Oh Jesus, no, Scott. I guess you haven't heard." Neal's
twin brother, Larry, she told me, had been killed in a freak
accident that afternoon in New York and Neal had flown
back. I expressed my sorrow, though really it was more than
I could absorb at the moment. I hadn't seen Larry in over
fifteen years, and we'd never been close. As a teenager with
a genius IQ, he'd been an insufferable intellectual snob. I
found myself drifting out as she told what had happened.
Since Yale, Larry had become a novelist who after years of
struggle had finally sold a book to Hollywood for a huge
sum. By way of celebrating, he'd gone out and bought an
expensive vintage automobile, "a yellow something-or-
other," she said, "like the car in _Gatsby_." A jack had slipped
while he was under it.

"Scott, are you okay?" she said eventually, no doubt disturbed by the preoccupied tone of my response. "Why aren't
you at the reunion?"

"We were there for a while," I said. "But it was dull. We
left." Without asking for Neal's New York number, I got off
the phone.

I stood there a minute trying to decide what to do next. It wouldn't take long to track down one of Neal's law partners. And there were always Melvin Belli and F. Lee Bailey.

But I saw the cops grinding my face into the cinder-block wall of a strip cell. I saw the endless courtroom scenes, and the weight yard at San Quentin, the Aryan Brotherhood tattoos.

I went back into the den. Sharlene didn't say much as I told her about the call; she didn't seem all that disappointed. When I suggested without much conviction that we try talking to another attorney, she sighed wearily, leaned back, and closed her eyes.

Louise stepped over, inspecting me again. "Oh, Sharlene," she said. "Now that he's all nice and clean, I do see why you like this man."

I grinned. Though she was being facetious, I caught an undercurrent of genuine desire, and was flattered. "You know, Louise, there are very few stars who can still awe me. I mean, I met Mick back in sixty-eight. Nice guy, but small. Elvis? Hey. Just folks. But you, Louise. I mean, let's face it, you are *the* ultimate erotic icon of the twentieth century." I brushed her arm. "It's almost like touching the sun."

She shrugged. "You're silly. I'm only a woman. Sharlene, does he talk this way to you?"

Sharlene nodded as she lit a cigarette.

"You're a woman-plus, Louise, and you know it. You must realize the place you occupy in millions of American male psyches."

"I know. I saved a generation of white boys from the Lennon Sisters."

"And a generation of white girls from *becoming* the Lennon Sisters."

She smiled. "Yes, I'm a fan of yours, too. I listen to you sometimes on long hot summer nights when I'm restless. Oh, I know everybody thinks I've got a brand-new man each night. But many's the time I get all lathered up on the stage, only to face a cold empty bed."

I smiled, assuming she was still being facetious. But with Louise, the line between humor and truth seemed thin. "I know what you're talking about. Many's the morning I leave the station all revved-up and pent-up and busting at the crotch with no place to go. It's too bad you never called me—"

"I tried several times. Your line was always busy."

"We could've gone out for breakfast. Pancakes at Denny's. Dripping with syrup."

"Ooohh. I like brown sugar on mine. You like brown sugar?"

"It's my favorite song."

"What about the flip side? You remember that?"

"'Bitch.' Yeah, I like that too."

"Ooohh."

She glanced at Sharlene on the sofa. I did too. Sharlene was staring into her drink, ignoring us, or trying to, as if she wanted a few moments alone with her own thoughts.

"Yeah, your voice knocks me out," I said to Louise. "When you sing. And even when you speak. It always conjures up images of cotton fields and orange plantation skies."

"Well, it should," she drawled softly. "Seein' as how that's where I grew up. Oh, it was a run-down plantation, to be sure. A few miles from Biloxi, the smell of crawfish wafting through the humid breeze. A decrepit Twelve Oaks full of fucked-up white folks. An alcoholic general who eventually blew his brains out. Three daughters, the oldest a sad old maid, the middle one a schizophrenic ballerina, the youngest one the town nymphomaniac. There was a son too, who liked to suck off all the black boys, even though he was married to a voluptuous, unsatisfied vixen-in-heat. I grew up with my father, out in the backhouse. What used to be the slaves' quarters and in many ways still was. Old Jim.

That's what they called my father. He was gelded, I guess, but I loved him. Many's the night he'd play his beat-up old guitar by the fire, singing every Robert Johnson song he knew. Everything I know about the blues I learned from him, till he smashed that guitar the night he found Jesus, convinced that Robert Johnson had gone to hell. He became a real prude and a tight-ass after that. Which was why I ran off to live with my mother."

"Where was she?" I asked.

"New Orleans. She was a madam in a house of black ill-repute. I grew up there in a plush red room with a peephole in the floor. It was there that I began to sing at the old upright piano. Though I had no ambitions in mind. Then one night in 1960, when I was fourteen years old, I heard Ike and Tina Turner on an old Philco radio, and said, if that girl can do it, I can too."

"You've come a long way."

"I've been lucky. But I try to give back some of what I've got."

"That's what I've heard. You do a number of benefit performances. And didn't I read somewhere that you do a lot of work on behalf of animals?"

"Oh, I take in a stray now and then. As a matter of fact, I've got one now. A stray biker. I found him on the freeway near Fontana. Pressed against the chain-link fence. Stiff with terror."

"Yeah, I passed him on the way to the john. He was still stiff."

She glanced off up the hall. "Then I guess I'd better get back to him. Before he starts to whimper." She strode off up the hall.

I dropped to the sofa next to Sharlene, exhausted. "She's really something, isn't she?" I said.

"Yeah. She's great," Sharlene said, but she sounded bleak.

"So, anyway," I said, matching her tone.

"It *was* self-defense. You *were* defending me."

"That's right. I'm going to be cited for heroism."

"There *were* witnesses."

"Most of those witnesss hate my guts, Sharlene."

"What do you mean?"

I didn't want to go into it. "I just don't think we can depend on their account. The fact is, I'm the one who showed up with a gun. That tends to make me look bad."

She thought about that for a minute. "They're probably going to take a hard look at Dennis now."

"I'm sure of it."

"If they find the bullet in his body, it'll be just our word that I was even locked in. They might not believe us now."

"I'm not optimistic about any of it." I rubbed her arm.

"Why don't we just get the fuck out of the country?"

"You may be onto something."

"Louise says we can stay at her house in Mazatlán for as long as we want."

"Whoa. No way, baby. Not Mexico."

"You got a better idea?"

"Anyplace but Mexico. France."

"France?"

"Sure, why not? I'll get a job at a Paris oldies station, spinning Edith Piaf discs. And you can become the Jerry Lewis of rock and roll."

"Right. I can sing 'Love Me Tonight' wearing false buck teeth. No, France sucks. It's picturesque but the people are all stuck up. Except Catherine Deneuve, she's okay. Scott, this house in Mazatlán sounds great. What's wrong with Mexico, anyway?"

"Nothing per se. But trying to reach the border is the ultimate kiss of doom. Don't you know anything about film noir?"

"Film what?"

"Trust me. Fugitive couples who make a run for the border invariably get mowed down at a roadblock. They die in each other's arms, Sharlene. If they're lucky, an insipid priest reaches down from the clouds and helps them up to heaven."

She looked incredulous. "I have no idea what you're talking about. Look, what do you want to do, turn yourself in? I hear county jail's a real pajama party."

"It is. They listen to old Leslie Gore records and fuck each other in the butt." I sighed. "I've got about twenty dollars in my wallet. What are we going to live on?"

She held up her hand, flashing the ring.

"Sharlene, you couldn't. Not your wedding ring."

She laughed. "This ought to keep us in tostadas for a while."

"But what about the sentimental value?"

"Are you kidding?" She twisted it off her finger. "I hate this fucking thing. I only wore it 'cause he made me. Once I threatened to flush it down the toilet. He said if I did he'd cut off my toes and flush them down too."

"He sure was a character, wasn't he?" I took the ring from her and examined it under the lamp. "How many carats?"

"Seventeen-point-nineteen."

I whistled.

"It's flawless. We can sell it in Mexico and live for years." She took it back from me. "Now"—she did a dementedly coy little voice—"where can I put this where it'll be safe?"

I laughed. "It might not be too safe there. Those Mexican matrons with the latex gloves don't fool around."

"I thought they only searched people coming back to the U.S."

I rubbed her leg with mine. "I think a lot of people would invent any excuse to search you." I noticed that her ankle was bare. "Where's your anklet?"

"I don't know. I lost it somewhere." She put the ring in my hand. "Maybe you'd better hold on to this."

"I wonder where *I* should hide it."

"Please. Don't get gross."

"You're right. It's been a tasteful evening so far. No need to spoil it now." I put my arm around her. She leaned against my chest. "So what will we do when the money runs out?" I said.

"By that time I should have my share of the estate. They have to give me half, no matter what's in his will. That's California law."

"They might want to ask you a few questions, Sharlene, before they make a disbursement."

"With what we get from the ring we can hire some Century City lawyer to cut through all that."

"Lawyers have a habit of cutting very slowly. Oh well, if worse comes to worst I can always get a job in Ensenada stuffing the horseshit in the tuck and roll. It's dirty work but it's honest."

"They've got radio stations down there that reach back to L.A."

"That's true. There's one that drives the FCC crazy. Pumps out a hundred thousand watts, blows the beautiful music station right off the air. Some schmuck's floating down the freeway in his Cordoba to a violin version of 'Feelings,' when suddenly FOOM! It's the Angry Samoans screaming 'You Stupid Asshole.' "

"So," she said softly, "there you go."

"What about you? Can you sing 'Love Me Tonight' in Spanish?"

"I know 'Guantanamera.' "

"Great. You can play the Hilton in Managua."

"Why not? I'll become a kind of Marxist Suzanne Somers. Have a bunch of Cuban soldiers carry me in on their shoulders."

We laughed.

"If worse comes to worst," I said, "I can always become a gigolo in Acapulco—"

"Maybe if you get your eyes done."

"And you can write a best-seller about your life as a prisoner in Malibu."

"Yeah, right. A new genre. Rock gothic."

We laughed again. I was happy we were laughing at all.

We watched the cable news sation for a while; it was too late for the local news. There were reports on the L.A. fires but they were general and hours old. There wouldn't be anything on the reunion till morning.

Louise came back out long enough to ask us if we were hungry—we weren't—and show us to what she called the Aladdin Room. There were no slot machines or black velvet portraits of Wayne Newton, but there might as well have been. It was as garish as any Jon Hall/Maria Montez set. I lowered the pink and blue lights.

While Sharlene took a shower I padded off to the kitchen to get a beer. Passing Louise's bedroom on the way back, I saw her in bed with her young friend. He was holding her from behind, a devil tattoo on his bicep. I couldn't see his face but for a second I was jolted, because he seemed to be crying. Louise patted his hand, as if to comfort him.

He probably just had a cold. My mind was still so distorted I didn't know what was going on.

Sharlene and I lay together naked on the canopied bed, lightly holding each other, talking for hours. For a while we were insulated; the possibility of a future together began to seem quite real. I *could* get a job at one of the Mexican radio stations. The notoriety that was imminent might even work in my favor. With the money from the ring we could pay off the authorities, and avoid extradition forever. Sharlene could record again, on her own. She could sing her own songs, choose her producer, or produce herself, and choose the musicians she wanted to work with. I could see her taking charge of her own career, emerging finally strong and assured. I knew that was in her. She was strong. She'd survived so far.

"You know I wrote a song for you on Catalina," she said at one point.

"Really? When?"

"I guess it was Sunday morning. When you went to the store. I was going to surprise you with it. I worked on it some more that Monday, right before I left. I think it was pretty good."

"Can you sing it for me now? What's the tempo? I'll slap my knee in time."

She laughed and shook her head. "I don't remember how it goes now. I left the lyrics at the house."

"Jeez, Sharlene. I must have really meant a lot to you. What was it called? 'Dear Vomit Bag'?"

"No," she said softly, putting her fingers to my lips. Then she kissed me.

We made love, gently and tenderly at first. She winced when I brushed her bruised cheek.

"Sorry," I said, and kissed her forehead.

She kissed me hard on the mouth. "Come on," she said. "Really fuck me now."

I grinned and leaned back against the upholstered headboard, my big-block 427 rumbling as she grabbed my vibrating stickshift. I floored her, cupping her Cadillac breasts as we roared full-throttle down the slick highway. Her brakes squealed as we smashed through the detour sign and hurtled off the end of the half-finished bridge. Her engine screamed as we flew through the air and I blew my transmission. We hit the water hard and sank like two tons of steel, rolling up the power windows just in time.

16

I got up around six, pulled on my laundered white Levi's, and padded off to take a leak. Stepping from the bathroom, I heard a blast of music—Junior Walker and the All Stars' "I'm a Roadrunner"—coming from the patio. It was hard to believe anyone else could be up at this hour but I crossed the hall to the arched patio door and saw Louise doing stretching exercises by the leaf-filled pool. She wore blue panties and bright red lipstick, that was all.

"Hi, sex machine," she said when she saw me.

"Good morning."

She broke into a languid dance, snapping her fingers to the beat. Her breasts shimmered.

"Where's your friend?" I said.

"Paul? Oh, I've got him chained to the bedpost. Don't worry. The chain won't reach this far."

"You're wearing panties. What's the occasion?"

"It's Bo Diddley's birthday."

She was perspiring heavily in the morning heat. The hard sunlight made her svelte body glisten like satin. Her panties were drenched with sweat.

"I'll give you this pair when you go," she said. "As a souvenir."

"Might be a life-saver. If I break down in the desert, and I'm dying of thirst, I can wring 'em out over my mouth."

She winced, pretending to be shocked. "Who taught you that kind of talk?"

"You did. Twenty years ago."

"Twenty years ago? Weren't you listening to Petula Clark back then?"

"No way, baby. In fact, I was picking up on you when you were still a Honeypot back in 1961. There was nothing on the white stations then. Just a bunch of Philadelphia wop-pop. Real stick-your-finger-down-your-throat time. I used to crawl under the covers with a flashlight and tune in KGFJ. I felt like a member of the French Resistance with a secret shortwave. One wrong yowl and my dad was liable to kick the door in and rip off my dick."

She laughed. The tape segued to Otis Redding and Carla Thomas singing "Tramp." A bead of sweat dripped from her nipple. "Those were the days," she said.

"I always thought it was a real shame when all those slick, cleaned-up Motown groups came along and stole your thunder. I mean, let's face it, the Supremes were to the Honeypots what Pat Boone was to Little Richard."

She danced along the edge of the pool. "I know. I was bitter about it myself at the time."

"You came back with a vengeance, though. I still remember the first time I heard 'Squat on It' when you went solo in sixty-three. I couldn't believe my ears. I still don't know how you got that song past the censors. I guess you did slur some of the raunchier lines."

She danced back to me. "I had something in my mouth. I think it might have been a Milky Way. I remember one thing." She snapped her fingers. "It was big and fat and sticky."

"To be frank, the first time I heard that song I was pounding my pud. One of my favorite pastimes in those days—"

"Those days?

"It was a grim period. My dad liked to sing along with Mitch."

"And you liked to beat it to Louise. What a naughty boy you must have been." She did a mean little grind. Only

her bemused smile kept it from becoming totally obscene.

"That was my favorite of all your periods, though, the
early sixties, when you were still basically into R & B. To
be honest, you got just a tad trashy during the psychedelic
era."

"Yes, I know. Bad management. Never listen to a fifty-
year-old lawyer in love beads."

" 'Thigh-High Vinyl Boots (People, They're a Gas)' *is*
something of a kitsch classic."

"I know. It's embarrassing, isn't it? And I was so sincere at
the time."

"I did like the heavy-metal stuff you did in England
around the turn of the decade. You could be *brutal!* Your
version of 'Inna-Gadda-Da Vida' makes Iron Butterfly sound
like the New Christy Minstrels."

"Let's not talk about minstrels, okay?"

The tape changed to Aretha Franklin's "Respect." She
moved up to me, doing a shimmy.

"Come on, Scott. Let's see if you can shake it."

A challenge. I began to dance, pretending it was midnight
in a smoky club and I was drunk. I had to show her I was no
white klutz.

"Your Led Zeppelin covers were pretty horrendous too,"
I said, doing a dirty hully gully. "The first time I heard
'Trampled Under Foot' I thought somebody'd set off a string
of firecrackers in my jockstrap."

"I see you're not wearing one of those this morning."

I grinned. So did my cock. Her eyes were goosing me.
This was jive, but serious jive.

"Even your Euro-disco period wasn't half-bad," I said,
doing a modified cool jerk. "You beat Donna Summer to
the punch by a good year. I mean, *Rieperbahn Fever* in
seventy-five was extremely prophetic. If somebody had to do
a disco version of 'Suspicious Minds,' better you than Rod
Stewart."

"That single put my third husband through Harvard."

"Your new-wave period was mercifully brief. Just that cover of 'Sex Dwarf,' as I recall."

"I changed managers again after that. Never trust a lawyer with rings in his tits."

"This is really your time again, though. At least you're basically doing R & B again, even if it is the slick stuff."

"I like slick stuff. Don't you?"

She bumped her crotch dangerously close to mine.

"I'd rather hear you sing 'Squat on It.' "

"Sing it?" she said. "Or do it?"

Whoa. This was no jive at all. I tried thinking of Pat Boone, hoping my erection would subside. I pictured him all right. But he was grinning like a crazed fiend.

"But the high point of your career—thus far, of course— I mean the true lacerating, ultimate moment, was 'Tidal Wave of Flame.' "

She scowled and snapped her fingers hard. "Please. I don't even like to think about that song."

"But, Louise, you have to know it may well be the single greatest moment in the history of rock."

"Oh, I know that's what all the rock critics say. The intellectuals. The ones who like to quote William Blake when they talk about my body. But they're so silly. It was only rock and roll."

"It was far more than that and you know it, Louise. The way you scream at the climax is a true moment of spiritual/ erotic catharsis—"

"I feel like screamin' like that right now," she said, as the music changed to Marvin Gaye's "Let's Get It On."

"Oh yeah? Why's that?"

She slipped her arms around me, lightly, softly now. "Because you're bein' such a tease."

I slipped my hands down her smooth, sweaty back as she moved against me. My cock was a lead pipe and her crotch was a magnet. I kept us dancing.

"This has always been one of my fantasies, Louise. To dance with you . . ."

Her nipples were hard against my chest. "This has always been one of mine," she said, and kissed me lightly on the mouth.

"Scott?" We heard Sharlene's voice calling from back in the house.

For a moment I couldn't move. Then Louise smiled, and laughed as if to indicate she'd known all along that nothing was really going on, that it had just been play. She pulled away.

"Oh, there you are," Sharlene said as she came to the door. "What's going on?"

"Not much," I said. "Louise was just showing me a few dance steps."

"Oh yeah?" She smiled, but I saw that she noticed the bulge in my denims. "Like what? The dry hump?"

"She provoked me, Sharlene. Look at her. I know I'm old-fashioned, but bare tits still excite me. I can't help it."

"This guy came on to me, Sharlene," Louise said. "With a lot of dirty talk. Telling me how he used to beat his meat to my old forty-five's."

"She was trying to rape me. I want to talk to a sympathetic cop."

"He was asking for it. Look at how he's dressed."

Sharlene checked us both out. "I think you're both full of shit," she finally said. Then she smiled again.

As we walked back to the bedroom, she said, "I guess I should've warned you about Louise."

"Really. I'm not used to being treated so cheaply."

She gave me a funny look out of the corner of her eye. "Don't press your luck," she said.

A short time later we put on our traveling disguises. Sharlene slipped into an aqua polyester pantsuit with gold-thread embroidery that made her look like a dumpy mid-seventies housewife. But the heavy makeup she put on to hide her bruises made her look like a fierce Vegas whore.

I didn't look too sharp myself in a slinky polyester body-shirt not unlike Bill Holtner's and a tight pair of linty black Dacron slacks. I tried to imagine I could pass for some sort of jazzy neo-bohemian, a romantically lowlife Tom Waits type or something. But I just looked like a sleazy Dacron dork from Gardena.

I wrapped Sharlene's ring in a Kleenex and stuck it in my pants pocket, where it rubbed against my balls.

Paul brought breakfast out to the patio, a platter of scrambled eggs and sweet rolls. I was jolted when I got a good look at him. One side of his face was severely burn-scarred, a mask of pink-and-yellow potato-chip skin. The other side was handsome.

We were alone at one point—I could see Sharlene and Louise in the den in a girl-talk huddle—when he said, "Smashed up my bike."

"I beg your pardon?"

"My face," he said. "Most people wonder. Gas tank blew up."

I didn't know what to say. I looked off to the den, where the girl talk seemed to have turned serious. Reacting to something Sharlene had just said, Louise covered her mouth. In shock? I wondered what could shock Louise.

"Louise is all right, though," he said. "She's gonna pay for the plastic surgery. I know what you're thinking, but I love her, man. She's some woman."

I saw that there were tears in his eyes.

Then Sharlene screamed. "Oh my god, no!"

I ran into the den, where she was kicking the sofa in a fit of rage. "That goddamn fuck! God damn him. Goddammit!"

"What is it?" I said, and saw what was on the big screen TV: a shot of the Contrelle house, the Romanoid columns and statues blackened, but the Egyptoid house itself intact.

"They found Dennis," Louise said, and you could almost say she looked pale. "He's alive."

"What?"

"God damn him! That fuck!" Sharlene picked up an ashtray to throw at the screen. I stopped her, and shushed her so we could hear.

"—found by his bodyguard and rushed to St. John's Hospital in Santa Monica, where he is in fair condition—"

"Fair condition? His brains were all over the floor." But then I realized: not his brains. The dogs'.

"—after allegedly shooting Contrelle, Cochran then appeared at his high-school reunion—"

"*What?* After *I* shot him?"

"—where, according to witnesses, William Holtner, a former classmate and an officer with the Redondo Beach Police Department, attempted to disarm the suspect when he brandished the gun. An altercation ensued, Sharlene Contrelle entering the fray. It was then that Cochran allegedly shot Holtner, critically wounding the off-duty policeman, who's something of a local hero in the South Bay—"

My breath was knocked out. "This is fucked up. This sucks. This blows dead dogs."

Sharlene was stunned too. "They probably just assumed you shot Dennis. He's probably still unconscious and hasn't been able to tell them what happened yet."

"I don't think we can count on him, Shar."

My old schoolmate Steve's florid face filled the screen, a microphone at his mouth. "I knew Scott was crazy the minute I saw him. He had that look. I think he was just going to start shooting at random." He got teary. "Bill's a great guy. He saved a lot of lives."

"You fuck, you rancid fuck," I was thinking out loud. "I *should've* just started shooting. Half the guys in that room had it coming. They all fucked her, whoever she was. They all killed her. They all got away with it. With all of it."

Louise stared at me. She definitely looked pale. Sharlene

was staring at me too, wondering what the hell I was talking about, and afraid to ask. I was afraid to tell her, though I wasn't exactly sure why.

"We'll get it cleared up," Sharlene said, which seemed ludicrous.

"Yeah, you can write a long letter to the L.A. *Times* once we're in Mexico," I said, as a new reporter described our freeway chase.

"I will," she said, watching the injured cops being removed from their car on the freeway shoulder. "You don't have to take the blame for what I did. I don't regret it. I just can't believe he's still alive." She was blank now. "I just can't believe it. I thought I was finally free."

I put my arms around her. "You are."

I saw her exchange a funny look with Louise, who had her fingers pressed to her lips as if to seal them. From the doorway Paul shook his head. "Shit city," he said.

A while later I followed Louise out to the five-car Bagdad garage.

"Anything but the Mercedes," she said. "I don't think I could take it if that one got riddled with lead."

I couldn't blame her. It was an immaculate pale blue '56 Gullwing. Next to it was a '64 Jaguar XKE, also pristine. It was violet.

"This one's nondescript." I ran my hand over the pricklike hood of the Jag.

"It has a bad habit of dying in the fast lane."

"Frankly, I may never take the freeway again."

The last car was a gutted '68 Firebird convertible, metallic green, the white top shredded.

"That one might be your best bet," Louise said. "I don't think he's ever coming back for it. He went back to Des Moines. To recuperate."

"Does it still run?"

Barely. It had a full tank of gas, but the battery was dead,

and the oil hadn't been changed since the fall of Saigon.
Paul gave me a jump off the Mercedes, and the engine
coughed to life in clouds of black exhaust. I pulled around
to the front of the house, threw it in Park, and got out to
pull down the top, the engine idling roughly.

Louise watched from the steps. I went up to her. "What
were you and Sharlene talking about before the news came
on?"

"*You*," she said seamlessly. "What else could possibly interest us?"

"I'm serious."

"So am I." She reached under my shirt. "She told all
about what a great lover you are. Till I got so wet I had to
ask her to stop."

I knew it was pointless to press it. "Look, Louise, I really
appreciate your help."

"I'd do anything for Sharlene," she said, and for once she
was serious. "I love her dearly."

"I know."

She took my arm. "I hope you're gonna treat her right."

"I'll do my best." I thought of the Boy Scout pledge.

"You gotta do your *very* best. You know, she needs a lotta
love."

I felt a soul rap coming on.

"I gotta lotta love to give," I said, feeling very white.

"And when I say love, I mean love. I don't just mean the
sex part, though God knows she needs that too. But what
she really needs is tenderness. She needs a guy who's tough
and strong, but who's got a gentle side too."

"That's me."

"And she needs a man who's patient. She'll probably get a
little crazy now and then. You know, Dennis messed her up
real bad." She hesitated, editing herself. "She needs love because she's been lonely a long, long time. *I* know. She's got
a lotta love to give too. A whole lifetime's worth, stored up."

"I love her. I don't know what else to tell you."

"Well, I *know* she loves you." She smiled. "Shit, I'd say you got it made."

"Yeah, I'm sure we'll live happily ever after. If we don't get our brains blown out between here and San Diego. Louise, listen, I know this morning was a little weird, but—"

"Weird?" Her sardonic attitude returned. "In what way was that?"

"I just mean if I wanted to die with a smile on my face, I know who I'd come to."

She sighed. "Oh my. You white boys have such strange fantasies." She started unbuttoning my shirt. "I'll let you in on a little secret. Some days, being the sexiest black woman in America is just plain hard work." She slipped her hands up over my bare sweaty back. "But then, we've all gotta make a living."

I smiled. And she gave me a deep, engulfing kiss. I didn't exactly resist—until I saw Sharlene coming out. Though Louise and I were still pressed together, Sharlene seemed preoccupied and unconcerned.

"Are we ready?" she said.

I stopped at a gas station to put air in the tires, then headed for the Harbor Freeway. We had to go up to Hollywood first so I could stop by my bank and get some cash from the machine. As I got over for the on-ramp, Sharlene said, "Oh Christ, no. You're not."

After last night I really couldn't blame her. I took Vermont north instead.

"We're going to have to get on the freeway eventually," I told her. "PCH turns into a freeway near Oceanside. There's no other way to get to Mexico."

"There has to be. Scott, I really can't handle the freeway. I'll freak out, I mean it."

I didn't argue. But I was exasperated. If we really avoided all freeways, it was going to take us forever.

Sharlene smoked silenty, the hot wind tossing her hair, morose behind her dark glasses.

We'd have listened to the news but there wasn't any radio, just a hole and loose wires. The sun was broiling, the temperature in the high nineties. By the time we took a left on Sunset, we were stuck to the scalding vinyl seats in drenched Dacron.

"I just don't see how he survived," Sharlene said as we shot past the Sunset/Vine tower. I rubbed my brow like a movie star at a stoplight, fearing somebody from the station might be walking down the street.

"Where'd you hit him?"

"I don't even know. I just pointed the gun and pulled the trigger, just trying to get all three of 'em. Including the dogs, I mean."

"Yeah, it's funny. I like pets as a rule. I cried my eyes out over *Lassie Come Home.* But for some reason I never really felt a thing for those dogs."

The engine wheezed as I gave it gas. I was beginning to wonder if it would make it to Mexico.

"This *does* change things, though," Sharlene said.

"What?"

"Dennis being alive."

I waited for more, but she said nothing. "Don't tell me. You want to go back to him."

"Are you kidding?"

"I can shoot you on out to the house if you want. It's a beautiful day for a drive up the coast."

"Don't you know I'd rather die first?" She was serious, but when she realized how melodramatic it had sounded, she laughed a little, as if to show she hadn't lost her healthy sense of humor. I laughed a little too, to show the same thing. We were both frazzled. We should have tried to get some sleep.

My hand kept reaching for the radio that wasn't there. I needed something badly to cancel out my thoughts.

Inevitably she asked the question: "What did you mean at Louise's? About some girl being killed?"

"Oh, it's just something that happened a long time ago. A girl got raped and killed at the beach when I was in high school."

"A girl you knew?"

"No, I didn't know her. Apparently nobody really knew her."

She stared at me. Certainly she could tell I was lying my brains out by omission. But I just wasn't up to telling her the Cheryl Rampton story, not right now. I'd tell her later, at a leisurely, indulgent pace, when we were both drunk on a breezy Mazatlán veranda.

Dammit, I wanted to turn up the radio and shout: "Hey, my favorite song!" even if it had been "Mandy."

"So why were you and Norrine dressed like that last night? And your haircut—"

"Check it out," I said as we passed the Chateau Marmont. "Hey, Belush! My man!"

"Scott, answer my question."

"Sharlene, quit badgering me. My nerves are shot and there's something seriously wrong with this car." Going up a light rise, the engine lugged and almost died.

"I'm not badgering you. I'm just curious. I mean, the way she looked especially—"

"It was nostalgia, that's all. I thought it might be fun. You know me, anything for a laugh."

"It's just that in a way, she looked like me. I mean, the way I looked back then."

I felt relief. So that's all it was. She thought I'd been making fun of her old image.

"Shar, *everybody* looked like you back then. There was even a guy on our football team who looked like you—"

"Actually, she was more pre-Stingrays. Dennis would never have let *me* be caught dead in a trashy little outfit like that—"

"Shar, those happened to be her best clothes—"

"I mean that tough-slut look is pure Angel. That's what knocked me for a loop when I first saw her, you know, when we caught up with her on PCH. For a second I thought it was Angel, running from the fire." The laugh that came from her now was tinged with hysteria.

I felt as if I'd just driven off a bridge. "What are you talking about?"

"What do you mean?"

"*You're* Angel."

"*Me?*"

Oh fuck, no. "Shar, I saw your picture up in the garage bedroom. You'd signed it 'Angel'—"

"You mean the Observatory picture? Where James Dean had the—" She let out a guffaw. "*That's* not a picture of me!" Sarcasm twisted her voice now. "Are you telling me he took you up there and he didn't tell you all about Angel? What did you guys do up there anyway, just listen to his oldies collection?"

"What are you saying, that there was some other girl?"

"Some other girl! Ha! Yeah, right! You could *say* that. Yeah, there was some other girl. Only the *love* of his life." She said *love* the way most people would say *slime*.

"Somebody he knew before you—" My breath was punched out.

"Yeah. Before me. Since me. Now, then, and forever. His eternal, undying *love*."

Her personality change scared me almost as much as what she was saying. She was evil now, vicious and smirking.

"Well, if *you* don't know about *Angel*, then *you* don't know *anything*, *do* you? He never gave a flying fuck about me! You know what he told me the first night we met? He said I reminded him of a girl he once knew. I thought it was just some bullshit pickup line. You know something? I should have listened. He wasn't lying. *That's* what the Stingrays were all about! He modeled everything about me after her. The clothes, the hairstyle, the whole look. I didn't know what he was doing. I thought he was doing it for me. I was fourteen! What the fuck did I know? The songs—everything he ever wrote, it was all aimed at her. He was still in love with *her*. 'Love Me Tonight'—that wasn't to me, like everybody thought. That was to her. I was just a *thing*, a little doll, a little fucking Angel doll that he moved around the stage and got to act out his sick little fantasy. When he got tired of it, when he'd said all he cared to say, he didn't need me anymore. I was nothing, I didn't even exist. The guys were lucky. They got away. Even Bobby—" Her voice broke. "*But I married him!* That's how stupid I was. I thought he was doing it all for me. I thought he was doing it because he loved *me!* And I fucking adored him!" Tears ran down her cheeks. "It broke my heart when I found out the truth. It broke my heart and it fucking killed me! *That's* what Dennis is all about! It's all Angel, everything, all of it! Angel!" She laughed harshly. "She must have been one hell of a fuck."

We were still on the Strip, but I was barely conscious of my surroundings. Sweat dripped into my eyes. I was so distracted I could have had a wreck at any moment. "She's dead?"

"Oh yeah. She's dead, all right." The rage turned into a cold toughness now. "There was a crash. That's what's funny about it, if you like black humor. 'Angel on the Highway' came first, of course, over a year before they even met. He gave her the nickname 'Angel' after his first big hit. The kiss of death, you might say. It was the endless summer of sixty-four and he was building the Malibu house. Their dreamhouse and all that. So romantic. One night they drove out to check on the progress but it started to rain. On the way back Dennis took a turn too fast, and the pavement was slick and he shot off the road. He crashed down the cliff and smashed into the rocks and Angel was killed, sob-sob. Not quite like the song. I mean, she didn't go back for her highschool ring. Knowing her, she was probably copping his joint and he stepped on the gas as he came. It was all a big joke, that's the sad part about it. She didn't love him, you don't have to be a genius to read *that* between the lines. He was her meal ticket, that's all. She had no talent, she couldn't sing, act, nothing. He only knew her for a couple of months. All she had was her cunt. She was nothing, believe me. Just some little lowlife slut from Lomita."

I felt the engine die, but it didn't seem to matter. The immediate physical world was unreal. Without giving it much thought, I turned through a yellow light at San Vicente, coasting to a stop in the gas station across from the Whisky. I think I was laughing softly to myself.

"Yeah, Cheryl," I said. "Wasn't that her real name? Cheryl Rampton?"

I watched Sharlene start to disintegrate and knew there was nothing I could do to stop it. A confused, terrified little girl took the place of the hard bitch. "What? What are you . . . *What?*"

"I knew her before she met Dennis. We went to high school together. She was the girl I thought had been raped and killed at the beach. For twenty years I thought that's what had happened to her. It wasn't till last night that I—"

She covered her ears. "I don't want to hear this."

"I loved her, too, Shar. She was very special—"

She screamed to drown me out.

"Shar, listen—" I touched her arm and she flailed at me, still screaming. I threw up my arms to shield my face. If she'd had a weapon then I'm sure she would have killed me. If it had been a knife she would have kept stabbing me long after I was dead. Finally she bolted from the car.

She took off running up the sidewalk. In her cheap clothes and heavy makeup she looked like a whore escaping the wrath of her pimp. A gas-station attendant shouted at me as I took off after her. She saw me coming and cut across the street. If there hadn't been a lull in traffic she would certainly have been hit. Before I could cross after her, more cars came. I lost sight of her as she rounded the turn by Tower Records on the opposite side of the street. Finally I crossed and ran up the sidewalk, but she was gone. Then I heard her scream.

I looked up and saw a life-size poster of her in the Tower Records window, a promo picture for "Premature Burial." She towered over me, arms crossed, feet spread, in black T-shirt and jeans, hair ratted high, a mint-condition Sting-ray with glaring blue eyes. Another scream, like burning brakes. She was inside the store.

I ran around to the entrance but I couldn't get in. The place was packed with kids there to see some group making a public appearance. I tried to push my way through as she screamed again. I saw her, far back in the crowd, trapped. The band's record was blasting from the overhead speakers, a synthesized remake of "Don't Worry, Baby." The young blond singer looked stunned. He'd recognized Shar. Other people were laughing, though—nervous, excited laughter. Some crazy lady, some garish whore, was really pulling out the stops.

I pushed through the crowd, trying to get to her. I stepped on feet, and elbowed a girl who snarled, "Hey, watch it!" Sharlene was totally berserk now, clawing her way through the crowd like an animal with its foot in a trap. Briefly we made eye contact, but I don't think she recognized me. She was gone. Screaming. Shattering, piercing, shredding screams. In a horrible way, it was just like the climax of her song. She was buried alive in a marketplace mob, drowning in a sea of hostile young faces, suffocating in a quicksand of unhinged agoraphobic terror. She gasped for breath and screamed again, her hair flying as she whirled and slammed through the cringing crowd.

I almost caught her in the oldies section. My fingers touched her shoulder, but she flailed wildly and clawed through the crowd toward the plate-glass windows in the front of the store.

She wouldn't. But she did. She slammed into the window with her poster on it, back-lit in reverse by the sun, and the glass came down in a lacerating crash. People groaned in that sickened way they do when somebody jumps off a ledge. She hit the sidewalk a few feet below.

By the time I reached the window there were sirens in the street, cop cars pulling up. I couldn't see Sharlene over all the heads, but I saw a line of blood run down a crack in the sidewalk. Cops were jumping from their cars and running over. I called her name and one of the cops looked up, recognizing me. His hand went to his gun. The music was still blasting "Don't Worry, Baby" as I dug a path back through the crowd.

17

Sharlene recovered. She'd suffered multiple lacerations and spent the next five days at Cedars. The D.A. delayed filing charges against her, pending a full investigation.

Dennis recovered too, from his "superficial scalp wound." He was released two days before Sharlene. When she finally stepped into the glare of the Minicam lights, he was gripping her arm. A new squad of professional bodyguards ran interference as Dennis steered his troubled wife through the press. She wore lollipop shades, a butterfly bandage on her forehead, and looked drugged. She ignored the reporters' questions as her long-suffering husband guided her to the Cadillac, Big Willy at the wheel. Then the car swept away, taking the tragic couple back to their violated beachfront Shangri La.

Bill Holtner remained hospitalized in stable condition. His face was going to require extensive restorative surgery before he could show it in a singles bar again, but miraculously the doctors had managed to save his tongue. He was the object of a national outpouring of sympathy. It would be some time before he could actually speak again, but when the President called, he held the receiver and grunted. He also held up a blackboard on which he had printed: God Bless You All. If he'd been running for office he would have won in a landslide.

I was elected sociopath of the year. Former classmates,

witnesses to the horror in Redondo Beach, described me as having always been "unstable." An anonymous source characterized me as a "deceptively charming but deeply enraged macho anachronism, a disturbed misogynist in the guise of a ladies' man." (This could only have been Lynn.)

I was saddened, but not really surprised, when Neal turned on me as well. "In retrospect you could see it coming," he told TV reporters upon his return from New York. "The last time I saw Scott he was joking about mass murder." He shook his head gravely. "You know, people don't joke."

The Contrelle attorney, a debonair Century City sleaze, described how I'd become "obsessed" with Sharlene, how I'd manipulated myself into Contrelle's favor simply as a ruse to gain physical proximity to his fragile wife. Then, even after my intentions were revealed, I had continued to "hound" and "stalk" the poor woman, despite Dennis' attempts to rationally dissuade me. Finally, on the night of the fire, I'd broken into the Malibu house, clearly intent on sexually assaulting the object of my fixation. Dennis had acted as any brave husband would've, but I'd gotten the gun away from him. Then, after shooting him and gratuitously killing his pets, I'd kidnapped his terrified wife. Emotionally troubled to begin with, Mrs. Contrelle saw no alternative but to accompany me on the next leg of my crime spree, for fear she would share her husband's fate. By the time we reached Redondo Beach, her capacity was diminished and she was under my evil spell. How else to explain the weird twist of psychology (that is not uncommon in terrorist situations) whereby she actually appeared at the reunion to take my side? Clearly she had come to believe that her own continuing survival depended on mine. Was this so dissimilar to the twisted thinking that caused Patty Hearst to rob a bank on behalf of her captors, when, according to unsophisticated logic, she might just as easily have turned her weapon on them? I think not, your Honor. In summation, ladies and housewives of the jury, hasn't this poor endlessly victimized woman suffered enough?

I couldn't blame her, exactly, if she went along with that, not if it would keep her out of prison. I couldn't see that she had much choice now that she was back there with him. I couldn't really blame her for hating me either, for thinking I'd only loved her because she looked like Cheryl. And I wondered myself if that had really been the case.

I had a lot of time to think about it. I had come back to the house on Catalina—at first just because I was exhausted and needed a safe place to sleep. I had reached the island about six hours after Tower Records, entered the house, and collapsed on the brass bed. Only to jump up yelling in shock as my arm touched something cold on the sheet. But it wasn't a slug or a snake, as I'd imagined. It was Sharlene's silver anklet, left the weekend we'd spent here.

I looked at it closely under the lamp and saw a tiny indentation in the clasp. I'd made it myself, twenty years before, opening the clasp with my teeth the day I'd given the anklet to Cheryl for her seventeenth birthday. I gibbered to myself for some time about this before I finally fell asleep.

In fact, I gibbered to myself in general for several days. I felt burned out, lobotomized, running on empty with a cracked block. I couldn't think clearly about what had happened. Or didn't want to.

I vegetated on the sofa, watching MTV, the sound barely audible, the endless pictures washing over me, *The Boys of Summer, Cruel Summer, Suddenly, Last Summer.*

Against that background, as my mind cooled off, I began to try to figure out what had happened. In a way it was a relief to understand now that I had not simply projected my own feelings about Cheryl into the Stingrays' music, that the resemblance between Cheryl and Sharlene had never been coincidental. It had always been deliberate, obsessively cultivated and emphasized. Dennis had known Cheryl, he had loved her, and he had created the Stingrays as a living

memorial. Perhaps on some level I'd always known that was
the case, that it had to be so, though rationally it made no
sense, it was impossible, when I believed Cheryl had died
that night at the beach. But then, I'd never been totally
convinced of that. The Stingrays' music, capturing some
ineffable spiritual essence of Cheryl, evoking her with an
uncanny specificity, had always been the seemingly irrational proof that she had lived.

How *had* she lived, how had she and Dennis met? I felt
like a film editor shown to a vault filled with rusty
CinemaScope cans, including outtakes and work prints and
fading Technicolor footage, and told to cut together a new,
logical, and definitive ending to the Cheryl Rampton film.

Where does she go the night of the gang rape? Who takes
her in? A Lomita girlfriend perhaps, giving her fresh clothes,
a few dollars, and a sympathetic Hollywood address.

For it must be in Hollywood that the meeting takes place,
as she makes a new life for herself in the seedy glitter-stucco
flatlands of that city, an evil mecca for runaways, for girls in
trouble, then as now.

Perhaps she gets a job as a waitress in, say, Barney's
Beanery, wearing a starched blue uniform that matches
her eyes. One look over his *Billboard* into those blue eyes
and Dennis forgets all about the blue-plate special. I want
you. With everything. To go.

Or maybe she's a manicurist by day, sharing an apartment
on Fountain with a couple of stews, by night a prototypal
British Invasion groupie in a Twiggy hairdo and op-art dress,
frugging along the Strip. One night in Gazzarris she spots
the handsome blond genius in wraparound shades leaning
bored against the bar. She watusis up to him and asks for a
light in a bad cockney accent to the strains of the Zombies'
"She's Not There."

There was another, much cheesier possibility, but given
her age, her beauty, the fear and bitterness she must have
felt, it also made the most sense. The moment I considered

it, the rest fell into place, moving through my mind with a flawless luminosity, Cheryl's last wide-screen summer restored.

She runs along the night shoreline, her legs bare in the moonlight, her pink blouse torn, waves crashing as she disappears into the Redondo mist. Fade out.

Fade in. Perhaps a week later we see her through the neon-reflecting plate glass of Canter's Delicatessen in Hollywood, counting out the last of her change for a jellyroll, oblivious to Artie at the counter beside her as he tries to look down the front of her blouse. Artie of the gold jewelry, of the open shirt and hairy chest. Artie of the ingratiating personality and cheap toupee. Artie, who cracks a joke now, eliciting a tentative smile from Cheryl. Is she new in town, does she need a place to crash?

Artie fucks her that night on the round bed in his highrise Sunset Strip apartment. They smoke cigarettes over the lights of L.A. as he speaks of his music-business connections, a world of parties and marijuana, the famous people he claims to know. He speaks of introducing her around.

Which he does. Because Artie is a pimp. And she becomes a high-class whore. That is, she never sees the money. Artie takes care of everything, feeding her, providing a bed, buying her nice new clothes for the parties he takes her to. And she does fuck a famous name or two, as well as many middle-aged executives with wedding rings and names like Ralph and George.

One afternoon Artie drives her into Echo Park to get an abortion. In the run-down bungalow living room he's opening up a *Playboy* centerfold when there's a Mixmaster sound far back in the house, and he winces as Cheryl cries out.

Then comes the night at the Bel-Air party when she sees the handsome blond genius through the smoky din and catches his bashful glance. She approaches him and sets him at ease, and leaves with him in his glossy blue Sting

Ray, swooping down the curving roads. And she doesn't go back to Artie's again, not even to pick up her nice new clothes.

One thing is certain, she's with Dennis by mid-June for the Vectors' "Rincon" sessions at Sunrise Sound. Their eyes closed at the microphone, Mark and Gary hit high blissful notes, riding the shimmering multitrack wave of rapture in this song only ostensibly about surfing, as here in these sessions, in this moment, the true Contrelle Sound is born. Everything before has been clever imitation, the early Vectors his copy of the Beach Boys, the Beehives his version of the Shangri Las. But the age of derivation is over. The cerebral wunderkind has discovered sensuality. The genius is in love.

Beside him at the board Cheryl presses a Coke bottle to her wet cherry lips as his hand moves up her soft white thigh. Her sweet perfume intoxicating him, he steals a kiss as the music swells rhapsodically. Aroused, he squeezes his luscious cheap angel, his trash madonna, his succulent muse.

Now they make love on the bunk bed in the house in Hermosa—his parents recently shipped off to Florida—their small bodies drenched with orange sunset light, Cheryl's eyes hot with pleasure, his dazed with awe. Compulsively he kisses her, a man starved for kisses. "Angel," he whispers, lost in her. "Angel," he sighs as he comes hard and deep, as he never will again.

Now they laugh in the sun-drenched Hermosa kitchen, Cheryl making waffles in a skimpy bikini where his dowdy mother once stood. They swim naked in the small kidney-shaped pool. Make love on the patio, in the living room—where later he gives her a gorgeous and useless fur coat. Where he gives her flowers and records and jewelry, never coming home without a gift for his Angel. Where he leads her, with her eyes covered, to the front door. Now she can look and she squeals at what she sees. It's a Mustang, a new

Mustang convertible with a red pony interior, the car he will eventually pass on to Sharlene.

Now she has fun, in this summer of fun, soaring down the freeway, hot blood-red vinyl against her bare thighs, smoking and singing along to "Rincon" on the radio, squeezing every last thrill she can out of this summer of profane thrills and impending wrath.

For they have now entered their sun-drenched days of Methedrine and roses, their cobalt-blue nights of speed and romance. In a pastel Hermosa bathroom, a slim Big Willy injects Dennis in the shoulder. Reeling, Dennis watches through dilating pupils as Cheryl lowers her bikini bottom, Big Willy poking her just below the tan line in her perfect coy Coppertone butt.

Breathless with chemical elation, they float into the bedroom, dropping to the bunk bed in a brain-scorched kiss. His inhibitions seared away, Dennis spreads her ivory legs, gluing his mouth to her sweet, sticky cunt.

In such a state of pharmaceutical bliss they surge up the coast in the Sting Ray one bright enameled Sunday afternoon, squealing up to the half-finished house in gales of giddy laughter. Happily they step through the framework, yammering excitedly about their future, pausing frequently to kiss and caress. Eventually they settle into the concrete conversation pit, where Dennis pulls out a fat roll of joints. The hours slip away as they smoke the marijuana, so locked into one another they don't even notice the storm clouds rolling in, until they hear the thunder and the downpour comes. Loaded, disheveled, and giggling, they stumble back to the Sting Ray, drenched by the time they climb in.

Surging back down the slick highway, "Rincon" on the eight-track, the wipers slapping time, Dennis steals a cherry kiss after such an afternoon of stolen bliss. As their lips meet the music crests and the pavement drops away.

The rocks and roiling night sea come up at them, as if in a process shot. Safety glass shatters in a blinding barrage of glimmering crystals. Blue fiberglass cracks, the cockpit crumpling in around them like a trap. The music dies with a painful screech as Cheryl's neck snaps.

In the rain-spattered aftermath, Dennis lies slumped unconscious over the wheel, blood trickling from his head. Cheryl is thrown back on the seat beside him, blood matted in her beehive and on her pale broken neck. Waves crash through the shattered windshield, receding red with blood.

Now at dawn the rain has stopped as a fireman breaks Dennis' window, reaching in to feel his neck for a pulse. A final long shot of the blue wreck wedged in the rocks, the fire truck and sheriff's cars on the edge of the yellow bluff, the clear blue sky ready for a searing-red credit roll: after twenty years of mystification the authentic ending of the Cheryl Rampton film.

Imagining that ending, I felt a kind of sadness that was not really grief. How could I feel grief now, when I'd already imagined her death so many times, when I'd already grieved so long? It was right that her death seemed stylized now, remote and artificial. Cinematic. My sense of loss had become diffuse, permeating the form itself. By the end of the last shot the color dyes would always be turning, the yellow bluff becoming a muddy vermilion, the blue sky changing forever to a grating iridescent pink.

If the last reel of Cheryl's life had been a CinemaScope Technicolor movie, what came now was in grainy sixteen-millimeter color-reversal stock, culled from hundreds of hours of suppressed D.A. Pennebaker documentary footage, the fluid tracking movements of Cheryl's life replaced with the grittily hand-held realism of cinema verité.

It would begin with a shot of Dennis bandaged and sedated in his hospital bed after the crash, his skin tinged green under the flicker of fluorescent lights.

Now a close shot on Cheryl's fake California driver's license as the coroner removes it from her wet billfold. CHERYL HORTON it reads (her real father's last name), and her birthdate is given as 1946, adding a year to make her eighteen. But the ink has run; the license is clearly a forgery.

Now the coroner accepts cash from a nervous young record-company flunky. And in the next shot Cheryl's death certificate is signed, its information in accordance with her false ID. Thus it is that her mother never learns of her death.

Now a box containing Cheryl's ashes is placed in the moist earth of Forest Lawn. In the next shot the gravestone is in place, repeating the lies, as a shadow falls across it. We pan up to see Dennis, some days after the crash, a cap hiding the stitches on his scalp. In some way he must be grateful that the record company has protected him from scandal, from the legal repercussions of a sex-and-drug summer with an underage girl. Still, this just isn't right. The love of his life cannot simply be censored out of existence. In disgust he turns from the grave and walks back to his car.

To his blue '63 Sting Ray split-window coupé, flawless and gleaming in the hot July sun. Can this be the same car we saw shattered and wedged in the rocks? If so it has been repaired with obsessive perfection, though more likely it is a replacement, identical in every detail to the car in which Cheryl died.

As he replaces the car, so will he replace the girl. Not that he's consciously looking for a replacement. It's not a matter of choice. Cruising through the beach cities in his new, or resurrected, Sting Ray, he sees her everywhere. Specters in other cars. Phantoms in record-store windows. Girls with Cheryl's hair, her pale skin. He will never be free of these illusions. The funeral denied him—the chance to touch her waxed hand and know with a tactile certainty she is gone— a part of his mind will never be completely convinced she is dead.

Now he roars through the turn on PCH where the car

went over before and he is so tempted to jerk the wheel. But his creative instincts save him from impulsive suicide. He will not go to Cheryl. He will bring her back to him.

But the proper invocation does not come. He sits staring at the piano, wadded-up papers on the floor. In numb grief he walks through the empty Hermosa house. He stares at the bunk bed in the cold blue bedroom. He holds Cheryl's silver anklet, watching it glimmer in the overcast light.

Then one fateful August evening he's streaming aimlessly through the L.A. suburban flatlands when he sees the Century Drive-In marquee up ahead against the garish orange horizon. A *Hard Day's Night* read the red letters reflected backward in his Baloramas. Perhaps hoping for a momentary escape from his sorrow, he pulls in.

There is no escape. Parked in the thirteenth row, he stares at the screen, the images dim through his dark glasses, the happy energy lost to him. Every song reminds him of Cheryl, every song. Finally, as Paul sings "And I Love Her," for the first time since Cheryl's death he sobs.

But a face at his window invades his grief. A zitty baby face matched to a stupid greaser voice. Bobby, who has recognized him, babbling on about a demo, about some group called the Darts, a girl singer.

How can Dennis hear this shit now, how can he care?

Until he sees a ghost in the sideview mirror. His heart stops, so do his lungs, as he watches her approach. Her pale skin glowing in the movie light. Her sweet mouth cherry red. Her eyes as liquid and blue, the same blue, as his car. His Cheryl coming back to him, his Angel descending from heaven, a gift from Jesus and God. The love of his life returned to him in only the thinnest disguise. He takes off his shades as she steps to his window, and takes her small warm hand in his.

The invocation begins days later at Sunrise Sound. In a white heat Dennis pours out his longing for Cheryl, constructing a rapturous model of their lost life, creating in those six relentless days the basic tracks of everything the Stingrays will ever do. In the rush of elation over their discovery, the guys are inspired, playing literally as they never will again, giving Dennis everything he wants—Sharlene giving him so much more. "Love me tonight," she wails through the glass as Dennis nods ecstatically in the booth, and it's obvious to everyone she's already in love with him, in love for the first time, without fear of rejection or hurt. "Love me tonight," she cries through the churning, euphoric wave of sound, and even Bobby, who is already futilely in love with her, must acknowledge the transcendent joy of the moment, whatever its source. But the mood moves beyond joy as Dennis provokes her to new extremes of emotional abandon. To be present at these sessions is to be a kind of spiritual voyeur as she gives him more and more, holding back nothing, protecting nothing, until with naive adoration she has in effect given him her soul. "Tonight, baby. Please, baby. Yes! Love me now!"

And at last, her desire captured on vinyl, he does. Taking her back to the house in Hermosa. Into the blue bedroom. To the bunk bed. Loving her so tenderly, kissing her sweet cherry mouth. Pretending she's Cheryl. Whispering "Angel" as he comes. As her sacrificial blood flows, staining the cactus spread.

A delirious imminent stardom montage as Sharlene is made over. Her mousy brown hair is teased up into a fierce Cheryl beehive. She's poured into sexy blouses and too-tight capris. As Dennis charms her mother, Sharlene steps into the dingy Arcadia living room in a chic, slinky snakeskin sheath. As Dennis gives instructions, her makeup is designed to accentuate her resemblance to Cheryl. She emerges finally as a glamorous movie-star version of her prototype; not that she suspects for a moment he's working from a model. She believes he's doing it all for her. She believes he's just as desperately in love with her as she is with him. What else can she think, the way he fusses over her,

flattering and pampering her, loving her more tenderly than
she has ever been loved before? Stardom and a handsome
blond prince—how can she not feel she's living in a dream?
She questions nothing. Her only desire is to please her love.
If he wants her to wear a certain sweet perfume, she just
does it. Dennis knows best. Clearly. He was right about the
name change, the sleek romanticism of the Stingrays replacing the lumbering stodginess of the Darts. "Love Me Tonight" is already surging up the charts. By September the
guys are slouching in their slinky shirts and shades and Sharlene is glaring from the cover of *Fuel-Injected Dreams*.

The Stingrays take America in a smear of limos, a barrage
of Instamatics, Sharlene wailing in sweat-drenched chiffon
over an endless sea of hysterical teenage faces. Then the
dash to the car, the escape through the streets, the last
screaming fan receding in the rearview mirror, the collapse
by the TV showing *Shindig* in the Holiday Inn.

Pink Kleenex, red lipstick, green heart-shaped Dexamyls.

A view of the Mailbu house completed in 1965, his Egyptoid palace intended for Cheryl. He leads Sharlene out to
the garage. Together they climb the interior stairs. She gasps
when she sees the blue bedroom, transplanted from the old
house in Hermosa.

"I wanted to preserve this room always," he tells her, "as
the first place where you and I made love."

Her eyes mist up. This is so sweet, so sentimental, so
typical of the man she loves—this brash, commanding genius with a private, gentle heart. Of course, she will make
love with him again on the bunk bed, just as they did that
very first time. Just as he did then, he loves her so tenderly,
whispering her nickname as he comes.

Album covers trace the next two years:

Teenage Utopia, released August '65. They're grouped
around the Sting Ray at a neon drive-in, Sharlene in pink
capris, Bobby lighting her cigarette, the only one of the guys
still wearing his shades at night. This is their leanest album

that kinetic summer of "Satisfaction" and "Ticket to Ride," Bobby's Stratocaster leads mixed prominently for the first and last time.

Pacific Coast Highway, March '66. On the highway at Zuma with their thumbs out, waiting for a Microbus, but even the most gullible college kid might hesitate to give this crew a ride: these sinister punks with greasy pageboys, round shades, and too-tight pipestem slacks, with switchblades hidden in their fruit boots, peddling acid laced with strychnine. And this girl, a red mouth above a tight black top, black miniskirt, black tights, an evil biker angel taunting you into a joyride that can only end with a severed spinal cord. But this album is their biggest seller, the Contrelle Sound returning in all its seething grandeur, with an overlay of tambourines and Byrds-like guitars.

Freeway Euphoria, their last album of "new" material, released in November of '66. An "artistic" Avedon-style cover photo, Sharlene looking pensive and world-weary beyond her sixteen years, the guys appearing "sensitive" and "poetic," these grease-pit Rimbauds—except Bobby, who spoils the effect by grinning goofily, wastedly, painful red smears under his dilated eyes. The elaborate density of the overdubbing—the Berlin Philharmonic on Desoxyn crossed with *Blonde on Blonde*—doesn't hide the fact that these songs are the dregs of the original sessions back in '64. Despite Dennis' promises to record them again—to produce some of Bobby's songs, to let Bobby sing—he never has and never will.

So Alive dies a sloppy death upon its release in 1967. A calamitous, pile-driving concert recorded late in their last tour in the spring of that year, the cover proves controversial. The front is a picture of a racing Corvette engulfed in flames, the form of the burning driver clearly discernible. The back cover is a photo of a dead stingray rotting in the seaweed on a beach.

Although they've never been bigger, the last tour is a

florid nightmare of accelerated decay and gratuitous self-
immolation, Dennis and Bobby at each other's throats.

"You're a moron! Your songs all suck! I'm *never* going to
let you sing!" Dennis screams in Bobby's face in a San Fran-
cisco dressing room a second before Bobby tries to strangle
him. Big Willy intervenes, getting Bobby in a choke-hold.

They move across America like a screaming panzer unit,
gutted Holiday Inns in their wake. Frank and Jimmy are
arrested in Kansas for pissing out a window on couples
headed for a prom party below. In Houston a camera cap-
tures Dennis slapping Sharlene for the first time. By the time
they reach Florida Dennis is psychotic, receiving secret mes-
sages from *Green Acres* on TV, spitting incoherent orders
into the phone as he fondles his gun. That night he breaks
down Bobby's door and tries to kill him. Big Willy gets the
gun away in time. In a Pittsburgh hotel Sharlene locks herself in a bathroom, screaming into a towel. On the other
side of the wall Bobby searches for a vein among the rivulets
of blood on his thin white arm. The needle's on empty by
the time they reach Chicago. The engine dies forever in
Detroit.

But in the tranquil aftermath the stink of burning fuel
recedes. One afternoon as Dennis and Sharlene lie recuper-
ating in the Malibu sun, he raises up on his elbows and
casually proposes marriage. Her look of shock is followed by
a shriek of glee heard from Rincon to La Jolla.

The flowery Beverly Hills wedding, most of the rock world
dressed in white. Ringo catches the bouquet. Mick kisses
the bride. Keith Moon makes a joke about using the cake
knife to get at Sharlene's diamond ring. Even Dennis
laughs.

The ultimate Riviera honeymoon. Languid days at Saint
Tropez, fireworks reflected in the diamonds of sex.

But no sooner have they returned to Los Angeles than the
darkness descends. Alone, Sharlene paces through the

empty Egyptoid mausoleum, chain-smoking Eves, playing *Sgt. Pepper* for the three hundredth time, then diddling at her piano, sketching out songs for the solo album Dennis has promised to record. But he seldom comes home anymore, except to sleep for twenty hours straight.

He's at Sunrise Sound, obsessed. Alone in the control room at four in the morning, he hunches over the board, chapped lips split, skin yellow in the dial light, black holes for eyes, as he replays the same bit of tape, studying, weighing, evaluating the same five-note guitar riff again and again for hours, through the next day, into the next night. This was to be his ultimate statement, a three-record concept album described once as a "rock-and-roll *Vertigo*." The Vectors were there for a while, till he called them queers to their faces and threw them out. Most of the greatest musicians of the time have come and gone as well, their tracks junked, redone, phrases punched in, junked, redone again, strings and horns and choirs added, deleted, tracks fussed over endlessly until he can fuss no more. His brain as charred as a hamlet in the path of the Tet offensive, his veins as torn up as the Ho Chi Minh Trail, he eventually destroys all the tapes in a paranoid fit, believing the music has somehow been responsible for prolonging the war in Vietnam. Two years of work, a masterpiece described by those who heard parts of it as being of such dementedly baroque but overpowering grandeur as to render Phil Spector, Brian Wilson, and the Beatles rock minimalists by comparison, is lost forever, gone with his sanity, brain cells, and teeth.

He takes a cure in early 1969 at a Santa Barbara sanitarium. Toward the end of his stay he strolls through the grounds, his arm around Sharlene, his faithful soothing madonna. Surely this is where she suggests they have a family, seeing it as a way to save him. Yes, a family, a return to normalcy, a reason to live. These must be the private thoughts she shares with him now, for abruptly he takes her

face in his hands, kissing her as tenderly as he ever will. He
has been through the fire, but his blue eyes are clear again.
The nights of psychotic agony are all in the past.

Or so it seems as they make tender love in the blue bedroom again for what will be the last time. So it seems as she
announces her pregnancy and he lifts her up in a swirling
embrace. So it seems as she decorates the nursery, as Dennis hugs her joyfully in the bright morning kitchen, as he
presses his ear to her stomach, the perfect loving father-to-
be, as Sharlene smiles, flushed and glowing in a delicately
embroidered maternity dress, her dream marriage real at
last.

Then in October he returns to the studio to record Louise
Wright. By the third day the Red Army is in the suburbs.
The bunker is sealed. Götterdämmerung has begun.

Perhaps it happens like this. Perhaps one afternoon late
in her husband's absence Sharlene is out watering the flowers alongside the garage, trying to stay busy in the peaceful
Malibu sunshine, though her thoughts are with the man she
loves locked in battle far away. How she wishes there were
some way she could stop what he's doing, but she knows she
cannot. Why must creativity and self-destruction always be
bound together for him?

Idly, as she waters the pansies, she notices that the padlock is off the garage. She does nothing at first. He's made it
clear there's no reason for her to ever want to go up to the
blue bedroom without him. But perhaps now more than
ever she may need a reminder of his sweet, gentle side. She
drops the hose, and taking care not to strain herself, lifts the
garage door.

Carefully gripping the railing, one step at a time, she
climbs the interior stairs, blades of dusty sunlight rippling
over her swollen maternity dress.

She steps into the blue bedroom, and opens the shutters,
drenching the shrine with ocean light. How she loves this

sentimental room! Wistfully she wanders about, spinning the globe, caressing the bedpost, affectionately regarding the lower bunk, that poignant sight of so many teenage longings which she alone made real for him, the place where the child in her womb was conceived.

She sees that "Love Me Tonight" is set on the spindle of the RCA 45 player. She turns it on, the record drops. As the music fills the room, the memory of that rapturous time floods back. How she loves him still, her crazy genius, as much as she did then!

As she sways to the music, her eyes are drawn to a point of reflected light—a shard of sunlight striking the knob of the door to the adjoining room. The key has been left in the lock.

She hesitates. She's never seen beyond that door. Though really there's no reason why she shouldn't look. It's just storage, that's what he's always told her, and what reason would she have to doubt him?

Does she have any sort or premonition, any sense of impending doom? It is highly doubtful. It must be only out of the simplest, most idle curiosity that she finally turns the key and opens the door to the room she has never seen.

Just what he said. Storage. Old Boy Scout equipment, pup tents and sleeping bags. A damaged surfboard, rusty power tools. An unpleasant, uninteresting room, windows covered with foil, the dead air thick with the smell of mildew. She's about to close the door when she notices the pink suitcase wedged behind the surfboard.

Pink. A girl's suitcase. But not hers, never hers.

Now she has a premonition.

She should just close the door. But she cannot resist. Besides, it's probably nothing. There's probably a logical explanation. The suitcase is probably empty anyway. She picks it up by the handle, shaking it a little. It's light, but there's something in it.

She takes it out to the blue bedroom, her voice swelling on the record player as she lays the pink suitcase on the cactus bedspread, snaps the latch, and lifts the lid.

Lingerie. And the sudden reek of her own sweet perfume. Black lace panties and French bras. The small bottle of Thrifty's perfume spilled by her jostling. Some of the panties are crotchless. Her heart is pounding now. These things are not, were never, hers.

Her breathing stops when she sees the packet of Polaroids. She removes the rubber band and leafs through the pictures, coppery black-and-white shots of a girl who could be, but is not, her. The girl with Dennis leaning against the Sting Ray in front of the house in Hermosa. This girl who could be her twin mugging at Hermosa in a fur coat. This girl in *her own* white Mustang, for God's sake! This girl who might be her double *here* in this room when it was still in Hermosa—Sharlene can tell by the view out the window. *Here*, striking a mock-seductive pose on this bed. Then laughing riotously, trying to block the camera, her blouse open, skirt up, her eyes, mouth, and vagina glistening in the flash. A jolting candid shot of this girl in the Hermosa bathroom, bikini bottom lowered as she pokes a needle into her perfect butt. Then a shot of this girl at the half-finished Malibu house, the sky over the ocean behind her dark with rain clouds as she smiles at the camera, beautiful but debauched, an air of poignance and doom about her, confirmed by Dennis' margin notation: "Cheryl's last picture." Under that, several color Polaroids of the Sting Ray after the crash, split-window shattered, bucket seat on the passenger side caked with blood.

And now, as the last chorus of "Love Me Tonight" swells, Sharlene removes the framed photograph of Cheryl at the Griffith Park Observatory, wrapped in a trashy pink negligee.

"Dennis, this is forever. Angel," the girl has written beside a lipstick print turned brown. And Sharlene understands everything now, understands that she was never more than a replica, a stand-in, a copy of this Cheryl, his true Angel, so perfect and dead.

Then, as the song of her love for him fades, against the silence she hears his winded breath.

He stands in the doorway, a walking corpse ten days without sleep, bombed-out cities in his charred blue eyes, a dub of his masterpiece on the cassette recorder he holds in his dead white hand. "What do you think you're doing, Sharlene?"

Though she is afraid, tears come to her eyes. "You never loved me, did you?" she says with an accusatory stare that infuriates him. "You never loved me at all."

"Come here," he says in a parched dead voice. "I'll show you what love is." And he sets the cassette recorder on the chest of drawers, pressing the red button, knowing this will be the last time.

Sharlene moves toward the door but he blocks her path. She tries to pass him, first on one side, then the other, but he counters each move again and again, laughing as her panic edges into hysteria.

Finally, as the cassette leader gives way to magnetic tape and begins to record them, he throws her on the bunk bed, pushing the suitcase aside.

He turns her on her stomach and tries to sodomize her. That's all she deserves, this cheap imitation who's spoiled everything now.

"Dennis, stop. You're hurting me."

"Am I?" His dry laugh.

But he is far beyond exhaustion, his flesh jabbed raw, his weapon a sore red stub.

And so he beats her, hammer blows coming down as she curls away from him, trying to protect her baby. A robot of rage, he pulls her from the bed. She falls hard on the floor. As she curls on the braided carpet, he turns into a kicking machine, the point of his cowboy boot jabbing her stomach.

Then he grabs her by her stiff hair and drags her to the stairs like a heavy bag of garbage. As if the men are waiting impatiently at the bottom to collect her, he gives her a quick, hard shove down the stairs.

She lies sprawled at the bottom, blood on her face, on her maternity dress, as Big Willy hustles into the garage. He stops when he sees her, and even he looks stunned and sickened. In the room upstairs, Dennis is talking angrily to himself.

At red sunset a flashing ambulance pulls through the electric gate.

Now Sharlene lies in a hospital bed, her face bruised, her stomach no longer swollen, as her mother sniffles into a handkerchief, heavy gold earrings (paid for with Stingrays money) framing the woman's overly made-up face. At the foot of the bed a young doctor stares at Sharlene's chart, saying something about a "nasty fall." Suddenly Dennis appears in the doorway, sobered, eyes filled with concern, as if he's just heard about the "accident." He steps to the bed, his eyes brimming with tears. He drops to his knees and weeps against Sharlene's hand, sobbing over the loss of their baby. "There, there," she says, stroking his hair mechanically, her eyes going to the bedside telephone as her mother and the doctor withdraw.

Now alone in the hospital room, she uses the phone, dialing Bobby's number. Bobby, the one person who can help her.

The phone rings in Bobby's apartment on a table strewn with used plastic syringes, snapshots of Sharlene, and the lyrics of dozens of original blues songs, all about love in vain.

The phone is still ringing as we see Bobby sitting stiff in the bucket seat of his shiny black '69 Camaro on a desolate dirt road behind a refinery in Carson. A needle hangs from his arm, flies perch on his white lips and about his open eyes. A burned spoon is tossed on the passenger seat beside a blue balloon containing brown heroin residue. Through the windshield, the refinery chimneys throw ribbons of smoke against the pink-and-purple sunset clouds.

Now, to a plaintive piano melody, a montage traces the next fifteen years.

We see Sharlene holed up in her bedroom as the seasons come and go. Painting her nails in the clear light of spring, curled up with a thick gothic paperback in the yellow light of autumn. Watching black couples do the hustle on *Soul Train* as rain beats against her barred windows. Her radio dial set to KRUF as she tosses under sticky satin sheets on hot summer nights. (Does her agoraphobia develop as an unconscious defense mechanism? If she's too impaired to even leave her room, let alone the house, she needn't face the risks of attempting an escape. And Dennis supports the idea that she's sick, paying for her doctors and therapists, a gesture of sympathy that may pass for a kind of tenderness in these empty, isolated years.)

For he never touches her again—at least not tenderly or affectionately. Or sexually. How could he, knowing how she would be watching him now, reading his thoughts of Cheryl? He has no more interest in her that way, or any way. But neither is he willing to set her free. She knows what will happen if she tells the doctors and therapists too much. Even when she hasn't, he may suspect she has and abruptly terminate their services. Of course his sympathy is a sham. He doesn't want her to recover. The agoraphobia is fortuitous. He doesn't have to lock her in when he goes out. The alarms are all in in her mind.

And he's gone a lot, holed up in the studio, building the tracks that will eventually condense into "Premature Burial," painstakingly polishing each nuance for nights, months, years, a decade, as the shrill Messerschmitts of speed give way in the seventies to the perpetual Mercedes precision of a lush cocaine exile.

In the thin Andes air of these years he may from time to

time discuss reviving Sharlene's career. If she ever recovers sufficiently to perform again. She nods at the breakfast table one morning, circa '77, as Dennis expounds on these matters for the dozenth time. They pretend to have a marriage of convenience now, a business relationship. But if Dennis is president of the company, Sharlene is a discontinued model. He has no intention of reviving her. This Stingray is permanently garaged.

And when she does become mobile again, when she is able to drive herself to the therapist, she is putting herself in great danger. For the cocaine proves less perpetual than once thought; his tropical hideout is soon discovered, his Mercedes is followed, there are clicks on his phone. Sharlene may return from a "victory drive" to the beauty parlor only to encounter a barrage of paranoid accusations that will culminate in a beating. To be followed by a listless apology, token reparations, and months of indifference. Only to erupt again when she's gone too long, or when she smiles at the gardener, or simply because the opiates that keep his pursuers at bay have temporarily run out. She's finally free of suspicion only when she stays in her satin cell.

Though even here she's not safe. The plaintive melody we hear is hers, we see now, an original song she plays at her piano, the sunset streaming through the barred windows behind her, encasing her in a halo of backlight as she begins to sing. The song is a wrenchingly fervent prayer, a spiritual release from her imprisonment. Sainted in sunlight, she wails with abandon, believing she is alone in the house.

But in the driveway below her open window the Sting Ray is cooling off. Our hand-held Arriflex moves past the car, enters the garage, and climbs the interior stairs. Rounding the corner, we see Dennis in the blue bedroom. On the bunk bed. His pants dropped to his ankles. Slowly masturbating with one hand, he reaches into the drawer of the bedside table with the other hand and removes a small bottle, skillfully twisting off its cap. Holding the bottle to his nose, he masturbates furiously now. For with one whiff of this sweet amyl nitrite of the heart, he can *feel* Cheryl's soft lips, her hot tight vagina, with an exquisite perfection Sharlene, his gross replica, could never provide. "Angel," he intones on the edge of orgasm, when suddenly Sharlene's plaintive wail blows in on the breeze, contaminating his vision. He ejaculates in rage through the fragments of broken fantasy, semen and perfume spilling. In a roaring red hatred he yanks up his pants, the spilled perfume soaking into the cactus bedspread as he charges down the stairs. (Even in careful moments he inevitably leaves traces of perfume.)

Up in her room Sharlene finishes the song. In the peaceful silence that follows, she rests at the piano, her face serene, so achingly beautiful in the peach-colored twilight. But she flinches as Dennis throws open her door, breathing hard, his fists balled up, his face a contorted red mask. Without looking at him, Sharlene's expression changes from contentment to terror.

That would be the last shot. Or at least that was where I would stop the film. There must have been so many similar scenes. I didn't want to watch it happen again.

I believed in the basic truth of that imagined documentary for several days. Some of the scenes were admittedly based on speculation, I might be wrong about a few of the details, but I was reasonably sure of its emotional accuracy.

But was emotional accuracy really enough? Was what I'd imagined finally less a documentary than a historical melodrama, using real people, incorporating well-known incidents, but inventing all the rest? It was a disturbing analogy, one I tried not to dwell on.

One night as I was sitting on the sofa polishing off a bottle of Metaxa I'd found in the kitchen, a virulent, cynical revisionism seized me. It was triggered by the image of Sharlene herself, not on imaginary celluloid, but in a real, grungy twenty-year-old sixteen-millimeter film.

It was an MTV *Closet Classic*, a 1965 promo film for the Stingrays' "Baby, When We Fight," one I knew existed but had never seen. Crude by current standards, the color was fuzzy, the editing choppy, a technical raunch that matched the subject matter. It began with Sharlene, curled up among her stuffed toys in a suburban bedroom, looking petulant as she lip-synched the lyrics of what was arguably the Stingrays' sickest song. Though it pretended to abhor the lovers' violence, it really wallowed in it, Sharlene riding a voluptuous wave of pastel pain. "Baby, when we fight," she wailed, "it really tears me up inside. It makes me cry all night and want to run away and hide."

The film cut to Sharlene fighting with drummer Frank, playing her boyfriend, in a suburban driveway, his chrome Harley-Davidson glistening behind them in dirty yellow sunlight. They sneer at each other in this *Scorpio Rising* outtake, Butch Wax trickling down Frank's mean red face. But it's just verbal until WHAP! goes his hand across her face. And SCRATCH! go her fingernails down his pockmarked cheek. She runs off as, astonished, he looks at the blood on his fingers.

"Baby, when we fight, it makes me do things I know aren't right." She enters a seedy beachfront ballroom now (an actual place in Orange County long since torn down), a desperate hungry look in her eyes. She zeros in on Bobby, the epitome of innocence here, in blue surfer Pendleton, blond hair degreased, the perfect foil to Frank's glowering macho biker sleaze. She brushes past Bobby provocatively, her tongue on her teeth, making eyes. Flustered but hooked, he shyly asks her to dance. "It makes me so crazy, baby, when we fight." Now she and Bobby sway. His transported look is too real to be acting. Her look is calculating, as she watches the door. She's not disappointed, for suddenly Frank bursts in. As soon as she sees him, and is certain he's seen her, she looks at Bobby alluringly and seems to sigh: Kiss me. He does.

"I know I made you jealous, baby. It was such a stupid game." In a rage Frank pulls the couple apart. Bobby's jolted, but stands his ground. Frank indicates that they should step outside. As they do, Jimmy and Billy, playing Frank's evil biker pals, are waiting. They grab Bobby from behind. Frank whips out a gleaming knife. We cut to Sharlene's look of horrified fascination as she watches what happens next.

"And now a boy is dead in his car," she wails, "and I'm the one to blame." And so it is, Bobby dead at dawn, not killed in a crash of some sort as the lyrics had always suggested before, but propped up at the wheel of his Impala, stiff in the sunlight just as he would be for real five years later in another Chevrolet.

"It makes me cry so hard when I think about the blood," she sobs, back in her bedroom now, tears painted on her face. "It makes the tears run down my cheeks as if there were a flood." The camera pulls back now and we see she's wearing a shackle on her ankle where the anklet should be, a chain running from it to the post of her pink satin bed. Now Frank steps in, towering over her, greasy biceps in a sleeveless shirt. She looks hurt and pouty as he crouches down to her. "There's only one good thing about it, baby, when we fight." He pulls her to him brutally, smashing his mouth to hers. "The way you squeeze me afterward. *Baby*, oh so tight!" But as he kisses her she pulls a razor blade from her stiff hair. A grisly close-up of Frank's howling face as she cuts him and the film ends.

This pretty much knocked my brains around the block. I sat there stunned, the empty Metaxa bottle stuck between my legs, oblivious of the videos that followed. I tried to tell myself it was *Dennis'* fantasy, she'd just been acting, giving him what he wanted. It was just a stupid promo film knocked out in a couple of days and forgotten. It didn't mean anything.

But I had an ugly, squirmy feeling, like maggots in a heart-

shaped candy box. It was not a noble emotion. It was similar
to what a redneck might feel if his girlfriend told him she'd
been raped by a black ex-con she'd "befriended." It was a
feeling I had from time to time that in spite of my experience
there were basic things I didn't know about men and
women, or that I was too nice a guy to want to see, or
believe. Perhaps I'd been tricked by words and ideas. Maybe
morons and bikers were closer to the truth.

Her voice. That tearful masochistic sob, so like her voice
the afternoon she sang "Hurt" here at the piano with tears
running down her cheeks. Crying for the man who'd beaten
her up, who'd imprisoned her. That babydoll voice so like
her voice on the cassette when I'd thought it was a record of
a game. Could I say for certain it wasn't? Had I in fact forced
the cassette to fit the assault and beating scenario, to serve
as a kind of documentary evidence, because I knew how
dubious that crucial scene really was?

I didn't *really* know what had happened in October 1969.
There was no proof that he'd beaten her then. She might
have lost her baby as a result of natural causes. There might
have been no need for her to violate his shrine and discover
the shattering truth of Cheryl, since she might have already
known. Could I really believe he'd kept all knowledge of
Cheryl from her for over five years? Wouldn't she have
known about the crash, about the girl killed in his Sting Ray?
She'd told me herself that he said the first night how much
she reminded him of another girl. Had she simply repressed
this key remark until later? She *must* have know about
Cheryl, she must have known from the start. She must have
know what Dennis was doing when he made her over in
Cheryl's image, but just gone along. Hoping that if she did,
he would love her as much as she loved him. And he did
give her stardom. But the time had come—with the demise
of the Stingrays?—when she'd been forced to see that he
didn't love her, never had, never would, that she'd sacrificed
her own identity in vain. *That* would be the moment that

gave birth to her colossal bitterness and rage. But why, after that, had she stayed?

My pseudo-documentary crumbled. If there'd been no beating in 1969, there would have been no hospital scene, no desperate call to Bobby for help. Then what was the meaning of Bobby's death, lacking the element of "suspicious coincidence" my bogus film had implied? Was it just as it appeared, a simple, accidental overdose that had nothing to do with Sharlene? Had he really died in his car? Or had he overdosed elsewhere, as rumors had it at the time, and been dumped in his car after the fact—making the '65 promo film an eerie prediction? But how eerie, how accurate the metaphor? *Had* his death in fact been outright murder, a needle jabbed into him instead of a knife? Or had it been suicide, as many fans believed at the time, the ultimate expression of his futile love for Sharlene? Of course, even those who saw it that way never blamed Sharlene. It wasn't her fault he'd destroyed himself. Was it?

I know I made you jealous, baby. It was such a stupid game. But was it the one the Contrelles liked to play? If Bobby had been their first chump, had I simply been the latest? How did I know there wasn't some truth to Dennis' allegations about Sharlene's provocative behavior? She was sure as fuck provocative with me. Christ, was that what had really been going on? Was that the stupid sick game I'd been sucked into? It made too much sense. She was bored, after all. And not getting it too much, if at all—I was pretty sure of that. Maybe she would come on to different guys, the hunky young poolman, the gas-meter reader—let's hope the stuff about her fat therapist is crap. So she fools around a little, making real sure Dennis finds out about it. Then the chump gets wasted—a virile blood sacrifice to their impotent *love*—and they have their big cathartic row. WHAP! goes his hand across her sneering face. SCRATCH! go her fingernails—I remembered the gouge mark in his forehead that afternoon at the Whisky. Why had I insisted on portraying

Sharlene as always the helpless victim, the poor battered wife cowering in the corner? What was all this Saint Sharlene shit anyway? The operative word was *fight*. What had she said after the reunion wrestling match? That she'd had a lot of practice? Yeah, I'll bet she had. Live from the Malibu Auditorium, Sharlene the Stingray vs. Dennis the Shrimp. She had a mouth on her, too. It wouldn't take more than a few choice words to send Dennis into a stiff red rage. Did she get off on that? Was the surge of adrenaline better than sex?

What *were* they doing up in the blue bedroom? Because *she was still* going up there. She had left the perfume scent on the bed. Dennis hadn't spilled it there while he was jerking off, that was bullshit. An obvious attempt on my part to spare Sharlene. Spare her from what?

What was their big dark secret? "Did she tell you?" he'd screamed at me. Had she told me *what*? That they did *what* up there? What was really in the adjoining room? Old surfboards and Polaroids, or bullwhips and muzzles? Did Big Willy's collection of bondage and S&M accoutrements reflect a similar obsession on the part of the master and mistress of the house? Did Dennis tie her to the bunk bed and watch her strain till her breasts popped the buttons of her blouse? Did he have her wear a studded dog collar and beg for his bone? Did he spank her butt with a black leather paddle till she cried big tears? Was it part of the game that she would eventually get loose and overpower *him*? Go after *his* bony butt with the bullwhip? Grind her heel in his crotch till he whimpered and peed? Bind him to the bunk bed in straps of tight leather till he could barely move? Then, when she had him at her mercy, *cut him* with a razor blade, cut him—just a little!—just in certain places, certain sensitive places? Did they have to see blood to come?

Was this what she'd meant when she'd said she was more fucked up than I knew? Was her agoraphobia finally less a defense mechanism than a pretext to stay, an excuse to pla-

cate what was left of her conscience? If I'd listened to more
of the cassette, what would I have really heard? A traumatic
assault and beating that explained why she had withdrawn
in hopeless terror for years to come? Or a recent ritual of
fetishistic pain that explained why she had chosen to stay?

Maybe a part of her had wanted to break free. Was that
why she'd finally shot him the night of the fire? But even
that scene was suspicious. She'd expertly taken out the dogs
with a single shot apiece, yet somehow managed to botch
killing him. Had she spared him intentionally? Or out of an
unconscious need, a primal compulsion to continue the
game? If so, her aim had been achieved.

She was back there with him now, back in the cage like a
lab monkey in a cocaine experiment, pressing the buzzer for
more and more even though it meant eventual insanity, self-
devourment, and death. She was back in her cell, her pastel
satin cell, and getting all set to hurl her shit through the bars
at me.

I still had her wedding ring. I looked at it under the lamp,
its facets sparkling in the amber light. Three hundred thousand dollars stuck on her finger for the last seventeen years.
Three hundred grand with her every time she had driven
across town, every time she was within a few miles of the
airport. Even granting that her agoraphobia was legitimate,
with what she could have gotten for that ring she could have
hired doctors to sedate her and fly her in limbo to Acapulco,
she could have hired bodyguards and lived in a walled villa,
whatever it took. If she'd really wanted to get away from
him.

Neal had been right. She was damaged goods. No, worse,
much worse. Damaged goods just sit in a warehouse. She
was virulent, poisonous, a fan shape with a spine on the
ocean floor where bare feet were about to step. Anyone with
half a mind could have seen what was coming. But I'd been
so dazzled by her phosphorescence I'd stepped where even
the stupidest surfer would have known not to tread.

I'd tried to help her but all I'd done was ruin my life. The reunion wasn't her fault, not exactly—though if I hadn't played into her little rescue game I would never have shown up at the reunion with Dennis' gun. At the very least you could make a powerfully convincing case that this bitch was bad luck.

She was a stingray, all right, and I had a ragged gash up the back of my leg to prove it. But I would heal. I was still relatively young. I still had my arms and legs, my wits and—no thanks to the Contrelles—my crank. I had her stupid fucking ring. Fair payment for what she'd done to me. I could go to Mexico, or anywhere I wanted, sell the ring, and start over. Spend every day in the sun, every night with a new brown-skinned girl who didn't speak English, the wrecked Corvettes of my American past forgotten.

That was what I would do. That was clearly the answer. I went into the bathroom and threw up a stomach full of ouzo. Then I washed my face and went to bed, where I slipped into a shallow, nightmare-riddled sleep.

18

I got up in the morning with a head full of sour feta cheese and washed down Excedrin with coffee till my nerves were shot. I watched MTV for a while, thinking the "Baby, When We Fight" video might come up again. When it didn't, I half-wondered if I'd imagined it. I wished I had.

I went for a walk around ten. The sky was dark; it was going to rain. I walked up the trail Sharlene and I had ridden, till I came to a lookout point where we had stopped. Looking down to the shore, I could just make out the roof of the house. I imagined Sharlene being grilled by the attorney in a Century City high-rise office. "And where did the two of you spend that weekend?"

"Some dump on Catalina."

I imagined a sheriff's SWAT team surrounding the house, calling to me over a bullhorn while I was in the shower.

I walked down to Avalon, staying on the beachfront, avoiding people as much as possible. I was letting my beard grow, but still. I definitely avoided the sidewalk café where Sharlene and I had eaten breakfast and fooled around under the table. I walked out along the pier.

A cruiser was about to leave for the mainland. I had three hundred dollars in my wallet and the ring in my Levi's coin pocket. There was no reason to go back to the house.

But I sat on a bench and watched the cruiser stream away.

I walked out to the casino. One of the grilled doors was open, a group of young architects taking pictures of the art-

deco movie theater. I entered as if I belonged there, and
went upstairs to the ballroom.

The drapes were open, but the sky was so dark it seemed
like twilight instead of noon. I stood where Sharlene and I
had swayed to the music on the janitor's radio till we'd
passed into a stupor of love.

Lightning flashed, thunder boomed, and the sky opened
up. Rain trickled through the dust on the windows. In a
stupor of memory, I went down the stairs, walking back
through the downpour. I was drenched by the time I
reached the house.

I stood in the living room. I could see the brass bed where
we'd made love. I looked at the leather sofa where we'd
laughed watching *Gidget*, doing silly voices, having stupid
good fun. I looked at the piano, remembering the afternoon
she'd sat there playing and singing, sunlight flickering
through the trees behind her. Rain battered those trees now.
I noticed a wadded-up piece of paper under the bench. I
picked it up and smoothed it out.

It was the song she'd written for me:

> Baby, you're my fantasy
> You're my dream come true.
> Through so many endless nights
> I've been dreaming of you.
> But are you everything you seem,
> as I sing this song?
> Are you really my dream,
> Or have I dreamed too long?

I knew it was stupid but I felt tears in my eyes. I still loved
her so fucking much.

I didn't care what he had done to her, or what she had
done, she wasn't soiled or spoiled or any of that crap. What
ever she did with him, it wasn't really willing. (The promo
film *had* been his fantasy, not hers.) It was fear, and only

fear, that had kept her there. Whatever she'd done, it was only to survive. I didn't care what it was, I just didn't give a shit. I loved her.

And I wasn't going to lose her by giving in to my doubts and sleazy suspicions, the way I'd lost Cheryl.

I didn't love her just because she reminded me of Cheryl. The resemblance was there, I could never deny it. I had made a kind of transference during the Stingrays years, when she had been my dream projection of Cheryl. But even then it was always her voice that I'd loved. *Her* voice. Not Cheryl's. Not Dennis' instrument. *Her* voice as she took his pap lyrics and made you believe them, whether they were abject or ecstatic. It was the actress I'd fallen in love with, the woman who could take his trash dreams and make them profound.

And she wasn't Cheryl when I finally met her. She wasn't Cheryl when we talked and joked. She wasn't Cheryl when we made love in the dark. She was only Sharlene.

Cheryl was gone, soggy ashes in a plot at Forest Lawn, red skin in a faded Technicolor print. A beautiful film at the time of release, but unwatchable now, the negative lost.

Sharlene was alive in all her fucked-up glory. She wasn't a film or a memory. Or an icon. She was real, flawed, agoraphobic, warped, scared shitless, enslaved, and whatever the hell else she was. And it was everything she'd gone through that made her the woman I loved. It was her essence, the beauty and humor within her that he'd never been able to destroy. Whatever she'd been compelled to do, she'd kept the most precious part of her from him. He had her body, that was all. Though she may have given it to him originally, at some point while he wasn't looking, she'd taken back her soul.

And she'd really loved me. It was there in her song. She hadn't been using me for a jealousy game. She'd loved me then, and she'd only gone back to Dennis that time out of fear, believing he would hunt her down and kill me.

And this time she hadn't gone back out of choice. She'd been caught again, trapped. Once again, she was just playing along to survive.

I understood now why I had come back to Catalina, why I was still here in spite of the danger. Because there was very little danger at all. Sharlene was the only other person who knew we had spent the weekend here. And because of what it had meant to her, what it still meant to her, she wouldn't tell. That weekend was our glimpse of the future. If she trashed that, she'd be trashing her own dream.

I realized with a clarity that went far beyond logic that in spite of what had happened, Sharlene still loved me.

I understood her hysteria in the car when she'd discovered I'd also been in love with Cheryl. But it was just that, hysteria. I believed that now that the dust had settled, she had to see her conclusion was wrong. I wasn't like Dennis.

I hadn't just wanted her as a visual echo of Cheryl, an echo that had if anything faded as I got to know her. And I was glad it had faded, relieved. The resemblance, finally, had always been more frightening than arousing. It was one thing when she'd been a Stingray, a remote media image of Cheryl. But if she had taken off her clothes and had Cheryl's exact body, every freckle in just the right place, of course it would have been a nightmare.

I had never wanted her to be Cheryl, not really. No Cheryl at seventeen, not Cheryl at thirty-four. I was sure she saw that now.

And I was sure she saw as well that I was her only hope. She was looking at hard time. The lawyers might save her from Frontera—even if convicted for her role in the reunion shooting, she would probably receive a suspended sentence —but she would be facing life behind bars at Malibu.

Unless I could come up with a way to bust her out.

How could I confirm this line of thought? Of course through Louise. I remembered she'd given me her private number before we'd left her house. I found it on a slip of paper in the Dacron slacks I'd worn that day and dialed it. No answer. I tried it several more times that day, at midnight and two in the morning, and again the next day and the next. I called again and again over the next few days, watching the rain come down. Could Louise be on the road? Had she taken a sudden vacation? I couldn't blame her if she had. There'd been no mention of her harboring us so far in the media, but a grand jury had been convened to investigate the case. She'd have to know something, though. Sharlene would surely have left some sort of message for me with Louise.

Like what? "Scott, I see the truth now. I still love you so much, baby." Or: "Fuck off and die, you dork!" In saner moments I considered that it could still be the latter.

I also tried calling Norrine one night. Her number was no longer in service.

I called a number I had for my mom in Guatemala and left a message. A few hours later she called me back. She wasn't drunk exactly, but you could tell she'd been partying. Yes, she'd heard what had happened. We had a nice long talk. For the first time somebody seemed to believe my side of things. But toward the end of the conversation she began offering advice I didn't want to hear. "Honey, forget about this girl. She's no good for you."

At about this same time the clicking began. Was there someone there who might be picking up an extension? No.

My heart started pounding. We'd been talking so long they'd had time to trace the call, pinpoint my location, get blueprints of the house, rehearse an assault, and eat a leisurely prestrike dinner. I got my mom off the phone as quickly as I could, promising to call again once I was safely "in Europe."

I was extremely paranoid for several days after that, certain the call had been monitored—by somebody. I found an old Colt .45 in my dad's rolltop desk. It was loaded but looked like it hadn't been fired since the OK Corral. Still, I

kept it on the bedside table at night just in case. But no one
came.

The rain was getting serious. After a week they were calling it the worst storm to hit Southern California in forty
years. Each news report began with tape of new catastro-
phes. Canyons had turned into raging rapids, carrying cars,
rotten Halloween pumpkins, pets, and people down to the
waterlogged flatlands. Stripped of brush by the fires the
month before, the hills turned to oozing mud. Rickety
houses perched on stilts collapsed like miniatures in *Rodan*.
A record surf bludgeoned the coast. Septic tanks broke and
leaked through the sand; if Gidget went surfing this year, she
would come out of the water with hepatitis.

The roof leaked in several places; I set out pans to catch
the water. I missed a leak one night over the piano. When I
got up in the morning it was drenched. The keys made a
damp thump. It would never play "Hurt" or "Point Blank"
again.

I slogged into Avalon a few times to hit the market, a small
Mom and Pop store run by an Asian couple. I wasn't too
concerned about being recognized anymore; my beard had
grown in fairly quickly. At least not until the night I saw my
picture on a tabloid by the register. It was a small picture,
an insert in a larger photo of Shar. "ROCK SINGER TELLS
ORDEAL," read the headline, though I doubted it. "DJ
STALKED, TERRORIZED ME," read the quote.

Those fucking rags. They probably hadn't even talked to
her. It was all shit, bullshit.

The next time I went in she was on the cover of *People*. It
was a pre-Tower Records photo, probably taken to promote
"Premature Burial." She had a glassy, drugged look, though
she was smiling. "SHARLENE CONTRELLE," the caption read,
"HER SECRET BATTLE WITH AGORAPHOBIA."

I nearly upchucked all over the Tic-Tacs. Christ, what

next? She was victim of the year, with the emotional disease of the season. She was going to do for agoraphobia what Karen Carpenter had done for anorexia nervosa. Of course it wasn't quite as good a story. They couldn't print her birth and death dates on the cover.

I kept calling Louise's number. I half expected Sharlene to call me—though rationally I doubted that she had the number. Or even access to a phone.

There were times when I realized I might be severely deluded to think she still loved me. But the fact that the cops hadn't come to the house yet seemed to prove that she hadn't told them about this place. Then again, maybe she had, and the cops were just waiting for a break in the weather. Then they would swoop down in the choppers, like *Apocalypse Now*, speakers blasting "Tidal Wave of Flame."

I considered different ways I might rescue Sharlene, but I couldn't really come up with anything that wouldn't get me killed. Approaching her now would be like stepping up to the President with a black plastic squirt gun.

There was always the Inglewood hair salon. I could disguise myself as a Latino hairdresser, blind the bodyguards with Aquanet, and escape with my beehived Princess Leia in a hell-bent Le Car.

In more pessimistic moments I could also see her taking one look at me and yelling to the bodyguards, "Oh Christ! It's him!" I would expire in a hail of hollow-point bullets, doing a death pirouette in my blood-soaked Diana Ross T-shirt and charcoal designer parachute pants.

Anything to do with the house was out of the question, of course. That place was an armed camp now. FDR would have had better luck trying to spirit Eva Braun out of Berchtesgaden tied across his wheelchair.

One morning I woke up to an unnerving silence. The rain had stopped. I looked out the window, past the dripping leaves. The sky was still dark; it was just a lull. But I felt anxious, uneasy. I didn't really expect a chopper assault, but if they did want to at least check out the house, this would be the time.

I made coffee and breakfast and watched an old episode of *The Adventures of Ozzie and Harriet* on TV. Adventures. That had always seemed odd to me. What adventures? They never did anything. Ozzie was looking for his misplaced car keys, the suspense almost unbearable, when somebody tapped on the door.

I dived from the bedroom, spilling my eggs, grabbed the Colt, rocked back, and aimed at the door.

"Scott?" It was Neal. "Scott, I know you're in there. I can hear the TV." He sounded stern, no-bullshit. "Scott, open the fucking door. It's all right. I'm alone."

I lunged for the window and peered through the lace curtain. He appeared to be alone. I unlocked the door. He stepped in cautiously, looking around for others.

"How did you know I was here?" I said.

"Just a hunch." He relaxed a little when he saw I was alone. "Scottie, what are you doing?" he said in his most pitying, parental voice as I stuck the Colt in my waist. "This is crazy. Why haven't you called me?"

"Haven't had time. Been working on a humor book. Mass-murder jokes. Knock, knock."

"Scott." He looked pained by this reference to his television remarks.

"Come on, say 'Who's there?' "

"Scottie, I was only reacting to what I'd heard on the news. What else *could* I think? You *had* been joking about doing something crazy."

"You might have waited till you heard my version." I went into the kitchen to turn down the coffee.

He followed me. "Scottie, look at me—"

I wouldn't.

"I *know* what happened at the reunion now," he said. "That's why I'm here. I can save you if you let me. There is a way out. But the absolutely essential thing you must do now is surrender."

"You hear about the Polish serial killer?"

"Scott, the longer you remain a fugitive, the guiltier you look. Especially now, your only chance is to surface and tell your side of the story."

"What do you mean, especially now?" I poured us coffee.

"Sharlene's been granted immunity. She's going before the grand jury on Monday. She's going to destroy you."

"I don't believe it." I still couldn't look at him.

"You don't believe it?" He laughed. "You'd *better* believe it. She's going to shove a Roto-Rooter up your ass, pal. Everything her attorney's saying, she's going to reiterate in spades. That you hounded her and broke in that night and tried to rape her. Maybe that you did rape her. Who knows how far she'll go? It doesn't matter what really happened, everybody's going to buy her version. Unless we counter now."

I sat down at the table, calmly sipping my coffee, but he was ripping my heart out. "I'm fucked anyway," I said finally. "Because of the reunion."

"Not neccesarily." He sat down opposite me. "It's true we're up against most of our former classmates. You know . . ." He laughed ingratiatingly, like Ronald Reagan. "I don't think most of them are even consciously lying. You were always a weirdo, Scott. And they've hated you for that for twenty years. They *want* to believe you finally flipped out, and came there with random killing in mind. But"—he leaned across the table —"there are a few people who saw something else. Who saw—Scottie, look at me—who saw the truth." He paused for the full effect. "Mary Ann James is willing to testify that Bill started the fight. That you were only protecting yourself and Sharlene. That Bill, in effect, shot himself. And Jeff Menton's willing to say the same thing."

"Bless their hearts," I said, and meant it, though I was

certain they would be outflanked by the others. "Of course, you know what really happened? I asked Bill about Cheryl Rampton, about that hot April night in sixty-four—"

He held up his hand. "Immaterial. Can't use it."

"But it's really quite interesting—"

"Scottie, what I'm trying to say is, I think we can make the best of an incredibly fucked situation. I believe I can convince a jury that you came to the reunion not with the intention of using the gun, but on the contrary, with every intention of surrendering it to me. For you had realized, albeit too late, how thoroughly you'd become entangled in her web, how callously and viciously you'd been stung."

I laughed.

He didn't. "Look, you're not going to emerge a hero. But better a schlub than a jailbird for the next ten years, right?"

I shook my head. "This is stupid."

"Scott." He gave me his sternest look. "That scheming little bitch used you from the word go. Shit, I saw that months ago. If you can't see it yourself, even now—then you're hopeless."

I held back my anger. "Neal, I don't think you understand our situation, I don't think you ever did—"

"I understand it, all right. I think the term's 'pussy-whipped.' It's too bad there isn't a legal equivalent. That would be our defense. Jesus Christ, Scott, she led you around by a piece of string tied to your dick."

"I think you're full of shit, Neal."

"No, you don't. You don't want to see it, but you do. It's an old plot, pal. I think Barbara Stanwyck pulled the same stunt on Fred MacMurray in *Double Indemnity*. That's who you are, pal. The Fred MacMurray of the eighties. And you know who I am? Edward G. Robinson. I smelled a rat from the word go but I didn't have the guts to warn you."

"You warned me. Anyway, that's not how that movie went. You're still full of shit."

"Scott, she set you up to kill Dennis, didn't she? Isn't that how it came down that night? Tell me the truth."

"*She* shot him, Neal. Just for the record."

This jolted him, but he tried to pretend it didn't. "Yeah, right. Great. But she lured you up there."

"I would hardly call it being lured. She was trapped in the fucking house and the fire was about to jump the highway. He had her locked in behind an electrified door."

"Oh, bullshit. That's just what she said to get you out there. She meant for him to catch you there. Maybe it didn't work out exactly as she'd planned. But whoever pulled the trigger, she always intended that you would take the blame. Scott, use your brains!" he shouted. "Do you know how much Contrelle's worth? Probably fifty, sixty million dollars! Why should she want to split that with anybody?" His voice dropped. "Although that's what she offered you, isn't it? That was the setup, wasn't it? Her hot little box and thirty mil."

I sighed disgustedly.

He raised his hand again. "No, don't tell me your version. I don't want to know. Better we just play you as the totally gullible, ignorant chump you probably were. Pity is a cheap emotion but if it cuts your sentence by a year or two, what the hell."

"Gee, Neal. I think you've talked me into it. Where should I turn myself in? Redondo Beach?"

"The thing to keep in mind, Scott, is that no matter what unpleasantness you may be forced to endure initially"— again the Reagan laugh—"in a very short time you're going to be living like a goddamn sheik."

"How do you figure that?"

"Scott, this is a big story. You can't be unaware of the commercial potential. For starters, this has all the makings of a big nonfiction book. It could be another *Blood and Money* or *Helter Skelter*. It's got all the elements: Malibu,

celebrities, murder, sex, drugs, and rock and roll. You mark
my words, pal, it's going to make one hell of a read."

"Who's going to write it?"

"Larry could've." He struck an expression of grief, though
I knew he and his late brother had engaged in a brutal life-
long competition, no amount of financial superiority ever
easing Neal's grueling envy of his inexplicably gifted twin.

"Right, sorry to hear about that," I said.

"It was a shock. I startled several people at the funeral.
They thought I was Larry. He'd grown a beard too, as it
turned out."

"It's sad."

"Maybe *I'll* write the book," he said abruptly, as if the idea
had just occurred to him. "With Larry's spirit to guide me."

"You?" I almost laughed.

"Sure, why not? If I really hit a snag, I can always hire
someone to help me. In fact, that might be the solution. I'll
write the book, and in effect, that'll be your way of paying
me." He looked at me hard, lying with all the earnestness he
had. "If there were any way I could just waive my fee in the
name of friendship, you know I would. But a case like this
—" He whistled at the expense. "Of course, there's an even
more exciting possibility."

"My juices are already flowing."

He cleared his throat. "I hope you won't overreact to this,
but I *have* been talking to Lynn."

"Lynn?" I felt a little sick. "You don't mean the multiple-
personality case I married, do you? Are you sure it was *Lynn*
you spoke to?"

"Scottie, she thinks this could be one hell of a film."

"What could be?"

"My book. I mean, your life." He laughed. "I mean, both.
The studio will buy the book. Naturally, you'll get a chunk
of that too. A nice chunk. It's probably way too soon to talk
about casting, but Lynn's thinking of people like Richard
Gere, or what's-his-name, the Australian guy—"

"Mel Gibson. An obvious choice. Who'd play Sharlene?"

He made a face as if anyone I might dream of would be right. "Debra Winger? What about Meryl Streep?"

"Naw."

"With her hair dyed? In a beehive?"

"Naw. What about Dennis?"

"David Bowie?"

"An English surfer? Come on."

"Scott, all that can be worked out later. The important thing is to get the ball rolling."

He stood, as though he considered it a successful meeting, and was planning to say a few final words and then go.

"All I need is your okay and I'll get on the phone to the D.A. You'll turn yourself in under the full glare of the cameras. Now, the bail is undoubtedly going to be a problem initially, but—"

"Neal, can I ask you something?"

"Sure, Scott, anything."

"Where were you the night Cheryl Rampton disappeared?"

He fixed me with his most earnest, deeply affronted look. "You know where I was."

"You went out with Vicky Stevens. To see *Goldfinger*—"

"You know I did. Why are you asking me this now?"

"Oh, just because I've known since about a week after it happened that Vicky Stevens had menstrual cramps that night and canceled the date."

He looked ill. "Bullshit."

"I heard her talking with a girlfriend at school. I guess we both know why I never asked you about it, don't we? I guess we both know why you felt you had to lie."

He was trembling now. He licked his dry lips. "Scott, I swear, I only *watched*—"

"Get out of here, you fucking scumbag, before I kill you," I said calmly.

Avoiding my eyes, he walked out the door.

I walked aimlessly around the house after he left, alternating between laughing and kicking the furniture in rage. I started in on a fifth of Cutty Sark, thinking that might calm me down, but it didn't, it only made me angrier and more paranoid. Maybe he was right about Shar, though. Maybe she'd always been planning to dump me once she got free of Dennis. What about the talk in bed that night, about needing time to herself? Had she been preparing me? The night of the shooting, had she known Dennis was coming back? For all I knew, he'd never left, he could have been there when she called. No, that didn't make sense. Or did it? Fuck it, I didn't know, and I didn't feel much like waiting around to find out. Fuck her, fuck him, fuck all of it.

I found a satchel, dumped out the Boy Scout relics, and packed it with some old clothes I'd found in the closet. Sixties shirts and sweaters, Levi's with the belt loops cut off—fuck, was I ever going to escape the past? But it was either that stuff or my mom's old cowgirl outfit, and I wasn't really in a Dale Evans mood.

I looked out the window. A mist was falling, another deluge imminent. I had no time to lose if I wanted to get off the island. I imagined Neal already on the phone to the FBI. "He's armed and psychotic. My advice is to shoot to kill."

Figuring Neal would be on the next chopper out, I called the Airport in the Sky, the strip cut through the interior hills. My plan was to get to the mainland, get a car, and make for the border. Yes, they told me, there was a flight to Long Beach leaving in thirty minutes. I ran out the door.

It was quite a hike. I arrived as the plane was lifting off the runway. Shit.

"When's the next flight?" I asked the guy in the office.

"That's it for today, pal. You might catch the chopper if you hurry."

He was talking to an old guy with a Sterling Hayden beard, who stopped me. "Where 'bouts you goin', son?"

"The mainland." I remembered him. He'd been on the chopper the night Sharlene and I came to the island, drunk, talking to himself. He didn't seem exactly sober now.

"Well, that's too bad. Now, if you'd said Mexico, I could've helped you out."

He was warming up his Cessna when on a hunch I used the airport pay phone to try Louise's number one last time.

"Hello," she said.

"Jesus, you're there!"

"No, sorry. Jesus just stepped out for a pack of cigarettes. This is the Virgin Mary speakin'. Can I take a message?"

"I've been trying to reach you for weeks."

"I've been in Berlin. Recordin' a new album of Big Mama Thornton songs."

"Look—" I wasn't even sure what I wanted to say to her now. Everything had changed. "Sharlene's been granted immunity—"

"I know. Say, listen, baby, where are you callin' from? Are you in Mexico?"

"No. Not yet—"

"Oh my. In that case I'm afraid I'm gonna have to sign off—"

Jesus, the phone was tapped? "Louise, wait. I've got to know what's going on. Have you talked to Shar?"

"Baby, really—"

"Louise, meet me." I glanced at the Cessna. "I'll call you back and tell you where." I hung up.

The old guy's name was Mr. Rachet. I think even his wife called him that. I gave him a story about a kid needing money to stay on a kidney machine, and he agreed to make a mainland stop.

I called Louise back. "Listen carefully. I'll be arriving with Paul McCartney's band." Wings, get it? This had to be the dorkiest code ever devised. "In the city where you opened for Jeff Beck in sixty-nine." I was referring to the Santa Monica Civic Auditorium.

"Really, that's quite a few miles back down the road. I'm not sure I remember—"

"Come on, Louise. *Think*."

An hour later I was standing under the awning of the Kitty Hawk restaurant, watching the Santa Monica Airport road, wondering if Louise would be followed. Did the FBI have computer access to her old playdates? It was raining hard again. Mr. Rachet was inside at the bar. Finally a violet dildo nosed up the road, her XKE. It slid into the restaurant parking lot. I dashed out and got in.

Louise was smoking a Sherman, radiating musky perfume. Though the car was heated to the point of stultification, she wore a heavy fur coat—it looked like blond-streaked chow pelts—over a slinky dress that didn't completely cover her muff.

"You should've gone to Mexico," she said.

"Have you talked to her?"

She exhaled smoke. A vein of lightning cut the sky over the runway. "You should go there now."

"I'm on my way. You didn't answer my question."

"Everything's gonna be all right." She cracked the window. Smoke whoshed out. "If you don't do nothin' to fuck it up. You go on down to Mazatlán. Chances are you'll have some company by Sunday at the latest."

My heart dropped a rod. "What are you talking about? She's going before the grand jury on Monday—"

"She'll be long gone by then if everything works out."

"What do you mean?"

She hesitated, as if she thought the car might be bugged too. "There's a young attorney with the firm. He's helping. He's good friends with this writer."

"Writer?"

She named the rock journalist who'd been eager to have me introduce him to Dennis. "He interviewed Sharlene in the hospital. Dennis doesn't know. He was still recovering."

Louise tossed her Sherman out the window and turned to me in the seat. "She told him everything."

A crazy elation rushed through me. "What do you mean, everything?"

"About all the times Dennis beat her up. How you came to save her from the fire. How she shot him. She told all about Angel, too." She lowered her eyes on that.

"How's she gonna get past the bodyguards?"

"She's goin' in with Dennis to see the attorneys in Century City this Friday. This young attorney with the firm has it all worked out for her to slip away while the bodyguards are waitin' in the outer office. Then this writer's gonna drive her straight to LAX."

"Jesus. What about the interview?" I was trembling with happy energy. "When's that coming out?"

"Next week. In *Rolling Stone*."

"Christ. Dennis is gonna shit."

"He'll do more than that." I caught a tremor of nervousness from her. "Listen, there's gonna be some pretty rough things in the interview."

"Like what?"

She wouldn't look at me. "I better let her tell you."

"It's about the bedroom over the garage." I saw her suppress a jolt. "What is it? What's he been doing to her up there?"

"Listen." She put her hand on mine. "You gotta understand. Sharlene was scared. Because of the miscarriage." She lowered her eyes. "And because of what happened with Bobby."

"What do you mean? What the fuck *did* happen with Bobby? Was his death really accidental, Louise?"

"Well . . ." She hesitated. "He hit himself up and OD'd, all right. But Big Willy slipped him a hotshot."

"It didn't happen in his car, did it?"

She shook her head. "After Dennis beat Sharlene, and she lost the baby, she told Bobby everything in the hospital.

Bobby tried to act like he didn't know, but Dennis saw that he did. That's why he got the hotshot. Then when Sharlene came from the hospital, she was walking past the nursery and there was a smell."

"Oh Christ." This was even worse than I'd imagined.

"She found Bobby under the crib. Already dead for several days. Stinkin' real bad. Dennis left him there on purpose for Sharlene to find. Like a warning."

"What did Sharlene tell him? It wasn't just about the beating—"

She looked out the window. "You'll see her Saturday. She'll tell you everything then."

"Louise, I want to know now."

She took my hand. "Look, you've got to understand. There's only one reason Sharlene went along. She knew it was sick. But she was terrified."

"What was sick? What?"

"Look, I gotta get movin'." She started her engine. "If the FBI was listenin' in when you called, they might figure out where I've gone. Jeff Beck, shit. I thought you meant the Forum. I almost went to Inglewood."

"You don't think you were followed?" I checked the road. No one had come in while we were talking.

"I doubled back around a few times just to play it safe."

"Well, you picked an inconspicuous car. There are so many violet XKE's around, it'd be easy for them to get confused."

"You're still being' mean to me. After all I've done for you."

"I do appreciate your help, Louise. I don't really even know how to thank you—"

"Oh, we'll figure out a way." She slid her hand up my leg. "I'll come visit you in Mexico. We can send Sharlene out on a long errand."

I grinned, and took her hand from my crotch. "You really are too much."

"So are you, baby. You gotta lotta soul for a spoiled white boy from the suburbs."

"Louise, coming from you that remark means more to me than a smutty postcard from Nancy Reagan—"

She stopped me with a wet, juicy kiss. "You take care now."

I ducked back to the Kitty Hawk as she slid away through the rain.

I was both elated and disturbed. I'd been right. Sharlene knew I loved her and she still loved me. Everything was going to be okay after all.

But what was going to be in the interview? How sick was it going to get? Was my resolve to love her no matter what she'd done going to be put to a grueling test?

I would pass it. All I cared about was seeing her again. And I was going to now. We were finally going to be together. Nothing could stop us.

Then I stepped up the the newsstand to get a pack of cigarettes and nearly shit. On the rack beside the car magazines, Sharlene glared defiantly from the cover of a fresh copy of *Rolling Stone*. "ROCK GOTHIC," the caption read.

"When did this come in?" I asked the clerk as I paid for it. "This isn't supposed to be out till next week."

"That? Oh, I think that came in this morning," she said blandly. "Yes, it's a little early this time. 'Cause of the holiday." The next day was Thanksgiving.

I stepped over by the window and tore through the article, too wiped out to read it word-for-word. I scanned the bold-letter quotes: "Yeah, I shot him. Too bad he survived." "Scott came there to save me, not to rape me." "Holtner was crazy. If he'd got the gun he would have shot us." "I freaked out when I learned Scott had also loved Angel. But he was naive. He didn't know the truth." "When I found Bobby in the nursery I went totally insane."

There were pictures: of Dennis, the Stingrays, the house, a shot from work of me grinning at a microphone. And pages

of interview, including, I assumed, the raunchier revela-
tions, which I'd have to glean some other time. I'd read
enough to know he was going to kill her when he saw this.
She'd done exactly what he'd always feared most.

I rushed into the bar and told Mr. Rachet there had been
a change of plans, that he should go on without me. I didn't
wait for his reaction.

I was crazy as I ducked from the Kitty Hawk. I needed a
car and I didn't have time to fuck around with Hertz.

I took it as a sign when I saw the '57 Bel-Air in the lot.
Restored to mint condition, white and pale blue, it was just
like the one I'd had in my teens. Toting my satchel, I dashed
through the rain. If the car was unlocked, it was meant to
be.

It was. I hot-wired it easily and roared away.

It had a full tank of gas, an eight-track of oldies, and a
plastic madonna affixed to the dash. The rain was horren-
dous now, traffic snarled. An hour later I was stuck on PCH.
Cursing, I inched forward, and finally saw what it was.
There's been another slide at Big Rock, closing the highway.
Traffic was being diverted up Topanga Canyon. *Shit!*

The next three hours were a nightmare of snaking mountain roads, churning rapids, and mud slides. Old Topanga
was washed out before it reached Mulholland. I took a one-
lane side road that soon ran out of asphalt and turned into
mud. I nearly got stuck several times, backed up, smashing
trees, finally reaching Mulholland, slogging through several
flooded-out stretches, taking Encinal Canyon Road down to
the coast, only to discover it was washed out a half-mile
before PCH. I had to double back up to Mulholland and
take Decker Road back down to PCH. The Chevy was a
gutted tank by the time I pulled into the gravel lot on the
bluff and saw what was happening to the mausoleum-by-
the-sea.

My vague plan to climb the beach steps and scale the gate

was no longer feasible. The steps weren't there anymore. Neither was the gate, or most of the back wall. Monster waves bludgeoned the bluff, eroding the garage foundation. The swimming-pool basin was exposed. The house itself was safe for the moment, but I wouldn't have made an offer on it.

I took the Colt .45 from my satchel, stuck it in my waist, and zipped up my powder-blue *Seahunt* jacket. I got out and ducked back to the grove of eucalyptus trees, soaked before I was halfway there.

As I approached the gate I heard an engine revving, then saw the car in the driveway, an Audi, waiting for the gate to open. A voice cut through the rain. "You chickenshit twats!" It was Dennis.

The Audi roared through the gate and past me, the four blond bodyguards wet and angry. I could see Dennis watching from the front door of the house. I didn't dare try to duck through the gate as it hummed shut.

I cut back through the trees and began working my way along the edge of the property toward the garage. I slipped several times in the mud, once almost falling against the fence. I wondered if the juice was turned off because of the rain—there was a twisted section near the garage I might have climbed—but I wasn't willing to test it.

Finally I had to climb down under the exposed garage foundation. Once I got past it, I could climb up to the patio and be on the grounds. But I saw now how precarious the garage was. Half the foundation jutted out over the cliff. It seemed to be balancing on the edge, waiting for a marble to roll across the floor and send it plunging into the roiling sea below. Waves smashed against the muddy cliff as I climbed under the foundation, holding onto exposed pipes. If a big wave came, it would wash me away.

I was almost to the patio when a big wave struck. I closed my eyes and held on. It smashed me back against the cliff.

For what seemed like a full minute there was nothing but frigid, bludgeoning surf. Through it I heard a tremendous crash.

When the wave receded I saw that the pool basin had cracked in two, half of it washed out to sea. I heard a crunching sound above me. Oh fuck, the garage was going to go.

I clawed my way up to the patio, reaching the remaining half of the pool basin as stucco crashed behind me. But when I looked back, the garage was still there. Only a portion of the back wall had fallen, partially exposing both floors of the building. It was like looking at an illustration, with part of the wall cut away to show what was going on inside. Or like looking at the back of a dollhouse.

There was the Sting Ray, gleaming as always. Its lights were on, cutting hard beams through the rain, its engine running. The garage door behind it was up. Somebody was warming it up for a drive.

A bare lightbulb swung over the interior stairway, Dennis' surfboard resting on the steps. The door at the top was open.

The blue bedroom was softly, romantically candlelit, the adjoining room still hidden. Rain blew in, soaking the braided carpet. The framed photograph of Cheryl had fallen from the wall.

Sharlene lay on the bunk bed, naked, in rigid repose. I knew the moment I saw her that she was dead.

The candles were grouped on the nightstand beside her. She was lying in state. In a gust of rain the candles blew out.

I wanted to cry but couldn't. I couldn't move either; I was too wiped out. Then I heard the sliding glass door open above me, the music-room door. I stepped back flush against the pool basin so I couldn't be seen from above.

Footsteps, running across the tile. Dennis, his black silk shirt drenched as he ran to the garage. He sprinted up the stairs to the bedroom, my view of the room now blocked.

I waited a moment, wondering where Big Willy was. Had

he abandoned ship as well? No one else came out of the house, and Dennis did not come back down from the bedroom. Rain gusted in my face. I climbed the pool ladder and crossed the patio to the garage. As I approached, there was just the sound of the rain and the crashing surf below, then the Sting Ray purring softly, as shiny as a photograph, as I passed it in the brightly lit garage.

I took out the Colt and climbed the stairs, as another wave crashed hard below. Partway up, I saw his shadow move across the wall and could tell he was standing by the bed. I took a few more steps and heard him talking. Talking.

"Don't worry, baby. You're going to be okay. I just have to get a few of your things here."

His tone of voice was casual, which I didn't understand. But then, what did I understand? I'd been so sure she was dead. But now she wasn't. He was talking to her; she was alive.

Reaching the top of the stairs, I heard his keys jingle as he continued, "I've got a nice place for you, baby. Out in the desert where it never rains. We'll be happy there in a cool dark room. Just you and me, baby. I'll never leave you, I swear."

I saw him now, his back to me, as he opened the door to the adjoining room. He flipped on the light and his image was reflected to infinity in the full-length mirrors that lined the walls. It was an elaborately feminine dressing room; some of the mirrors slid back to reveal racks of women's clothes, blouses and capris under plastic, rows of flats. Cheryl's clothes. He went to the closet, pulled a red vinyl raincoat from its hanger, and picked up its matching red vinyl boots.

Then he turned and saw me, stopping as if he were a robot someone had just switched off. The look on his face was not really shock or guilt. It was a vacant look, beyond conscience, as his dilated eyes went to Sharlene on the bunk bed, then back to me. Clutching the raincoat and boots to his chest, he smiled and shrugged sheepishly, like a little boy anticipating a scolding.

"Hello, Scott."

I looked at Sharlene and again I was certain she was dead. She lay so pale and still in the shadow of the bunk bed, in studied repose, her legs straight as a mannequin's, arms not folded over her stomach, but open at her sides in a stilted gesture of receiving. Her skin was *too* pale, as though something had been done to her beyond the mere fact of death. In a blade of dressing-room light her ankle seemed to give off an odd ceramic sheen.

I kept the gun on him, though I was the only one revved up for attack. He appeared drained, almost serene, as if the worst had already happened.

"What have you done to her?" I said.

"See for yourself." His tone was reverent.

I felt along the wall for the light switch. Cautiously he stepped to the door to follow my reaction, like a parent watching a child about to open a gift.

"You always knew she was here, didn't you?" he said as I switched on the light.

The bulbs in the overhead fixture were pink, but there was enough light to see. Oh, I saw.

"Isn't she *just* as you remember her?"

"Oh Christ."

It was Cheryl.

And he was right. She was just as I remembered her. Her sweet mouth as red as the last time I kissed her. Her thick-lashed eyes lightly closed, as if she were swooning in bliss, as if they'd open in a moment, those addictive blue eyes, and meet mine. Her creamy neck as soft as the last time we'd nuzzled, as the last time I'd kissed my way down to her high, sweet, perfect breasts. Her small waist, her Kim Novak thighs, gleamed in the light. At her crotch the glossy thatch of brown public hair was set forever in the hard clear polyurethane plastic that completely encased her—except that here, below the pubic hair, she was not perfect, not frozen in time or angelic at all.

I reeled when I saw the fresh blood glistening at her vagina. How could this be? How could an opening exist without leading to her putrefaction? Then I saw what it was. There was no opening. In the space between her legs, flush to the mound of her plastic crotch, he had fashioned a vagina of lean red meat. The battered lip of the meat was gooey with clear lubricating jelly and a streak of pearlescent semen. Beneath her hips a sheet of clear plastic covered the cactus bedspread, intended to catch the blood.

I don't how long I stood there. I thought I was dreaming or hallucinating or had just gone insane. I began to realize he was talking.

". . . . because she's so beautiful and I knew the minute I saw her there would never be another. And what would life mean without her with me forever? My Angel."

I felt a crazy rush of protectiveness. I wanted to cover her, as though she'd just died, or was sleeping. Or wash away the blood, or something. Anything. Rain spotted her face and trickled down her cheek. Under the plastic her brown hair was ratted high, creating a bubble, though the reflection of light made it look like a halo.

"How could you do this?" I said finally.

He smiled. "How could I not?"

He went to her now, as boards wrenched beneath us, lifting her stiff body, slipping the raincoat over her arms. I couldn't move.

"I'm surprised you didn't recognize her voice on the cassette," he said, buttoning her raincoat with a fussy air. "Though it *was* poor quality. An eight-track originally. The only record of her voice I still have. I'm sure you would've recognized her if you'd heard the whole tape. She laughed toward the end. It was all a game. I wasn't *really* hurting her. How could I ever hurt my Angel?"

The foundation lurched. I grabbed the door frame to keep

from falling; he held on to the bed. Bottles fell off a dressing-
room shelf and broke, drenching the air with sweet tropica
perfume.

"Oh, hey, Scottie," he said jauntily. "I think this place is
just about to go." He stuck Cheryl's little red boots on her
stiff little feet and pulled her upright. As he did, the mea
slid down her legs and hit the floor.

This flustered him slightly. "I know what you're thinking
Scottie. I feel bad about the steak, really, I do. It's such a
cheap substitute. Almost sacrilegious, really. But what else
could I do? I tried so hard to leave a way in. I really put on
my thinking cap, but that was one nut I just couldn't crack
I finally ran out of time. She was starting to rot." He made a
samurai grimace. "I do feel bad about the meat. But wha
would *you* have done?"

A monster wave crashed below and the building lurched
again. I steadied myself; so did he. As the wave receded, he
pulled Cheryl toward the door.

"It's funny, Scottie," he said. "I had a very strange feeling
about you right from the start. I always sensed we had more
in common than a mutual love of rock and roll." He
laughed. "But I swear I didn't know what it was till today."

Some version of reality pulled at me. He'd read the article
Shar.

The floor lurched violently, dumping the chest of drawers
into the sea. I held on to the door frame, blocking his path.

"Where's Shar?"

He ignored the question. "You know, Cheryl told me
about you," he said smoothly. "Though of course I didn'
know it was *you*. Her ex-boyfriend. The guy who got her
pregnant, then dumped her. Boy, did she ever hate you.
wanted her to keep the baby, that's how much I loved her
But she said, no, it's his, I don't want it. So they sucked ou
your son."

I shoved him back against the wall, Cheryl between us
reeking sweet perfume. I was insane. "Where's Sharlene?"

He smirked. "I really don't know. Try looking in the trash-bin. Oops, wait a minute. Today was trash day."

"You sick fuck. If you've hurt her—"

"If I've *hurt her?*" he said sarcastically. "That's all she's good for. That's what she likes. Haven't you figured that out yet?"

I hit him across the face. I hit him more than once. I blacked out in a way, making up for all the times I'd wanted to pound his face in and hadn't. I might have killed him eventually, if the building hadn't lurched again, this time dumping the vanity into the sea. Dennis and I hit the floor, taking Cheryl with us. I held him there, as he held on to Cheryl.

"Where's Shar?"

"I'm not telling. Fuck her. She's dogshit. And now I've wiped her off my feet."

"Where is she?" I pressed the muzzle of the gun under his chin. This didn't seem to impress him at all.

"She came up here once." His lip bled. "She interrupted us. Oh, sure, I got pretty mad, but it was her own damn fault that she lost that baby. Then she went and told Bobby." He flashed a grin. "She knew what would happen if she ever talked again."

"Where is she?" I pressed the gun flush against Cheryl's shiny face, for the first time noticing the blood in her hair.

His manner changed abruptly. "No," he said softly. "You wouldn't. You couldn't."

I cocked the gun. "It's just a twenty-year-old corpse to me."

"But it's *Cheryl*—"

My finger closed over the trigger. "Watch her dead brains fly—"

"*No!*" he wailed, and pulled Cheryl to him. "She's up in her room! Take her, I don't give a shit. She's nothing, she doesn't even exist." He held Cheryl to him and sobbed. "But please don't hurt my Angel. Not my precious little Angel. God, I love her so much!"

I got up and started for the door, leaving him there, holding his Angel in his arms. As I reached the stairs, the floor moved again, and he called out to me, "You're too late, though, Scottie. That's one little bitch who's sung 'Twist and Shout' for the last time."

I didn't understand what he meant.

He laughed. "From now on, she'll have to lip-sync her old Stingrays hits. Just don't expect any between-song banter."

Oh Jesus. Fuck. Like the dogs.

I lunged down the stairs.

I ran into the house through the music room, the Colt in my hand. The amps were on, the speakers popping static, as I dashed across the pink shag carpet. I ran up the red velvet corridor, the house itself beginning to creak.

On the foyer floor I saw the latest issue of *Rolling Stone*, ripped apart, the last page stomped with a muddy shoe. There was a telephoto picture of the garage I'd just left with the bold-letter caption: "ANGEL'S TOMB?"

The security door was open at the top of the stairs. I followed the muddy footprints up the shag-carpet steps, as the chandelier hanging from the foyer ceiling shook. I stepped through the security door and saw a bright light in Sharlene's room. It blinded me for a moment. Then I shielded my eyes and saw Sharlene on the bed.

It looked as though she'd fainted, but there was a spot of blood inside her elbow. Her pose was almost voluptuous, her hair loose across the satin pillow, her blue satin robe open to reveal her breasts.

Her head was thrust back on the pillow, her mouth open wide, the bright lamp adjusted to illuminate her throat. Protruding from her mouth, the stainless-steel handle of a long scalpel gleamed.

I started for her without thinking, and Big Willy, hiding

behind the door, grabbed me from behind. He twisted my arm till I dropped the gun, and was quickly forcing me to the floor, where I would be doomed, when in a desperate burst of animal strength I threw him. I still don't know how I did it. It was like a cricket throwing a Cadillac. His head struck the cabinet TV screen, a Cars video blowing out with a grisly pop.

As the cathode mist settled, he sat there holding his bloody face in his hands, moaning in disbelief.

I bent down to Sharlene and carefully removed the scalpel from her throat. There was no blood on the blade. I had stopped Big Willy in time. Sharlene was out cold. I lifted her up in my arms as the house erupted in a wrenching chorus of shrieks. The floor lurched as I moved toward the door. I braced myself against the wall to keep from falling, and heard a tremendous crash outside. I looked through the window in time to see the garage go. In an avalanche of splintering beams and cracking Egyptoid plaster, it crumbled into the surf.

As I carried Sharlene into the hall, the house moved again, and the security door began to sway shut before us. It stopped on its hinges an inch short of closing. I used my toe to pull it open as the house lurched again.

Glass and china crashed off shelves into the rooms below as I carried Sharlene down the stairs. As I reached the landing, the stairs began to wrench from the wall. I nearly dropped her. In a final swaying lunge I reached the foyer, where I saw the front door was now open. Dennis had left the garage in time.

His muddy footprints led back to the music room, where I saw his shadow on the wall. Watching for him, I carried Sharlene out the front door.

The Sting Ray was waiting in the driveway, halfway back to where the garage had been. Cheryl was wedged in the passenger seat in her little red raincoat, a little overnight bag hooked over one stiff arm—packed with a toothbrush and a fresh pair of panties perhaps. The engine idled smoothly, the Vibra-Sonic softly playing "Love Me Tonight."

I carried Sharlene out to the car. With difficulty I crouched down and opened Cheryl's door.

Rain blew in, battering her ceramic face. In the full light now she looked less than real. It was the chalky face of a doll, heavily made-up. There was no luminescence to that dead white skin. She could have been made of paper or wax. Only her lips still glistened with a terrible reality, a hurt poignancy still demanding an impulsive kiss. I saw again a time I'd kissed her in my blue bedroom, her mouth with the same pouty look. "Love me, baby," she seemed to say, though it was really Sharlene echoing through the Vibra-Sonic. "Love me now."

Hooking my toe under her arm, I pulled Cheryl from the car. Dennis screamed as she hit the mud, and came running around the side of the house, dropping an armload of tapes. Ignoring me, he skittered down in the mud to her in a paroxysm of abject concern.

"Oh Jesus, oh baby."

He lifted her up and cradled her in his arms. A gust blew back the flap of her raincoat, revealing her bloody crotch to the rain. As if she were still alive and modest, he quickly pulled the flap back in place.

"Oh baby. There, there, it's all right."

With his wet sleeve he wiped the mud from her face.

The front of the house cracked in several places. A cabinet smashed against one of the barred plate-glass windows, dumping shattered cupids and Kennedy plates into the driveway. At the edge of the property, more ground broke off, uprooting a royal palm. The asphalt beneath us was pulling apart as I placed Sharlene in the passenger seat of the car. Her eyelids fluttered. She swallowed and rolled her head, then went limp again. I closed her door. We were ready to go; there was just one problem.

"Dennis, how do I open the gate?"

He was on his feet now, pulling Cheryl back toward the house. "Fuck you," he said. "Go to hell." He knelt down to pick up a two-inch tape.

A crevice split the driveway and the waterlogged lawn, and one of the Romanoid columns came down. I watched him pull Cheryl to the Luxor doors, trailing a muddy ribbon of tape. As he entered the door the Horus steles on either side of it cracked.

I went in after him. From the foyer I watched as he carried Cheryl back to the music room. The house was a cacophony of wrenching beams and cracking concrete. Ceramic mementos crashed. Glass crunched. I called to him, "Dennis!" He ignored me.

I ran up the red velvet corridor, plaster cracking under the fabric, making it appear to undulate. As I reached the music room, a blast, a deafening roar, a monstrous crushing din of sound nearly blew me back out to the front door. I covered my ears.

"Tidal Wave of Flame" surged from the tremendous speakers in a blistering avalanche of ecstatic sound. Wave after pulsing wave of humming choirs, glistering percussion, armies of muted brass and keening strings, Africa sodomizing Brahms, mariachi bands bludgeoning Wagner, until Louise Wright entered like a screaming condor in flames. The sound level was unbearable; even with my ears covered it felt like two drills boring into my brain. Yet Dennis Contrelle appeared perfectly serene.

Surrounded by the vibrating speakers, he held Cheryl gently to him, as if she were shielding him as much as he was protecting her. Though she was covered with mud now, her sweet face appeared to glow with its old luminescence in the soft pink light. His cheek was pressed to hers as close as the polyurethane allowed. He seemed to be savoring the nuances of the music, sharing them with her, with the one for whom it had all been done, the one who had inspired this greatest work of his life. The bass line slammed through me like a G-force. Horns shrieked. I couldn't understand why he wasn't in agony.

Then as the second verse ended, the music dropped, preparatory to the ultimate climactic rise. In that brief lull there was just a muted percussion, a glistening sheet of synthesized brass, slick as a swell.

Plaster misted down. The wall that held his gold records and photographs trembled. And in this sublime moment, like the lull before imminent orgasm, there came to his face a look of unbearable sweetness and sadness, the expression of a purged saint.

"Dennis," I said. "I need to open the gate."

"Right there behind you, Scottie," he said in an easy, compassionate voice. "Just press that button and you're home free."

The music rumbled with nervous expectation. I found the red button hidden in the matching crushed velvet and pressed it. I looked at him again and for just a moment something in his charred eyes seemed to acknowledge the demented futility of what he'd done.

Then, as if in response to that thought, as if only one thing could begin to redeem the enormity of his transgressions, the music rose.

There would never be anything like these few moments of music. For all its digital perfection, his recent work had not even come close. This was dreck of a transcendent order, florid emotion transformed into a religion of the heart. Rising like an unforgivably stunning wave of shimmering blue fire, sucking the sea from the shoreline, destined to drown all below who now watched transfixed with astonished awe, all the tracks converged in a final blinding catharsis of bliss. Somewhere within in those few seconds, there was a trapdoor to heaven, an escape hatch to a place of infinite love and grace, a warp in mundane reality and suffering that transcended the world like a sustained orgasm or an addict's tatal rush. Legions of eunuch angels hummed with mortifying purity as Louise yowled along the edge of inexorable elation, building toward madness and excruciating joy, finally exploding over the edge in an endless lacerating scream of obliterating release as the crest of the burning wave seared her crotch.

Right then, at its blistering, destroying peak—it all died, yanked out, disemboweled, as the room went dark, the power cut.

My ears still ringing, I watched Dennis, holding Cheryl in shadow now. For a moment there was nothing but the sound of the rain and bludgeoning crash of the waves below. Then behind him the foil-covered windows shattered. Rain gusted in, the cold twilight drenching the room. It was an open gallery now, perched above an abyss. An eagle's nest about to collapse.

The floor cracked down the middle of the room, splintered floorboards ripping through the shag. Chunks of plaster came down from the ceiling, as the collapsing section of floor tilted toward the window, dumping everything into the pounding surf. The piano rolled squeakily across the soaked shag and careened off the edge. The speakers fell out, the amps. He and Cheryl were going too, when I grabbed for him, missed, but got the sleeve of Cheryl's vinyl raincoat. They slid down the slanting shag, but stopped as I held on to the raincoat, bracing my foot against the edge of the splintered floorboards. The raincoat was pulled up over her head now, as Dennis held on to her arm, which was all that kept the raincoat from slipping off her.

His fingers squeaked on the wet vinyl and his eyes fixed on mine with a terrible tenacity.

Polyurethane cracked.

"She's mine," he said, as the shoulder stitches of her raincoat ripped, and her arm itself broke off at the shoulder, and he fell, still holding her arm, down the debris-strewn cliff to the battering sea below.

Her shoulder socket dripped, the stench of formaldehyde fuming through the air. The wind blew her raincoat away from her head and I looked at her angel face for the last time.

"She's yours," I said, and let her go.

She slid down the cliff as another wave crashed, disappearing in the spray.

I ran back up the red velvet corridor as the music-room ceiling came down.

I ducked through the Luxor doors as beams and concrete fell, and saw that the front gate stood open. The way was clear. I ran around the corner to the Sting Ray. That was where I died.

The driveway had broken off and the Sting Ray was gone. I ran to the edge of the asphalt as the house came down in a shrieking avalanche of concrete and wood. Spray blew in my face as another wave hit. I stepped back to keep from falling. There was nothing below, no sign of the car, nothing but the crashing surf and the battered debris of the house. His mummy surfboard flipped through the air and smashed against the rocks.

She was gone.

I reached the Bel-Air and sat there awhile—how long, I really don't know. When I finally pulled away, there was nothing left on the bluff but a battered royal palm and the open front gate.

19

I drove to keep from going crazy, though perhaps I already was. All I knew was that I didn't want to think, I didn't want to give in to what I felt, not then, maybe not ever.

I was gone in a way, my mind was dead, I still don't know how I made it. It was as if I'd been programmed to follow a certain course, though it made no sense to me anymore, and whether I succeeded or not really made no difference at all. Maybe that was why I got away.

I drove through the rain for hours, up to Oxnard, then back down the 405, through wrecks and traffic jams, the eight-track playing, though I barely heard it. The border was a mess. They waved me through. I drove on to Mexicali, where I stopped at a run-down stucco motel and got a room.

I wrung my clothes out in the tub and hung them up to dry. Then I sat on the bed with all the lights on, as if that would stop the movies from playing. It didn't. My mind had kicked in with a vengeance by then, obsessively trying to find order and sanity where little remained.

I would see Dennis and Cheryl having sex on the bunk bed twenty years ago in the house in Hermosa, perhaps a few days before she died. The cassette recorder on the bedside table. "Dennis, stop. You're hurting me." "Am I?" She would let out a little fake cry and a stifle a yawn.

I would see the crash, Cheryl's head striking the window frame in a splash of blood. In the aftermath she would be

dead, but Dennis, with only superficial cuts, would climb
out of the car. Dazed, he would walk through the rain and
call Big Willy. Together they would remove Cheryl's body
from the Sting Ray. There would be a visit to a seedy Watts
mortuary, where money would change hands, and Cheryl
would be embalmed. Then he would take her home, back
to the house in Hermosa. To the garage. Eternity poured
from a gallon can. Her death would never be reported.

Sharlene had never known.

Until the day five years later in 1969 when she climbed the
stairs to this *private retreat* for the first and last time. I would
see her halfway to the top—pregnant, gripping the rail—
when she heard Dennis talking, as I had, and thought he
was up there with another girl. Then she would continue on
to the top, enter the room, and see what he was with. Then
he would see her. He would come at her and beat her to the
floor. Kick her as she curled on the carpet.

I would see Bobby at her bedside in the hospital room as
she told him what Dennis had done to her. And what she
had seen. With tears in his eyes, he would kiss her hand. An
escape would be planned. But Bobby would never come
back. Instead, Dennis would come and take his wife home.

Where she would find Bobby dead in the nursery, a paci-
fier-tipped syringe hanging from his arm, flies on his baby
face under the crib.

I would see Sharlene withdrawn in her room through the
years of fear. I would see the beatings—the only way he ever
touched her again. There had been no sadomasochistic
games. She had never again violated the sanctity of his blue-
bedroom shrine. What would he need of his gross public
simulation, when he had the real, perfect Cheryl preserved
forever in waves of perfume on his bed? All my suspicions
about Sharlene had been groundless. Her only secret was
that she'd known his. That was the big revelation she'd made
in the pages of *Rolling Stone*. There'd been nothing else to
reveal.

But for fifteen years she'd lived with that secret, under the threat of what would happen to her if she ever told again, knowing what had happened to Bobby the one time she had. She hadn't even told Louise until she'd thought Dennis was dead. She couldn't tell me on Catalina. I saw now that she must have known it was Cheryl's voice on the cassette. But she'd been willing to let me assume it was her voice, captured in a private version of "Baby, When We Fight," rather than reveal the truth that would have exonerated her. Why? Had her fear also become guilt, a sense of complicity because she had known and hadn't told, because she had known and yet she'd stayed? Maybe she explained all this herself in *Rolling Stone*. Maybe someday I would look at that again.

One thing I knew: she'd finally overcome her fear once I'd been there to help her. That was all she had ever needed, a sense of what her life could be like beyond the prison wall. Somebody waiting down the beach at the wheel of a getaway car.

I saw her with a frightening clarity standing on the wooden steps to the beach the night I'd helped her escape, the pink Samsonite suitcase in her hand, the wind pressing her aqua silk dress to her body, the bright moonlight in her eyes—

I got up to stop the film there. I knew where it was going to take me, and I couldn't go through it here. I lit a cigarette. The walls were thin. I could hear a couple having sex in the next room. He was grunting earnestly, she was crying halfheartedly in a Spanish accent, "Oh baby, yes, baby, oh baby, yes," as I watched a fat black cockroach crawl across the faded rose-patterened carpet. I stubbed out the cigarette after a couple of puffs, put on my damp clothes, and hit the road.

The storm had burned away by midmorning. By noon it was clear and hot. I barreled down the highway, sweating now, the rich green jungle moving past my dirty windows, the eight-track blasting to drown out my thoughts.

I reached Mazatlán late that night and got directions to Louise's address from an American drunk.

The house was on a bluff a few miles out of town, a simple whitewashed place glowing in the moonlight as I pulled up the gravel drive.

I broke a window to get in and switched on a light. It was musty, a tomb with rattan furniture and lots of plants, all dead. I picked up the phone. That was dead too.

There was food in the freezer, booze in the bar. I peeled off my shirt, grabbed a bottle of Jack Daniel's, and collapsed on the sofa. That was when I saw the album propped by the stereo, a scuffed copy of *Fuel-Injected Dreams*. The color had faded severely, the Sting Ray and Sharlene's eyes turned a pale chemical green.

That was when I broke down and sobbed.

I stopped and drank for a while, then broke down again. It went like that the rest of the night, images of Sharlene flooding back. The way she had looked in the sun-drenched Avalon ballroom, the way she had smiled. Her mouth glistening in the Century Drive-In movie light a second before I'd kissed her. The way she'd looked as we'd made love. Her sweet tenderness in the dark.

When the bottle was empty I threw it at the wall. Then I took the thick translucent blue vinyl disc from the album jacket and broke that.

At dawn I reeled out onto the balcony. The day was clear and windless, the ocean as still and dead as the day I'd come upon Sharlene out by the pool. I looked at the rocks below. It was nothing like Malibu, maybe a twenty-foot drop at most. But I was pretty sure if I went headfirst I could feed my brains to the seagulls. I was thinking about it. I was just fucked up enough to do it.

It was so still it was frightening. I jumped when a bird

squawked. When an engine revved and gears ground in the distance, I heard that too.

I leaned out over the railing, nearly slipping, and saw the filthy car lurching up the road that stopped at the house. It was a Corvette, a '63 Stingray split-window coupé. It looked as if it had been driven through a mud slide. But you could still see that under the dirt it was phosphorescent blue.